D1596372

The
Jardin
des
Plantes

THE
JARDIN
DES
PLANTES

CLAUDE
SIMON

Translated
from
the
French
and
with
an
introduction
by
Jordan
Stump

Northwestern
University
Press
Evanston
Illinois

Cet ouvrage, publié dans le cadre d'un programme d'aide à la publication, bénéficie du soutien du Ministère des Affaires étrangères et du Service Culturel de l'Ambassade de France aux Etats-Unis. This work, published as part of a program of aid for publication, received support from the French Ministry of Foreign Affairs and the Cultural Services of the French Embassy in the United States.

Hydra Books
Northwestern University Press
Evanston, Illinois 60208-4210

First published in French as *Le Jardin des Plantes*. Copyright © Editions de Minuit, 1997. English translation and translator's introduction copyright © 2001 by Hydra Books/Northwestern University Press. Published 2001. All rights reserved.

Printed in the United States of America

10 9 8 7 6 5 4 3 2 1

ISBN 0-8101-1723-1

Library of Congress Cataloging-in-Publication Data

Simon, Claude.
  [Jardin des plantes. English]
  The jardin des plantes / Claude Simon ; translated from the French and with an introduction by Jordan Stump.
     p. cm.
  ISBN 0-8101-1723-1
  I. Stump, Jordan, 1959– . II. Title.
  PQ2637.I547 J3713 2001
  843'.914—dc21

                                                2001001856

The paper used in this publication meets the minimum requirements of the American National Standard for Information Sciences—Permanence of Paper for Printed Library Materials, ANSI Z39.48-1984.

CONTENTS

TRANSLATOR'S INTRODUCTION

Claude Simon's life would appear to offer first-rate material for an autobiography. The world has changed a great deal since his birth in 1913, and his life intersects with some of the more notable upheavals—both political and intellectual—of the troubled history of the past eighty-eight years: the Spanish Civil War, the brief and catastrophic engagement of the French and German armies in the early days of World War II, the rise of the French "New Novel" of the 1950s and 1960s. Simon has reached an age when he might justifiably consider himself a grand old man of French letters—a status confirmed by his Nobel Prize for literature in 1985, recognizing a string of astonishing novels such as *The Flanders Road* (*La Route des Flandres*, 1960) and *Conducting Bodies* (*Les Corps conducteurs*, 1971), among many others—and we might now expect from him some sort of summing-up, some reflection on the paths he has traveled to arrive at this point.

And indeed, *The Jardin des Plantes* (*Le Jardin des Plantes*, 1997) takes as its subject a series of moments from the author's life; nevertheless, it is not an autobiography, nor a reminiscence, nor a memoir. It is, as the cover of the French edition reminds us, a novel. The moments that make it up are considered not in their immediacy but in their distance, and they are assembled not chronologically but according to the capricious, associative, non-linear workings of memory; the assemblage thus created stands not as a catalog of events but as a meditation on the process by which those events are recalled (or produced) by the remembering mind. Which is to say that *The Jardin des Plantes* is, in Simon's words, a "portrait of a memory"—of a capacity for remembering, that is, and of a set of memories, and of the rambling and subjective mechanisms by which a memory operates. Like any other, the memory depicted here works in curious ways. It recalls some events with breathtaking clarity, others uncertainly, or only partially, or even erroneously; furthermore, as anyone who has tried to look back on a distant childhood already knows, it is not always easy to draw a line between recollection and invention, between memories sincerely and spontaneously recalled and memories elaborated, arranged, not felt but *written*. Little wonder, then, that *The Jardin des Plantes* looks so much like both an autobiography and a novel; perhaps there is no real difference between the two. And perhaps that blurred distinction is the very subject of this book.

That subject finds its emblem in the Parisian park from which the novel takes its title. The Jardin des Plantes lies on the left bank of the Seine, not far from the Latin Quarter, the new French national library, and Simon's apartment. It is one of the most expansive and agreeable of the many parks of Paris, but its name is mildly deceptive, for it is not one garden but several: it encompasses a formal French garden, an English garden, and an alpine garden, as well as a small zoo and a remarkable museum of natural history. The French garden shows us nature in a domesticated state, geometric and orderly; the English garden offers up nature in all its glorious, aleatory wildness. The one is overtly artificial, the other glorifies the natural and the real. But of course the English garden is no less carefully planned, shaped, and maintained than the French garden; and that French garden is, despite itself, subject to the same uncontainable and random sort of growth that the English garden glorifies. Again the line is blurred: is one more authentic than the other? Is memory less authentic when it is shaped and arranged? Can it be otherwise? And yet can that arrangement be true to itself when it relies on something by definition partial and random?

The memories that fill the pages of *The Jardin des Plantes* continually pose such questions. They are disordered, fragmentary, digressive, like all spontaneous memories, but at the same time they bear all the hallmarks of something written, of literature: recurring images (wedges, disintegration and reunification, the straight, the sinuous, and the diagonal), consistent preoccupations (light, leaves), rhyming situations (censorship, marginalization). We also find here a very literary sort of attention to the registers of language (telegraphic, lyrical, descriptive, oneiric), and this leads us to one of the novel's central concerns. The multiplicity of tones in which the novel is narrated—and the frequency with which the narration returns to the same images, endlessly seeking some new and perhaps more effective way to put them into words—poses a difficult question: what is the language in which it becomes possible to communicate a memory or an experience? Simon's answer seems to be that there is none, that language is capable of many things, but communication of a reality is not one of them. There is always more to reality than language can express, and the language with which we struggle as we attempt to say what we have seen can so easily be misunderstood, oversimplified, or distorted in the mind of its addressee—even if that addressee is the speaker himself. This is not to say, exactly, that Simon seeks here to show us the difference between the real and the represented; rather, what emerges from these pages is a strong sense that, like the two aspects of the Jardin des Plantes itself, each is always interlaced with the other.

Be this as it may, it cannot be denied that Simon's memory has some intriguing real experiences to communicate (to attempt to communicate) to his reader: not only the great historical moments I have already mentioned but also his early childhood, his acquaintance with Picasso, the Italian artist Gastone Novelli, the poet Joseph Brodsky; but also the 1985 Nobel ceremonies and a later trip to Gorbachev-era Russia in the company of Peter Ustinov, James Baldwin, and others; but also innumerable journeys (to India, South America, North America); but also academic conferences, interviews, museums, readings (Proust, Rommel, Dostoevsky); but also life in his own apartment, with a view over a small Parisian square, ever changing, ever the same. Reading this list, we may well feel a certain astonishment at the degree of engagement with the world that it suggests, but we must also note the place that the speaking voice persistently occupies throughout these reminiscences: a place outside of or on the edges of the events being recounted. No matter how momentous the incident, Simon (or S., as he often calls himself here, as if he were not even willing to commit himself to his memories in the fixed and certain form of his own name) is never quite in the center of things, never entirely involved, never fully within the fold; his gaze is aimed not directly toward the action, but toward its margins, and from the margins. Whether turning his attention to the light shining over the trees as a fatal wartime episode unfolds, or staring out the window during the premiere of Picasso's play *Le désir attrapé par la queue,* or refusing to join his fellow intellectuals in signing a pompous proclamation at the end of his tour of the Soviet Union, or watching from his apartment as Paris bustles, or looking back with irony, bemusement, and uncertainty on his own lifetime, his position remains constant: never central, never undistracted, never entirely convinced.

Strands such as this—and others I have mentioned—run throughout *The Jardin des Plantes,* unifying and consolidating the diverse patchwork of which it is composed. But this patchwork quality is as central to the novel as its unity; again, like the Jardin des Plantes itself, the dual nature of Simon's novel cannot be reduced. The workings of this patchwork are intricate and complex, as will become apparent from the first page. The text is split into blocks, from a few words to many pages in length; some of these blocks coalesce to form longer stories, while others soon fade; some are narrations, some citations, some meditations. Some are written in a jagged, fragmentary style, some in long, looping, run-on sentences, some in a perfectly traditional descriptive mode. Why these incessant shifts in the novel's tone, the reader may ask? I put that question—in a rather more convoluted form—to Claude Simon, expecting a similarly convoluted answer. But what he then told me is, I think, something the reader would do well to keep in mind as he or she experiences this text: *Je fais comme je peux*—"I do as I can." In spite of it all, that is, and perhaps beyond anything else, this novel seeks simply to express the reality of an experience, outside of theory or aesthetic ideology, in full awareness of the impossibility of the task, but also in full awareness of the beauty that can result from that impossibility. Hence, for instance, the frequent recurrence of parenthetical remarks, and of parentheses within parentheses within parentheses: anything can be restated, anything can be said differently, and while one comes no closer to the truth with each successive reformulation, the act of restating, or of attempting to restate, has a certain truth and beauty of its own.

No matter how it may appear at first glance, then, this is not a "difficult" book; it is a perfectly accessible rendering of a lifetime's memories, not abstract but sensuous, not Olympian but unfailingly human. It is at the same time a set of recollections and a meditation on writing, censorship (official and otherwise), history, and memory itself, in addition to that, though, it is simply an intense, fascinating, complicated string of images and evocations. And of course there is more to *The Jardin des Plantes* than I have said here; but I will leave the readers of this endlessly compelling book to discover that for themselves.

Before doing so, I have only to thank a number of people without whom this translation would not have been possible. Let me first acknowledge three translators whose work I have cited here: Constance Garnett (Dostoevsky's *The Possessed*) and C. K. Scott Moncrieff and Terence Kilmartin (Proust's *Remembrance of Things Past*). I must also extend my most grateful thanks to M. J. Devaney, David Carroll, Melanie Kemp, Thomas Ritter, Eleanor Hardin, and especially Claude Simon, who answered my endless questions with patience and humor, and who has given me some of the most absorbing work I have undertaken as a translator.

The
Jardin
des
Plantes

No one has a definite understanding of the shape of his life; we can conceive of it only in little pieces. . . . We are all patchwork, and of a makeup so formless and diverse that each part, each moment acts on its own.—**Montaigne**

1

To drag the intimate nature of my soul and a pretty description of my sentiments into the literary marketplace would be in my eyes unfitting and low. I imagine, nevertheless, not without displeasure, that it will probably be impossible to avoid descriptions of sentiments and thoughts (perhaps even vulgar ones) altogether: so much does any kind of literary work corrupt a man, even if it is undertaken only for himself. — **Dostoevsky**

struggling in my bad English

maybe I'd had too much to drink only the effect was the opposite of what they were probably hoping for

Frunze Kyrgyzstan heart of Asia A "forum" they called it five days verbiage declamations peace between nations love fraternity etc. by invitation of the great writer winner of the Lenin Prize Hero of labor etc. presiding over the verbiage meditative pose or rather weariness weight of his thoughts crushing no doubt (or just dozing maybe elbow on table heavy head supported by one hand) after opening speech invocation of the Old Men of the Mountain then falling asleep At the end caviar sturgeon smoked tongue vodka and then like a bill discreetly slipped in with the dessert that blather

second husband of the most beautiful woman in the world I nudged him with my elbow showed it to him struggling in my bad English he looked annoyed irritable pout he shrugged his shoulders said Yes I've read it Oooooh it's no big deal I said Jesus sign a load of claptrap like this you think it's

on the stage the two Harlem
Brothers had broken off
their comic act

all of them
looking at me

black sheep

finally I stood up
from the table
and left

hadn't seen him
leaving the ban-
quet room Ran

landed before dawn the fifteen guests
scarcely awake hadn't slept in fact night
flight gritty feeling under the eyelids blinking gray dawn gray countryside poplars
gray silhouettes hurrying whitewashed cot-
tages trucks now and then a man on horseback suddenly in the beam of the headlights a road sign Tashkent 700 km the
horizon beyond the city blocked obstructed
by something like crushed diamonds sparkling pink and white marvelous touched by
the first rays of sunlight Then in a daze
sleepwalking in the middle of the apartment two hundred square meters I measured it furnished in antique Niçois-style
false Louis XV veneer false mahogany false
bronze false Oriental rugs Opening the
doors two bathrooms Finally I stepped
onto the terrace I couldn't see the rushing
river only hearing it unending hiss imagining it frenzied mane tossing flying down the
marvelous mountain The morning breeze
shook the leaves on the tall poplars gilded
by autumn sometimes carrying them off
lazily slanting snow Beyond on the opposite bank now the sunlight was touching the
side of the mountain first foothill rounded
barren yellow ocher On a path leading up-
hill parallel to the torrent two men were
walking slowly conversing both wearing
something like long dark caftans tall bon-

8

straight into him
Tolstoy without
the beard in the
vestibule semi-
darkness

nets on their heads the air was as if washed
clean transparent light Central Asia Roof
of the World Trying to remember the
names of those two philosophizing characters Persian Letters

the last guy I wanted to meet up with

naturally he was the author of the masterpiece drivel Future generations Harvests that we will have sowed We
all know that we must die but we want to put it off as
long as possible etc. etc. two pages like that final motion blather Pay the bill

tired (faint or drunk
maybe?) Seemingly asleep
Or pretending wisely ab-
sent at the strategic mo-
ment?

but he'd recognized me
anyway

trapped!

a moment brief fan of light
through the opened swinging
door along with the uproar the
laughter The two Harlem Brothers had probably resumed their
comic act then the door swung
shut drowned them out I was
hoping that in the semidarkness

waving at me patting with an inviting hand the place
next to him on the couch sitting or rather slumped at
one end of it thick voice Trapped like a rat I obey

(still in a daze brushing my
teeth lips pulled back white
foam between them long string
hanging from my chin I said No
I'm getting it all mixed up I'm

tired That was this morning in Moscow the apotheosis him with the birthmark the port wine stain on his forehead Great honor private meeting all fifteen of us around a table but only there and nothing but tea biscuits mineral water no caviar no vodka interdit strictement interdit streng verboten pericoloso sporgersi I don't know how they say that in Russian)

hiss of the invisible torrent the two men walking quietly tall headpieces caftans talking Montesquieu name on the tip of my tongue something like Ousbeck or Usbek what about the other one?

maddening

heart of Asia Pamir poplars shedding careless golden snow eyes burning sounds washed out Remembering another awakening or rather a half-sleep in Delhi after another sleepless night on an airplane there too air and sounds as if washed out strange cries from birds imagined strange ultramarine with long curved beaks imagined among the foliage giant leaves giant flowers peppery from one of his scents plumed trees poisonous fruits the pockets took sound of the air vultures acting as garbage a little bottle men they say devouring trash carrion in or vial rather Bombay apparently there is or used to be a Elixir he said tower at the top of which they used to set out secret blend cadavers for the vultures undertakers herbs from the magic mountain put it in my hand closed my fingers over it thick voice cures everything

I laughed again foam on my lips toothbrush in midair White lacquered bathroom tubes pipes lacquered red vermilion red vermilion toilet tank vermilion door head neck shoulder filling three quarters of the mirror above

the sink In the other quarter I could see her sitting behind me on the edge of the bathtub nude mother of pearl
pointed breasts propping herself up on her two arms
smiling incredulous amused pout her eyes like two slits
the line of my shoulder cutting off her body at the knees
I looked at the time on my other wrist This morning
more or less no just twelve hours ago now with time
change Yes Great honor

a second time brief fan of light through the swinging
door pushed open just as the uproar the laughter
erupted The two Harlem Brothers were still doing their
gay routine This time it was the interpreter with a face
like a ferret a cop rug merchant he was holding that
goddamned gibberish in his hand harvests

future generations et cetera invoice two   Usbek   Persian
hundred square meters false oriental rug   women   steam-
plus vodka caviar smoked tongue I was   baths harems I
hoping that in the semidarkness but he   imagined as a
walked straight toward me brandishing   schoolboy cheeks
the open pages I hear you don't want to   afire caresses
sign why? The Tolstoy Old Man of the   Turkish bath
Mountains was pretending to have fallen   seraglio intrigues
asleep again   Spirit of Laws

what intrigues what vizirs what de-
tours what corridors what hairpin
turns had led him here now sitting at
the end of this table vodka verboten elegant vest Italian tailor they say Italian
shirt tie idem speaking of abundance
visibly quite pleased with himself more
gibberish proclaimed values of human-
East Berlin 197...   ism must now come before values of
(check this) subway   the proletariat What? No let him talk
station Stadt-Mitte   what's the use so satisfied with himself

amid the ruins once every seven or eight minutes a passenger emerged silence She came out pink dress walked away alone at the foot of the fa-çades long charred wall brown black

his tie proletariat probably no longer human beings to him value zero probably something like calves cows worms drunkards pigs vodka verboten Yes I'm done Rinsing my mouth wiping my face washing the glass the toothbrush She hadn't moved still watching me with that same amused look

with gaping windows against the sky orange setting sun reddening vermilion velvety disappearing little by little the pink spot of her dress dancing very small now in the empty distance gone

I said Very pleased with himself also declared once again his country now open to everything proletariat calves cows worms

pigs drunkards right to read anything see anything hear anything foreign books foreign magazines foreign newspapers records films Coca-Cola et cetera et cetera everything absolutely everything Except! He said Except! Face suddenly severe not jovial at all now no more humanism Coca-Cola Unyielding resolute inflexible: Except pornography! Pornography streng verboten Like vodka absolument interdit pericoloso strictly forbidden The two gay Harlems very impressed respectful Second husband of the most beautiful woman in the world also very respectful As for me already proven lost lamb black

finally I took the paper crumpled it and shoved it into his hands I said There now leave me the fuck alone Maybe I'd had too much to drink I might have shouted I was exasperated but it was beginning to be fun The big friendly interpreter came along conciliatory I played at indignation Overdoing it

sheep pig She was still in the
same position amused incredulous

later I looked at a map the rushing torrent was
marked in blue heading west and north shaky dotted
line finally disappearing swallowed up empty space
marked Bet-Pak-Dala Steppe

water glass on the shelf thick emerald green
striated by diagonal fluting wrapping around
it twisted the toothbrush handle pink transparent plastic its reflection in the mirror
blocked the naked body I finished wiping my
mouth I turned around Now I saw all of her
mother of pearl slightly pink at the knees the
ceiling light cast long triangular shadows beneath her breasts I said Except pornography
eyes still like two slits laughing bold I came
near her I placed my hand flat on her stomach marble I

what god is it with the high
oval headpiece ending in a snail
sculpted in bas-relief on a black
marble column small temple at
Karnak shown in profile no arms
his entire body like a sort of boot
with something emerging from the
middle like a branch a tenon his
stiff horizontal member fertilizing
with his sperm a lettuce plant (tradition or bad translation? in reality
a leafy plant on a long stalk)

Arrested by the Germans
Gastone N—— was
sent to the Dachau ex-
termination camp and
tortured Afterward he

said he could no longer bear the sight of a German or a uniform but also not even the sight of a so-called civilized person So he left for Brazil and undertook a search for diamonds (or gold?) in the Amazon basin Abandoned in the middle of the virgin forest by his Indian guide he managed to win the trust of a primitive tribe and studied their language Later back in Europe he began painting again

old-fashioned bathtub faucet handles made of brass with spokes in the form of a star each one ending in a little ball like the pearls on a crown One of them not completely turned off was dripping in the silence Blip making tiny undulations over the water's surface propagating concentric growing larger very pale green water ring around the drain also made of brass undulating as they passed as if it were moving up and down

paintings almost all constructed on a system of horizontal and vertical lines forming a sort of checkerboard the lines spreading apart or coming together like the tiles at the bottom of a basin a swimming pool whose surface is rippled with undulations losing their form

Titles of some of the works he showed in Rome (Galleria La Salita):

Un goccio di vita (A drop of life)
Piuttosto terra che cielo (Rather the earth than the heavens)
Strappo (Torn)
Raccattato in terra (Picked up from the ground)
La Grande Bestemmia (The Great Blasphemy)
Interpretation of erotomania

14

Aaron's rod marble silky pink rock opening up suddenly fountain Oh Moses! Began to breathe more quickly through the
nostrils

Other titles (The Allan Gallery—New York):

One of the rooms in the Museum
Sister Caroline
In the folds
The road to recovery

dark gray so low you could see the white cross edged in black painted on the fuselage not even aggressive indifferent quite slow dropping it as they passed by more like birds relieving themselves in midflight doing their business caca-yellow droppings

road of discovery long hillside pavement three of them flying low sharks bush of dust dirty brown crackling as if hanging above the ground surge of muscles between my thighs gallop the mare bolting the air breaking like glass a thousand pieces a thousand triangles collapsing explosions so violent that the windows rattled yellow stars blinking on and off amid the thick wreaths of smoke I was sure the glass would fly into pieces I said to Brodsky I hate fireworks The guests were clustered around the windows in the great hall white ties décolletés tiaras bare shoulders bare chests satin silk faille The four of us had stayed behind in the little parlor paneled in natural oak decorative bouquet on the table in the center her delicate Italian profile him aquiline nose crow condottieri looking more Tuscan than Jewish

"Now at last the slowly gathered, long-pent-up fury of the storm broke upon us. Four or five millions of men met each other in the first shock of the most merciless of all the wars of which record has been kept." (Winston Churchill)

"a la cinque de la tarde" about five o'clock yes probably death in the afternoon except that there was no one there to watch me no spectators no arena no little trumpet no applause only the cheerful green springtime countryside cheerful May sunshine so let's say five o'clock me calf-deep in the stream swearing like a mule driver pulling on the reins of that mare that wouldn't jump or even step into the water like comical English engraving foxhunt rider black cap red coat white pants boot tops folded down whiskey label same position except in this case the fox was me millions of men first shock the most merciless Good fortune of finding myself in the best seats the front row Little iron-gray balls began to rise up here and there in the field

I stepped into the transparent water Nile-green pale it only came up to my calf foot cut off undulating deformed the ankle as if elongated angle of refraction boot god fertilizing rigid tenon She leaned over I was caressing her hair her shoulders Along the enameled sidewalls of the bathtub the water lapping reflected a moving web network of bright yellow veins polygons dancing stretching out contracting splitting up coming together again I lost my balance staggering trying to catch hold of the faucets tumbled into the splashing water

In 1961 Gastone N—— painted a large canvas, more or less square, which he entitled ARCHIVIO PER LA MEMORIA. The upper part is filled by three rows of women's breasts against a white background, drawn in profile and numbered from 1 to 34. They are schematically rendered by two curved lines, one descending, the other ascending, facing right and coming together to form a pink-ish-brown point, some of them darker, some lighter, which represented the nipple, occasion-ally indicated only by a small circle. Most of the nipples point upward. Some of the breasts have shadows beneath them; one pair is underscored by what appears to be lace, of the kind used to decorate the neck-line of an evening gown; another pair is shaped like the swollen teats of a goat, oval and pendulous. Beneath, in the center of the canvas, rising from the bottom, the viewer can make out the form of a monumental erect penis, its head ogive-shaped, like a col-umn supporting the frieze of breasts. It is nearly concealed by a smear of creamy white paint, which has dripped here and there, forming an irregular dribbling fringe. Along the axis of the penis, as if to mask it further (or to re-place it in its function as a pillar), the painter has stacked up a series of rectangles, edged in various colors, some pale, some violent (pink, black, green,

So busy strug-gling with that horse that I don't even remem-ber hearing the explosions: only those balls of gray cotton that had begun to appear here and there in the field not close together just here and there as if at random carelessly so to speak as if those god-damn airplanes were dropping their bombs just to get rid of them, it seemed, as they passed by on their way home to supper Abendessen Mortar shells probably now, at least that's what I thought, and only for the pleasure of firing their weapons God how beautiful war is or else, perhaps, firing at the three small truck-mounted machine guns which seemed to be returning their fire from the higher road if so they weren't very good shots but in any case it would red, salmon), while on either side of the nearly invisible ogive arch thin horizontal lines sketch out something like the elongated rungs of two ladders. Between them, here and there, we find uneven rows of letters or numbers, as if put there by some unsteady hand scratching words into the surface of a wall with a tack or a nail, the lines moving closer together or further apart, undulating, the characters hastily engraved. "La superficie pittorica torna ad essere veramente une superficie, senz illusionismi de scorci e prospettive."(Preface to the catalog)

only have taken one here and there to get me how do they say it in English Killed in Action DSO Distinguished Service Order Talk about a distinguished act of heroism this was one for sure trying to get a stubborn mare to jump a stream Death on the field of honor probably in the metro tomorrow the commuters would be reading the story of the battle newspapers folded in four assuming of course that as I pulled at the reins of this horse I was involved in a battle then I remembered it was Sunday I stepped out of the stream undid the knot on my sword and still holding the reins I whipped at her flank shouting at the same time to keep away two stallions who were trotting around the field looking light as feathers like in a slow-motion movie bouncing rubber apparently unconcerned by the cotton balls much more interested in my mare thinking Grotesque the very definition of grotesque killed Maybe one of the little shells had fallen nearby and frightened her because all of a sudden she jumped without stepping back for a running start throwing me off balance hanging onto the reins dragging me staggering into the stream into the middle of the splashing water glints of light sparkling May sunshine

trying to tell him the story jokingly in my bad English Kyrgyzstan Roof of the World old man of the mountains Harlem Brothers future harvests He just shrugged Read somewhere that he was known for a certain arrogance Simply re-

18

served I think The Italian woman with her delicate profile also reserved or haughty Quattrocento Maybe he was suspicious of me Western intelligentsia more or less fellow traveler or something like that I'd sent them packing but they'd sent him to prison camp so it was probably just impossible for him to laugh about that

paintings in which against that same creamy white background he continually returned to a checkerboard composition whose lines seemed to undulate each square occupied by some geometric figure triangles disks arrows snail or else a little black and white checkerboard or else inscriptions with uneven irregular letters half rubbed out such as for example:

sort of thing At the end a bouquet several enormous explosions great cracks one after another simultaneously golden rain lighting up the great hall apotheosis not only the windows but the entire palace shook all of Stockholm too The Swedish physicist told me the next day that his children had been awakened frightened even though distant neighborhood Fireworks courtesy of the city of Barcelona the program said

IL PIU

BEL C (illegible)

CHE IO

ABBIA

MAI V

ISTO

or else awkward depictions or rather suggestions of entangled limbs folds thighs bellies splashes of light shooting out around us fell out of the bathtub overflowing puddles or else the letter A repeated over several rows filling up an entire square like this:

AAAAAAAAAAA
AAAAAAAAAAA
AAAAAAAAAAA
AAAAAAAAAAAA
AAAAAAAAAAA

or else shapes that can scarcely be made out (breasts, thighs, genitals, tufts of hair). Like the limbs, the organs, or the positions depicted, the clumsy or repeated letters, often difficult to recognize, suggest the broken words exchanged by breathless lovers in each other's arms. We can understand as the title of one of his large canvases this collection of words painted at the bottom in tall capital letters:

UNA DELLE SALE DEL MUSEO MENO (illegible)
PROBABILE: I RICORDI MIRAGLIOSI E IMPROBABILI
II (illegible) ADIZIONATE NUOVA COLLEZIO
NE DI RICORDI DAI PIU SEMPLI (illegible) DISOCIETA
III ALLI CONSEGENZE DE PIU MODERNE (illegible) CAPABILE

managing nevertheless to right myself still holding fast to the reins getting a foothold alongside her on the opposite bank jumping on her back kicking my spurs and galloping back up toward the little woods the spot where the refugees had told me they'd seen some cavalrymen enter when three of them came out full speed visible atop the ridgeline I rode over toward them I didn't recognize any of them one had blood streaming down his face I shouted The squadron where's the squadron In that little woods? Without slowing his galloping horse one of them shouted The squadron you've got to be kidding you asshole the woods are crawling with Krauts I shouted Where you going He shouted Where do you think asshole they're going to blow up the bridges over the Meuse We were about fifteen kilometers away When the horses got out of breath we had them trot for a little while then gallop again At one point a small car full of mounted dragoons passed us there must have been ten of them stuffed in there we shouted to them to take the wounded man they laughed out loud they gave us the finger they told us we were a beautiful sight on our old nags we'd never make it in time Ha ha ha! they seemed to be drunk one of them threw a bottle in our direction which broke against the road From far away they were still gesticulating in our direction laughing then at a turn in the road they disappeared In the fields the shadows of the trees were starting to grow long the countryside was deserted silent abandoned Sometimes passing by a farm we could hear cows lowing One of the cavalrymen said Poor old things there's no one to milk them

décolletés bare shoulders bare chests faille satin silk explosions burning bush Fireworks courtesy of the city of Barcelona Old photo from the archives showing the façade of the Hotel Colon arrogant building arrogantly requisitioned headquarters (star-shaped bullet holes still in the ground-floor windows) of the PSUC (Partido Socialiste Unificat de Catalunya) as is proclaimed by a muslin banner stretched between two balconies on the fourth floor on either side two gigantic portraits one of Lenin goatee smooth skull shining polished limpia bottas the other of I don't know who Stalin maybe mustache but slender or else what was the name of the Spanish Lenin back then a name like the name of a bird something like cormorant no Comorera I think From one of the balconies supporting the muslin banner I watched the funeral procession of a chief of police In their newspapers the extremist organizations accused each other of his assassination or more conveniently for everyone they blamed the notorious Fifth Column Mountain of red flowers The presi-

I couldn't remember the statue one of those figures faun or that sort of thing which they used to put in public gardens pale with slightly blurry features a ghost as if radiating a milky light an outmoded relic perhaps even a vestige of a vanished world ridiculous and voluptuous left there as if forgotten or rather renounced pushed aside out of the way so it won't block the view waiting to be thrown onto the scrap heap replaced by the effigy of one of the new divinities so far only in paintings monumental scale later cast in steel sculpted in granite bald or mustachioed the pale marble thanks to a respite from time from history still perpetuating the naked body of the model who had posed among the anatomical casts dusty dent of the Generalitat was walking at the head of the procession his face ashen What was most striking from the balcony was the crowd of men on the esplanade most of them bareheaded black pomaded hair shining crows' wings Further to the left but you can't see it in the photograph there was a café with a sign BAR DE LA LUNA In the end the hotel burned down a bomb or more likely arson archives to be eliminated Where it stood on the corner of the Paseo de Gracia there is now a bank polished marble façade All very far away now legs feet arms in the sculptor's studio some gymnast maybe mustachioed like the ones you see in the earliest photographs or I don't remember what they're called kinephotographs analysis of movement walking jumping successive positions overlapping woman also pale running naked black chignon pubic hair or perhaps some effeminate hoodlum maricona or else a docker a welder revealing as they undress a milky body with tattoos four points of the compass in dirty blue the mustachioed head of the gymnast or the hoodlum replaced by conventional academic horned face Panpipes or grape cluster against albino lips

transparent water in the bathtub Nile-green in the deepest part a light Veronese green in other words reminding me of one of the stamps of that same green stuck to the postcard mailed from Port Saïd 6/25/08 and arriving in Perpignan 7/9/08. On the almost-square stamps a line-engraving depicted the pyramid of Giza with, in the left foreground, the head of the Sphinx, its face not mutilated, eroded, flat, enigmatic, but meticulously embellished with a nose, a mouth, and two pensive eyes like those on a

mannequin in the window of a dress shop, POSTES EGYP-
TIENNES — DEUX MILLIEMES written in French on two
sides, in Arabic on the others, the second stamp worth
only one millieme showing the same drawing but closer
to reality, that is, light brown like the water of the Nile,
more precisely a muddy yellow, about twice as wide as the
Seine, at least at Luxor where, after lunch, the director of
the archeological mission had coffee served for us on his
garden deck by the banks of the river which flowed past
about two meters below us, lined with bushes and reeds
into which small ripples on the water's surface disappeared. It measures about two hundred meters wide. The
current is not particularly swift, comparable to that of the
Seine as it passes through Paris, perhaps even a little
slower. Tufts of greenery, bushes pulled from the banks
upstream drift along on the current. The largest ones form
small islands sometimes inhabited by birds. On one a
wading bird (heron? stork?) with a long beak was standing on one leg. Two boats passed by while we were there,
their decks laden with tourists. You could hear the tap-
tap of the engine from far away, slowly growing louder,
coming closer, then very close, mingling with the sound of
the water displaced by the prow, bubbling up behind in
great eddies that spread wider as the purr of the engine
faded and fell silent, replaced once again by the quiet
whisper of the river. After the boats had passed, the tan-
gles of grass trapped in the reeds along the bank went on
moving up and down for a moment with the waves created by the boat's wake, which splashed against the bank
with a fresh sound. On the other bank, fields of cotton,
beans, or clover stretched off to a line of dirt-colored hills.
Between the first and second of those peaks lies the Valley of the Kings. The late February sun was already hot,
and several times I had to move my chair, following the
shadow of the eucalyptus that sheltered me. The temple
reminds you more or less of a city, an immense maze of

colonnades and murals strewn with obelisks. You walk in a fine gray dust, like ash, which comes up to your ankles. When the Egyptian army reached this place in their pursuit of the Mamelukes, only the tops of the structures

scarcely dried off brown puddles on the linoleum feet leaving damp prints behind them in the shape of an elongated guitar crowned with pearls hunger for each other crossing the room unable to let go connected the two bodies linked Siamese twins like some mythological monster animal with eight limbs two heads four arms four legs tangled staggering falling onto the bed

could be seen above the desert of sand beneath which they had been buried and about ten meters up you can see carved in large letters on the sides of the pylons the names of the soldiers who camped in their shadow: Doverchain, Mauduit, Lemoine, Gaubert, Renaud. On one of the black marble columns in one of the little secondary temples since uncovered the form of the god reduced to a sort of boot is engraved, without arms, as if he were bound with straps from head to toe, except for his penis, long and thin, horizontal, whose sperm falls on the plant he is fertilizing

the library of the University of Salamanca has in its collections an original copy of Erasmus's *Colloquies* in which the Inquisition censors have concealed many passages under a thick layer of black ink These rectangular blots sometimes cover whole pages sometimes only a paragraph at other times two lines or no more than a few words

the explosions had stopped there was one more little pop not much louder than an ordinary firecracker one last lingering star falling to earth trailing sparks like a comet and its tail through thick brown smoke streaked with yellow whose billows we could see slowly sinking from the windows of the gallery I tried again to tell Brodsky how the fat jovial interpreter had intervened how I'd feigned indignation played the victim of an affront poor buggers in the end that was how they earned their living But he listened to me blankly the fireworks were over now the King and the Queen had left the gallery was emptying out From the ballroom came the sounds of an orchestra We left the little parlor Beneath the gleaming chandeliers a throng of young men in rented evening clothes were dancing with student girls I asked him if he didn't miss Russia He watched the dancers still without expression he said No not at all I said Now they'd surely give you a tourist visa you could go back He said No I'll never go back There was no anger in his voice he was very calm Most of the girls were wearing white caps with patent leather visors coquettishly set sideways on their heads they had long blond hair that fell over their bare shoulders the couples were dancing or rather oscillating in place crowded up against each other

hail of bullets not a cliché not that they come in bunches but the sound they make when they pass by very close a crack dzing! like the first hailstones of a thunderstorm falling separately at first with a metallic ping bouncing off the metal gutters Galloping crouched over the horse's neck I thought naively incompetents they're shooting too low thinking those metallic clinks were when they hit the horses' shoes it was the sergeant who later told me the truth I still had a lot to learn that was only the beginning From time to time a cavalryman fell from his horse or rolled to the ground along with it but no one turned around Years later a journalist asked me how we managed to live with the fear I told him You know everyone does what he can it's not like Stendhal cavorting merrily among the cannonballs at Waterloo. He said Not Stendhal: Fabrice. I said No no Fabrice was following behind in the supply wagons you don't think Stendhal would have missed the chance to show his much-vaunted courage it's like Faulkner in his wonderful fighter plane. He said What are you talking about? Faulkner never . . . I said Yes yes Under the name of Sartoris A real Southern gentleman would never dream of doing such a thing except under the cover of a pseudonym noblesse oblige incognito But he kept the photograph of himself in the uniform of a Royal Air Force lieutenant I've seen it A photo doesn't lie The uniform looks a little too big for him, but . . . And then he was an excellent shot he never missed an opossum or a bear In his later days he loved hunting parties buck deer fox red hunting jacket white cravat top hat he was impeccable I've practiced that kind of sport myself riding hell for leather through the countryside you ever tried it? Tally-ho! Tally-ho! Tally-ho! Quite exhilarating jumping obstacles ditches streams Except that I was the quarry that gives you a different perspective it's . . . He cut me off irritated he said That's exactly what I wanted you to tell me about. . . .

what do they call that photographic technique for studying movement a camera whose shutter opened and closed every fraction of a second imprinting on a slowly unwinding roll of film the postures the positions of the body the limbs a horse trotting galloping a phase revealed for the first time in which all four legs come together the front and back hooves almost touching which up to then no illustrator no painter had been able to catch however quick his eye horses always shown frozen in an extended position stretched out as they leap flying over the ground Epsom derby Géricault whence no doubt the expression *ventre à terre* Then a sudden discovery on those narrow strips where the wan naked bodies of male and female gymnasts walked ran jumped before a black backdrop their translucent limbs unfurling like the leaves of a fan contracting relaxing overlying each other radiating from the joints hips knees elbows shoulders what a tangle the two bodies Siamese twins interlaced or rather melded together or rather one body with two heads and eight limbs further multiplied as they walk precariously falling when as she moves in reverse her heels and calves hit the side of the mattress falling backward then thighs against her torso the other body bent forward crawling hands holding like a cup chalice her two

in addition to the volume of Erasmus with certain passages shrouded in a black shadow by the ecclesiastical censors the library in Salamanca holds a number of precious documents You enter through a door of the kind found on bank vaults, consisting of a circular steel portal about fifteen centimeters thick and studded with cylindrical locks Above it remains the following inscription:

HAI EXCOMUNION

RESERVADA A SU SANTIDAD

CONTRA QUALESQUIERA PERSONAS

QUE QUITAREN, DISTRAXEREN, O DE OTRO QUALQUIER MODO

ENAGENAREN ALGUN LIBRO,

PERGAMINO, O PAPEL

DE ESTA BIBLIOTHECA,

SIN QUE PUEDAN SER ABSUELTAS

kneeling learned to keep my hands beneath the cloth covering the communion table spreading out my fingertips to form a sort of little platter or rather a hollow a little cup to catch it if by accident the priest dropped it between the chalice from which he took it and my mouth This is my Body which he set like a pill a tablet on the outstretched tongue a little flat disk about the same diameter as a five-centime piece Real Presence do not chew under any circumstances wait for it (Him?) to dissolve in the acid of the saliva With a roar like ocean waves the pain crashed against my eardrum it was something furious relentless pitiless vicious it had awakened me in the dormitory long before the bell rang it rushed forward with every beat of my pulse dug in like a sharp wedge drew back burst forward again I said You who can do anything make it stop make it stop make it stop but I still had to wait for the end of morning study to go to the infirmary the doctor wouldn't be there before nine o'clock he looked like a seal he had huge drooping yellow mustachios a blinding electric light on his forehead I knew he would put that little metal cone into my ear and that when he began to probe around with his long needles I wouldn't be able to keep from screaming Fructis ventris tui on her back her thighs clasped around my head "Chalice a botanical term external envelope in the form of a cup which encloses the corolla and the sexual organs of the flower" (Littré dictionary)

As for learning what that character was doing there living in that traveling salesmen's hotel in a city hardly thirty kilometers from the border which he seemed very careful never to cross and how and why he alone could with a single telephone call have his will done by the captain and the crew of that anarchist freighter rusting in Barcelona harbor and how and why his friends who for the moment held absolute power in that country not to say that they were the government (for that word (government) or rather the very idea that it signifies or implies set their teeth on edge (but to tell the truth so did the idea of power), they who when by chance (or by accident or by grudging concession to the desires (to the superstitions) of some fiancée) found themselves legally married were very careful never to say my wife but my companion (although language itself betrayed them since after all like it or not they were forced to use the possessive pronoun) with the same concern for respect and purity that also caused them to set fire to churches and hunt down priests like dangerous predators) . . . and not only (power) over the city but also over the entire province from the Pyrenees to the Elbe (and even beyond) even in the tiniest villages where all the town halls they'd taken over displayed the red-and-black flag above their front doors—the two colors not in two bands but side by side diagonally—as for learning, then, why and how that omnipotent power (or government which refused to call itself by that name) could not simply issue an order to the old tub's captain but was forced to act through the intercession of a character (Italian to boot) who lived (hid? from whom?) on the other side of the border in that second-rate hotel called the Terminus or something like that (chosen perhaps for the ease with which he could duck out of it should the need arise, without even taking time to pack his suitcase) where I'd finally located him (after all the "whys" were not really my concern . . .) and not without difficulty because with all my comings and goings from one side of the border to the other the only thing I'd managed to get hold of apart from his name was the name of a café near the courthouse and the hour at which another character (a Latin teacher they told me but he could just as well have passed for a wine broker or some minor functionary nearing retirement) came every evening to drink an *anis* and who, taciturn wary obese unshaven his eyes half closed and his lids heavy, continually brushing from the folds of his vest the ash of the cigarettes that he lit one after another, had finally not without hesitation and only after a long string of questions given me the address Avenue de la Gare where sitting at a little table covered with a paper tablecloth shoved up against the right-hand wall of a restaurant as dimly lit and narrow as a hallway and what's more smelling of tar because of the woodstove I would find dining alone the man who went by the name of Comandante

To this day I carry with me as one of the most painful blows dealt to my self-respect the memory of a 4 × 100 relay race which I was accused of having cost my school team, a memory made all the more bitter by the knowledge that the charge was justified except that it didn't happen the way my detractors claimed, which was that I'd been unable to keep up the pace, when in fact running in the third position and in the second lane I had gained distance, finding myself at the turn alongside the runner of the strongest opposing team who was in the fourth lane which meant that I was ahead by several meters, disaster striking at the end of the turn just as the baton was to be passed when misjudging the distance still separating me from him I shouted to the last team member to begin his sprint, and was then unable to catch up with him, so that in order to allow me to reach him and extend the baton toward him within the legal limit he had to slow his pace, which cost us the race but, from afar, from the central judges' stand, they couldn't make out just what had gone wrong and they said that I'd run out of steam. In the locker room and afterward I tried to explain what had happened, not without cynically intimating that the fault lay as much with him as with me, claiming that he'd miscalculated the distance between us and shouldn't have started off at such great speed, but he maintained that I had simply shouted too soon, which I knew was true, and more than the reproaches or disdainful shrugs with which they answered my explanations, I remained profoundly and inexorably humiliated before myself.

The anticipation before the event, the restless, impatient feeling in the legs, the damp, dark locker room, walking down the dark hallways of gray cement on our heels to protect the cleats, the stairway with steps also of cement which we climbed up with our toes turned out and which, up at the top, seemed to give onto the sky, the clouds, and in the opening of which appeared little by little the bleachers, the billboards, the arena where shouts of glory or defeat awaited us.

the cavalryman with the bloody face had taken a bullet in the knee as well and from time to time a bit of bright red blood seeped through the torn fabric of his breeches adding to the crust that had already coagulated, dark brown, disappearing into his leggings. At a gallop there was no problem but when we slowed the horses to a trot to let them catch their breath he didn't have the strength to post. Clinging to the pommel, tossed from side to side in his saddle like a bundle, he must have been suffering horribly and we could hear him groaning. I think there must have been tears flowing along with the blood that covered his face. Teeth clenched, he kept his eyes fixed on the road stretching out before us as if at every turn he was hoping to catch sight of the Meuse. When one of us asked him if he wanted someone to hold him up, he answered without taking his eyes from the road and

30

scarcely opening his lips something like I'll be all right! But we had no choice but to let the horses catch their breath from time to time. Even at a trot we could see how exhausted they already were.

> bathing naked in the freezing cold water of the lake concentric ripples around her legs her thighs her body over the smooth surface mirror reeds near the banks silver circles spreading over the dark burnished reflection of the deep woods silence only the fresh sound of the splashing water when she dives into it a bird somewhere
>
> a string of drops that fell like beads from her elbows when she came out of the water raised her arms to wring her hair

we stayed there for more than an hour on top of that hill our guns unlimbered waiting sitting or lying in the grass chewing the stem of an umbel-flower the horses more or less hidden behind a hedge From there at one point we could see the third squadron to our right fleeing at a gallop in extended order pursued by artillery fire mortars probably whose little shells exploded at long intervals We looked down over an entire landscape it was like one of those papier-mâché relief maps reconstitution of a battle-field of the sort you see in certain museums with copses made of dark green cotton except that those maps are usually dusty gray-ish whereas all around us the countryside was as if varnished jade English green emerald The exploding shells also looked like lit-tle balls of gray blue cotton the galloping horses and their riders were like tiny lead soldiers that could be knocked over with one clumsy movement of the hand the cuff of a sleeve yet we never saw one fall As it happened the shells were exploding a little be-hind them By the time the gunners had adjusted the trajectory they had disappeared into the woods I said to the lieutenant We're going to be outflanked He was also looking toward the spot where we'd seen the cavalrymen fleeing worried He said to me Yes but we haven't received the order to withdraw He was very young and in the reserves just out of Saumur before the mobilization with a pink baby face over a long spindly body or rather atop it and naturally a noble name He was doing his best to sound detached only a little put out as if he were in a drawing room somewhere When he spoke he sounded as if he were sucking on a piece of candy Unlike the other officers and cavalrymen of the regiment whose boots and leggings were mahogany colored he wore long black boots still gleaming he looked a little like a wading bird Everything was quiet again when a moment later a courier arrived climbing the hill on foot pushing his vehicle beside him I don't remember now if it was a motorcycle or a bicycle whose tires slid over the luxuriant grass As soon as he was within shouting range he screamed furious red panting Jesus Christ what the fuck are you still doing here you should be Where's the captain? Almost immediately the NCOs shouted On your horses!

"At the high point of this examination of Mademoiselle Raimonde's madness, the door of the theater box opened to allow the passage of etc."

In a marginal note to the manuscript, Stendhal writes:

"The reader who knows his way around will read: sitting on Leuwen's knees who had his hand I know not where and was about to j—— her off. Make the reader understand: had her on his knees."

Except pornography

On the way from the Holy Sepulchre to the Wailing Wall you follow a long souk, sometimes open to the sky, at other times under a vaulted ceiling, which runs down a gentle slope through the Arab neighborhood. An occasional tourist wanders by, sometimes slowing down to glance vaguely over the displays of baubles, rugs, postcards, or local craftworks, whose merchants, sitting on chairs or squatting at the entrance to their shops, sought more by reflex than by conviction to attract their attention, chanting or making lazy gestures of invitation, their arms falling limp, their voices falling silent as the strollers went on their way. Most of the shops were closed, in fact, their steel shutters lowered over their doors, and in places the souk was nothing more than a narrow corridor between those gray panels of corrugated sheet metal, some of them covered with black paint, carefully applied in a thick layer in most cases, but elsewhere as if in haste, so that through it you could make out, like a face behind a mourning veil, the colors of a flag with green, yellow, and red stripes into which, on one side, a triangle dug like a sharp wedge which the overlying paint made still blacker.

I don't remember if it was the waitress or the hotel manager (by then I'd already walked from one end of the dining room to the other) who pointed out from behind (from behind: he was facing the entrance—maybe so that he could keep an eye on it, the better to make a quick escape through the kitchens if need be) a figure sitting alone at a table in that narrow dining room with its cheap-restaurant smell and only five or six customers who looked like traveling salesmen, three of them engaged in an animated discussion. I remember that salt-and-pepper hair, carefully smoothed back, falling over the black velvet collar of the overcoat which he hadn't taken off, the ridiculous idea flashing through my mind that maybe he didn't even take it off to sleep, went to bed like that fully clothed and with his suitcase close at hand, as if the shoes, the overcoat, the salt-and-pepper hair parted on the side, the dark suit, the discreet necktie (and perhaps a concealed revolver) were one with the face which he turned toward me (giving a start when I said his name, beginning I thought to make a gesture, but in any case if I'd come to shoot him down it was too late for him), impassive, looking mildly surprised, even, eyebrows raised, as if I'd mistaken him for someone else, until I spoke the name of those who had sent me, then losing some of his coldness, still not relaxing entirely, still wary, his upper body moving, leaning forward, as he pushed his chair back with his legs, standing up, saying or rather whispering in a low voice Not here! walking toward the coat rack, taking down his hat, setting it on his head with one hand on which he wore a heavy signet ring while the other clasping my arm like a vise carried me more than it pushed me toward the exit, then both of us walking side by side along the avenue, deserted at this hour (and maybe a whistle, the puffing of a locomotive being shifted, the echoes of the buffers crashing together), as I explained the situation to him, surreptitiously glancing (standing, he was nearly a head taller than me) by the light of the few street lamps, half hidden by that hat with its curved brim, of the kind diplomats wore in those days, at the face I had briefly seen in the restaurant and which was something like the opposite of what I was expecting, that is, with those regular features, scarcely dulled by middle age, those bags under the eyes (eyes whose perpetual moistness I would later come to know, a sort of continuous watering that made them seem less metallically cold), that flushed face, and those nascent jowls, something more like an Irish face than an Italian one, forming, with his well-cut clothes, the impeccable crease of his trousers, his impeccably polished shoes, his manicured nails and his gold signet ring (about that there was no question: it was real) a whole from which emanated an impression of lavishness, violence, and irreparable sadness at the same time, of the sort exuded by rich, idle travelers killing time in the lobbies of luxury hotels, surrounded by the aura of starchy, neurasthenic, supercilious respectability characteristic of former Eton or Cambridge boys, retaining the puritanical stiffness of their upbringing, along with the brutality that finds release in the mud of the playing fields—or rather the fighting fields.

Nevertheless, resembling as he did an elegant diplomat (he claimed to be (or to have been) an officer in the Italian army and insisted on being addressed as Comandante) and at the same time a mortician ("Or what he probably is," someone who didn't like him later said to me: "Did he really impress you? an adventurer—or just a gangster, a vulgar little Napoleon or rather Neapolitan and if he was ever a 'comandante' anywhere, it wasn't in the Italian army but in something like some Mano Negra or Cosa Nostra: the type who thinks it's elegant to dress up like an undertaker and with tears in his eyes follow the funeral procession of a colleague he's had done in: the type that's always available whenever there's dirty work to be done somewhere . . .") . . . nevertheless, Oxford-schooled diplomat or mobster, he was the only figure in (or rather outside) a country mired in civil war who could exert any decisive influence over the crew of the only boat that seemed to be available along the entire Spanish Mediterranean seaboard, and three days later a decrepit little tub was in Sète, moored or rather stuck to the side of that Norwegian freighter whose freshly painted forecastle towered over it, blinding white, its hull also repainted (and at one point the clouds not so much parted as tore open slightly, the wan disk of the winter sun appeared, creating, along the black flank of the ship, a gleam as brilliant as if it had been coated with wax and polished with a chamois cloth), the filthy, pitiful little boat, its modest structures, also once painted white, now streaked with a dirty yellow, listing slightly, half rusted through, looking like some stunted sickly animal, some runt calf grown prematurely old, clinging to its mother's side or rather, as the Italian said, now standing (still wearing his fedora which he held down against the wind with one hand, still wearing his elegant overcoat, impeccable, impassible, and disgusted) in the dinghy bringing us aboard, the oarsman fighting a slight swell, the dinghy lashed from time to time by the spray, like fine raindrops, of the waves breaking on the other side of the dike, rising up in dirty white plumes (the gray sea, the gray sky, the damp, cool early-winter wind) and crashing with a limp sound, like wet laundry) . . . or rather, he muttered between his teeth, like an old mule trying to get herself knocked up by rubbing against an elephant, whereupon he swore again, but in Italian, grumbling that loaded down with the contents of the Norwegian ship's cargo hold her old hull was going to take on water past the waterline so that once she was out of the harbor the first wave would sink her like a stone: now we were getting close and I could read the name, partially worn away and also urinous yellow in color, of that half wreck, which (CARMEN), evocative of guitars, castanets, flounced skirts, and lustful glances, seemed to participate facetiously in what was being played out there, relegated as if to a secondary stage in that outer harbor where on the pretext of the danger of explosion the maritime authorities had forced the two ships to moor, sheltered from the dirty gray assault of the sea only by the dike protecting the roadstead, the Italian giving up cursing through his teeth only as he began to climb the gangway ladder atop which, pausing a few rungs below, stunned, I watched the tall Quaker-minister silhouette above me embrace, patting him on the back, a little old man who seemed to be the very materialization in human form of the floating junk heap he commanded, a childlike smile illuminating a weathered face, reddish-brown, etched with wrinkles, wearing the sly look of a professional smuggler, merry, topped with a filthy beret and emerging from the collar of a bulging overcoat made of rough cloth, it too as if eaten away by rust, while, hunched over the railing, dark, unsociable, and indifferent, three or four men, tall and lanky, coal trimmers probably, with the inevitable half-red, half-black kerchiefs around their necks, spat into the water.

Unlike large cities in Europe (London, Berlin, Paris . . .) which, so to speak, come unraveled around the edges, fray, seem to scatter a series of suburbs, ever less dense, at their periphery, pieces of cities, like an archipelago of little islands, ever more sparse, dropping off like beads as you move away from the center . . .
    (For example, starting from the Gare de l'Est, noted successively:

    Engine sheds—Freight stations—Profusion of tracks
    Warehouses—Housing projects
    Signal box
    Vacant lots—Factories
    Suburban houses—Gardens

Gas holders—High-tension lines Pylons
Factories—Cement-slab fences
Suburban houses brown buhrstone or gray black
   roughcast
Cement works—Pink laundry drying (watchman?)
Brick garage: yard full of junked cars
Green river—Barges
More houses, gardens, orchards
Tracks crossing over each other (bridge)
        running alongside each other
        joining up with each other
Slope, high embankment, hiding
Machines (bulldozers), painted yellow
Pink freight cars
More huge warehouses—rusting things, metal carcasses,
   crates
Sports field
Poles with crosspieces lying pell-mell alongside the track
First expanse of countryside—Mauve woods (a few
   black-green pines)
Park—View—Brick chateau
Sandpits—Worksites
Public landfill
Junkyard, stacks of cars—Mountain of carcasses with
   motors removed
Storage building full of ironwork (girders)
Undergrowth (thickets, brambles, pink carpet of dead
   leaves)
Mountains of cylindrical oil drums ringed with various
   colors blue yellow green rust
Another little woods
Plowed fields (in the rain the slopes of the furrows
   compacted by the blade shiny blue (marl?)
Then nothing but countryside: fields, hedgerows, stands
   of trees, etc.)

. . . Moscow comes to an abrupt end. Turning around, I could see the receding lights of the tall new apartment buildings that ring the city. A sort of rampart. In his capacity as driver of an official car, my chauffeur seemed to know only one way to drive: pedal pressed to the floorboards and furious blasts with the horn whenever he passed someone. The car bounced wildly in the potholes, but I'd come to know how the roads are in this country and I'd sat down in the front seat next to him. Everything was dark. From time to time we passed or met an occasional car or truck whose headlights blinded us, momentarily summoning up from the gloom, pale, ghostly, the car's four occupants: the driver with his doglike jaw, hunched over the wheel, stiff, as if hypnotized, swallowed by the darkness, and in the back the anemic-faced woman who had served as my interpreter and her boss, the jovial fat man, bending forward to talk to me. He asked what I had thought of our reception that morning with the Secretary General. I said it was very nice, that he was very likable. He told me we were lucky, that the Secretary General was very busy and that it was very rare that he took time out to speak with visitors like that. I said that it really was a great stroke of luck and that he was a very interesting man. Sometimes a lurch of the car threw the fat man off balance, and he'd laid his hand on the back of my seat. I could feel his breath on my neck. I liked him. He had put on that act with the other one, the ferret-faced one, but after all he was only doing his job. He asked if I'd enjoyed my stay. He seemed uncomfortable. But maybe it was only fear caused by the speed at which that idiot was driving, sitting there as stiff as if he'd been carved out of wood and as if fascinated by something he was staring at, straight ahead of him in the dark. I was expecting the fat interpreter to bring up the business about the signature, but instead, between two jolts, he asked me about my publishers. He wanted to know if they might publish a translation of their great writer, the one who had presided over these four days of interminable speeches that no one was listening to. He was insistent. He said that the great writer's latest book was very interesting, that it was a long dialogue between Christ and

Pontius Pilate. I don't remember what I mumbled in reply. I hurried to ask if we were still far from the airport. There was not a single light to be seen.

(Thick voice. Elixir, little vial, I remembered how he'd closed my hand over it and held it like that for a moment, in his grip. Like a little bird that might fly away. Precious.)

From the air, as far as the eye can see, Kazakhstan presents an ocher surface without visible relief, no cities, no villages, not even a farm, a road, a path. The only sign of human activity is, at one point, a railway line stretching into the distance, perfectly straight, as if drawn with a ruler, without a single curve, without even the slightest meander, apparently coming from nowhere and leading nowhere, like the absurd dream of a mad engineer. Here and there ponds can be seen (or maybe lakes: how to know from so high up? . . .), most of them more or less circular. When the rays of the sun reflect off their surface it looks like tin, a film over a blind man's eye (frozen?). Above it, also as far as the eye can see, hanging static and regularly spaced, rows of little white clouds, also circular and all the same size, lined up like an army in battle formation. From their motionless shadows on the ground where they repeat the same military configuration you can see that no drift, no wind carries them along.

The airplane was descending, preparing to land. Flying over the lake, it passed over the north side of the city. It was about noon and, with the light behind it, reflecting the autumn sun, the lake was like a sheet of gold. Near the shore, towering above all the others, stood a skyscraper, not perfectly rectangular like its neighbors but similar, on a gigantic scale, to one of those scaffold towers (derricks?) they build over oil wells, that is, in the form of an elongated and truncated pyramid.

Iron beams ran diagonally, crossing over each other, from one edge of the building to the next. The whole thing was painted black. The gold of the lake seemed to be melting: Chicago.

"Those who read a book in order to learn whether the baroness will marry the count will be confounded." (Flaubert)

In the country, we had the little cellar whose roof was about to collapse demolished, leaving a large empty courtyard, about ten meters by twelve, in which we planted a bay tree and an acacia along the north-facing wall, a climbing jasmine along the west-facing wall, a fig tree along the south-facing wall, then a stand of reeds, then a pomegranate tree, and finally a magnolia. With the beams salvaged from the cellar's ceiling we made two benches and, set upright in the ground, little tables for drinks. The fig tree is now over two meters high and its rough, raspy leaves with their sinuous and deeply incised edges rub up against the stems of the reeds. The latter spring from the ground at a slight slant, bending away from the wall then turning straight up in curved lines that sway limply. Some of them, the tallest, droop after a storm under the weight of the drops still clinging to them, diamondlike, or sometimes even stay bent toward the ground, lying horizontally, like the neck of some exhausted horse, their long pale green tapering leaves hanging like a mane. In the afternoon, the sun casts their interlaced shadows on the ground, and the forms of their leaves cross over each other in slender black triangles that move, clash, extend, or retract. The magnolia, which had difficulty recovering after being transplanted, is covered this year with healthy fleshy leaves, as if varnished, gleaming in the sun, grouped together in tulip shapes. The Virginia creeper planted three years ago clings to the wall, now covering a large part of it with dense, layered leaves, deep green with blue highlights, the largest ones heart shaped, like the hearts on playing cards, the others divided most frequently into three points. The young acacia has grown too fast and will have to be trimmed in the fall. Its branches spread outward, by turns bending under their own weight, rising up, and sinking down, undulating in the slightest breeze, as if it were beating its wings, shaking its plumes, its multitude of oval leaflets light green, like feathers.

If you look up, you can see swallows, with curved, black, daggerlike wings, flying like arrows over the walls. They appear suddenly, very low, just above the roofs, one, two, three, then spread out in a fan shape like the thousand sparks of a firework, shaped like crossbows, their paths crossing, diverging, suddenly turning with a quick beating of the wings. More of the same at various heights in the sky which they sometimes completely fill. If you watch closely, you can follow the path of the ones soaring high above, motionless, describing long sinuous curves then suddenly breaking away, still motionless, probably taking advantage of the updrafts, sometimes quivering a little. A few sparrows pass by now and then from the top of one wall to another or from the ivy to a roof, in one sudden movement. Toward the end of the day, fairly high up, seagulls fly past, heading unhurriedly but in a straight line from east to west, that is, from the sea inland. Their angled white wings beat slowly. Everything about them contrasts with the blinding speed of the swallows. When their flight suddenly changes direction their bodies swing sideways and for a brief moment the declining light of the sun illuminates their lustrous bellies, like metal, like silver.

In his *Notebooks*, published after his death, the German general Erwin Rommel sets out one of the principles—if not the sole principle—of his strategy. It is a simple one, and can be summed up in an axiom frequently put into practice by street toughs: hit first, talk later, replacing the word "talk" with "go and see." For he had taught his soldiers (manning a tank or mounted in sidecars) to systematically open fire without letup on everything which (hedges, stands of trees, edges of woods, buildings, etc.) might serve as an entrenchment or camouflage for the enemy, who, in this way, if that is where they're hiding, will think they've been spotted even before they've made their presence known, and thereby find themselves demoralized, immediately placed in a position of weakness. Similarly, when, not yet fully recovered from his wounds, convalescing, he learns that he is under police surveillance, expecting to be arrested from one day to the next, and goes walking in the woods around his house, he hands his service revolver to his son, who accompanies him, saying: "When you see the slightest movement shoot right away: they'll be afraid and miss their shot."

Chicago is known for its fires. They've even built a Museum of Fire, I was told, which unfortunately I did not have time to visit. Nevertheless, from the windows of the French consul's office, on the thirtieth floor of a skyscraper, I was able to see a conflagration shooting up in the distance, as dusk fell. Black smoke and flying sparks spewed from deep red flames, undulating, twisting upon themselves, almost at the horizon of the great brown mass of the city, seeming to rise high into the sky. Here and there neon lights were coming on, electric blue, acid green, cherry. As the dusk deepened the high flames seemed even higher and redder. The consul told me there was a fire like that at least once a week.

A thick fog prevented the takeoff of the plane that was supposed to bring me back from Urbana to Saint Louis, where the passengers were finally transported by bus. The endless plain of Illinois is uniformly bare, uniformly flat, without the slightest hill, the slightest depression. Sometimes you see farmhouses built of wood, painted yellow or brick red, with green or black copper roofs, like in Scandinavia. Apparently the majority of the region's inhabitants are descended from Swedish or Finnish immigrants. We don't know just what Shatov and Kirillov did in the United States after they went there together, if they hired themselves out as seasonal workers on farms like this, or worked wherever they could find jobs in construction or perhaps in factories. Dostoevsky says that when they returned home they avoided each other. Although they stayed in more or less close contact with the Russian revolutionaries, Shatov seemingly evolved little by little toward a sort of angelism while the refusal of the established order led Kirillov to an individualistic conception of freedom which could find its only logical expression in suicide, but in the one case no less than in the other the question of the existence of God seems to have occupied a central place in their preoccupations.

I didn't find the young brown-haired whore all that attractive The skin of her buttocks was slightly grainy On the other hand her entire body was like stone I was inside her when he threw open the door and came in or rather stood there on the threshold He was naked too his long cock hanging in the middle of his graying thatch a stray lock of his hair which he always kept carefully smoothed back formed a sort of cowlick a plume I pulled out of the girl I said Well come on in don't be shy what the fuck are you doing here He said you've got a nice dick I said What are you a faggot? He said No I like to watch He had his arm around the waist of the girl he'd gone upstairs with She was completely naked as well I looked at the blond hair of her not triangle but sort of light mossy patch She didn't know whether to laugh or what she winked at me I said Get the fuck out of here! I'd gone completely limp I said Comandante! what do you command? He began to laugh Wouldn't you like all four of us to fuck together? Wouldn't you like to have this one? I repeated Get the fuck out of here! Still I liked the blond more than the one I was with but he'd laid claim to her with that sort of authority he had I don't know where it came from She was tall and thin she had slightly sagging breasts but rounded oval like goat teats the nipples surrounded by large areolae of a very pale pink She smiled at me The madam appeared in the hallway She wasn't undressed yet she said What's all this shouting about? She had a likable face a reasonable air She pushed them aside and came into the room then turned to face him and pushed him out saying in a friendly way Come on now I don't want any trouble come on Monsieur don't make trouble you can see that your friend He began to laugh With his long ruddy overly pink face almost purple the bags under his eyes he looked more than ever like an Irishman

When he didn't think he was being watched he had a sad look desolate even with those permanently moist pink-rimmed eyes His white round stomach was divided in two by a thin line of gray hairs like a chain of upside down circumflex accents Come on the blond said to him She winked at me again Finally he turned his back disappeared down the hallway with her Come on I'll suck you you'll see I'll make you hard again said the little brunette She sat on the edge of the bed jerked me off a little first then leaned over brought her open mouth toward me and swallowed my cock Her head went up and down determinedly but it wasn't working I said Forget it She drew herself up and looked at me crestfallen Damn! she said Poor dear Who is that guy he made you Is he a friend of yours? I said Yes a friend She went on jerking me off mechanically Don't you like me? she said Would you have preferred Lili? I said No no you're very cute I patted her hair I'm just tired She went on looking at me with curiosity perplexity I tried to smile Finally she made up her mind to speak What are you doing here? I said What are we doing as you see we're out on a spree we're living it up She said Living it up? She hesitated again her hand had stopped moving What was with those Norwegians? I said Those Norwegians you mean those guys who were here when we got here? I took one of her breasts in my hand They were small with lilac brown nipples I squeezed she said Hey you're hurting me I let go and rubbed the back of my hand over her nipple pushing it inward a little as my hand passed over it afterward it sprang back elastic She said You tried to talk to them I could see there was something going on there I said You're imagining things we were just having a laugh that's all She said Having a laugh The boss told me the newspaper said the freighter's full of weapons what are Your friend he could be your father Why did you call him Comandante is he Spanish what does I said Irish he's Irish You're cute Take me in your mouth and make me come like that

Once, at dusk, one of them crashed into the window, behind which the lights were burning. I opened the window. It was lying spread

out on the bricks, huge, black, wild. I could see its wings, sharp
as knives, its forked tail.

KIRILLOV: . . . Have you seen a leaf, a leaf from a tree?

STAVROGIN: Yes.

KIRILLOV: I saw a yellow one lately, a little green. It was de-
    cayed at the edges. It was blown by the wind. When I was
    ten years old I used to shut my eyes in the winter on pur-
    pose and fancy a green leaf, bright, with veins on it, and
    the sun shining. I used to open my eyes and not believe
    them, because it was very nice, and I used to shut them
    again.

STAVROGIN: What's that? An allegory?

KIRILLOV: N-no . . . why? I'm not speaking of an allegory,
    but of a leaf, only a leaf. The leaf is good. Everything's
    good.

On the tenth of May, at five o'clock in the morning,
the Germans launched their offensive along the French,
Belgian, and Dutch borders. The brunt of their attack
was directed toward a front about seventy kilometers
long, between Sedan and Namur, where they had
concentrated a total of thirty-three (33) divisions, including seven (7) armored divisions, in response to
which the French sent into Belgium, in forced march,
only nine (9) divisions, whose fastest-moving elements, composed of cavalry regiments, half of them
on horseback, crossed the Meuse at about noon on
the eleventh. The next day, Pentecost Sunday, the
Fourth Light Cavalry Division, overwhelmed, retreated in disarray, and under fire from the enemy air
force managed with difficulty to recross the river in
the evening. Without ever having had the chance to
fight, the division had in just one day lost about a
quarter of its men.

One part (the oldest) of the Jardin des Plantes, in Paris, was laid out according to a geometrical design in the form of a rectangle about four hundred meters long by fifty wide extending from the quays along the Seine to the main building of the Natural History Museum, of no great architectural interest. The vast esplanade is framed by two alleyways running between rows of plane trees, whose branches, thinned every year, form two unbroken, rectilinear walls on either side of the lawns and the flower banks, which change from season to season. It is clear that here man has set out to domesticate, so to speak, to tame nature, working against nature's exuberance and heedlessness in order to bend it to a will for order and domination, just as the rules of classical theater enclose language within an equally artificial form, contrary to the disordered manner in which the passions naturally find their external expression. To this rigid decor are added, on the north, a botanical garden, a little alpine garden with artfully arranged boulders, and a zoological garden where one can see exotic birds, snakes, monkeys, bears, felines, and, in times past, a giraffe and elephants. Where the garden touches the first slopes of the Montagne Sainte-Geneviève, they have constructed a belvedere, a little conical butte about fifteen meters high. Along its sides snake paths leading to a cast-iron lantern, reached by a stone staircase. In contrast to the strict alignments of plantings and floral decorations, this part takes its inspiration from what is known as an English garden, avoiding symmetry at all costs. Great trees, hundreds of years old, among them a cedar with dark foliage, grow there surrounded by a varied, unfettered vegetation which seems to have come up by chance: bamboo, climbing ivies, bushes of various species create an environment suited to the contemplative taste for Nature that was in fashion toward the end of the eighteenth century, illustrated by writers like Jean-Jacques Rousseau or Bernardin de Saint-Pierre, whose statue in fact graces the lower slopes, wearing a riding coat, sitting meditatively in an armchair while two children play at his feet, sheltered by broad

Invited to dinner in Madras by the wife of a car man-

46

ufacturer who is said to be the Indian Ford. Servants with dark faces, dressed in white, with turbans on their heads, stand at attention beside the door to a large garden with alleyways lit by lanterns at the far end of which stands the single-story house. The hostess is a woman of about forty, very beautiful, wearing an olive green sari edged with a gold ribbon. She is with her daughter, who has an agreeable face but not the aristocratic beauty of her mother. The furniture (armchairs, sofas), fitted with orange cushions, is made of a dark wood (ebony?) minutely hand sculpted with exuberant plant motifs. On one of the walls hangs a clumsy oil copy of *Paul and Virginia Fleeing before the Storm* by Madame Vigée-Lebrun: the young boy is trying to shelter his companion under a sort of veil, billowing in the wind. The banana-tree leaves, also cast in bronze. Oxidation has covered the latter with a pale green color, spread indiscriminately over the undulating leaves of the banana tree, the children's cheeks, their clothes, the riding coat, and the closed fist on which the pensive face of the writer rests, brushed by the end of a branch from a pine tree that bends dangerously under its own weight, whose trunk they had to support with an iron trestle. On a little zinc plaque held by a stake thrust into the ground at the foot of the tree, the words Aleppo pine can be read. On the other side of the alleyway the branches of a large tree extend outward and droop majestically toward the ground. A sign is nailed to its spotted trunk, with the inscription Anatolian plane tree, planted by Jussieu in 1785.

sky is black, the veil yellow. The painting is surrounded by a heavy gilt frame bristling with moldings in rococo style. Too large for the canvas, it leaves a gap between its own edges and those of the painting. At dinner, around the table, servants also dressed in white and wearing turbans move silently. The plates are made of silver, in the form of deep platters. Forks and knives are laid out for the two European guests while with their long, fine fingers, brown with pale nails, the two women pick up the food and lift it elegantly to their mouths. On the wall of the dining room hangs an unfolded publicity pamphlet, about a meter and a half long, of the sort you see in the windows of travel agencies, showing a full-color panoramic view of the Alps including the Jungfrau, the Matterhorn, and Mont Blanc. It is held up only by pins stuck diagonally into the wall.

we were coming down the hill in single file at a walk the haunches of the horses swaying stiffly from side to side the way they do on slopes the upper bodies of the cavalrymen tilted backward slightly the sun had gone behind a cloud I was still halfway up the hill when I heard the shots they must not have gauged the height correctly because at that point I didn't hear a single bullet go by we began to gallop I caught a glimpse of them on the road beyond which the third squadron had fled a little earlier they were jumping out of their vans in bunches and running to the ditches to lie flat on their stomachs so they could shoot taking us from the side I very clearly saw the figure who seemed to be their commander oddly dressed in a sort of long tan duster half hidden behind a tree and gesturing with one arm Between the buildings of the hamlet we were safe from attack the horses were turning circles without direction running into each other no one seemed to know what to do and at one point there was an explosion in the middle horses and men thrown to the ground later someone said a grenade thrown from one of the windows who knows people said that among the Belgians there were But all at once the leader Ostertag shouted Get behind me full gallop toward the railroad tracks I remember in a confused way that we jumped the ditch galloped across fields this time under a hail of bullets the sun had come out again the railroad tracks were bordered with tall bushes impossible to jump so we climbed back up the other hill still at full gallop and suddenly I saw the tracks gleaming down at the bottom of the railway trench now lying open before me the sun had gone behind a cloud again years later I remember the whole thing down to the smallest detail After the war I went back to see the place again the hamlet is called Lez Fontaine ("Fontaine" in the singular) that trench must be something like ten or twelve meters deep I remember having reflexively spurred her toward the back of her left flank and simultaneously pulled down on her neck with the reins on the same side so that we both went down the slope on our sides but when we reached the bottom as she stood up she threw me off I got up right away I took a step forward I touched the reins with my fingertips she also took a step I almost managed to get hold of the reins again but suddenly she took off at a gallop other riderless horses passed by us also galloping but I couldn't manage to catch one they suddenly turned away every time I saw the last of them disappearing so I began to run along the tracks trying to aim for the ties

No name (or perhaps in incomprehensible idioms dialects with strange sonorities, savage, guttural, or silky in the way a bird's call can be, the call of an eagle, of some supernatural animal, gentle and bloodthirsty—and in fact that was what it resembled: not what we usually call mountains, a simple barrier of inert stones, of needles, or of inert névés, but something living, somnolent and terrifying, from the saurian or reptile family, having the same sort of wrinkles, and which could probably kill without even taking the trouble to move, simply waiting, with the peaceful and monstrous indifference of one of those animals covered with scales or a shell, lying in wait, asleep in their immobility, suddenly striking, then falling back into their slumber—and unviolated, except perhaps by some more or less scientific expedition: a half dozen men stooping under the weight of surveying and measuring instruments, there not for the sake of some athletic feat or media event but sent by some governmental institute, geological or geographical—or political: perhaps charged with the mission of establishing some absurd or hypothetical borderline amid that chaos, wearing clothes, hats, shoes, and gloves of animal skin, panting beneath their burden in the thin air, their eyes protected by thick glasses, digging out a path with their ice axes, step after step, in the glistening snow, perhaps finally with their frozen hands planting some flag that the wind will have ripped to shreds before they have even made it back to base camp—or maybe, for greater resistance, made of zinc) . . . no name designated the peaks or rather the pile, the endless succession of ridges, the sort of solidified tempest, blinding, of which, in the little airplane whose interior was furnished like a drawing room, the jovial interpreter said, pointing to it, that very nearby, then (but nearby what, starting from where? ran the invisible dotted line established through surveyors' lenses in accordance with time-honored conventions between nomadic tribes (there must be, invisible, hidden in the depths, the folds, places that resemble valleys, gorges, defiles, a few passages that can be crossed, at least for two or three brief weeks, in summer . . .), a few caravan drivers or a few bandits with slanted eyes, also protected by animal skins, and later solemnly signed and sealed on a map by other bandits in silk robes, wearing a peacock feather on their heads or soberly dressed in European style: but what path did it take through this chaos, the piles of ice and shining walls that have arisen here, jostling each other, as if in the center of a continent (or rather of two adjoining continents), between two steppes, two deserts, in its monstrous and silent solitude and thousands of kilometers from any liquid surface, any sea, there had arisen a desert even more deserted, even more implacably hostile, unlike oceans, to any penetration and to any form of human or animal life), . . . very nearby, then, the head interpreter said, was China.

Whereupon one of the fifteen guests (the fifteen guests chosen as if at random, from a directory of what are known as VIPs and which included in their number a diplomat straight out of a toothpaste commercial, two Turks, an Ethiopian painter in tribal costume, an elegantly turned-out Cuban, two Black Americans, an economist, a futurologist, the second husband of the most beautiful woman in the world) . . . whereupon one of them (an actor who had played Nero in the movies) told amusingly of a recent visit there, of having been welcomed on his arrival by a chorus of young girls with slanted eyes intoning the Ode to Joy which gradually (he was an excellent actor and he mimed the scene hilariously) lost its rhythm, went astray, began to wander aimlessly, to undulate, transforming itself, whiningly, into a sort of Oriental threnody.

One night, on the plains, it snowed. But in the autumn sunlight, still warm, the layer of pale blue snow had melted by afternoon. They were photographed along with their interpreters, bunched together in front of the main building of the cluster of little houses where they were lodged, scattered throughout a huge park planted with orchards and poplars. The park was ringed by a high impregnable grillwork fence and its entrance was watched over by armed men in brown uniforms who emerged from a guardhouse to lift the barrier when their cars arrived in procession. Although they could clearly hear the tumultuous rush of the nearby torrent rolling its waters straight down from the glaciers, no one was allowed through the gate to go and see it and it remained invisible, haunting, like the relentless cavalcade of some herd of wild animals jostling, leaping, struggling to get ahead of the others, tossing their manes. The same little airplane whose interior resembled a drawing room brought them to the banks of a lake with a Mongol name surrounded on all sides by the enormous mountains. Young girls in embroidered costumes and toques welcomed them on the threshold of a tent, also embroidered, where they were offered piles of brittle sweets. Some slow-moving doves were released, quickly caught by falcons that fell upon them like stones and killed them. They were also shown wrestlers, races between Kyrgyz horses, for which the nobility of the ancien régime used to pay a king's ransom. The little grandstand was full of men with slanted eyes, with round, weathered, yellow faces, with hats like the ones worn by Tyroleans but made of white felt edged with a black ribbon. Several of the older ones wore military decoration ribbons on their jacket lapels. Evening was slowly falling from the top of the mountains, gradually growing dark, across the lake which seemed still to preserve the last glimmers of the setting sun.

Kirillov and Shatov might also have worked in one of those gold mines whose abandoned structures can still be seen in the Rocky Mountains, surrounded by the little clusters of ruined buildings they call Ghost Towns. Entryways into the tunnels, more or less blocked off by boards, trestles, rusting windlasses with tangled wires hanging from them can still be seen on the hillsides, lying on cones of rubble, like the bones, the gnawed skeletons of a frenzy of money, violence, and greed. The silence is only broken now and then by the silken sound of the light breeze playing through those metal harps, that debris, those twisted railroad tracks hanging over the void, their carriages lying upside down, half buried. Most of the wooden houses have lost their roofs. Their splintered walls allow a glimpse of empty interiors, with beams and rafters lying in piles. In contrast to cities that have been bombed, burned, or ravaged by riots, there is no visible trace of destruction by human hands: time alone has slowly eaten away the paint, the wood, the iron. As if some invisible monster, in-dolent, unhurried, and voracious, had mercilessly pursued (con-tinued to pursue), silently, showing itself only in the gentle vi-bration of the air among the interlaced cables, the weeds, a relentless project of recuperation, of assimilation, reducing to their basic components (oxides, fibers) materials taken from the earth or the forests, seeking to absorb them into its cast-iron belly, to erase little by little even the memory of every trace of life, every dream. Only one of the buildings, for the sake of the tourists, has kept its tall wooden façade, on which the word SA-LOON peels and flakes, with a bar inside where grizzled actors sit, pretending to drink and talk, wearing huge hats, checked shirts, and leather jackets with fringe hanging from them.

Also in contrast to the ruins left behind by past civilizations, whose traces can still be seen (temples, forums, ramparts, are-nas), the materials used here (wood and iron) are doomed by their perishable nature to be attacked and destroyed little by little, either by rust or by rot, meaning that unlike those sanctuaries, colonnades, or agoras, there will one day remain absolutely nothing, not a tunnel, not a windlass, not a wagon, not a house, of what was built by a furious and impatient appetite for gain. The soil will grow arid again, only mounded a little over the last remnants, then simply bare, returning to its primitive state.

The university at Colorado Springs displays in its museum a collection of Christs of Mexican origin, carved in wood and painted. The welts left by the scourges, the various wounds, the puncture in the side are represented with a realism at once self-indulgent and naive: where the skin is torn from the knee, the inflamed flesh swells to form a sort of roll that makes a pink, bruised crater around the exposed bone. Without explaining why (too human?) Dostoevsky writes somewhere that the contemplation in the Dresden Museum of the dead Christ painted by Holbein can make you lose your faith. It's a highly elongated painting, narrow, whose surface is entirely taken up by the body of a man lying on his back, naked and thin, stretched out flat, a short black beard pointing upward from his chin, his head bent back. In all of *Remembrance of Things Past,* Marcel Proust never speaks of the existence of God.

One of the most renowned thinkers in French equitation, General L'Hotte, writes that the objective of the rider must be to obtain a horse that is "calm, forward, straight." General L'Hotte adds: "The order in which these three goals must be pursued is invariable, absolute, and one must never seek the next before the preceding one has been attained."

On the morning of May 17, 1940, followed by only two cavalrymen, two officers (the colonels of a brigade) are walking their horses along the road from Solre-le-Château to Avesnes, whose borders are lined with the wake, at once sad and repulsive, that war leaves behind, formed of all sorts of vehicles, abandoned or destroyed, some of them just burning out (little flames still playing tag over the carcasses, stink of burning rubber), dead horses, crushed suitcases, the most varied sorts of objects lying scattered and dirty. The hips of the two officers so perfectly absorb the movements of their mounts that their backs remain absolutely straight, stiff, as if the two men were sitting in a vehicle running on tracks. Valéry tells of a famous riding master at Saumur who, visited by a young major known as a brilliant rider, says to him: "I'll show you how I ride," has a horse brought to him, climbs into the saddle, crosses the length of the riding grounds at a walk, comes back, jumps down and says: "There you are. I'm not bluffing you. I'm at the peak of my form: I walk without making a mistake." The two colonels have thus covered about five kilometers when one of them is shot at almost point-blank range by an enemy sharpshooter hidden behind a hedge. By a curious reflex, just as he is hit by the volley of shots, he unsheathes his sword and raises it full length: horse and rider thus fall to one side, together.

Other titles of Gastone Novelli's paintings:

> Vuole dire caos (Means chaos)
> Al di sopra delle stelle (Above the stars)
> Paura clandestina (Clandestine fear)
> Ora zero (Zero hour)
> Giornale intimo (Diary)
> Le cose nell'uovo (Things in the egg)

Nothing could be more different from the Mediterranean south, dry, windy, and dusty, with its monotonous expanses of vineyards, its roads lined with plane trees, its overly blue sky, where I lived as a child, than the Jura Mountains toward which I set out with my mother almost as soon as school had ended in the summer. The hamlet with its long mauve roofs as if hanging over the eyes of the houses, at the bottom of the steep-sided valley overlooked by rocky cliffs, themselves crowned with a mane of trees, of bushes. The steep slopes, wooded, haunted by animals evoked as a way of frightening me, fantastic in my childish imagination (wild boars, lynxes, foxes), and whose carcasses, eyes closed, fur matted with blood, hunters sometimes proudly exhibited in the village square. Place names: *Fontaine aux oiseaux, Chemin des bêtes, Tour aux vipères.* A river snaking between the fields, beneath the low branches, glittering over its pebble-lined bed, still ice-cold as it emerged from the source only a little higher up. Unbroken noise of the springs. Cascades. Stone bridge. Gray trout undulating over the streambeds of tufa or ocher pebbles. Fields, umbels, mint, watercress, and the smell of the mushrooms we foraged for in the damp undergrowth the roads still white amid all that green, lined with bushes covered with blackberries that left violet black stains on your hands. Trout still in the places where the river's current slowed, sleeping, the water as if thickened dense green now which the rays of the sun, filtered through the leaves, could scarcely penetrate, the sought-after trout the same shade of green, a little darker, or rather black, fleeing swift arrow disappearing with a flick of the tail under some stone.

He took out his wallet, opened it, pulled out a photograph and handed it across to me. As I looked at it, I could sense that he was watching me. It showed a hanged man. Since they had attached him to the low crotch of a fruit tree, it couldn't have been his own weight that had strangled him and they must have had to push down (several of them at once?) heavily on his shoulders. He was sitting on the ground, one of his legs folded back, as if broken, beneath the other one, which was stretched out full length, flat against the ground of the orchard. It was a man with short cropped hair, like many peasants of Aragon, with a thin neck (or grown thin, distended by suffering—or by the downward pressure). The rope had dug so deeply into his neck that it seemed almost to have cut through it, to be encrusted in it, the lower jaw standing out as on the desiccated head of a mummy. His eyes were closed, the hollow orbits of a mummy as well. He was dressed in a sort of dark pullover with short sleeves and a pair of trousers, belt

55

The shadow overtook the valley, the high limestone cliffs reflecting the glow of the invisible sunset, spotted with long blackish streaks, like ink, which, they said, was a sign of rain to come the next day. A time when the roads were simply made of stone, dusty in the summer sun. Oxen with light pelts, almost white, walking slowly, chained two by two to mountains of hay or dragging the long trunks of pine trees newly stripped of their bark leaning on each other shoulder against shoulder bent forward diagonally their foreheads girdled with a fringed strap to protect them from the horseflies which nevertheless clustered in knots around their pale-

unbuckled, which seemed to have slipped down over his hips. It wasn't clear whether his hands were tied or not. They were joined together, clasped in a protective gesture over his genitals. His lower lip protruded and the corners of his mouth sagged unnaturally, like those fish (groupers?) that wear an expression at once spiteful and unhappy. Around us, in this downtown café to which he had led me as we left his hotel, the few customers were talking peacefully. Wearing caps on their heads, four regulars played *manille* and noisily slammed their cards down on the marble tabletop. Now and then one of them lit a damp cigarette butt using a lighter fitted with a long yellow wick. Outside you could hear the tinkling of the bell in the movie theater next door, announcing the beginning of the next show. He was looking at me with a mocking gaze. I managed to conceal any emotion. I only said to him as I handed back the photo: "Did you take it yourself?" He didn't answer. He went on looking at me with a mocking air. He folded the photo away in his wallet and put it back into his pocket.

lashed eyes, on their pink snouts from which hung glistening strings of drool. Women out strolling carrying puce-colored parasols whipping themselves in the shoulders with a frond from a walnut tree to keep the flies away . . . Attracted by the color black they say. Ten years afterward they were still wearing mourning for my father who was killed on the Meuse. Shadow of the walnut tree unhealthy they said. Don't fall asleep there. Brown stains of crushed walnuts, wild mint with fleshy little leaves, puffy, giving off a smell when pinched.

I repeated his question: How do you manage to live with the fear? I said Hey! You don't have any choice! . . . He said What I'd like you to . . . I said You're afraid, that's all. Although . . . I tried to find the right words. I wondered what the words "war" or "fear" could possibly mean to this man who hadn't even yet been born back then, for whom the word "airplane" meant nothing more than a means of transport, and who visibly had never missed his three meals a day. He was about forty years old. He was dressed more like a businessman than a journalist, that is, without that slightly ostentatious carelessness, more or less bohemian or artistic, that the latter sometimes affect. He had an air of efficiency about him, precise, wore a discreet tie and on his wrist a square gold-plated watch, or maybe real gold, with a black face on which several little dials were pressed in together, like moons, each of them indicating I suppose the month, day, hour, minutes, and seconds. The band was made of fine slivers of the same metal, parallel and interlinked. He said The theme of war recurs insistently in your work. Some have even called it the keystone, underlying everything you've written, and that . . . I said that Ooh that was a bit of an exaggeration, a bit reductive, that after all I'd written a lot of other things and that . . . But he cut me off, he said All the same, you must recognize that . . . From behind the rectangular lenses of his glasses, in their gold frame, that too, he watched me attentively, professionally, neutrally, like a doctor. He might just as well have been a traveling salesman sizing me up in hopes of persuading me to sell him my apartment or trade in my old car for a new one. I said that Yes it was true it often came up but . . . He said Why? I said that You know I don't have much imagination so except for my very first books which weren't anything much the next ones were always more or less based on things I'd lived through, my personal experiences, or else old family papers, that sort of thing. . . . He said Yes that he knew but that's just what interested him: my personal experience, and I said that Well, as it happened among other experiences there was the war and it must have made a strong impression on me, maybe because I was too emotional, or too fragile, or else maybe because I hadn't had time to get used to it, because for all practical purposes I was only involved in it for eight days and . . .

He said Only eight days? I said Only that. Yes. I tried to strike a joking tone I said But on the other hand I had a good seat, in the orchestra stalls, as they say in rugby jargon of the heavy-weights that fill out the forward lines. Except that I wasn't in with the heavyweights but in one of those divisions they call light which according to the 1870 rules of military engagement must be the first to reach the front, so as to get the conversation started break the ice so to speak but unfortunately the other side didn't seem to have read the 1870 manual and they were the opposite of light and as for conversation, it was rude words right from the start Ha ha ha! . . . But he was looking at me in a reticent way, as if he were embarrassed, even reproachful So I said all at one go that to get things straight once and for all we had to agree on what the words mean, that for instance when I said I'd fought in the war I should make it clear that the word "fight" was very rel-ative given that I hadn't even fired one lousy shot with my rifle so it would be more accurate to say not that I'd fought in the war but that I'd simply found myself caught up in it as you find your-self caught in a storm or a cataclysm and that even there those weren't the right words (storm, cataclysm) because they proba-bly give an impression of devastation, of a ravaged landscape, lu-nar, whereas in fact it was green, lush, pastoral, except that at certain moments without warning this thing was suddenly upon you: the explosions, the crackling of the machine guns, the deaf-ening noise, the shouts, the orders, the counterorders, the whinnying, the panicked horses, after which it all returned to normal and then there was nothing left for you to do but try to catch your breath and count your men. Slightly fewer every time. And so, that when it was all over, on the morning of the eighth day, the colonel brought back with him only two men from his entire regiment, following along behind him. Me among them, and that's it.

He repeated in the same reticent tone of voice That's it? I said again Yes, in the end, that's it. I said that You know it could have been worse, that next to him there was another one (another colonel): the one from the regiment with which we formed a brigade. He didn't have anyone following him at all. Not even a horse. Everyone from his command group had been killed and he was forced to walk all night until he stumbled into ours, where he was offered the horse of a dead soldier. As for the general commanding the brigade (or rather who had commanded the brigade), it was even simpler: he'd blown his brains out the night before. But I didn't know anything about that until later. For the moment, all I knew was that a little earlier the retreating regiment led by the colonel had fallen into an ambush, which thanks to an incredible sequence of lucky breaks I'd managed to get out of alive, without a horse again, that I'd walked westward through the woods using the sun to guide me, and that suddenly, by pure coincidence once again, around the bend of a road I'd found the colonel or rather the two colonels who, side by side, looked as though they were out enjoying a ride, followed by a cavalryman leading two horses, one of which the colonel simply ordered me to mount and follow along with them. Only . . . But I've already told this story, I . . . He said No go on it's very interesting, I . . . Would you mind if I recorded this? Without waiting for an answer he had already taken from his briefcase a little tape recorder which he examined and then set down between us on one corner of the table. I said I don't much like those machines. I have no talent for speaking. In fact, that's probably why I write, I . . . He said We'll take care of that, it's only to help me remember, afterward I . . . Listen, I'm sorry, but could we close the window? . . . Because the noise from the street . . . I said Yes of course. I stood up, I walked to the window. It had rained. The damp trunks and branches of the plane trees stood out darkly, as if varnished, against the leaves, also washed by the rain, colored soft green. The leaves now concealed the large nest that two magpies had built a few years before in the highest branches of one of the trees, to which they return toward the end of March or the beginning of April. They shore it up and for ten days or so are forced to defend it against two crows who try to take it over. The same thing happens every year. It's a strange spectacle, in which there is no fighting in the strictest sense of the word, no direct confrontation—at least I've never seen one—but rather a sort of campaign of intimidation, each of the four birds landing here or there on the branches, still bare, which bend beneath their weight, then taking flight and landing again a few meters away, one of them sometimes flying off, disappearing over the roofs, then returning a moment later, the vacant nest constituting so to speak a focal point for that sort of parody of war which seems to have its own rules, its own conventions, and a predetermined outcome, because when it's all over it's always the magpies that, although smaller than the crows, win out and end up occupying the spot. But when the trees have put out their leaves, everything is hidden. I closed the window against the roar of the cars and I came back and sat down. In the meantime he had dealt with his machine. He leaned over it one last time and said If you don't mind let's start now. Yes you've already told that story. But the fear, I mean how is it exactly, what do you do to live with it, to . . . I said You know, you get used to it. And immediately after I said that No, that wasn't really true. That you don't get used to it. Never. That you're always afraid. All the time. Before or after, that is. That is, when you're not running, or galloping, throwing yourself to the ground, standing up again, mounting your horse again, jumping to the ground again, running on all fours . . . And it's like that from the first shell that suddenly falls next to you. I say suddenly because you've been riding for two days,

60

you've been moving along without anything happening except, sometimes, on the right or the left, or even behind you, sounds of explosions, fairly distant, and until then it's only apprehension, along with something like curiosity, excitement, and toward noon, the second day, you've crossed the Meuse, then, a little further on, a little town with a gazebo in its central square— you know: one of those gazebos made of lacy cast iron, painted sky blue—and people who watch you go by without a word, with nothing but an uncomfortable look, and you have nothing to say to them either, nothing to do but look away when your eyes meet theirs, and in the silence the only thing you hear is the clattering of the hooves over the paving stones of the square with the gazebo, and a little beyond the far edge of town the word starts to spread from platoon to platoon that the enemy has been sighted, and just then there's something that clenches up inside you, but when you're in the countryside again no matter how you squint, no matter how closely you listen, you can't see or hear anything resembling shots or explosions that might lead you to believe that you're approaching some danger—because you suppose that there must be someplace from which you would hear at least a few machine-gun shots, a few rifle shots, even isolated ones, fired as they retreat by the soldiers that had spotted the enemy, but nothing, still nothing: so imagine the peaceful end of a spring day where everything looks as though it had been varnished, fresh, enameled, the rays of the setting sun slanting through the leaves of the trees lining the hillside that the squadron is climbing at a walk, and apart from the sound, still, of the hooves, there is silence, no one speaks, you simply watch the first groups of refugees coming up the road toward you, and suddenly, without anything having happened, without any apparent cause, you hear them shout, or rather scream, the piercing screech of the women, too sharp, almost indecent, to the point where you wonder with a sort of pitying condescension What's their problem, what's their problem? at the same time as you see them all, women, men, children, abandon the carts, bicycles, or baby carriages that they were dragging along and throw themselves into the ditch and then, without your having even heard the approach of the three high-flying planes, all at once that sort of bush of dust in the field, a few meters away, sparks crackling with a deafening roar or rather a crash, and the shockwave striking you from the side like blows from a fist, and then, since that's what you're asking about, that's when it comes: fear. Animal, uncontrollable, as uncontrollable as your bolting horse whose muscles you vaguely feel tensing and relaxing between your thighs at the same time as, paradoxically (it's comical, perfectly ridiculous, since after all that's what you're there for), . . . at the same time as you feel something like a sort of scandalized indignation: What the hell they're trying to kill me! What the hell they really are trying to kill me! And from that moment on . . .

He said Excuse me, do you mind? As he stretched out his arm to pick up the little tape recorder his sleeve pulled up, fully revealing that large wristwatch with its dials for the seconds, the minutes, the hours, its hands turning circles. As if time did not move forward, spun on itself, always came back to the same places, ran in place so to speak. In any case, even if the dog stops chasing its tail, it still drags it along behind.

He said Let's see if it's working the other day this thing didn't . . . He pressed a key, then another, and I heard my voice come out—or rather not exactly: a metallic voice, resonant, not mine or at least not the one I hear when I speak, saying: . . . a sort of scandalized indignation what the hell they really are trying to kill me and from that moment on . . . Then his—but that one was the same as the one I'd heard: Excuse me do you mind . . . He said Right it's OK, once again pressed two keys and said Let's continue. Go on. I said It must seem ridiculous to you? He said What? I said That a soldier could feel indignant, scandalized because he suddenly realizes that the people on the other side are trying to kill him? . . . He said No not at all on the contrary that's a perfect answer to my question go on. Sitting as he was on the couch facing the windows, the light reflected off the lenses of his glasses most of the time, so that I couldn't see his eyes. As if I were speaking to a blind man. Again I wondered what all these things I was saying could possibly mean to him. Since a watch can never go back in time. Only the tape recorder could do that. Although that wasn't exactly my voice. . . . He said And after that? I said After that? . . . Well, after that, once you've managed to get your horse under control again and yourself as well and when you've realized that the airplanes can come along just like that at any moment, wherever you are and with no way of defending yourself, then that's it, the fear is there, it takes root, once and for all. Like a natural state, one of the givens of your existence—or rather of the precariousness of your existence . . . I sat silently for a moment. I was trying to remember. But even for me it was now like something foreign, unreal. I knew I was wasting my time, that it was as if I were speaking to him in a language he didn't understand. But I tried to describe it for him anyway: for example in the evening, when little by little everything slows down, that little by little, more or less distant, the explosions and the crackling of the machine guns become less frequent, sometimes start up again, as if outraged, like a last volley of insults, raging for a brief moment, then grow more sporadic again, finally stop altogether, and that then the silence settles in, night begins to fall, the peace of the evening, the air growing cool, the slight bluish mist that rises from the damp fields, the woods growing dark, and then, in that tranquility, because the tension is subsiding, something difficult to describe, maybe the most unbearable of all: a sort of distress, of despondency, a feeling of abandonment, of physical and spiritual misery. . . . Because you know that the next day, as soon as it grows light, it will all start up again, that in those woods, behind those hills, the enormous machine is settling silently into place, that it will be unleashed again, will scream and rip the air. . . . He said "The sound and the fury"! I said No. A lot of sound but no fury. Another thing that depresses you even more. That is, that the people from the other side seemed to be doing all this as if it were only an exercise, like a task carefully, methodically performed, without getting worked up. Because it didn't take long to understand what was going on, and that what was going on was exactly as if someone had organized a match between a youth-league team and a professional team. . . .

On May 13, at dawn, Rommel, having reached the Meuse the previous evening, set out without delay to force his way across it at Dinant (letter to his wife: "Dearest Lu—Everything is wonderful so far. I've come farther than the other officers. I'm completely hoarse from giving orders and shouting. I've only had three hours' sleep, and a meal only now and then. Apart from that, I'm in fine shape").

bold slipping out of my grasp pushing me down on my back putting her leg over me Dryad straddling me now with a twinkling eye a sort of challenge weight of her buttocks on my thighs slowly turning first then bending one leg her foot flat on the bed knee level with her breasts flattening one of them her upper body now leaning forward the folds of her stomach like marble then the other leg as well sitting or rather squatting on me each time she pulled herself up I could see buried inside her that swollen cylinder appearing and disappearing shining its roots sunk into my groin she began to breathe more quickly first only through her nostrils then beginning to moan then

"That everything important in us is done by means of tubes."

windpipe bronchial passages lungs growling only a little at first teeth clenched trying to keep control of my throat only lips clenched them too pride He said All right now don't panic it's just going to burn a little the operating room plunged into darkness my arm tied to a sort of gibbet He looked inside me with a sort of periscope illuminating my darkness is it red or what He said You must be very careful not to move I might puncture one of your lungs I was still clenching my teeth succeeded at first

64

that growling like a dog then I gave in all at once I heard myself
shouting

> AAAAAAAAAAAA
> AAAAAAAAAAAA
> AAAAAAAAAAAA
> AAAAAAAAAAAA

feeling like I was about to faint thinking good thing nothingness
but the nurse monitoring my pulse stuck a needle into my arm
injected I don't know what brought me back I didn't care about
anything now went on screaming AAAAAA His eye still at that
sort of periscope his hand guiding the electric scalpel I heard him
saying There . . . There . . . It'll soon be over just two or three
more and it'll be over but it kept going it kept going that burning

It was still light when they brought me back upstairs papery
rustling of the nuns' starched skirts their waxy faces their waxy
hands they laid me in the bed propped up by pillows Take care
to stay sitting up very straight be careful otherwise the lung might
fuse with the pleura they said a technical word something like
symphysis you understand it's full of blood in there now so be
sure not to go to sleep we'll give you something so you won't
sleep don't lie down I said All night? they said All night yes we'll
give you a pill Through the window I could see the leaves of the
trees along the alleyway which the setting sun was beginning to
gild the pink brick walls hear the children playing running after
each other shouting wildly on the grassy banks of the river their
cries reaching me as if from far away

He writes in his *Notebooks* that the fire from the French units set
up on the left bank was so heavy that he had to leave his armored
command tank and walk down to the river on foot with his staff
officer, concealing themselves in the woods. Although several
times rehearsed in maneuvers on the Rhine, the operation was
not brought off without difficulties. He tells of the inflatable rafts

punctured one after the other by shots from the machine guns or drifting downstream with their dead occupants, the cries of drowning soldiers, the officer asking over the radio for permission to be evacuated ("General, I must inform you that I've lost an arm"). Lying flat in the grass and looking through his binoculars toward the bank where the French have taken up position among the rocks bordering the river, he orders his men to set fire to several houses (he doesn't say whether he sent a detachment to drive out anyone who might have been inside or simply ordered them to fire the incendiary shells), so that the smoke, soon filling the valley, from which, he writes, "rose the sound of battle," would allow his riflemen to cross the river and take up position on the opposite bank (imagine the scene: it's a magnificent day, the deep valley between high hills in shadow at first, later the glinting of the water in the sunlight, the dead men, the wooded slope held by the French, the crackling of the machine guns and the artillery, the balls of gray cotton made by the shells exploding here and there in the greenery, the geysers of water or earth sent up by enemy fire, a number of his tanks have been hit, some of them are burning).

A photograph (taken by him?: throughout the war, he never stops taking one photograph after another with his Leica—until his luck changes, at least: "I don't photograph my defeats," he would later say to his son) shows the pontoon bridge that his engineering battalion manages to construct, over which the first tanks will begin to roll the next day. More than one hundred fifty airmen, both French and English, sent to destroy this bridge and two more built upstream, will be killed without accomplishing their mission ("in desperate and devoted attacks," Churchill will write). In that one day the British air force will lose 268 of the 474 airplanes that were engaged there. The antiaircraft installations that shot down a great many of them cannot be seen in the photograph. Everything seems to have grown calm. In the foreground, on the right, an officer (Colonel Rothenburg?), standing ensconced in his brilliantly glistening boots, is watching the operations. The cloth of his tunic forms fan-shaped creases across

66

his broad and rather fat back, starting from the armpits. He is not wearing a helmet (he has neglected to wear . . .) and does not seem to be worried that he might be fired upon. Resistance from the enemy on the left bank has probably ceased. Perhaps, from time to time, he lifts his head to watch as a plane is shot down, one of the many fruitlessly attacking the bridge in successive waves. Along the other bank stand a few modest houses, which do not seem to have been damaged in the battle. They are probably part of a suburb downstream from the city that survived intact, because the exhausted, starving prisoners who are led through the city itself a few days later on the way to their prison camp will see a good third of the houses destroyed, the rubble shoved aside to make room for passing trucks: as if by intentional irony here and there on the shattered or blackened façades of bakeries or candy shops hung an abundance of shattered signs or advertisements for a kind of pastry which was a local specialty.

The cannons have long since fallen silent. For more than a century, high atop a monumental stone pedestal, its base protected by garlands of chains, decorated with emblems and allegorical figures, the statue of Queen Victoria has sat enthroned in the center of Calcutta, her diadem on her head, in a full dress with folds and embroideries of bronze. The gaze of the metal eyes, their irises incised into the plump, majestic, and vaguely outraged face of the old lady in eternal mourning, seems to be lost in the distance, like that of some anthropomorphic divinity, fleshy, fattened on puddings, as if it embraced, beyond the façades brought from London to the swamps, that immeasurable kingdom of islands, peninsulas, seas, straits, ports, docks, jungles, palm forests, and deserts of ice or sand upon which the sun never set, the base of the monument as if surrounded by an invisible phalanx of ghosts in scarlet tunics, Quaker ministers, admirals, planters, mutton-chopped bankers, explorers, slave traders, and Bible peddlers. She does not see the ragged, mended tents of the families who now camp before the proud, peeling arcades modeled after Regent Street. Nor does she see the vultures and ravens flying in circles over some mountain of garbage, disputing its ownership with a group of naked children, gingerbread colored, or the schoolgirls, also with faces the color of gingerbread but wearing clothes from London, playing a fiercely competitive game of field hockey at the other end of the huge esplanade, no more than they are seen by the adversaries engaged in kite battles, impassive, severe, intense, who, standing at the foot of the monument, hold fine ropes at the end of which, far away, no larger than pieces of candy, the little colored rhombuses climb, swoop toward the ground, fly up again, turn in circles. Only a connoisseur can appreciate the maneuvers and the subtle struggles taking place up above, in the sky grown white with the heat. Serious, solemn, like the officiators at some ceremony, the kite fliers (rivals?) are grown men, some of them even quite old. With imperceptible movements of their wrists, sometimes only of one finger, they command the motions of these docile cloth birds in their struggle to destroy each other. The kites are small, no more than a meter high. Waiting their turn (or the chance to enter into the battle), two or three other competitors are testing their own kites, flying them for a few moments over a short distance, bringing them back to earth, carefully adjusting the curve of the light reeds that underlie the canvas. On the bare playing field at the other end of the esplanade, the young schoolgirls in white blouses and pleated skirts, their legs sheathed in plaid knee socks, continue to run from one side to the other, striking an invisible ball with their sticks. Muffled and delayed by the distance, their shouts of victory or excitement resemble the shrill cries of birds.

As dawn breaks over Siberia it spreads a pink tinge over a range of low, rolling hills that stretch out in a vague bluish expanse as far as the eye can see. For several hours they slowly slip by beneath the airplane, monotonous, identical, and deserted, with no trace of human life (road, railway, city, or hamlet) while little by little the light sharpens their flattened contours, soon lemon colored on the faces exposed to the sun, more deeply blue now in the folds that separate them. Seen as a whole, it resembles the thick skin of some monster, some old pachyderm, gray, seamed with scars and wrinkles, with a scattering of thin hairs. Sometimes, heading north, the convulsive meanders of some gigantic river snake along, already covered with ice, whose whiteness contrasts with the dusting of early autumn snow over the hills. Imperceptibly their forms grow higher and tall mountains sprout from them, with ice-covered slopes whose rocky peaks give them a ragged look. Eventually they come to a stop and on the surface of the ocean, glistening like a sheet of tin, appear the first islands of Japan, which seem to have been laid out flat, like overturned oyster shells, nubbly, sharp, like imbricated pyramids.

Flying back again, the vermilion disk of the sun hangs over the horizon for a long time on the left side of the airplane. By its dim light, the endless expanses, devoid of any trace of life (perhaps the airplane is following some route along the far north of the land?), sometimes crossed by the writhing meanders of the monstrous rivers, seem uniformly blue-gray.

When he escaped, it took Trotsky an entire week to travel seven hundred kilometers: "There were no roads along the Sosva. . . . Beyond Berezov the country is utterly wild. For thousands of versts there are no police, and not a single Russian settlement, only occasional Ostyak huts. No sign of a telegraph. There are no horses along the entire route, as the track is exclusively for deer travel. The police could not overtake one, but there was the possibility of getting lost in the wilderness and perishing in the snow. And it was February, the month of blizzards. . . .

"I was transferred with my small luggage to a light deer sleigh. I had on two fur coats—one had fur inside, the other outside—fur stockings, fur boots, a double-lined fur cap, and fur gloves. . . .

"Early in the journey the drunken driver had a way of falling asleep frequently, and then the deer would stop. This promised trouble for both of us. In the end he did not even answer when I poked him. Then I took off his cap, his hair quickly froze, and he began to sober up.

"We drove on. It was a magnificent ride through a desert of virgin snow all covered with fir trees and marked with the footprints of animals. The deer kept up a lively trot, their tongues out at the side, breathing heavily with a 'chu-chu-chu-chu. . . .' Amazing creatures, knowing neither hunger nor fatigue! . . . In the darkening twilight the woods seem even more gigantic. I cannot see the road; the movement of the sleigh is hardly perceptible. The enchanted trees rush toward us, the bushes run away on all sides, slim birches and old stumps covered with snow fly past us. Everything is filled with mystery. Chu-chu-chu-chu resounds the even breathing of the deer in the wooded silence of the night."

crossing through the apartment staggering toward the bedroom then falling together onto the bed backward tongue in my mouth over her breasts slipping stomach navel descending spreading with the tip the moss tongue that sees pale mauve lilac then brighter pink folds face crushed nostrils crushed her breathing very quickly in little gasps opening wider index and middle finger in a V shape spreading wider seashell carnivorous flower now holding her under her backside a cup to my mouth lapping chalice lifting her up descending lower rut marble growing shadowy tinted dusky secret bronze finally host on my outstretched tongue my eyes closed

There is a photograph of Brodsky "sentenced to five years' hard labor in a distant region." With a friend, he is standing in front of a post to which a sign has been nailed, bearing the word НОРНHCKAЯ (Norinskaia) in large letters, probably the name of the camp (or hamlet) to which he has been banished. The ground is covered with a layer of snow, as is the irregularly shingled roof of a wooden shed whose wide door stands open. Like his friend, Brodsky is wearing a fur bonnet. His hands, hanging at his sides, are protected by mittens. He has grown a short beard; his mouth is slightly open, and unlike his friend, who is looking toward the photographer's lens, his face is turned to the right in three-quarter profile. The sun is shining, because the shadows are sharply defined, and the cold must be bitter. Far in the background, on the right, you can see the dark shapes of bare wintertime trees surrounding a little clearing, also snow covered.

"Eat and drink, do this in memory of me." He held the chalice in his two hands, using only his middle finger, ring finger, and little finger, spread in such a way as to leave both thumbs and index fingers free, with which he had broken the host before consuming it. I poured the small amount of wine left in the cruet over them. He rinsed them off, rubbing them together, then brought the ciborium to his lips and drank. Blood and little pieces of the body of Our Lord. Then wiped the inside of the ciborium with a white cloth, which he carefully folded. Over his surplice he wore one of those strapped chasubles that make them look like they're wearing a sandwich board, green embroidered with pink INRIS. I set the cruet down, went to the altar, and picked up the heavy missal and its stand, walked down the steps, genuflected as I passed behind his back, climbed the steps again, and set it down on the left-hand side for the reading of the last Gospel. It was customary for several of the pupils to raise their hands and volunteer at the end of the evening prayer. To be chosen was considered a favor and an honor bestowed by the prefect of studies. I carefully observed the final phases of the service, and when I was more or less sure of myself I also raised my hand. Although visibly unhappy, the prefect acquiesced, and except for a few small mistakes which he corrected in a low voice I got through it fairly well. From that day on, at more or less regular intervals, hoping to find my way into his good graces, I repeated the gesture. A ploy. A game, in which several factors came into play: one had to take great care not to let this eagerness to volunteer be interpreted as what, to a great extent, it was, which is vanity and a desire for favor. On the other hand, not to make the request, which was considered a sign of fervor, was to give oneself away either as a pupil of lukewarm faith or as a rebel. Finally, for the prefect of studies, even if he suspected the baseness of pupil's motivations, to refuse the request would have openly betrayed the little faith he had in that ardor and that dubious piety, placing himself in the position of showing an overt hostility which he could not allow to be seen, not to mention the risk of alienating from the faith, through his refusal, a young soul which, perhaps (how to know?), aspired to nothing else. This ambiguous game went on for an entire school year, each of us reciprocally concealing our disdain, hatred, or ill will. In the next year's class, fortunately, there was a new prefect. The last year, I deliberately chose the priest who taught Latin class as my confessor, to whom I went every Friday to tell the number of times I'd masturbated in the previous week.

When the window's double reflection on the lenses of his glasses wasn't hiding his gaze from me, I could see his eyes still staring at me or rather scrutinizing me with that same curious look, still doubtful, reserved. From time to time he looked toward the tape recorder sitting on the table between us. He said Yes but when you were running in that railway trench as you've told it or when you were knocking yourself out trying to jump that stream on the mare and what you call little balls of cotton were rising up out of the field here and there after all you must have been afraid then, weren't you? I said No. Not then. With the mare and the stream it was just Jesus fucking Christ! Jesus you stupid idiot horse are you going to do it or aren't you? Jesus Christ! I think that what exasperated and depressed me the most was how grotesque the situation was, how laughable: to be killed in such a ridiculous position, in the water up to midcalf and fighting with a mare who didn't want to ju . . . He said OK but what about the rest of the time? I said The rest of the time? I've already told you: in the evening, at the end of the day . . . He said You told me it lasted eight days, right? I said Exhaustion. He raised his eyebrows and said Exhaustion? I said Yes exhaustion more than anything. He said Exhaustion more than fear? I said Yes For example when you can only manage to walk, not run, when you're being shot at Simply because you've reached the end of your strength He said in a slightly indulgent tone But that was only one incident. Again I wondered how much of all this he could possibly understand, him with his doctor's glasses his Swiss watch his tasteful tie and his shirt fresh from the laundry. No more than he could grasp what it's like to spend ten hours in a service saddle then to drop still fully armed to the tile floor of a kitchen then to mount the horse again before dawn to spend another full day on the horse to be attacked by airplanes in the evening to sleep again still fully armed on the floor of a barn if you can call that sleeping then to get back on the horse then to find yourself surrounded to flee at a gallop to end up at the bottom of a railway trench without a horse to try to run along the tracks then to resign yourself to walking to steal a bicycle to pedal until you're out of breath to find your horse again to struggle with it to make it cross a stream to jump on its back again then to cover another ten or fifteen kilometers at a gallop all that carrying between your hobnailed shoes and your helmet a full load of gear carbine cartridge belts gas mask flask haversack whose straps half strangle you not to mention the long heavy cavalry coat which whips at your calves the whole thing weighing at a conservative guess something like twelve kilos. I said Can you imagine what that represents in terms of physical effort alone not to mention the effect on the nerves? I said No it wasn't a paradox Fear exhausts it exhausts you terribly and since that exhaustion comes on top of the purely physical fatigue I wouldn't say that it's canceled out but . . . He said Yes I understand I . . . I said No You don't understand You simply can't It's absolutely impossible But let's just say the fear well it's like the filthy stinking shirt you're wearing and which of course there's no question of changing no more than of washing it and it sticks to your skin and you can't smell its stench because it's your own stench and you don't even see that the collar and cuffs are black with filth but you can always feel its stiffness about as soft as cardboard but there you are it's your shirt and . . . Just then he raised his hand saying Stop stop! . . . The windows were rattling he picked up his tape recorder again and pressed one of the keys: my voice could only vaguely be heard behind a crackling sound that almost completely drowned it out I stood up I walked to the window again and opened it A long moving van was maneuvering its way around the corner of the square went forward and backward guided by the driver's assistant who was walking backward signaling to him with both arms Every time the driver moved forward or shifted into reverse he gunned the engine The sun had come out again The concrete of the esplanade reflected the blue of the sky the leaves on the trees still weighed down by the rainwater lazily swaying in a light wind shaken by slow contrary movements that is drooping down and rising up again limply in turns or rather in conflict that is some of them drooping down at the same time as others were already rising up again slow undulations passing over them A large puffy cloud brilliant white was still drifting by above the mansard roofs their slate washed with a hard blue color I could imagine the newsagent sitting in her kiosk her head framed by naked women on the color magazine covers Across the street I could see the *café-tabac* with its flashy red-and-gold decor After the tobacconist there's a beauty supply shop then another café but less gaudy then a shop selling takeout food then a shoe repair shop then a vegetable stand Across the street a bank a candy store then a hat shop then a baker then a shop that's gone out of business its windows covered with posters taped up by hand each announcement or advertisement trying to conceal the others superimposed over the rest such as for instance . . . ments for sale or ren . . . J. S. Bach The Passion according to Saint Eight days in the Antilles from Equitation week in Ber Dare to live your fantasies Josiane tel. 43 25 3 Rock concert etc. On the sidewalks the pedestrians came and went two dogs were playing at chasing each other through the trees on the esplanade an undulating race Lifted by the escalator people were emerging from the subway entrance most of them dressed in long robes slate blue brown one of them bright green all wearing little toques. All very tall and slender. Or maybe that was an effect created by those robes: rising up like that standing motionless still straight up toward their paradise. It was Friday. They gathered at the edge of the sidewalk, waiting to cross with the green light, like a group of statues with their vertical folds, then crossed the street, their long robes lifted up behind them by their heels. Kings. Melchior, Balthazar, and the third one whose name I've forgotten. The truck had finished its maneuvers and driven off down the street. I closed the window again, I said But they weren't Malians. He said Malians who do you mean? I said A convoy of vans in the middle of the night that stopped in the forest, lost. We tried to talk to them but they didn't answer. North Africans. Probably the division which they'd been saying for the past three days would come and relieve us. Fear, you say? Those poor bastards, poor goddamn bastards! Rounded up in their *douars* more than two thousand kilometers away just to . . . The next day or rather the following night, as we were retreating, we saw them again. Or rather what was left of them. The airplanes had made quick work of them. He said Precisely! Forgive me but I come back to my original question: fear. I was wondering what else I could possibly tell him when a click came from the tape recorder. He made a tut-tut sound with his tongue. I think it's time to put in a new tape I should have Do you mind? I watched him. Since he was having difficulties and it was taking some time I lit a little cigar and looked out the window again. I saw one of the magpies fly up with its wings outstretched, spreading them wide to slow its flight, both feet thrust forward, swoop down, hurriedly beat its wings as if to recover its balance and disappear into the thick foliage of the tree where they've made their nest. Probably the male. I suppose the female must have been sitting on the eggs. I thought again that then too it was spring. The green countryside, the flowers in the fields, the cool shade of the forests, the birds. And within that, the cavalrymen, terrified, exhausted, the exhausted horses, their flanks ripped by the spurs, and, under the saddles, raw wounds as big as your hand, the waiting, the orders that come too late, the frantic retreats amid a hail of bullets, the unending fear of the airplanes, the squadron, the regiment melting away like that, little by little, harried, surrounded . . .

He was done changing the tape, he said All right there we are, forgive me: we can start again. I said Where were we? He said Still about fear. I'd like to . . . I said Fear, fear . . . No I don't think that's the word It was far beyond that, something else, far worse. . . . Try to picture yourself five days into the battle, sitting on a dead soldier's horse (and for the second time) and following the two colonels of your brigade at a walk down a road that's something like a slaughterhouse, and imagine that along with one other cavalryman leading another dead man's horse you constitute all that those two colonels are bringing back from their regiments, and on top of all that you're no longer facing the people from the other side but far behind them, because the people from the other side have advanced more quickly than you've retreated and . . .

He shook his head, seemingly irritated again. He said Yes Please, on that very subject: when you found yourself on that road which you've described so well in your novel and . . . I said Thanks you're very kind but I have to assume that I didn't describe it all that well, because one of the foreign publishers thought it would be good (or clever, commercial, enticing) to decorate the jacket of the book with an illustration showing the cadaver of a horse lying across a rutted, muddy road, dotted with puddles and lined with shattered trees. All that was missing was the classic bombed-out buildings, the classic walls, also shattered. But there too there were other publishers who thought of that. As a rule, the colors of the dust jackets tended to be red and black. Fire and darkness. That way the reader doesn't have to read, and if by some misfortune he does read the book he's going to be terribly disappointed because there (I mean on that road) if there was smoke it was only now and then, and only a wisp, and not black but blue in the sunlight, a few trucks or a few cars burning out, and the sky perfectly blue, and what was about to happen was simply a quiet assassination. So I must have told the story badly, and

I have to start again: the time of day, the look of things, the characters, their actions . . .

Dzerjinsky District—City of Leningrad, 36 Vosstania Street. Judge: Savelieva; February 18, 1964.

THE JUDGE: What is your profession?

BRODSKY: I write poems. I translate. I suppose . . .

THE JUDGE: Keep your suppositions to yourself! Stand up properly! Don't lean against the wall! Look at the tribunal! Answer as befits this court. (To a person in the audience) Stop taking notes at once or I'll have you expelled! (To Brodsky) Do you have a regular job?

BRODSKY: I thought it was a regular job.

THE JUDGE: Answer the question!

BRODSKY: I write poems. I thought they would be published. I suppose . . .

THE JUDGE: We don't care about your suppositions. Answer the question: why don't you work?

BRODSKY: I did work. I wrote poems.

THE JUDGE: That doesn't interest us.

Future generations Will reap the harvest that we are sowing After having presented me with the magic elixir of the old men of the mountain the hero of labor winner of the Lenin Prize had fallen back onto his sofa drowsing Or pretending The rat-faced interpreter who had followed me was holding some papers in his hand he said to me Why don't you want to sign? I said They never told me there would be a text or I don't know what do you call it to sign He raised his voice What do you find so disturbing in it? I couldn't tell him in front of the other man: Simply because this idiot I said I didn't understand when I got the invitation I thought and besides all these past few days there's never been any question of He cut me off he was outraged he forcibly thrust the papers into my hand poking at them with his finger Tell me what you find so displeasing in here why do you refuse to I took the sheets crumpled them up into a ball and put them back in his hand If that's the way you feel about it here you can Then he began to yell outright The great writer the new Tolstoy was still slumped on the couch as if unconnected to what was going on deaf I was beginning to feel genuinely angry but I was exaggerating it I began to yell also Hearing the raised voices the elegant Spanish diplomat dressed to the nines came out of the banquet room He cast a hostile reproachful look my way he said What's going on? I said What's the big idea with these who wrote these I nodded in the direction of the Lenin Prize winner Him? A weary look came over him said There must be mistakes in the translation The ferret-faced interpreter began to shout again I said If there are mistakes in the translation then they're . . . I was trying to find a word that wasn't too strong I was irritated but now I was having fun The ferret-faced interpreter was shouting You're the only one he's the only one who None of them but him why tell us why what is it that you don't want to sign? I was shouting also What kind of a way is this to treat invited guests If I'd known I wouldn't have come you The Spaniard was visibly furious as well but he was trying to contain himself diplomatic The fat jovial interpreter appeared said What's going on? I told him He turned toward the other one and spoke to him in Russian very quickly Finally he gestured as if to send him away He turned to me said Excuse us he I repeated What kind of a way is this to treat people? He said excuse us he's drunk he's not used to international meetings he'll be fired I said No it's nothing to do with him I turned toward the Spaniard I said Don't you realize that this is simply a tissue of idiocies I have no desire to become a laughingstock He said It must have been badly translated What I wrote was much shorter it's not my text The ferret-faced interpreter had walked a few steps away was standing there like a whipped dog The fat jovial head interpreter said Excuse us he's drunk I said Let's not talk about it anymore He probably thought he was doing the right th . . . The fat interpreter said No he'll never be sent to an international meeting again he'll be sent away Classic good cop bad cop routine I wasn't any angrier at one than at the other poor devils In the car as they were bringing me back to the main building my interpreter said But really why didn't you want to sign? I said Come on come on Good night sleep well She was looking at me as if I were some sort of animal, as if frightened On the way back to Moscow, in the airplane, the Spaniard asked me to come and sit next to him so he could show me another text It was only a little less ridiculous I shrugged I said with a sort of tremor in my voice We must learn to extend a hand through the bars. . . .

A lively discussion at the end of a dinner in the dining room of the Park Hotel in Calcutta between Roger C. and the director Antoine V. on the proper declamation of alexandrine verse, C. praising the famous enjambment *"escalier dérobé"* while V. defended the customary scansion in which the caesura is clearly marked, the dispute (beyond their respective arguments: C. criticizing the monotony of the succession of twelve-syllable lines, V. trying to explain that it was no different from those gardens, those parks with their alleyways of trees formed into walls, entablatures, language and nature having both been subjugated to the same royal desire for order, regularity, and the mathematical) taking an unexpected turn when as a professional man of the theater V. began to support his thesis with long tirades from *Andromaque* or *Athalie* and to his astonishment C., in turn, countered with equally lengthy citations of *Bajazet* or *Esther.*

Aléna C. had long since gone off to bed and the last diners had left the room where now, in the faded luxury of the Victorian decor, Iphigénie's tears alternated with Phèdre's confessions and the wrath of Pyrrhus, before a little audience of tired waiters with wood-colored faces standing and waiting near the pantry, whose leader, timidly, here and there, soundlessly, walking on tiptoe, went and turned out the lights one after another. As if, at the heart of this Orient full of British opulence, in the gathering darkness of the huge room, with its tables, now cleared away, once again covered with virgin tablecloths, there were some gathering of phantoms going on (and suddenly, outside, without a flash of lightning or any preliminary rumble, all at once, the tropical rain began to fall: not the nibbling sound or even the crackling with which a rainstorm sometimes whips the windowpanes, but diluvial, primitive, blind, vertical, with the majestic sound of a cataclysm and a disaster, similar to something like a liquid curtain which, in a few seconds, would transform the rutted streets into lakes, into rivers on which garbage and dead rats would float, dry again the next day, steaming in the newly returned, pitiless sun), the answering voices of heroes dressed in togas or crowned with feathers, of queens, of sultanas full of taunts and emperors ripping at each other in cardboard palaces or harems, through an alternating, elegantly cadenced succession of elegant sobs and elegant rages, set against a sonorous and powerful background of catastrophe.

> THE JUDGE: In a general sense, what is your specialty?
> BRODSKY: I am a poet. A poet-translator.
> THE JUDGE: Who decided that you were a poet? Who classed you among the poets?
> BRODSKY: No one . . .

Toward the end of his life, Marcel Proust, in the men's brothel he habitually visited, used to have rats brought to him, and he entertained himself by killing them, slowly piercing them through the bars of their cages with those long hatpins that women wore in those days (imagine their metallic blue-gray glints, their heads made of faceted jet studs). Proust seemed to take great pleasure in hearing their cries, as well as in the spectacle of their agonized writhing.

Although the sun had not yet set, fat gray rats were running here and there over the esplanade ringed with buildings whose façades stood tall in the stifling late-afternoon light. To one side a group of men in long robes had gathered, engaged in a vehement discussion, gesticulating, as if in the grips of some terror, of impotence and disarray. The robes, colored with vegetable dyes, were

80

ocher, lilac, bronze, daffodil, olive, saffron, one of them striped orange and gray like those cloth covers you see in Oriental bazaars, another one indigo and turquoise. Tired of the endless discussion, the shouts, two of the men finally walked off while others, beside them, tried to pull the children away from the half-naked body (maybe they'd undone her clothes to let her breathe) of a woman, her flesh already turning gray, who had collapsed on the ground. Impotent or curious, two men were observing the scene from a balcony.

As the sun sets the heavy copper-colored light grows dim, the façades grow darker in the gathering shadows, the last rays of the sun casting a salmon-colored glow over them. As it often happens at this moment of the dusk, or sometimes in a storm, the light seems to emanate, diffuse, from the people themselves, from the folds of their clothes. No one thinks of chasing away the rats scurrying here and there in sudden dashes, just as abruptly coming to a standstill, inhaling the squalid air, quivering, running off again in a different direction, unpredictable, busy, voracious, dragging their ringed, glabrous tails behind them. Its back hunched, tense with anticipation, one of them is standing, about to spring forward, beneath the pedestal of the fallen statue, the head and one hand lying separated from the body a small distance away. Poussin painted the canvas entitled *The Plague of Aschrod* during his stay in Rome, on the Via del Babbuino.

It is probably not long after taking the photograph of the pontoon bridge he has had constructed across the Meuse that Rommel climbs into his command tank to go to observe the situation on the left bank, where the Germans are still encountering a certain resistance: his vehicle then hit full force by two shells, of which a small fragment strikes him in the cheek: the blood dripping onto his tunic ("the wound was not serious but bled abundantly"), his attempt (the gunner having died?) to pivot the gun turret, made impossible by the angle at which the tank, thrown to one side, is leaning: he has to jump out and make a run for it under enemy fire. He narrates this episode in the impersonal tone of an official report and limits himself to adding in a memorandum: "If in the course of the afternoon the enemy had succeeded in infiltrating between the movements of the Panzers and of the rifle brigade, it was only because the latter had had a late start. The officers of an armored division must learn to think and act independently in the context of the overall plan, without waiting for orders."

He glanced again at his watch with its many dials. He said Forgive me this is a little off the subject of my question but if you will allow me to ask you about one little detail: how was it that you came to be in the cavalry Did you volunteer? I said Yes I was raised by a former cavalry officer They put me on a horse when I was twelve years old. He said But you never imagined . . . I said No I never imagined I simply liked horses. . . .

(frigid air sweeping through the stables rushing through broken windowpanes making the lightbulbs sway slightly their miserly yellow light scarcely reaching into the furthest corners inky dimness in which their forms could be made out most of them sleeping on their feet some of them lying down their haunches as round and opulent as those of an odalisque a *houri* animal smell ammoniacal also frigid stinging the nostrils and the constant noise from the chains attached to the halters light gleaming over their hindquarters most of them orange mahogany brown bay light bay a few of them chestnut also blond the officers' mounts isolated in boxes with walls made of whitewashed boards at either end of each row Guard duty two hours in rotation the rest of the time sleeping in the grain bins coffins Lazarus emerging from his tomb when you woke up your replacement ghost in his combat uniform made of coarse canvas tan almost white the earflaps of the forage cap folded down blinking sometimes running wooden clogs clattering over the stone floor hurtling forward shaking a pitchfork handle shouting *Hue Hôla Hooo* fights battles suddenly breaking out among the horses whinnying trying to bite each other wild superb Liboucha Altaïque Amiral Avril Edgard kicking sometimes getting

82

caught in the bars one leg stuck between the wooden beams that separated them panicking tearing the inside of their thigh tender delicate skin there like glazed kid leather quickly then throw open the bolt on the chain they're hanging from other horses waking up then sometimes whinnying one to the next here and there then everything growing calm silence again broken only by the clinking of the chains the frigid air suddenly gusting through one of the open doors the NCO on duty helmeted bundled up chin strap face invisible in the dark shadow of the visor that covered it one of the men from the post carrying a lantern the NCO cradling the coquille of his sword in the hollow of his arm shouting Guard! the night guard running in clattering of clogs saluting the helmeted silhouette turning around his spurs clinking walking away silence again sometimes a cascade long stream of urine the mare standing legs apart her hindquarters slightly lowered splashing bubbles atop the yellow urine flowing over the paving stones then the mare standing up straight again the colors are umber chalk white straw yellow Above one of the doors a clock indicated the time its face framed in black wood sometimes the snow came whirling inside but the flakes melted right away It snowed several times that winter When they went off for their exercises the low sun cast their shadows elongated apocalyptic wading birds pale blue over the sparkling crystalline ground Shooting exercises every two weeks mound in a nearby forest invigorating ozone smell of the snow they were lying in mingling with the smell of gunpowder and hot oil from the rifle breeches sharp clap of the shots being fired echoes detonations rebounding through the bare winter woods mauve turning blue-gray as the day waned the horses in a group some distance away little clouds of bluish mist spouted from their nostrils like mythical mounts rattling of their hooves on the way back over the paving stones of the narrow streets around the cathedral with its bulbous baroque bell towers melancholy sound of the trumpets lights out brass notes launched into the night all the lights going out soon after except the ones in the stables rows of narrow bunks with brown blankets the swords shining dimly in the rack the sleeping bodies lying parallel Even from outside you could hear the slight incessant clinking of the chains only sound in the black silence always two or three of them awake scraping the bottom of the trough or nervous puffing scratching at the wall with one hoof muted blows resounding through the masonry the other ones asleep also parallel maybe they're dreaming)

THE JUDGE: And did you study for that purpose?
BRODSKY: For what purpose?
THE JUDGE: To become a poet. Did you not try to undertake some advanced study in order to prepare yourself . . . to learn . . .
BRODSKY: I didn't think it was a thing that could be learned.
THE JUDGE: How does one become a poet, then?

Scents summer smells the air wafting into the room in the clinic along with the visitors The women with their suntanned skin alive standing uncomfortably at the foot of the bed in a hurry to leave probably The smell of ether of formalin driven out for a moment one of them in a mauve sleeveless dress bronze arms tufted black wild bushes overflowing from her armpits Where her arm met her breast the heavy golden skin formed three little folds in a fan shape then disappeared and the ether again.

Later, I would remember this: one of those old-fashioned offices of the sort that a provincial *notaire* might have, dark, lit only by a lamp with a shade in the form of an opaque glass cupola, bil-liard-table green, on one end of the desk, casting a violent light over the papers, over the hands as they lay them on the table or added a signature, while in the surrounding darkness you could vaguely make out the shelves full of flat-backed notebooks, all identical, marked only with a number or a letter of the alphabet, or both together (and maybe not a *notaire*'s office: the office of an agency, like a forwarding agent or a charterer or something of that sort), the man sitting behind the desk lit only halfway up his chest, his shoulders and head in the green shadow, the visi-

tors (now only the Italian who called himself Comandante un-
earthed in that traveling salesman's hotel on the Avenue de la
Gare in P . . .—the anarchist pharmacist from Narbonne had
gone home—and a third person who'd arrived a good fifteen
minutes late and whom the *notaire* (or the forwarding agent) had
called Colonel as he stood up to greet him: a character of the kind
you still met back then at horse tracks, in the enclosure, wearing
a bowler hat which he did not take off, gloved, dressed in a short
coat of dark blue ratiné which he did not unbutton (the room,
the agency office, symbolically heated by a tiny electric radiator
whose elements glowed faintly red), sitting magisterially in the
only armchair without a word or a glance for the people he'd
kept waiting, listening as the man behind the desk spoke, asking
two or three questions, removing the glove from his right hand
when his turn came to sign the papers (the light reflecting off the
white sheets briefly illuminating an impassive face, already
plump, which could just as well have belonged to a bookmaker
as to the owner of a stable), immediately afterward taking his
leave of the figure sitting at the desk, who stood up to show him
out, him with his hat still on his head, his coat still buttoned up,
his imperturbable face, his gaze that seemed to see no one, entering and leaving as briskly as if he'd come to a house of ill re-
pute, the Italian saying (now we were sitting in a first-class compartment (he had bought the tickets magisterially, just as he had
dealt with the whole affair magisterially) in the train coming
back from Marseille) . . . saying I thought those weapons firms
only employed retired generals. But maybe for us they thought a
colonel would be enough? bursting out laughing, grumbling in
Italian, saying something like He can go fuck himself! yawning,
saying We've got a three-hour trip ahead of us, wake me when
we get there, then both of us standing on the dock (in Sète now),
looking at the two freighters, still moored in the shelter of the
outer breakwater where they'd been relegated by the port authority, the Norwegian ship and another one that had come from
Barcelona, about half its size, with, on the prow, that name
straight out of an operetta (Carmen), the damp, cold wind blow-

ing in from the sea, the cold, gray water lapping at the dock, the Italian stifling a curse, then (now it was night: from the portholes of the little enamel-painted cabin they could see, sparkling in the dark, the lights of the city, twice: motionless and reflected, blinking on and off, in the slightly rippling water of the basin) . . . then three again, the Italian (he had taken off his curved-brim hat, at the same time slicking back a lock of his impeccably parted hair, seeming, with his few gray hairs, his long pink tired face, the bags under his always slightly watery eyes, like some ceremonious diplomat or—as his enemies said—like a gangster in a funeral suit), me, and now the commander of the Norwegian freighter, a man of about thirty-five, affable, discreet, courtly, the Italian asking the Norwegian in a bantering tone what he would do if he were ordered to put out to sea, the Norwegian answering in the same tone that he obeyed the orders of his Company, the Italian saying But what if he were forced? the Norwegian answering in the same joking voice that he didn't see how anyone could force him, the Italian saying that it might just happen that way, the Norwegian still smiling saying that they'd have to put a gun to his head, the Italian saying that if that was all it took he could easily get hold of a gun, the Norwegian saying that his first mate and crew would have to see it too, the Italian also laughing, saying What did he think the crew would do? the Norwegian saying Why don't you ask them? both men looking each other in the eye for a few seconds, smiling, the slightly heady odor of hot oil and wet paint in the little cabin, with its dollhouse bed, its dollhouse desk, everything tidily arranged, in its place, polished, the Norwegian finally asking if he could offer them something, the Italian saying Where's the crew? the Norwegian saying Ashore, except for the men on watch, the two men smiling looking each other in the eye for a moment more, silently, then once again the cool, damp sea wind, almost cold, night, darkness, in which, sometimes, by the weak lights glowing on the deck of the freighter, you could see plumes of grayish foam shooting upward then falling like rain as the waves crashed against the other side of the dike, then the Italian and I staggering in the dark, colliding with the winches and capstans on the deck of the rusting freighter, then three again (four with the oarsman, the third now a small man of indeterminate age, with a round face, placid, weathered, and wrinkled like an old apple, wearing only a beret on his head, in a twisted old overcoat (but without stripes on the sleeves) open over a woolen check shirt with no tie, its collar kept closed by one of those imitation mother-of-pearl buttons which in the uncertain light of the harbor you could sometimes see throwing off pink and pale green glints, looking like some sort of sly, crafty peasant, except that it wasn't dirt or mud that had incised or rather slashed, like scars, the wrinkles that furrowed (or rather scratched out) his face but visibly an accumulation of layers of salt and it surely wasn't beets or pigs that he sold in markets or transported in the holds of his rusting junk heap and unloaded onto the docks in ports, or rather, at night, in discreet little coves), three of us, then, in the dinghy, whose oars, each time they plunged into the black water (and at one point, even though it was broken, the swell coming through the outer breakwater rocked our little boat back and forth, and then it grew calm again), pulled strings of small phosphorescent bubbles along behind them, the three men watching the silhouettes of two customs agents growing larger on the dock, the Italian saying No? Why? saying again They won't? saying What? Because people will say we're bandits Ha ha ha! . . . saying Do they want these weapons or what? saying And what if I say it's impossible, what if I say that he (he said the name (Paco, or Ferran, or Luis, or Pablo) of the small man with the wrinkled face) can't carry a load of this sort, that it's too much for his old tub, if I tell him to go back to Barcelona? saying What? I can't do that? Who had him come here? Who . . . saying What? I might be shot? Ha ha ha! Ha ha ha! the two customs agents above us bending down, reaching out to help us off the dinghy, all three now standing on the dock while the dinghy headed back toward the pile of rusty sheet metal looking more than ever as though it were clinging to the side of the Norwegian freighter, the Italian now negotiating with the two customs agents, then coming back to join us, triumphantly brandishing something like a calling card between his index and middle finger, saying It's called Madame Rosa's (or Rosette's, or Nina's)! Where else do you think they would be? Let's go. It's very close by. We only have to follow along the dock, cross the canal, go straight ahead and then turn right at the next dock, then suddenly the warmth, the huge room, painted with chrome yellow enamel, with café tables and moleskin-covered benches along the walls and two girls, one in a black skirt and white blouse like the maid in a bourgeois house, the other wearing one of those transparent printed voile dressing gowns like they sell in open-air markets, with nothing underneath, dancing in the empty space to the sound of a phonograph, and at the beer-stained tables men between twenty and forty years old with vacant faces, one with his head between his arms, collapsed among the glasses, as if asleep, and next to them a few sour-faced girls, trying to shake the drunk awake, the two dancers breaking off their waltz, saying Men it's about time! saying Look at these guys drunk as skunks Can't understand a word they say Only one of 'em even bothered to go upstairs you have to wonder what for He could hardly hold himself up to walk all they do is drink, saying to the Italian Well hello handsome Where'd you come from? the Italian, the pink of his furrowed face made brighter by the wind, the cold, his moist gaze wandering around the room, the drunken sailors, the small man with the wrinkled face looking around him placidly as if he were simply in a café or on his rust pile, or at the market, the Italian seeming to wake up, shrugging his shoulders, indifferent to the bare arm that the tall blond girl in the dressing gown had already thrown around his neck, looking at the small man with the wrinkled face and bulging overcoat standing next to him, then shrugging his shoulders again, muttering something between his teeth (an oath or something like: Zero for me!) in Italian then suddenly bursting out laughing, taking off his hat which the girl immediately took from him, saying Very well, saying While we're here we might as well have a drink, beginning to unbutton his overcoat too which the girl also took off his hands, saying (now he was watching the motion, beneath the transparent fabric, of her breasts with their large pale pink areolae): Isn't there anything else to drink around here but that fucking beer for Norwegian drunks?

In one of the boxes of the chessboard compositions upon which the paintings of Gastone N—— were almost inevitably constructed, two female breasts were drawn in a deliberately clumsy fashion, shown head on, with large lilac nipples. Below them was written, in uneven, chaotic capital letters, the words LAR DEL LAPE. His studio was also in the Via del Babbuino. It's a narrow street, surfaced with flat cobblestones, near the Piazza del Popolo. We walked along the side of the piazza, where two baroque churches stood, toward the car parked close by on the Via della Penna. When he saw us, a little boy ran forward,

I haven't been back to Rome since. Maybe they've managed to solve their traffic problems by now but back then it was something completely anarchic, really astonishing. With its colossal ruins, its profusion of palaces, cupolas, and churches amid which the waves of cars moved (or found themselves immobilized), it brought to mind the bones of some predatory monster of a species long extinct, with an army of shelled insects relentlessly gnawing at whatever flesh might be left clinging to those stone cliffs, those arcades, those baths, those swollen hollow domes. Like the

gesturing with a rag and a squeegee toward the windshield, which he had washed. He was wearing a faded pink tee-shirt with the words CALIFORNIA UNIVERSITY. While the two women were getting settled in, N—— searched through his pockets and gave the child one of those crumpled bills, so dirty, fuzzy, that it was impossible to make out the color, greenish gray I think. As we drove, he told us that in Naples you were lucky if you didn't find your car with a flat tire and two kids like that obligingly hurrying forward to help you change it. He even claimed that in service stations there they knew how to puncture a tire buildup (the ambitious cyclopean accumulation of architraves, pediments, cornices, scrolls, trophies, tombs, canopies, pietàs, and gilded angels) left behind by successive dynasties of figures with the same pensive, hairless, and pitiless faces sculpted in marble, crowned with laurels, tiaras, or cardinals' hats. That made him laugh. He said that nothing had changed, that they were still the same sort of bandits except that today they were illiterate, wore three-piece suits, and their only ambition was to fill their pockets by building shit piles made of reinforced concrete meant to last for twenty years or so at most, after which they were no longer fit for anything but demolition.

so that it would lose its air very slowly and go flat after you'd driven a certain distance where this time it was two young toughs who came and relieved you of your wallet and anything worth taking in the car. To get to the Ostia exit, he had to drive almost the entire length of town from north to south. He went on making the two young women laugh by listing all the ways you could be robbed, and when we were stuck in traffic I took the opportunity to read the catalog of his latest exposition in Milan which he had given me as we left the Via del Babbuino. I've kept the catalog. Despite the jolting of the car I was able to make out a few random lines written by the author of the preface: ". . . Il problema, in sostanza, non è di riferirsi a una nattura apparente da imitare, ma di saper cogliere nella propria esperienza più complessa: la pittura comme atto, che si serve di segni . . ." On the last page was a list of paintings on display:

Senza sonno (Without sleep)
Il sole nudo (The naked sun)
Cada vez mas (Each time more)
Visibilità 2 (Visibility 2)
La luce nelle mani (Light in one's hands)
Poco per poco (Little by little)

The long sandy beach, deserted on this weekday, was rather dirty, with waxed paper, plastic wrappers, and cellophane from cigarette packs scattered here and there. The women went right off for a swim, but he said he'd rather wait awhile, that he didn't like to fling himself into the water just like that. I then asked him to translate a few of the passages in the catalog that I hadn't entirely understood. After the preface he began to translate the titles of his paintings as well. I told him that those I'd understood but he continued all the same and suddenly, when he'd just read Vuole dire caos and Paura clandestina, he stopped. He was still holding the catalog open in his hands and seemed to be still reading the titles to himself when suddenly he told me that at Dachau they had hung him by his wrists until he fainted. Maybe he would have told me more, but just then the two young women, one Greek and one Spanish, emerged from the waves and came back to us, wringing their hair. Drops of water slid from their raised elbows and disappeared into the tufts of their armpits. The drops also slipped down from their bathing suits over their thighs, where they snaked along in thin silvery streams, sometimes suddenly changing direction. He stood up and said he was going to swim a little. He had a powerful, athletic body, and despite the choppy sea he swam with a butterfly stroke. After that, he never again spoke of his arrest, the prison, or what he had undergone in the camp. His centurionlike face, his very slight Italian accent when he spoke French. A few years later I learned that he had died at the hospital in Milan, in unclear circumstances (there was some question of counterindicated medication taken after minor surgery—someone intimated that he had committed suicide). I remember seagulls flying overhead, some of them virtually motionless, their wings outstretched, turning their heads right and left, weightless, held aloft by the light sea wind. From time to time they let out hoarse cries. One of them landed very close by and began to tear at a piece of wax paper half buried in the sand with its beak. I was surprised at its size, its enormous hooked beak, its wild, rapacious look.

"Our speed (about 60 kilometers per hour) raised a huge cloud of dust behind us. . . . Without delay and still at great speed, we headed toward the heights west of Clairefontaine where we found Colonel Rothenburg with the forward units of the Panzer Regiment. When it arrived, the column was deployed as quickly as possible and without lingering in this place."

large gulls flying low silently in the half light of the arctic night some of them with black heads as if wearing hoods They didn't cry out occasionally one would land on the deserted road run forward then take off again still silent gray in that immobilized pearl gray light time as if immobilized also suspended and leaving the nightclub all of us a bit dazed by the noise the music and then not night but this thing that was neither dusk nor dawn someone suggested we go and round out (but round out what? not the evening the night since that didn't exist) at his place (or was it one of his friends'?) and six or seven of us then in a rather small room with a couch some sitting on the floor backs to the wall legs crossed like students although it was a long time since we'd been students and the clinking of the bottlenecks against the glasses jiggling against each other and one of the young women a little drunk or playing at it staggering or pretending to a little tipsy no doubt a little disheveled brunette unlike the others with their blond or chestnut hair hers a raven brown in fact lively Gypsy-like rather unusual in a country like this triangular face perhaps distant Turkish origin since somewhere in the capital the Turks have a cemetery of their own ended up there who knows how came up from the south through the steppes to buy or sell furs sable marten fox so pretending to stagger her glass in her hand adjusting her husband's tie the Viking giant with the broad pink face jutting cheekbones mustache and dull blond hair and she was making puns in French about the *noeud,* the necktie that some men automatically straighten when they enter a living room or a public place unsure of themselves sign of an impotence complex she claimed and the Peruvian writer said that was an invention another fairy tale told by psychoanalysts and one of the young women said Oh no don't start boring us with Freud after all those speeches we've been hearing all day show some mercy! But someone said No, no! saying that now it was fashionable to decry Freud that it was the latest thing of course but Freud really was For my sake they were all speaking French even the Peruvian as they used to do in Russian high society Only the one wearing the apricot-and-peach-colored dress spoke nothing but English She said laughing that she couldn't find shoes large enough for her feet asking permission to take off her shoes putting her feet up on the couch In the distance through the open bay window you could see a tall smokestack, square, made of brick, standing out against the dark green of a hillside planted with pine trees Her bare feet were long and muscular the nails gleaming with a nacreous polish that made them seem lighter than the skin rubbed pink along the sides slightly orange at the heel the others were still laughing at the young brunette's double entendres the tone changing little by little though the conversation drifting turning imperceptibly into one of those more or less muddled discussions of the kind people who've had a little too much to drink sometimes have at two in the morning Freud Marx Jesus Strindberg etc. but it was not so much drunkenness the drinks as that strange absence of night of any reference point in time in thought the terrace not lit by a lantern but bathed in that sort of milky daylight and Ippolit's interminable reading the wall of the Mayer house Ganya Lebedev the Apocalypse the Wormwood Star the network of railways the death of Mme Du Barry Yvgeny Pavlovich Ptitsyn and the wall of the Mayer house again and Ippolit does not announce that his suicide will take place at first light since the light has not gone away but when the sun reappears and when Myshkin goes early in the morning to the park where Aglaya is waiting for him on the green bench he has not been to bed since the day before and she probably hasn't slept either.

It must have been about three in the morning when the Viking giant drove us back to the hotel through the deserted avenues where the gulls with their black-hooded heads were still flying silently ghostly running then taking off again Long feet rubbed pink with apricot heels.

Long after the death of N——, as I was looking through a magazine, by chance I came across a photograph showing, on the left-hand side, two men dressed in something like striped pajamas hanging by their wrists from tree trunks, their hands bound together. Their arms, pulled behind them, form an acute angle, about thirty-five degrees, with their backs. Their shoulders are raised and their heads thrust forward. Despite the poor quality of the photo you can see that the faces of the victims are contorted in pain. In the foreground the inanimate body of another victim lies full length on the ground. His head is shaved. They have untied his hands and his right arm is stretched out beside him, his head turned to one side facing the photographer, one cheek against the ground. His expression is peaceful; he seems to have fainted. A man in an officer's uniform, his cavalry breeches ballooning above his carefully polished boots, is standing next to him. His hands are on his hips and from one of them hangs a sort of long curved baton, like the sheath of a sword but more likely a black rubber nightstick. His head slightly bowed, he is looking at the body stretched out at his feet as if evaluating his condition and waiting for him to stand up again. His slender waist is cinched by a belt whose buckle shines in the sun (because the sun is shining). The collar of his tunic is black, with a silver edging, like his epaulets. He is wearing a kepi on his head, tilted over one ear, its concave crown rising disproportionately high in the front over a stylized eagle with outstretched wings. He is resting his weight on his left leg, the right one angled slightly to one side, his foot invisible, hidden by the body of the victim, whom he seems to be kicking with little blows as if to bring him back to consciousness or force him to stand up. The sun brings out a rectilinear gleam along his boot. In the left foreground you can see the trunk of the tree from which the body on the ground has just been untied, its bark spotted with black, like a birch. In the background lies the edge of a wintry forest of bare trees. The man in the uniform pays no attention to the other victims, still hanging.

A few kilometers outside Madras there is a dancing and music school in a woods of widely scattered trees whose grayish leaves, also sparse, cast only a slight shadow onto the ground, where the foot sinks into a fine, loose, sandy dirt. The motionless air has what could be called that intestinal, fleshy warmth characteristic of India, laden with those uncertain odors, at once vegetal and animal, which, in the morning, before the stifling blast furnace of the afternoon, seem to hang like the gentle exhalations of herbs of unknown natures and species. There are small buildings here and there with walls of whitewashed adobe, about ten meters on a side, entered through an opening with no door, and a floor of compacted earth inside. The music teacher sits on the ground in the middle of a circle of young girls who sit cross-legged, swathed in saris dyed the colors of flowers and fruits: geranium, indigo, carmine, periwinkle, cherry, crimson, saffron, pomegranate, old rose, lemon, reseda. They do not hold their violins clasped between their shoulder and cheek as in the West but vertically, the body pressed to their thigh, the scroll near their shoulder, the bow coming and going horizontally. The sound of the instruments undulates, rises, falls, multiple, at once violent, plaintive, tense, and tender. A few of them have a length of their sari, some edged with a gold ribbon, folded over their heads; others have thrown it over their shoulder and you can see their black, shining hair pulled back, gathered at the nape, exposing their delicate faces of gold or bronze, the forehead, between the eyebrows, sometimes marked with a vermilion circle.

There is a photograph of Rommel, probably taken outside a city (or village) in the north of France, a little after his division had taken Clairfayts. The area has not been damaged in the fighting and a few cars, white with dust, can be seen moving along the road that runs past the house near which he is standing next to Army

Corps General Hoth. The house, intact (where Hoth's command post is probably set up), is of recent construction, made of bricks whose joints have been carefully painted white, like the metal garden fence that extends from either side of the façade. Hoth is wearing a forage cap, like an ordinary soldier, and his weathered face, thin and sly, similar to a peasant's face, is illuminated by a half smile. The collar of his tunic is black, embroidered with silvery leaves. The iron cross edged with silver hangs between the points of the two officers' collars. Rommel's face has not yet become that macabre leather mask, bony, burned by the African sun and topped with motorcyclist's goggles, which will later become famous from the propaganda photographs. Although lower in rank than Hoth and much younger, he stands confidently in the foreground, in a flattering pose. His face is slightly plump, his chin oval, his nose short and straight, his mouth narrow and well formed. His cheek bears no trace of the wound that he says in his *Notebooks* he received only a few days before ("the wound bled abundantly but" etc.). He is visibly savoring his recent triumph and boldly (proudly) stares into the photographer's lens, his gaze nonetheless hidden by the shadow of the gleaming visor of his kepi, whose peak, ornamented by a stylized eagle, rises disproportionately high.

The dance classes are given in a similar little building, with the one difference that no music accompanies the movements of the three young girls standing before the teacher who sits at a table (or hollowed beam) which he strikes alternately with two pieces of wood held in either hand, underscoring the sequence of postures struck by the dancers, who pass without transition from one to the next in a series of sudden movements, jerky, extremely violent. No other sound than that of the blows coming at quick intervals, except the panting breath of the dancers. They are dressed only in a short vest that leaves their navel exposed and a wide skirt that swirls around them, allowing their legs to move unhindered. Their hieratic, stylized poses recall the sculpted friezes whose figures raise or lower their arms, elbows pointing away from their bodies, palms upturned in a gesture of offering or on the contrary turned toward the ground, fingers together, outstretched and curved backward, forming a right angle with the forearm, the legs alternately joined at the heels as well, thighs and shins forming a diamond shape, or suddenly lunging to one side, the soles of the feet slapping flat against the compacted dirt floor, like the feet of dueling fencers. The attitudes follow one upon the other in quick succession, the teacher allowing the students no rest. The dancers' faces are completely devoid of expression, their gaze vacant, absent, sweat trickling over their temples and cheeks. Neither the teacher nor the students take any notice of the curious visitors who, walking away from the little building, can still for a moment longer hear the dry, regular sound of the blocks of wood knocking together.

Escaped. Wild visits to the brothel. After which went to the barber's next door every morning for a shave. The walls hung with floral wallpaper. Just two chairs facing two mirrors in Louis-Philippe style, their molding rounded at the upper corners and bordered with a string of pearls, the whole thing painted in flyspecked ivory enamel. The pivoting basins made of black marble veined with white, the copper faucets crowned with spokes ending in a little ball like ducal crowns. On the walls ads for perfumes or lotions: women's heads with pink faces and luxuriant red serpentine manes against a sea green background, inhaling the scent of a flower. The smell of cosmetics. Violet. A mother sometimes bringing her kid in for a haircut, the child then sitting on a plank placed over the arms of one of the chairs. After a month though I'd

In the camp, the black huts, the difficulty of waking up, the endless roll calls even in the middle of the night. We only shaved on Sundays, squatting outside if the weather was good or straddling a bench. In the mess kit we ate from. Soapy water with a bluish crazed film over the surface, and black whiskrs floating on top. The inside covered with a sticky coat-

97

ing, impossible to remove, even when scoured with the sandy soil of the Saxony plain.

managed to calm down a little and bought a razor.

I felt no pain. Lying on the bed, eyes open, exhausted, I was thinking of that thing inside me, red (or what did it look like?). Cavern. Watching the sky slowly grow light in the frame of the window, listening to the first noises of the day inside the clinic, the nuns' quiet footfalls on the red-brown linoleum in the hallways, the rustling of their heavy skirts, the door of the *tisannerie* creaking. Little by little also the first cars outside on the quay. Then full daylight, the thin ray from the sun rising in the east, first orange, then yellow, then growing thinner, then only a thread which seems to sparkle for a moment, then disappearing from the enameled wall to the left of the bed. A little later the cool, husky, voices of the fishwives, singing, shouting Lovely sardiiines Who wants lovely sardiiines, the shout sometimes interrupted, suddenly breaking off: probably some housewife sweeping her doorstep or calling down from a window. After a moment the shout started up again a little farther off, repeated at regular intervals, weaker every time, not so much heard as suspected, finally disappearing, and I knew that soon the nun would come in with her thermometer, her, her bland face, her bland smile, her bland voice, that she would say not How do you feel? but, neutrally, How are we feeling this morning? and that later they would enter in turn, dressed in their carefully buttoned white smocks, in the wake of the fat little surgeon with his short arms like penguins' wings, with small manicured hands, and that they would gather around the foot of my bed, looking at me with their curious gaze, sympathetic, but curious more than anything else. One of them was Asian but they all seemed to have the same flat, smooth faces, the same slanted eyes behind the same wire-rimmed glasses, like alien creatures that had come here, along with the sound of the cars and the fishwives' shouts, from another planet, from another world, unreal.

98

"appointments made for having it off—Rodolphe's stimulations—the way she loved him, thoroughly debauched—after the f——ing goes and has her hair done—smell of hot irons, falls asleep under the peignoir—something obsequious about the hairdresser—Emma comes back to Yonville in a good physical state of normal f——ing—It's jam season—pink manure. Homais's beet-red anger."

After a description of the way his miners demolished the first bunkers barring his path, Rommel writes: "The light was now beginning to grow dim. As night fell there were farms burning here and there, toward Clairfayts and farther west. At that point I gave orders for an immediate penetration into the fortified zone and an advance, as swift as possible, in the direction of Avesnes. . . . There was nothing left but to climb into our command tank and start off."

Le esplorazion geografiche . . . . 70 × 90
Il gioco volante . . . . 27 × 41
Di che occuparsi se non dell'uomo? . . . . 135 × 135
Le cose da conservare . . . . 100 × 100
Chiuso per restauro . . . . 100 × 120

Suddenly against my chest a violent shove from her muzzle, her damp, warm breath. The street was not much more than two meters wide. I'd stepped aside to let her pass and if I hadn't had my back against the wall I think she would have knocked me over. Then, at the same time as I saw the lateral movement of her jaw, I felt her pulling at the necklace, made of those heavily scented orange flowers, musty and sweet, that they had put over our heads. Our guide shouted, managed to move her aside. She walked away, serene, unhurried, the petals still emerging from the corners of her mouth as she chewed, the pointed bones of her skinny haunches protruding one after the other with every step. Sacred cow. A wandering Io, holy, starving, and indifferent. Suddenly all the lightbulbs illuminating the little shops went out but just as I heard the guide telling us to put our hands over our pockets little flickering lights began to go on one after the other in the shops. In contrast to the fixed immobility of electricity, all these glimmering lights filled the street with a multiform life, as in fairy tales, legends. The electricity had come back on when, later, we passed by a larger shop or rather an open room giving onto the street, from which it was separated only by a grillwork fence, like a cage. Inside, on rugs and cushions, sat young women, almost children it seemed to me, smiling at us. If not for their silence, you might have mistaken them for birds, glistening, fragile. I didn't understand what it was at first. Graceful copper bodies. I was wondering if here too they were shaved. "Enjoy yourself in the land of shaved cunts," writes Flaubert to Bouilhet as he is leaving for Algeria. I would gladly have retraced my steps but maybe the guide wouldn't have let me enter, just as he clearly didn't want to take us to see the funeral pyres, but, I don't know how, A. went into a house that must have been something like a monastery or a small temple because she came out a short time later with a monk who was tucking away the banknotes she'd given him under his robe and who led us through the maze of little streets to a terrace beneath which a pyre flamed in the night. Among the flames, we could make out the almost carbonized form of a body which two half-naked men were turning over and over with long poles. The monk also showed us the gigantic scale used to weigh the sandalwood for the pyre, which the families of the deceased paid for by the pound. It's a primitive instrument, whose two trays are formed by two crossed planks. The Ganges could not be seen in the darkness. By the light of the pyre, we could only see two or three forms wrapped in shrouds and laid out on stretchers, lapped at by little waves of black water. Farther downstream there was a tall terrace overlooking the river, lit with garlands of multicolored electric lights. A shrill chant emanated from it, amplified by powerful loudspeakers and underscored by hand claps. The priest (bonze?) told us a marriage was being celebrated there.

To replace the shirts they had taken from us, our guards had given us something like pullovers made of a papery material, grayish. The stitching made a good hiding place for lice, which, on Sundays, sitting on the ground in the sunlight, our backs against the walls of the huts, we patiently hunted down and crushed between our grooved, black-rimmed nails. The lice were colored the same gray as the papery fabric of the pullovers, their bodies, as if transparent, ringed with legs similar to white whiskers. The others said they weren't dangerous, except the ones with a black Lorraine cross on their backs, which carried typhus. Impotent, dripping with sweat, piled up on three levels in the airless, stifling huts, we could feel the obstinate, tranquil, voracious little animals swarming over our bodies. Like a tangle of worms, he thought. Like on a corpse. As if we were already dead, as if . . . Finally falling half asleep, still thinking: Gulliver. And when I wake up they will have tied me down and their king will come and speak to me, standing on my chest, armed with a spear no bigger than a pin, and I'll say: Yes. Serial number 28982, yes, what do you want from me, lousy fucking vermin, fucking . . . Then falling completely asleep, a heavy sleep, opaque, dreamless. None remembered, at least.

Nightmare damned Dante's Hell that street in old Cairo dragged along by my guide, exhausted, a succession of little shops or rather steel-shuttered compartments lit blindingly by large electric bulbs hanging naked at the end of their wires in a deafening tumult of hammer blows metal on metal Copper at the beginning of the street trays Oriental bazaar and those tall conical things appliances for smokers tea or what decorative stoves hammered anvils striking with all their might engine parts or plows pistons cylinder heads hanging from chains striking with all their might blinding lights forced to keep our backs against the wall at the narrow intersections jammed with hand carts donkey carts vans cars interlocking game of jackstraws Mosque empty cube cupola dripping water rugs or rather carpets or rather worn damp pieces of carpet shoes left at the entrance wet socks cold two or three worshipers at most men one of them praying prostrate reminding me of those three in the dark on a patch of grass at Kennedy Airport facing east kneeling prostrating themselves standing kneeling again prostrating themselves standing in the middle of the traffic the buses the cars spinning around the rotary headlight beams low-flying airplanes skimming over the roofs of the buildings their little red lights going on and off roar of their engines them indifferent still kneeling prostrating themselves standing After a moment though one of them probably tired simply stayed on his feet the two others continuing A little earlier in the afternoon Fourth Avenue bus stopped in traffic behind enormous truck with sides painted cotton-candy pink polished like mirrors reflecting the skyscrapers undulating trained serpents rubbery In each of the windows of the bus was framed the head of a rabbi black hat black beard the same exactly identical repeated as if they'd been painted on also impassive Cultural attaché known as "the God nut" tireless pitiless forcing me to climb to the top of the minaret dark spiral staircase hand feeling the way damp stone steps wet feet From the top view of Cairo terraced roofs used as dumps covered with all sorts of trash rubble grayish garbage a white goat tied up on one of them a chicken house brightly colored laundry drying on a rope the street below like a narrow illuminated trench blinding lamps the sky growing dim vaporous pink here and there prayers rose up from other minarets other domes I said I beg you could we not find a taxi go back to the guest house wet socks damp cold Nightmare.

The tribunal takes its place again and the judge reads out the decree:

"As his frequent changes of work demonstrate, Brodsky has systematically tried to shirk his duty as a Soviet citizen, which is to produce material goods and personally assure his subsistence. . . . From the reports of the commissions on the work of young authors, it is clear that Brodsky is not a poet. . . . Consequently, in accordance with the decree of May 4, 1961, the tribunal orders that Brodsky be sentenced to five years' hard labor in a distant region."

Very elegant, very diplomatic, hidalgo. He was smiling full blast to mask his exasperation. But I'd realized that he was the one who had put together this whole thing with the Russians and had written that ridiculous declaration with their help. He said: We must learn to extend a hand through the bars! I said Is that what you call extending a hand? Is it to pull them out or to push them farther in? Just because they've made this country a sewer that's no reason to . . . After all, this was once the land of Dostoevsky and Chekhov. So try to make it a little less . . . Good God! "future harvests"! You think I'm going to sign something like that? He cast another furious glance my way. I left him busily crossing out and erasing words on the sheets spread out over his little tray table and went back to my seat. I looked out the window. For the past hour the landscape hadn't changed. It was flat and ocher as far as the eye could see. As we passed over, the sunlight glinted off the frozen surface of the little ponds as if they were made of tin, then they turned gray again. Also as far as the eye could see the little round white clouds, fluffy, hovered over the steppe as if they'd been set out at regular intervals along parallel lines also separated by regular intervals. I've never seen such a formation anywhere else. Their round shadows seemed to stud the earth, as if laid out by a surveyor. Kazakhstan.

The tall windows of the school chapel were divided into two vertical, parallel sections, each of which held a series of stained-glass panels, one atop the other, representing edifying scenes such as, for example, a missionary holding up a crucifix before a group of savages kneeling on the ground, or a charging brigade of pontifical Zouaves. Ringed with the leaden came that emphasized them in black, the outlines of the characters were crudely drawn, without style, the volumes (bodies, drapery) shaded with little curved ripples, sepia for the flesh tones. These images were violently colored, with no thought of harmony or unity: the stole of the holy priest was of a gaudy violet, the azure cuirass of Joan of Arc highlighted with silver glints, the pontifical Zouaves wore short boleros of a harsh blue color and wide puffy red trousers. The cannonballs exploding in their midst were ringed by vermilion and yellow flames. The assault was led by an officer wearing a tunic ornamented with frog clasps. One leg half bent, the other extended, he held up his sword in the direction of an invisible enemy, his upper body very straight, his face turned behind him, his mouth open as if to encourage his men, the nearest of whom, no doubt hit by a shell fragment, was falling backward, one hand on his chest, the other dropping a long rifle. A strong, heady odor of incense spread through the chapel, coming from the altar, where the priest officiated dressed in a voluminous green chasuble and surrounded by choirboys in lace surplices from beneath which hung their scarlet or mauve skirts.

Rumpled nightgown billowing almost up to her armpits revealing the crevice at the small of the back, curving inward as it goes up, fading away at the level of the kidneys, one of the two buttocks slightly flattened by the weight of the body, the other one rounded above the line of shadow.

"At the same time, my unhappiness found consolation in the idea that my love etc. I think I must have corrected that on the proofs," writes Proust to Berthe Lemarié. "If I did not, you have only to replace the word 'unhappiness' with the word 'grief,' leaving the rest as it is."

"The road west was now clear. The moon had come up, so that, for the moment, we could not count on full darkness. The plans for breaking through the defenses called for the lead tanks to spray the road and the surrounding area with their machine guns and cannons from time to time. All of our guns were armed with tracer ammunition and the regiment crossed over the second front spreading an immense rain of fire throughout the countryside on either side of us. The confusion among the enemy was total. Everywhere French soldiers were lying on the ground, every-where cannons, tanks, and other military vehicles were crammed into the farm buildings. Nowhere was there any attempt at resistance. The enemy tanks that we met were put out of commission as we advanced westward, never stopping. In their hundreds, the French troops and their officers gave themselves up as soon as we appeared."

In October 1916, Proust writes to Gaston Gallimard: "And since the word 'war' has found its way 'under my pen,' I think (but then this is of no practical interest, since there's nothing to be done) that I was wrong to insist on delaying publication of the book until after the war. . . . But [my reasons] now that I've thought the matter through (and here again it's still purely theoretical) are that at a time such as this when (not me but nearly everyone) people have got used to the war, they scarcely read anything but the official bulletins, if that, and perhaps they'd like something else, they might be interested in a long work. After the war, Peace, victory, these will be new things to them, delicious things, and that's what they'll want to think about, rather than reading. And then the war itself, already seen in retrospect, will become the object of the imagination's interest, which it never aroused when it was a daily reality whose progress was imperceptibly slow."

The cannons hadn't fired for more than an hour, and now it was night. The moon had just come up, and the leather saddles on the horses standing in the clearing gave off dim bluish gleams in the darkness. The gunners, who had hitched up their weapons, were waiting for the order to detach them. From the open door of the radio car, against the silence of the night, came the sound of static, nasal voices, and, now and then, dance or opera music. A convoy of vans, apparently lost, pulled to a stop near the artillery. I walked toward one of them and, from the back end where the cloth covers were folded up against the sides in a triangle shape, I looked in. As it happened, I could only make out the two who were closest to the opening, sitting on benches facing each other, parallel to the direction of travel. They were holding their rifles vertically between their knees. I asked them what regiment they were from, but no one answered. They seemed not even to be breathing. Two of their officers had got out of the first van and were speaking with the artillery commanders. I heard one of them say that the Germans had crossed the Meuse. He added in a falsely carefree voice that it would cost them dearly. Once again I tried to speak to the black shadows sitting motionless inside the van, but I got no response. Someone said that they were the North African division whose support we'd been promised for the past three days. I repeated the number of the division in a loud voice asking them if that was it but they remained silent. Maybe they'd been forbidden to answer questions, but you sensed that there was more to it than that. All of a sudden one of the horse guards who had also come to the van shouted in a voice at once tremulous and angry that it was about time what the fuck had they been doing all this time while we were getting ourselves blown up that now it was their turn to have a taste of it You'll see you Wogs it's a piece of cake Ratatatatat Boom Boom It's . . . From the group of officers a voice shouted out What's going on? Who's that yelling? From under the cloth cover emanated not an odor but something indefinable, subtle, at once warm and frozen, like cold sweat. As if something were closed up in there with them, in the dark, one of those iron-colored reptiles, like the ones you see inside glass cages in zoos, coiled, excrementlike, around barkless trunks or wrapped over themselves, as motionless as the stumps or stones, deadly.

"For *Within a Budding Grove,* would there still be time to add three lines to one page and an infinitive to another? I'd be very happy if this could be done," writes Proust on July 25, 1918, to Berthe Lemarié of the Éditions Gallimard, and on August 1, "On page 81 line 12 it says: into one that was quite small, empty, with one window lined with sunlight. I stayed there etc. But that 'lined with sunlight' strikes me as horrible and 'I stayed there' as inelegant French.

"Therefore, I wish to modify line 12 in this way: into one that was quite small, empty, its windows beginning to dream already in the blue light of afternoon. I was left alone etc."

Or perhaps (I don't remember exactly) it was the officer that had been hit by a fragment from those shells ringed by red-and-yellow flames exploding in the midst of the attacking group of pontifical Zouaves, collapsing in midsprint, the sword that he was brandishing a moment earlier still hanging from his wrist by the knot, his legs now joined, knees bending, while his face remains turned toward his men and his mouth remains open, the shout (the attack order) issuing from it suddenly mutating into a gasp of surprise, of pain, of short-lived agony, each of the images (the missionary converting the savages, Joan of Arc, the holy priest of Ars) in a frame of stone (or more probably plaster) imitating Gothic style, that is, with four lobes, the gaudy colors (blue, the green of the palm trees, the violet of the stole), the chorus of juvenile voices rising up intermingled with the odor of incense, spreading out little by little. Kyrie Eleison Magnificat Parce nos Domine

Soldiers on leave, back from the front for a few days, drawn there in hopes of making a little money by satisfying Charlus's tastes (Proust's tastes, actually), share their impressions as they wait in a parlor of the men's brothel that Jupien runs. There is a small sailor among them as well. They speak amongst themselves of the "fancies" of the customers. One of them tells the rest that he has to say he beats his mother and steals from her. Proust skewering the rats imprisoned in their cage with hatpins, entirely naked (his white, flabby, sick man's body) or simply without trousers (his bulging eyes, his hooked mustache, his impeccable center part, his curled bangs undone and hanging loose) jolted by the assaults of the "wild boy" he has chosen: "You have a great big bum!" says Jupien lovingly to Charlus, with mingled admiration and respect.

She said in English: "Well! There's your bloody plane!" We were sitting in the cafeteria on the balcony overlooking the central hall.

"May 16 at 1130 hours, Captain A. de V——, Cmnding Off. of the 1st group of 1913-model 105s of the 104th R.A.L.A., arrives at the command post of the 3rd battalion of the 84th R.I.F. at RAMOUSIES (Battalion Chief B——). This group (9 or 10 elements in firing condition) is already deployed at Le Muid in RO-CAINSART, facing CLAIRFAYTS, 2 elements on the north side of the road, 7 or 8 on the south. The targets and the order of fire are worked out. The group is ready for action at noon. It had left NAMUR at noon on the 15th, arriving at LE MUID before dawn on the 16th. Captain V——, full of confidence, predicts optimal performance from his men. Cmdr B—— is pleased that he has arrived.

"Statement of Lieutenant D——, of the first group of the 104th R.A.L.A., 3rd Bry., imprisoned in Oflag IV D: The morning of May 16, Lieutenant D——, mechanical officer in the 1st group of the 104th R.A.L.A., leads several trucks full of ordnance to the artillery installations and does not unload them because at the same moment he receives the order to take them away again.

"1500 hours—Captain A——, Cmnding Off. of the 9th Co. (command post LE MUID), telephones: 'Engines heard in CLAIRFAYTS, a group of tanks has been spotted in the village.' The 105s are alerted and open fire (Shot no. 9 on the firing chart).

"1645 hours—20 at a time, the enemy tanks emerge from the woods around CLAIRFAYTS, regroup, and cross the hillside diagonally, moving toward the installations at 'LA FERME AUX PUCES.' The 105s fire shot number 8 then, by telephone, Captain V—— warns Cmdr. B—— 'that he has no ordnance and is retreating.' Consternation of Cmdr. B——, who strongly pro-

tests and puts in a call to MAUBEUGE. General B—— orders the group to hold its position. Captain V—— had spent the entire winter in the area, he was surely not unaware of the location of the munitions depot, and yet he had brought with him at most 150 rounds. In the order, 2nd part, received from Lieut. Colonel R——, Cmnding Off. of the 104th R.A., the § on ordnance delivery must have been dealt with.

"Colonel C——, commanding the A.L. of the 5th C.A. was in MONT DOURLERS. What did he do?

"Someone in authority is responsible, a heavy artillery unit cannot be sent into battle without ordnance, for this lack of ordnance alone allowed one Panzer to penetrate the line at CLAIRFAYTS, after destroying the installations and gun turrets." (Appendix no. 1 to the Field Log of the 84th RIF—S.H.A.T. = Service historique des armées de terre—Château de Vincennes)

"Now that, from one artist to another, I have given you my reasons," writes Proust, still to Berthe Lemarié, "here is the passage to be added. It's on page 128, line 27. The line begins with these words: Autrefois de Swann . . . Here is the passage to be added, with no change of paragraph, immediately afterward: Then becoming Odette again, she began to speak English to her daughter. Immediately it was as if a wall had hidden a part of Gilberte's life. In a language that we know, we are able to substitute for the opacity of the sounds the transparency of the ideas. But in a language that we do not know . . ."

Your bloody plane.

Along with the paintings of Gastone N——, the Alan Gallery showed a certain number of canvases by Enrico Baj:

> Profile with Orange
> Man Happy with His Social Position
> Excited Person

Little Portrait with Fruit
General
Excited Woman
Person Facing His Destiny

Rommel writes that at dawn on the 17th, as he was approaching Landrecies, he captured a French lieutenant colonel who, he says, proved particularly irritable when asked his name and assignment. He had him taken to Colonel Rothenburg and the latter ordered him into his tank but, since the Frenchman refused to obey ("sharply," writes Rommel), rather than sending him to join the other prisoners, Rothenburg ordered that he be killed ("we had to resign ourselves to shooting him").

Summer nights, I sometimes stayed awake long after she had fallen asleep. Raising myself up, I could see the milky prairie sloping down to the lake surrounded by the dark clumps of pine trees and the light trunks of the birches. Halfway down the hill, a stand of trees whose trunks diverged in a V shape stood out against the calm surface of the water, which seemed to contain and concentrate the light falling on it, as if phosphorescent, as if the water were the very source of the light, had stored it up and was now sending it back into the Nordic night (as if when it reappeared it would come not from the sky but from the lake, brighter than the sky, with the colors of an opal: green, almond pink). I could hear her breathing quietly. She was asleep, lying on her side, her back to me, her legs bent, her nightgown rumpled and pulled up to the middle of her back, exposing her waist, the curve of her hip, and her buttocks, also pastel blue in the half light. The room was hung with a pale-colored wallpaper, the furniture (the chest, the wood of the sofa, the head of the bed) lacquered white, like the broad planks of the floorboards.

The train has been traveling for two days since it left Stalag IV B near Mühlberg an der Elbe, in Saxony. Each of the cattle cars that make up the train holds forty prisoners belonging to colonial reg-

iments which, for propaganda reasons, the Germans are trans-
ferring to a Front Stalag. A few French prisoners born in the
colonies (mostly *pieds-noirs*), on the strength of their birthplace,
have managed to slip in with them. They are all dressed in the
same khaki uniforms and coats, dirt stained, sometimes torn. It
is late October, the nights are already cool and naturally the wagons are not heated, but the prisoners, after five months in the
wretched conditions of the camp, stacked up in huts, covered
with lice, underfed, and forced into hard labor eight hours a day,
scarcely notice the cold. With only forty of them in each wagon,
they can lie or sit down, and a sufficient amount of food was distributed before the train left. Through the two little windows on
either end of the cars they toss away the improvised receptacles
(tin cans or simply paper) in which they collect their excrement,
which is in any case not particularly abundant, and the train
stopped once, at the Dijon station, where the guards threw open
the doors so the Red Cross women could hand out loaves of
white bread. Brief but violent battles suddenly break out here and
there among the prisoners, over the distribution of the bread and
other matters, but everything grows calm in the evening when,
sitting in silence, they listen to one of the oldest men among them
telling a story in Arabic in a monotonous voice. When on the
evening of the second day the train arrives in Bordeaux, the
guards once again unlock and open the sliding doors, but apparently only in order to let in a little fresh air, because there are
no women from the Red Cross this time. Beneath the station's
glass ceiling everything seems much as usual, bustling, except
that the platform where the train has stopped is off limits to civilian travelers. Through the wide-open doors, beyond the main
hall, the prisoners can see the square in front of the station. It is
late afternoon on a warm autumn day, and the sunlight is lingering on the façades. On the café terraces customers are sitting
at tables with aperitifs and waiters in white aprons are coming
and going, bearing trays. Some of the customers are talking in
groups of two or three. Others, sitting alone, are reading newspapers or smoking cigarettes whose blue veils rise up in the fad-

ing sunlight. On platform 1, travelers, some with children, some not, their bags sitting next to them, are waiting for a train. They look blankly at the convoy of prisoners, at the dark, emaciated faces appearing at the doors of the wagons. Finally the orders are barked out by guttural voices, the doors of the wagon are closed again and locked from the outside. A moment later the train lurches forward.

Eventually we managed to transfer the entire contents of the Norwegian ship onto the rusting old freighter. There were even crates sitting on the deck. I still wonder what miracle kept it afloat, but fearing the Italian air patrols from the base in Majorca (or maybe the captain with his old-smuggler face was afraid that a simple sea swell would send it to the bottom) he did not go on to Barcelona but unloaded the weapons at Palamos (or maybe it was more convenient for the "Comandante" and his friends there). But I never heard of him again. He had openly boasted to me of being a double agent and had shown me two photographs, in one of which he was in the company of Garcia Oliver, one of the leaders of the Anarchist Federation, and in the other surrounded by Francoist officers. I suppose that one or the other group must have had him shot at some point.

I told the journalist it was an assassination. But the fact is that he'd just thrown the entire squadron whose command he had assumed into that ambush, and (that great plodding off-horse that he was riding bareback—a sign that he was probably no longer in his right mind) we might legitimately believe that, consciously or not, he was seeking an honorable death.

Your bloody plane.

Strange birdcalls in my half sleep I imagined them strange with long curved beaks perched among the branches strange exotic interlaced enameled blue like on porcelain vases from Delft or what? Strange odor as well peppery at once warm and cool permeating the room where I was gradually waking up after the long airplane trip Rustling of paper slipped under my door: *Indian Times*

At dawn on the 17th, Rommel had traveled nearly 80 kilometers from the previous evening's point of departure. He had taken ten thousand prisoners, not surrounding them but simply sweeping them up as he passed by. At Landrecies, he crossed the Sambre without opposition. On the left bank there were barracks full of French soldiers. His aide-de-camp, Lieutenant Hanke, walked into the yard and ordered the officers to assemble their troops and lead them eastward.

They were so white, so regular, and he flashed them every chance he got in such a self-satisfied way that I wondered if they weren't false. With his tanned face and those dazzling teeth, rather than a diplomat, he looked like a torero or a gigolo. "Extend a hand through the bars! . . ."

At sunrise, they took us for a boat ride on the Ganges, which, at Benares, flows more or less north to south. At the very edge, you could see, lying on stretchers and half submerged, the bodies of the dead who would be burned when night fell. A hundred meters downstream a wide stone staircase descends to the river, where during the day beggars stand exhibiting their amputated limbs. They say that the poor mutilate their children so they can bring in some money. In Bombay, I saw one whose forearm had been cut off and the skin was sewn up so skillfully that the radius and ulna emerged, separate, to form a sort of pitchfork. At the bottom of the stairs men and women were bathing, walking into the river up to their necks, splashing water over themselves. Some of them, their two hands brought together to form a cup, thrust them into the water and drank. Most of the women were elderly. They were fat, and their soaked saris clung to their bodies forming undulating folds between which the light, translucent cloth plastered against their skin appeared pinkish brown.

Where they were thicker, the sinuous folds of the wet cloth were light gray, twisting, moving apart from each other, toward each other, over their breasts, their stomachs, their thighs, as on statues. In the east the enormous disk of the sun climbed little by little over the horizon, orange red.

Could it be suggested that Dostoevsky sublimates a sensuality that he cannot restrain by conferring upon it the status of an act of defiance against God?

After the guards had locked the doors of the wagons the train lurched forward and soon stopped again. We spent the entire night on a siding track. In the morning we moved on again for about a half hour, after which the train made its final stop and they had us get out. It was good to walk in the cool air after those three days and two nights closed up in the wagon. The camp to which they led us had probably been built in a hurry, because it was only surrounded by a minimal fence made of one single row of posts, about two and a half meters high, with widely separated strands of barbed wire running between them. The next day I escaped. Since they locked us into the huts as soon as night fell, I had to make my attempt by daylight. Two or three people had tried it before me but they had been recaptured (or in any case, knowing how flimsy the fence was, the guards had spread a rumor to that effect, even going so far as to specify, since a knife wound is more frightening than a bullet wound, that one of them had had his thigh run through with a bayonet). But I thought it would be now or never.

Person facing his destiny.

From the balcony, where the cafeteria was, we could see the huge front hall of the airport. It was built entirely of wood, polished and gleaming. I don't know why it made me think of the inside of a musical instrument. The lights of the shops selling furs or duty-free goods were reflected in the glowing parquet floor.

Now or never The arrival of the trainload of prisoners was probably badly timed and with no food to distribute the Germans let the Arabs collect and cook the acorns that had fallen in the oak forest running along one edge of the line of barbed wire Bent double I pretended to be looking for acorns as well coming going keeping one eye on the sentinel the lower strand of barbed wire ran about forty centimeters above the ground The sentinel turned his back Now or never I don't know how much distance I covered like that on all fours in the bushes expecting at any moment the shock of a bullet or shouts a pursuit the pain that a bayonet stab must cause until I had to stop breathless stretched out full length on my stomach hearing no sound but the air noisily entering and exiting my lungs the pounding of my heart beating violently When I was able to get moving again I continued on my elbows and knees but not as fast I probably went another two or three hundred meters like that Finally I listened again Everything was calm After a moment I stood up carefully From where I was now you almost couldn't see the huts Now it was ferns Almost as tall as a man Already going brown And pines The rays of the setting sun streamed between their thin vertical trunks in parallel, diagonal bands of varying widths I began to walk

Your bloody plane!

As if floating in midwater, like some ancient, blind sea monster, some whitened cetacean emerging from prehistory, vaguely phallic, the uncertain shape of the front end appeared, slowly materializing in the darkness amid the snow squalls, the snow also imponderable, sometimes lazy, then suddenly frenzied, shooting diagonally, the closest flakes lit by the lights of the hall, golden, then, further away, simply white, then grayish, then simply imagined, eddying, innumerable, filling the darkness as far as the eye can see with impalpable moving particles crossing over each other, slowly sinking earthward. Through the thick glass you could just hear the roar of the engines fading away. Across the table, her face, lit from below by the little lamp that made her cheekbones stand out even more. She hadn't touched her cup

of tea. Something glistening, trembling, in the corners of her al-
mond-shaped eyes. But maybe only an effect of the light.

Replace the word "unhappiness" with the word "grief" leaving
the rest as it is.

Still trying in my bad English to . . . Sudden voice in the loudspeakers twice first in that language that sounds like barbed wire
the third time in English She said Now they're announcing your
flight You bastard Go on. I took my bag and stood up. Through
the whirling snow squalls you could see the headlights of the two
plows busy clearing the runways coming and going pushing their
cones of yellow light before them. At the stop in Stockholm a
worker on a rolling scaffold circled the plane, armed with a wand
that sprayed an antifreeze liquid over the wings.

When you fly over them at night all you can see of the Nether-
lands and Belgium is a vast network of lights Beads strung out in
lines crossing over each other diverging sometimes running parallel (triangles stars intersections constellations) as far as the eye
can see Mesh of a net stretched out over the darkness where
sleeping. Density of the population. Scarcely, every now and
then, an occasional dark patch (or perhaps a cloud concealing?).

In the daytime, once, from an airplane, on the way to Cologne,
I tried to spot the places. Clearly saw the Meuse at the bottom
of its valley. Trying desperately to orient myself. The roads the
villages that railway trench where I ran unhorsed bullets passing
by with the sound of hornets. Breathless. Quite simply kept walking despite still hornets. Anyone who says danger or fear gives
you wings has never It seemed to me it was there but airplanes
fly too high too fast nowadays. Everything far behind already
slipping away carried off. Pleasant countryside.

2

367 different demonstrations of Pythagoras's theorem have been catalogued.—Elisha Scott Loomis, THE PYTHAGOREAN PROPOSITION

From the windows of the white-and-gold succession of molding-laden parlors the guests saw the honor guard snap to attention while at the same moment they heard the metallic rustling of sabers being pulled from their sheaths, their blades glinting in the sun. For a moment nothing happened, the honor guard stayed frozen in place with their whiting-coated leatherwork, their black tunics, their red fourragères, their gleaming helmets, like a joyous, carnivalesque, showy mockery of combat uniforms, the tidy, optimistic antithesis of the mud of the battlefields, the dirt-colored uniforms, and the suffering.

Then there was a sort of jostling (an exchange of blows, even, it seemed) among the dark-clad group of press photographers who had been waiting in the June sunshine for an hour and who now tried to push forward, restrained more or less by the police contingent, also kitted out in fourragères and, passing through the gate, the long black automobile slowly pulled to a stop just alongside the doorman with the heavy silver chain who opened the door, backing up to let the Queen out of the car.

No one had noticed the corpulent man in the middle of a little group (a former railway employee, drawn by caricaturists with the head of a monkey) who stepped away from the few silhouettes gathered at the foot of the stairs, walked forward to meet the sovereign, bowed (it was not clear if he was kissing her hand), and, gesturing broadly with his arms, invited her to climb the red-carpeted marble steps.

She disappeared, reappeared a little later at the far end of the string of parlors which, a moment earlier, still buzzed with the polite murmur of the many guests, primarily men, mostly middle-aged, some of them still young, speaking in quiet tones, some in little groups, others standing separately in couples, of agreement protocols or ministerial rumors, like some secret society, a meeting of insiders, a little too controlled beneath their affected carelessness, all dressed in the same dark suits, like a uniform, with their immaculate shirts, their sober neckties, their impassive faces, and, like iron filings attracted by a magnetic field, but nevertheless without pushing, hurrying calmly, they had clustered together in silent ranks as she advanced, smiled, briefly slowed her pace, gave a slight nod, started forward again: not an ordinary woman, not even an ordinary queen but (she whose father had reigned over a third of the planet, who herself reigned over nothing more than a half-ruined nation, become the vassal of richer cousins) something affable, fragile, and formidable, with some of the qualities, in her clothes, her dress, her hydrangea-colored hat, of a rare but somewhat faded flower, and, in her posture, of the prow of a battleship and the pediment of a bank, albeit a broken one.

Now as far as the eye could see the column of tanks was raising long plumes of yellow dust in the May sunshine which the breeze spread over the gently undulating landscape covered in places with woods, sprinkled with lakes, with villages whose names (Cerfontaine, Sivry, Clairfayts, Eppe-Sauvage), evoking by their sound an idea of moving waters, coolness, and shade, seemed to contradict the very idea of war, of death, but for, here and there, in the fields ("No sound came from the enemy, even though at regular intervals our artillery sent shells toward points situated far inside their territory"), the corpses of a few cows struck by a stray fragment, vaguely obscene, lying on their backs, their stomachs distended by the gas, their teats swollen and pink, their four legs sticking up in the air like pikes in one final mute gesture of protest.

"People said that an age of speed required rapidity in art, precisely as they might have said that the next war could not last longer than a fortnight."

As it happens, the paths followed respectively by S. and R. will merge for a short distance (about five kilometers), each of them, a few hours apart, following the road from Solre-le-Château to Avesnes, more precisely, from the spot known as Le Trianon to the western edge of the little town of Beugnies, where one of the two colonels followed by S. (who, at that point, will constitute along with another cavalryman their entire escort) will be shot. It will be about ten or eleven in the morning. It will be a beautiful day and the springtime sun will be shining down on the fields, the flowering hawthorn hedges, the orchards, casting a salmon-pink tint over the smoke rising here and there from burned-out vehicles, glinting off the slate roofs of the farms. Rommel will have passed this way during the night at the head of his division and, forging ahead, will have continued straight on toward Avesnes, Landrecies, and Le Cateau, setting out on the victory-studded trail which will lead him four years later to bite into a capsule of cyanide.

And also in May, and the same grillwork fence with its gilded spikes, the same entryway, the same steps, but without the red carpet this time, with no honor guard and no photographers (unless they discreetly—or rather secretly—brought him in through some hidden entrance, a service entrance so to speak, since he himself was coming here so to speak as a service—although as Prime Minister he obeyed no orders but his own, that is to say those which through innate courtesy (or tradition) he was pretending to elicit from the five or six grave personages who had designated him (by whom he had caused himself to be designated), fully prepared to disavow him and remove him from office if things went wrong): and then perhaps only some private secretary next to the doorman (the latter without a silver chain this time, no doubt) who opened the door of the car from which he emerged, the cheery May sunshine darkened by the wreaths of black smoke which, merely furrowing his brow a little, he pretended not to see, perhaps chewing (or throwing it aside before stepping forward) the eternal cigar which seemed the indispensable complement to his eternally fat baby face, muttering a greeting, then following the private secretary, climbing the steps, then crossing through the succession of white-and-gold parlors with their mirrorlike parquet floors, treading over the rugs decorated with leaves flowers and fruits: on the Roman-numeraled face of the gilded marble and bronze clock in the middle of the marble mantelpiece the gilded filigreed hands were pointing to a little after five o'clock in the afternoon when, carefully closing the door behind him, the private secretary left him standing alone before an ordnance survey map surrounded by three grim-faced men, among them a general in uniform, his breast adorned with a rectangle of small colored ribbons.

Although Proust gives no explicit indication of the time, we can deduce from the context that it must be about five o'clock in the afternoon when, accompanied by her daughter-in-law, née Legrandin, the Marquise de Cambremer (whom the liftboy of the hotel insists on calling Camembert) comes and sits with the narrator and Albertine on the terrace of the Grand Hôtel. "We gazed at the calm sea upon which, here and there, a few gulls floated like white petals," writes Proust, which suggests (as will become clear over the course of the narration, in which the gulls gradually change color as time passes) that when the marquise and her friends sit down the light (it is May) is not yet tinted with the iridescence it takes on as the sun declines: "Because of the level of mere 'medium' to which social conversation reduces us, and also of our desire to please not by means of those qualities of which we are ourselves unaware but of those which we think likely to be appreciated by the people who are with us, I began instinctively to talk to Madame de Cambremer, née Legrandin, in the strain in which her brother might have talked. 'They have,' I said, referring to the gulls, 'the immobility and whiteness of water lilies.'"

The following scene takes place about twenty years after the episode of the colonel's death from a sniper's bullet: a girl (or a very young woman) dressed in pink emerges from the Stadtmitte (City Center) subway station in Berlin. The city stretches out in a vast expanse of ruins with an occasional building still standing here and there, intact or damaged, balancing precariously, held up by beams, in which, nevertheless, in a few remaining windows, curtains can be seen hanging, tenacious, paradoxical evidence of habitation. There are no vehicles passing by in the streets (or in what were once streets), which have nonetheless been cleared of rubble, and a strange, unbroken silence hangs over the scorched walls and piles of stones or bricks among which, soundlessly, the two or three commuters that emerge from the subway entrance every ten minutes or so go their separate ways and disappear from sight. The entrance is not far from the former Akademieplatz, which could be seen from the windows of the hotel where S. once stayed, before the war. On either side of the square, in those days, stood, in symmetry, two perfectly identical churches in seventeenth-century baroque style, decorated with pediments, entablatures, columns, and which, having been hit by bombs and set ablaze, are now blackish red, the color of baked bricks. Thanks to an exuberant growth of shrubs, bushes, and weeds that has taken root in the broken entablatures, they resemble those ancient ruins beloved of Romantic artists, or of the kind you sometimes see in Poussin's paintings. The girl in the pink dress coming out of the subway is elegantly attired, as if for some rendezvous, or as if she were on her way to a party. With a graceful walk, she makes her way between the piles of rubble toward what is now nothing more than an empty space, bordered on one side by shapeless mounds of bricks and on the other by a series of façades, still standing, with nothing behind them, like a theater set, the sky showing through the empty windows. Only occasionally does the sound of distant traffic break the silence, coming from a part of the city that has been rebuilt, like a faint rustling, no louder than the whir that accompanies a silent movie. The long wall of façades, which have probably also burned, is dark brown. The silhouette of the girl in pink gradually shrinks as she walks along this wall, her skirt swinging with the graceful rhythm of her steps. Soon she is only a dancing spot, continually shrinking, a point, then nothing, vanished. It is June. The disk of the sun, orange red in the light summer haze, gradually sinks over the broken walls, redder and redder, velvety, as it slips downward, with a bite taken out of it by some cornice, by the ironwork of some balcony hanging over the void, finally disappearing in its turn.

". . . and (continuing to imitate the language of her brother, whom I had not yet ventured to name) added that it was a pity that she had not thought of coming a day earlier, for, at the same hour, there would have been a Poussin light for her to admire."

The Queen is wearing a hydrangea blue hat swathed in a twisted ribbon, a hydrangea blue dress with buttons down one side, a three-strand pearl necklace, and a diamond on her ring finger. She looks much younger than in the magazine photographs. At dessert, she will read, perfectly at ease, in the gentle voice of a well-bred schoolgirl and with no trace of an accent, the speech that has been written out for her in French. All the Englishwomen in her retinue (the wives of the principal members of the Embassy no doubt) are wearing large hats; one of them, very thin, wears a red dress and a wide-brimmed black straw capeline. The former railway employee, promoted to the rank of Prime Minister, who will commit suicide less than a year later, is sitting next to her among the more distinguished guests on one side of a long table, their backs to the windows, facing the other guests who are divided among separate tables. The meal consists of whole truffles in *feuilleté*, young pigeons, a salad, cheeses, and strawberry ice cream. On the cover of the menu, which is printed in an elegant script, is a color photograph inside a gold-ringed oval showing the fireplace of one of the parlors of the palace where the reception is being held. Made of white marble, monumental, its false columns, its entablatures, its consoles, are laden with an exuberant profusion of bronze ornaments, with garlands and cupids surrounding the face of a clock set into the pediment, topped with a tall statue of a woman in marble veils, one hand lifting the flame of a torch toward yet more gilded cornices. The same cornices, the same profusions of gilt run above the large bay window to which the Queen, among the distinguished guests, sits with her back turned, in the filtered sunlight streaming through the translucent plastic blinds. Mingling with the clinking of the forks and knives, a polite murmur of conversation runs through the room. The butlers come and go silently amid the tables where former ministers, generals, ambassadors, or members of the Académie Française discuss the good and bad points of various diplomatic posts in London, Beijing, Jakarta, and the means of transport, more or less luxurious, trains or airplanes, that service them. At dessert, standing, a glass of champagne in his hand, the Prime Minister evokes the memory of the soldiers of the two allied countries whose bodies, he says, lie side by side in the cemeteries. Monotonously repeated, in bronze or in plaster, on the clock stand or over the mirrors, naked children with fat folds of flesh, with simpering gestures, carrying garlands or pointing a plump finger toward the face of the clock, seem to be so many versions, vaguely bacchic, of domestic angels fluttering among the cornices, framing vague coats of arms, like laughing allegories of time, fecundity, and love.

"But the name of Poussin, without altering the amenity of the society lady, aroused the protests of the connoisseur. On hearing that name, she produced six times in almost continuous succession that little smack of the tongue against the lips which serves to convey to a child who is misbehaving at once a reproach for having begun and a warning not to continue. 'In heaven's name, after a painter like Monet, who is quite simply a genius, don't go and mention an old hack without a vestige of talent, like Poussin. I don't mind telling you frankly that I find him the deadliest bore.'"

There were no crosses, only stakes hastily cut from the nearby thicket (sometimes only a floorboard pulled from the rubble) thrust into the ground at the head of little mounds, the freshly shoveled earth an ocher color, already growing pale in the May sunlight, standing out against the enameled green of a field, sometimes at the edge of a woods, or near some charred ruin, sometimes singly, but most frequently in clusters of six or seven—not much more—the little rectangles side by side, the stakes side by side topped with the helmets of two opposing armies, the muted rumbling of explosions already far away, and once more the twittering of birds in the hedges, the faint rustling of the leaves, the peaceful woods, and only here and there a few blackish spots sullying the grass, sometimes a mutilated tree or two, or a house with no roof, with coal black walls, and already, stretching out along the roads, the first columns of prisoners in their dirty uniforms, unkempt, with several days' growth of beard, their eyes red from lack of sleep, their faces drawn, vacant, their shoulders slumped, sometimes passing alongside a string of vehicles, burned out or overturned in the ditches, walking past some machine with shredded canvas covers, a cannon, a dead horse, already beginning to stink.

After setting up the machine-gun rig on a kitchen table, the corporal commanding the squadron goes outside to urinate. As he is buttoning his trousers, he hears the whistle of a flying shell. Rather than throw himself to the ground, he stupidly jumps into the building through a ground-floor window. The blast of the explosion knocks him flat on his stomach amid a hail of plaster and broken glass. As he stands up, he glances at his wristwatch, whose crystal bears a star-shaped fracture. The hands have stopped at 5:45 P.M.

126

The same plaster cherubs with their gold-veiled nudity, with the same dimples, the same mischievous faces, repeated on either side of the fireplace, above plaster pediments and capitals, the same enamel-faced clock, with Roman numerals (I, II, III, IV, V, VI, . . . X, . . . XII . . . , as if time, History, must always be marked off by these bars, these geometric signs, these wedges, these crosses engraved by Caesars), the gilded bronze hands, intricately worked, pointing to five-thirty in the afternoon when, having just emerged from the plane that brought him from London, he made his entrance.

He did not say whether a doorman with a silver chain hurried forward to open the door of his car. Chain or no, he probably wouldn't have seen it. No more than the chandeliers, the tapestries decorating the long succession of parlors that he passed through, slightly hunched, like an animal running full speed, head thrust forward, hearing but not listening to the voice of the short man with the small face, with a flat skull, with a rat's snout, with the look and the clothes of a departmental manager, constantly at his side, repeating expressions of welcome which he answered without even thinking of it with that mechanical and excessive politeness which thanks to his upbringing and his birth he had learned was owed not so much to one's inferiors but to every living creature, human or animal, general, horse, statesman, or dog born beyond the borders of his island with its perpetually gray sky, its perpetually gray rain, and its lawns clipped and rolled over the centuries. Afterward, he told about that (not the plaster, the gilt, the false columns, the cherubs—although he was vaguely aware of them, perhaps even appreciated them (he only said that it was "nice"): perhaps because the cornices, the fat cherubs, and the garlands corresponded to the image he had in his mind of this land of cocottes, operettas, Trianons, novels of adultery, and mustachioed generals—or perhaps simply, after all, because that was his taste as well, his concept of pomp, opulence, art, like the hydrangea hats worn by his sovereigns, or the evanescent Ophelias or Beatrices displayed in the Royal Academy: in his spare time, he himself painted: landscapes imitated from Monet (rocks, haystacks, seasides) with pale mauve shadows, with plastery highlights applied in small strokes—and later, when it was all over (when things became normal again, when, still as massive as ever, placid, formidable, with his eternal bow tie and his eternal cigar, looking as though he'd just come from his club with its private stock of port, he sat down in the folding chair that had been set up for him in the middle of a desert of ruins in the garden—or rather in what had once been the garden—of what had been the last den in which the last leader of those who for nearly five years he referred to only as the Huns had gone to ground), when it was all over, then, everything back in place, then you could see photographs of him in the newspapers, his baldness protected from the sun by a straw hat, sitting on a folding chair before a portable easel, his brush in his hand, busy mixing on his palette the jamlike colors of sunsets or of the glimmering of the sea in whatever port chance had brought him to, aboard the yacht of some billionaire or some soprano): he told, then, of this: the last parlor into which he entered, where the first thing he saw was, on an easel of the kind you see holding up the chalkboard in schoolrooms, not a flamboyant sunset or haystacks with the violet shadows of a freshly harvested field, but a map of about, he said, one meter by two, around which was standing, waiting for him, a small group of men (only three, in fact), the one who began to speak (the general who commanded three million men—although not really anymore) sporting not those manly whiskers, one of those mustaches of the kind worn by drum majors or NCOs in the colonial army like the one he had known twenty years earlier, with his pitiless wooden face, flat cheeks, dry voice, but (the current general in chief) clean-shaven, soft, slightly plump: a sedentary man, a frequenter of parlors and ministers' offices, having reached the high position he occupied thanks not to some talent for strategy but apparently to his aptitude for waiting patiently in vestibules.

"'Anyhow,' Mme de Cambremer went on, 'I have a horror of sunsets, they're so romantic, so operatic.'"

Half of the regiment consisted of very young cavalrymen, those who were in the middle of their military service when the war broke out, and the other half of reserve officers who'd been called up, whose average age was no more than twenty-five. The majority of the soldiers were peasants from the Marne, the Aube, and the Yonne, and to this was added a small number of city dwellers, shop boys or office workers, placed in the cavalry as if through a mistake (or a joke) of the recruiting offices, drowning among the farmhands, day workers, and beet farmers. No doubt, for all of them, after the first shock of the mobilization, the long winter months, spent in an inactivity scarcely enlivened by routine maneuvers, during which their principal concern was to protect themselves from the cold, had little by little softened them up, but, in any case, what they suddenly came face-to-face with in that paradoxical, cheery springtime setting was so different in its violence and speed from what they could have been prepared for that there was not, in the strictest sense of the term, any real combat, at least not to the extent that that word supposes two forces with more or less equal chances in mutual opposition.

Their first contact with gunfire was an extremely brutal one, and emblematic of the shape that would be taken (that was already taken from the beginning) by the entire battle which, in the space of one month, brought the Germans to the Loire and even beyond, that is, that the regiment literally flew into pieces, like a simple plywood panel struck by a thick beam, and in seven days, or more precisely five if we except the first two which were spent traveling in forced march to meet the enemy, it ceased to exist as a coherent unit.

On the sixteenth of May, just six days after the regiment had entered Belgium, the general in command of the brigade blew his brains out. On the seventeenth, after having thrown the squadron whose lead he had taken into an ambush, the colonel, isolated, found the honorable death he was seeking, after which there remained only a few scattered elements, with no communication between them, dragging themselves along on foot, their horses dead or exhausted, mixed in with the disparate debris of other units retreating (or rather repelled) in disarray, here and there, as they happened onto some bridge, some suburb, or some canal, entering into pathetic skirmishes intended to slow down the enemy, and immediately overrun.

On the twelfth alone, the cavalrymen having never at any time found themselves in a position to fire a single shot, the squadron's losses were already enormous. Those who, in groups or singly, pursued like wild animals, driving their horses to exhaustion, had managed to cross the Meuse again before the bridges were blown up were led westward in the evening, into a woods where, for the first time in three days, they could unsaddle their horses, worn out from the long walk to get to the battle site and from galloping at full speed to escape the machine-gun fire. Under the saddle blankets abscesses had formed and burst, so that when they undid the straps they found patches of raw flesh amid the sweat-matted hairs, deep red, black around the edges. They spent the day counting the number of missing, tending to their animals as best they could, and digging holes as a protection against possible air attacks. Toward noon they lined up by the field kitchen truck which had made its way there from the rear and in which the cooks, eager to be off, keeping one eye on the sky and shouting at them, filled their mess kits with pieces of meat mixed with sticky rice, which they chewed slowly, sitting on the ground, their backs against the trunks of the tall trees, holding their mess kits between their widely spread legs, keeping an ear cocked, their spoons growing still, hanging in midair, whenever there was a sudden violence to the echoes of the explosions coming from the east, where the successive waves of airplanes flew circles through the sky. Later (and this was for the first and last time) they were given little gray-green cards decorated with two crossed tricolor flags and with the words POSTAGE EXEMPT printed diagonally in one corner. On the other side, beneath an invitation to buy Armament Bonds, holding the cards on their knees, they wrote their families to tell them not to worry, that everything was going well and that they were in good health, then they stayed there, among the holes that they had dug like little graves, their gaze empty, lost, while the buffeted air continued to bring them the incessant echo of the explosions, some of the men wandering around aimlessly, pausing occasionally to listen to some braggart or some show-off, surrounded by a small group, perorating in a nervous voice, too loud, too fast, then no longer listening, setting off again, mute, dejected.

"The dowager marquise . . . had two remarkable habits, due at once to her exalted passion for the arts (especially music) and to her want of teeth. Whenever she talked of aesthetic subjects her salivary glands—like those of certain animals when in rut—became so overcharged that the old lady's toothless mouth allowed to trickle from the corners of her faintly mustachioed lips a few drops of misplaced moisture. Immediately she drew it in again with a deep sigh, like a person recovering his breath."

Toward evening, the order came to saddle up and stand ready to move. Once it was formed, although amputated of one platoon, the squadron set forward again, heading south at first, parallel to the Meuse. The sky had grown overcast and darkness was slowly falling. On the way, they met a continuous column of refugees, which they had to nudge to the side of the road, some of them riding in carts, others pulling little wagons or pushing bicycles, and watching them pass by in silence, with a dead, inexpressive eye. As evening fell the echoes of the bombing in the east became more widely scattered, and the battle seemed to grow calm, either because the ceiling of clouds was hampering the airplanes now or because all resistance had stopped. At one point, the squadron followed a stretch of road that must have been part of a car-racing circuit, because it was lined with barricades and billboards bearing, in letters of faded yellow and green, the brand names of tires or lubricants. To the right stood the skeleton of a little wooden grandstand. A cool wind had come up, almost cold. There were children with the refugees, sometimes walking next to the carts, sometimes, the youngest ones, in the arms of the old women sitting on the packages piled up in the cars, often protected by a red blanket. Similar blankets, of the same red and apparently new, could also sometimes be seen, folded in eight, on the baggage racks of the bicycles and a rumor coming from who knows where began to spread through the cavalry column that they were being used as signals for the enemy airplanes, so that at one point, as the captain and a non-commissioned officer stopped at the side of the road seemed to be questioning a cyclist, several cavalrymen said that he was a spy and would have to be shot. Also among the refugees were groups of nuns wearing long robes and curved starched wimples, and another rumor ran throughout the column that the enemy was dropping parachutists disguised as nuns or priests. Some even said that in Belgium all the religious orders and all the priests were German agents. A little later, the captain and the NCO came up alongside the column from behind, and, although no one had heard a gunshot, some claimed that they had taken the cyclist behind the grandstand of the racing circuit and executed him with one pistol shot.

To tell the truth, it is difficult to see in what way the second formulation adopted by the narrator to describe the gulls "in the manner of the brother of Mme de Cambremer, née Legrandin" ("They have," I said, "the immobility and whiteness of water lilies") differs so greatly in its deliberate excess of preciousness from the one that he himself used a little earlier on ("We gazed at the calm sea upon which, here and there, a few gulls floated like white petals"), but it soon becomes evident that if he corrects himself in this way by introducing the word and image of water lilies it is in order to, on the one hand, concretize the Monet painting which will form the object of the conversation, and, on the other, make visible, through the successive descriptions that he will provide of the changing colors of the gulls as the sun sets, the passage of time as the exchange of thoughts on art is pursued, thoughts more or less influenced by changing fashions and by age (which is another way of evoking time) expressed alternately by the voice of young Mme de Cambremer and the toothless, drooling mouth of the dowager marquise.

Whereas in the north, along a front of about twenty kilometers, running from the Dyle to Namur, the French had positioned, next door to their allies, ten divisions, contrarily, in the south, between Namur and Mézières, that is over a distance three times as great, they had only set out nine, which found themselves facing thirty-three German divisions. As it happened, the only real battle, after which it can be considered that the war was essentially lost, was the one that took place on May 13 and 14, in which the Germans crossed the Meuse and immediately enlarged their bridgeheads.

A shell was bursting at the front line of the charge of the pontifical Zouaves. Various other subjects, such as Saint Louis (or Du Guesclin?) on his deathbed, Joan of Arc dressed in a silvery cuirass at the crowning of Charles IX, or a missionary baptizing the kneeling savages, were also depicted on the different panels that ornamented the windows. Their style was that of the last century, with, in the execution of the lead-ringed figures, a certain limpness and a conception of form very different from that of the stiff, hieratic figures of the Middle Ages. The explosion's flames were surrounded by gray smoke, whose center glowed like the heart of a petal with a vermilion gleam mingled with gold. The pontifical Zouaves were dressed in broad, puffy, madder-colored trousers, embroidered navy blue boleros, and fezzes with fringed tassels. The one in the foreground was frozen in a running position, one leg bent and thrust forward, the other full length, his upper body leaning forward, pointing a rifle fitted with a bayonet in the direction of the enemy. No doubt hit by a shell fragment, another soldier—an officer armed with a saber— was on the contrary shown standing, bent backward, off balance, one arm raised in an unfinished gesture, his saber already falling from his hand, held there only by the loop passed over his wrist. The juvenile voices of the pupils rose up along with the suf-focating billows of incense that climbed toward the painted vaulting, the censer being swung by one of the choirboys gath-ered around the officiant dressed in a voluminous Nile green chasuble with moiré highlights and decorated with a deep red Y-shaped cross on which, at the junction of the two branches, was a large medallion bearing, against a gold background, the letters INRI, interlaced, like thorns.

The platoons were reconstituted to fill in the gaps created by the losses incurred, and the corporal knew the cavalryman riding be-side him only by sight. He is a reservist, like himself, more or less the same age although with a face already showing signs of wear, and who speaks with the drawling accent of the Parisian suburbs. From the moment they climbed back into the saddle, he has not spoken a word: gloomy, taciturn, limiting himself to a shrug of the shoulders (or not even that—as if he didn't hear them) in re-action to the rumors of spies that were running through the ranks, only swearing sometimes, crudely, when his exhausted horse stumbles and he pulls it up brutally. When he hears the other man addressing him, the corporal says What? and looks at him. The cavalryman does not answer, does not even turn his head, as if he had been speaking only to himself, his gaze fixed, beyond the knobby expanse of helmets and backs, on the line of trees bordering a road which, from west to east, crosses the col-umn's path. There are no refugees beside the road now. When the cavalryman speaks again, he still does not turn his head. He says, louder this time, Where do you think we're headed? You think we're going back into it? The corporal does not answer. He too is looking at the straight line of trees which the head of the col-umn continues to approach. All the cavalrymen are looking in the same direction and nothing can be heard but the multiple clopping of the hooves above which the Parisian's voice rises again, at once furious, indignant, plaintive, saying They aren't taking us back into it, are they? Yesterday wasn't enough? Isn't it enough that we all just about bought it? Isn't it enough that we

. . . Neither the corporal nor any of the other cavalrymen answer him: only the same quiet clopping of the hooves in the silence, the gray plain, the sky an iron gray, and then once again the voice, whining now, like a lament, a plaint, rising up, saying If we turn left that means we're going back into it, if we turn left that means, the corporal saying without raising his voice Shut up! the other voice continuing now, as if impossible to restrain, as if growing frenzied, rising in pitch, breaking, saying, almost shouting, That's it they're turning left, they're turning left! We're going back! I knew it! They're taking us back to the slaughterhouse, they The corporal suddenly beginning to shout as well, shouting Will you shut up, will you shut up, will you just shut up? I'm scared too, everybody's scared! So what? Will you shut the fuck up? Will you . . . And suddenly the cavalryman riding ahead of the Parisian pulling sharply on his reins, making his horse turn around completely, digging in his spurs, running forward and colliding with the flank of the Parisian's horse, so violently that the second horse is shoved to one side, crashing into the corporal's horse with a sound of clicking stirrups, of weapons clanging together, the corporal nearly thrown off balance himself, the cavalryman's right fist striking the Parisian's face once, twice, three times, while at the same time he also shouts, although almost without opening his mouth, his lips taut, thin, whistling through his clenched teeth I'll shut him up, damn Parisian! I'll shut this asshole up for you! You about ready to shut your trap now? You done crying now? You better shut up by God, don't you think you've been bugging us long enough, huh? You want another smack, tell me, you want another one? . . .

"'. . . Monet, Degas, Manet, yes, there are painters if you like!' . . .

'But,' I remarked to her, feeling that the only way to rehabilitate Poussin in her eyes was to inform her that he was once more in fashion, 'M. Degas affirms that he knows nothing more beautiful than the Poussins at Chantilly.'

'Really? I don't know the ones at Chantilly,' said Mme de

Cambremer, who had no wish to differ from Degas, 'but I can speak about the ones in the Louvre, which are hideous.'

'He admires them immensely too.'

'I must look at them again. My memory of them is a bit hazy,' she replied after a moment's silence, and as though the favorable opinion which she was certain to form of Poussin before very long would depend, not upon the information that I had just communicated to her, but on the supplementary and this time definitive examination that she intended to make of the Poussins in the Louvre in order to be in a position to change her mind."

Later (in the shelter of the tent shading the deck: the blazing sun, the glistening sea, the billionaire's or soprano's yacht anchored in some cove whose transparent water laps gently at its sides, the cove itself nestled between two promontories of one of those islands whose position, for four years, surrounded by his counselors with their chevron-laden sleeves, a harassed look on his face but always imperturbable, he had so many times examined on the map—and now relaxed, still, as always, pink as a baby, his disdainful lower lip with its babyish pout thrust further forward than ever, the folds of his jowls framing the inevitable bow tie, his massive body dressed in a limp alpaca suit sunk into a rattan armchair and the secretary or stenographer swiftly laying down the little symbols on her pad of paper as he spoke—or perhaps at home, in his office with his Victorian furniture, walking to and fro, scattering ashes from his cigar here and there over the carpet, perhaps pausing in his dictation, pushing back a curtain, standing motionless at the window for a moment watching the gray rain falling over the city with its soot-colored walls, with its red-painted buses, its parks, its gray river, its wounds still open) . . . later, then, as he told it, no one (none of the four men gathered in the overgilded parlor) sat down, they all remained standing while the character with the flabby face, with stars on his sleeves and on his breast a plaque ornamented with hard-candy colors, pointed to the pocket or rather the paunch drawn by the line of the enemy advance on the large-scale map held by the easel. He said that afterward, for some time (he said "consider-able"), no one spoke. Perhaps, in the silence, they could then hear the tiny, implacable sound of the mechanism of the clock, the im-placable rotation of little toothed gears, the wild oscillations of the flywheel, the clicks of the little hook falling and rising, hold-ing back and then liberating the minuscule parcels of time one after another, the elegant golden hands, with their intricate or-namentation, imperceptibly progressing from one austere Ro-man numeral to the next, while the plump cherubs continued to frolic over the cornices and among the gilded leaves, until he de-cided (maybe clearing his throat, seeking, weighing the words that he was about to speak (at this point it must have been about six o'clock), maybe adopting a genial tone as when one speaks to children or cretins (or simply to people born on the Conti-nent), recalling memories of the last war, the breakthroughs that they had seen run out of steam, the flanking counteroffensives), saying finally (this time in French, he said, either out of coquetry or because he thought perhaps that he would be better under-stood by his interlocutors: the grocer, the rat, or the school-teacher): "Where is the *masse de manoeuvre?*" the general in chief then turning toward him, shaking his head, perhaps spread-ing his arms and letting them fall at the same time as he answered "There is none," silence settling over them again, the four men standing there, the little toothed gears continuing to move one after the other, still without haste, still inexorable, until, perhaps, he realized that the sound he was hearing was not that of the teeth, of the mechanism as it nibbled away at time, but, coming from outside, the crackling of the bonfire lit in the garden where he could see the old doormen dressed in black (or perhaps, given the circumstances, in those long gray smocks like ironmongers wear) dumping into the flames, one after another, the contents of wheelbarrows overflowing with archives, one of the sheets, blackened or still burning, sometimes rising above the flames, as if gripped by panic, climbing unsteadily through the smoke, flut-tering, sinking earthward, rising up again, spinning around, fi-nally carried off. Some of them, perhaps, fell at the foot of the

French doors. Almost whole sometimes, sometimes half consumed, the brittle burned part crescent shaped, like a scalloped brown bite mark, silvery black, embossed.

"As the sun was beginning to set, the seagulls were now yellow, like the water lilies on another canvas of that series by Monet."

Having come back to the table on which the machine-gun operator is lying, the corporal pulls out a chair and sits down. He and the sharpshooter look out the window at the deserted countryside. In one corner of the room, the artilleryman fills the clips with cartridges that he takes from a canvas bag in which they are lying loose. A five-day growth of beard covers their cheeks, and their eyes are red. For two days they virtually haven't eaten or slept. Another three or four shells fall on the village, but at some distance from the house where the three cavalrymen are staying, nevertheless they instinctively pull their heads down between their shoulders each time, after which nothing happens at all (adjusting their trajectory?).

Thick wreaths of black smoke, swirling, eddying, slow to dissipate in the sky, come from the smokestacks of the boats offering passage from one bank of the Bosporus to the other, moored at the quay near the Galata Bridge. The beige canvas tents stretched over the upper decks no longer protect them from the sun, now setting, reflected in a vertical golden bar along the tubes of the smokestacks, which have been painted black, as if rubbed with wax. A cool wind makes little waves in the water of the basin, indigo blue, kicking up plumes of foam here and there which break against the flanks of enormous barges loaded with sacks, on each of which a single boatman hunched over his oar is trying to steer. A bustling activity reigns over the water, where various little launches powered by a motor or a sail are moving along, no less than over the quays or the movable bridge where two rows of vehicles meet between the wooden sidewalks full of pedestrians, including a few women covered in veils. In a dinghy rising and falling with the slight swell, two men dressed in dirty pullovers, sleeves pushed up, with brown, bony faces, are using a portable stove to cook slices of fish which are bought by passersby who lean over or squat on the edge of the quay. The flesh of the fish is yellowish white in color, just as the oil with which they are impregnated makes deep yellow spots on the torn sheets of newspaper in which one of the two fisherman, acting as vendor, holds them up toward the customers. The customers also have thin faces whose skin, leather colored, is stretched over their protruding cheekbones. They move a few meters away, holding the torn sheet of newspaper in one hand like a plate and lifting the jagged pieces of fish to their mouths between their thumb and index finger. Their lips, pulled back, let their teeth show, very white, like dogs' teeth. Toward the setting sun, the domes and minarets of the large mosques stand out against the daffodil-colored sky, as if cut from sheets of blue-gray cardboard. The streets climbing toward the old city are very steep, but even so you can sometimes see men running up them, bent in two, their upper body almost horizontal under the weight of a packsaddle of the kind used on donkeys, carrying stacks of bundled pack-ages or suitcases, and sometimes a large piece of furniture, an ar-moire. People say that even when they've taken off their pack-saddle in the evening they can no longer stand upright. In the display cases of the porcelain-walled Topkapi Palace one can see collections of weapons, handworked saddles, porcelains and richly embroidered gowns once worn by sultans. One of them, made simply of linen, has a slash at chest level, a little below the base of the throat, made by a saber blow (or dagger?) in the course of a battle (or assassination?). The dried blood around it is still visible, a pale rust color.

"'Oh! They're flying away,' exclaimed Albertine, pointing to the gulls which, casting aside for a moment their flowery incognito, were rising in a body toward the sun."

"Als wir in das Innere des Bunkers kamen, konnten wir uns von dem Erfolg unseres Schusses überzeugen: wir fanden dort einen Toten und blutbefleckte Verbände," writes Rommel. (As we made our way into the bunker, we were able to gauge the efficacy of our fire: we found a dead man and bandages stained with blood.)

When the general in chief had stopped talking, dropping his arms in a gesture of impotence, of despondency, he simply stood there, silent, with his face like limp paste, his plaque of decorations in all the brilliant colors of glory, valiance, and victory, green and black, daffodil, emerald, azure, lilac, rust, fire, his brightly polished boots reflected by the brightly polished parquet floor, or sunk into some rug with an interlaced pattern of faded laurel boughs and pale fruits. The Englishman said that they stayed there, incapable of speaking a word, him incredulous, his eyes glued to the map without another thought (as if he had erased them from his mind and from History) for the three others, still not moving to sit down, as if in the silence, broken only by the crackling of the bonfires onto which the doormen continued to dump their wheelbarrows full of archives, two formidable adversaries were confronting each other in the aspect, on one side, of the incarnation in human form of some animal from the family of bulls or bulldogs, dressed in an impeccably tailored suit, his back slightly hunched, his head drawn down between his shoulders, as if he had been stopped in midspring, and on the other side, of a military map supported by that easel which, amid that riot of plaster, false columns, fluting, and acanthus leaves, seemed like a foreign body, some curious accessory, as if in that decor (the palace conceived on the eve of another defeat by a hapless emperor, completed and recuperated by a Republic greedy for pomp in the service of parvenus) war itself had crudely intruded, had cast down there that indecent, simple, and categorical piece of school furniture, impossible to reject or ignore, while with imperceptible jerks the bronze hands, similar to lace, continued to move over the enameled face of the Roman-numeraled clock.

"In the sunlight on the horizon that flooded the golden coastline of Rivebelle, invisible as a rule, we could just make out, barely distinguishable from the luminous azure, rising from the water, rose pink, silvery, faint, the little bells that were sounding the Angelus round about Féterne. 'That is rather Pelléas, too,' I suggested to Mme de Cambremer-Legrandin. 'You know the scene I mean.' 'Of course I do' was what she said; but 'I haven't the faintest idea' was the message proclaimed by her voice and features, which did not mold themselves to the shape of any recollection, and by her smile, which floated in the air, without support. The dowager could not get over her astonishment that the sound of the bells should carry so far, and rose, reminded of the time."

Reading the narration of these events that he later wrote up (or that he completed during the period in which, after his injury, convalescent, waiting for a new command or for his assassination, he wrote—or revised—his notebooks (documents which, afterward, his widow and his son hid, along with his letters, in various places, scattered here and there in little bundles: on farms, in cellars, under the rubble of bombed-out cities, in boxes, at the bottom of a buried suitcase, avoiding the frenzied searches of his assassins, and then of the enemy secret service (once, simply, of Moroccan infantrymen looking for chickens or pigs to slaughter), the thickest one, in spite of it all, finally discovered, sealed, sent across the Atlantic, locked away like precious metal or cakes of explosives in a safe guarded by armed sentinels, minutely studied by crew-cutted academics, finally returned after many years with the apologies of courteous diplomats and equally courteous generals with the faces of myopic Anglican pastors); there is a photograph of him taken at that time, no longer displaying that same arrogant kepi as the man with the nightstick, with its crown rising up in front, its sharp-beaked eagle, wings outstretched, its gleaming brim, no longer the black cross edged in silver hanging at his neck, but bareheaded, dressed in an ill-cut civilian suit, a tweed jacket (brown, his son says) and flannel trousers, sitting awkwardly (or cautiously: some other injury no doubt than the one that nearly cost him an eye?) on a low wall, looking, with his unusually high forehead, his unusually large head atop his narrow shoulders, like one of those spastics whose hair has been carefully combed and necktie tied by other hands, fragile, awkward, his upper body supported by his two arms anchored on either side of him, a few sheets of paper in one of his hands: his eyes are lowered, he is not looking at the camera lens (the same perhaps as the one he proudly used all through his victorious campaigns, avidly photographing explosions, burning buildings, ruins . . .). As if bending under its own weight his head leans slightly forward, a black dog is lying at his feet and, behind him (the wall seems to run along a terrace, the wall and the terrace made not of stone but of concrete, perfectly square, without a single chip or crack), the upper half of one of those houses with false slate roofs made of plaques of concrete, gray or earth red, with a zinc gutter, also perfectly straight, the same house, the same roof that can be seen, similarly set out in perfectly straight lines, all identical, in the hamlets or villages, also all identical, of Württemberg, Hannover, or Saxony, always desperately bleak, and, in the background, the pale slope of a hill, also desperately bleak, desperately gray. . . . But that might explain it, says the journalist. Explain what? says S. Boredom, says the journalist. Simply that: boredom. As I remember, there's a passage in Heine that describes a walk through the streets of Aachen, where he meets a dog who says to him: Kick me, and Heine says: Kick you, but why? It'll give me some entertainment, the dog answers. Yes: boredom. Maybe that's what compels them to demand that their philosophers give their life some meaning, to blow into fifes and every now and then, to go look for a little entertainment away from home. Even if it means getting themselves killed. Anything to escape the boredom . . .) . . . reading the narration, then, that he later wrote up, it is difficult to establish with any certainty the chronology and the sequence of events: only after describing the way he set about quickly breaking through the narrow row of bunkers lined up along the border ("An assault detachment from the Panzer company had managed to neutralize a concrete shelter. The men crawled to the entrance and threw a three-kilogram explosive charge through the peephole") does he provide some indication ("The sky was growing dark") which would allow us to assume that he launched his initial attack more or less at the same moment as, in the gilded-plaster parlor, the formidable personage with the Havana cigar found himself face-to-face with the military map set up on an easel. For its part, the field log of the only regiment which opposed him at that moment, stretched out over a twenty-eight kilometer front, states that at 4:45 in the afternoon "more than twenty enemy tanks emerge from the woods around Clairfayts and take up position facing the installations of the *Ferme aux Puces.*"

"The dowager gave her footman the address of a pastry cook where she had to call before taking the road, which was pink with the evening haze, with the humped cliffs stretching away into the bluish distance."

Although extending on one side as far as the brightly lit boulevard lined with cafés and bars whose nights were illuminated by American nymphomaniacs, philosophers from Central Europe, real or false poets, painters and their models, also real or false, the school, whose yards and buildings covered almost an entire city block, had its entrance on the opposite side, on a quiet street with a name both Marian and pastoral which, like that of the nearby church, seemed a fragile anachronism amid the apartment buildings, the more or less seedy hotels, and the movie houses and artists' studios that had little by little hemmed it in.

As if, with its lawns and tranquil gardens, its bland plaster statues, its dormitories lit by night-lights, and its chapel, the school as well, itself anachronistic, persisted there like a foreign body, impossible to expel, an island, a place under siege, impregnable, opposing the cosmopolitan agitation of the cafés and the bars with an invincible, severe, haughty silence.

To the left of the large main entrance, three steps gave access to a small door opening onto a tiled vestibule where a sculpted medallion hung on the wall facing the front door, representing in bas-relief and in profile the World War I ace, his automobilist's goggles raised up and resting against his aviator's hat, his head slightly thrown back in an attitude of courage and defiance, looking proudly toward the sky, as if he were endlessly scrutinizing it in search of some enemy, in order to come up on his tail and shoot him down. There was a rumor that he had been expelled from the school for indiscipline but the palm leaf also sculpted in the marble and which formed a graceful curve above him showed eloquently how little weight the missteps of a young boy carried, long since absolved, swept away in the apotheosis of glory that seemed to shine eternally from him, between those beige-enameled walls, like a permanent injunction, the permanent reminder not of the runt in puffy riding breeches, with his swaggering air, his kepi tilted over one ear, who, between two victories, sipped champagne in the luxurious restaurants of the capital, but of the very incarnation of some vaguely medieval tradition (single combat, trial by ordeal, Divine Judgment), something vaguely supernatural, like the immensity of the unsullied skies where in a sort of virgin assumption he had, without a trace, disappeared forever.

As if this biblical rapture in which he had been carried off on the wings not of seraphim but of a stinking propeller engine (in reality, by a pile of twisted, charred scrap metal, sunk diagonally into some beet plantation or plowed field with, at its tangled core, something like a little mummy, shriveled and coal black) had so to speak propelled him, neatly embalmed by the flames, out of the realm of human existence: a new Elijah, then, vanished or rather evaporated (no blood, no dismembered body) into the azure, thereby exempted from ending up like one of those men with the pudgy physiques of mechanics or automobile repairmen reduced to taking people for their first plane ride at air shows or ringing the doorbells of industrialists or newspaper publishers in order to beg, with the strap of an eye patch making a bar across their face, for money to finance some perilous trip across continents or over vast oceans, exempted too (in point of fact, because the undisciplined recalcitrant pupil had never earned this distinction) from appearing in the photographs of the school's best students, invited every year to the Saint Charlemagne banquet served in the huge gymnasium, displayed for the edification of their younger peers in great glassed panels on the walls of the corridor running off the right of the vestibule, offering the sight, in superimposed rows of medallions, of hundreds of little wan faces, doll-like or scrawny, their hair carefully slicked back, sometimes curly or spiked with a cowlick, with the same look of a little frightened animal, their necks squeezed into the same officer's collar of the same dark uniform, like a collection of postage stamps, the multiplication of one single portrait of the same boy, studious, devoted, and fragile, destined to a future as a student at the École Polytechnique, a ship's ensign, or a lieutenant in the cavalry.

But the boarders did not at first walk down this hallway when they were brought back to school on Sunday evening by their parents—or relatives of their parents—at whose home they had spent the day. Through a door to the left of the glorious bas-relief they entered one of the rooms of the visitors' area at the center of which, near a table covered with a green rug, stood a priest dressed in a long black cassock, with a pale emaciated face, his body no less emaciated, his gaze invisible behind the lenses of his glasses in their circular steel frames, who, without a word, with a simple nod of the head toward the parents, punched the exit pass of the student reentering the school.

Apart from a few cretins or incorrigibles, the despair of their families, regularly thrown out and then let back in (probably thanks to pleas and arguments of all sorts—monetary included —addressed to the archbishopric) and placed temporarily in full pension as a punishment by their parents, denizens of the sixth or seventh arrondissements, most of the boarders were provincials, with the exception of a few foreigners, Belgians, Spaniards, or South Americans, to whom their rich and pious families wanted to give the sort of prestigious education that in their minds was assured not only by the teachings of stern churchmen but also (they thought, perhaps) by the frequentation of numerous fellow students bearing noble names with a *de* or a *du*.

The dry, repeated clicks of the punch in the silence, the emaciated priest, the parsimonious lighting of the room, hung with green, Empire-style wallpaper, where, in the semidarkness, one could vaguely make out the rows of chairs lined up along the walls, had something monastic about it, something austere and inflexible, as if the future *polytechniciens*, the future naval lieutenants, the future Guynemers (or the future Argentinean generals) were crossing, as they left their families, their eyes still full of the traffic in the busy streets, of images of horse rides and Hollywood kisses, over the threshold of a world of recluses, dark, military, and categorical.

Alone or in little groups, they walked down the hallway where the hundreds of studious, meritorious, and well-groomed faces seemed to watch them pass by with their eyes as docile as those of a little animal, then went outside into darkness again to walk across the deserted yards to the sound of the bell, which, starting at five minutes to nine, rang at regular intervals, like some knell, like the signal, at once imperious and desolate, of the end of some festival and the announcement of a period of isolation. Apart from the *cour des troisièmes*, surrounded by high walls, and an unsightly, recently constructed addition made of buhrstone, there was nothing particularly severe about the buildings. Built toward the end of the last century, in the style, at once sober and romantic, that can be seen in old engravings in bishops' palaces or in presbyteries, covered with white paint, they opened onto two parks decorated with boulders and pale-colored Virgins. Chestnut trees, covered in the spring with white flowers standing upright like candles, ornamented the largest of the yards where, every year, in June, the Corpus Christi was celebrated at the foot of a monumental altar made of a pyramid of flowers. This same yard was separated from those of the Grandes Écoles preparatory classes by a series of little buildings including, among others, the salon occupied by the barber, who, for the price of a few chocolates, sold the students pocket combs, a pomade known as Argentina, and little round or oval mirrors, on whose plastic backs in pastel-colored monochrome, pink, almond green, or pale blue, you could see photographs of nude women smoking cigarettes or sitting at high vanity mirrors, their backs arched, their bottoms thrust out, the glass reflecting their image as they perfume their armpits, or sometimes lying languorously on divans.

Still not pursued by but accompanied by the regular tolling of the bell, the boarders walked across yards and playgrounds toward their respective buildings, climbing staircases and finally entering the study room where, indelible, intermingled with the mustiness emanating from the heaters, there hung a particular odor of ink, chalk, and blackboards that seemed the very smell of Latin verse, Racinian tirades, and algebraic formulas. Behind the tall rostrum stood a priest in a threadbare cassock, or some mustachioed proctor wearing an equally threadbare suit, who simply, with the gestures of a cashier, added the new arrival's exit pass to the pile accumulating before him as the boy returned to his place. The students of the Grandes Écoles preparatory classes, like those in the senior humanities class, were no longer obligated to wear the military-style uniform. At the same time, inside the school they were authorized to wear something like a forage cap, no less military in appearance. The colors were black edged with red for the Polytechnic, navy blue edged with azure for the Naval School, solid sky blue for Saint-Cyr, and bottle green edged with yellow for the École Centrale, the candidates to this last school, none of whom bore noble names, being the object of a certain disdain among the others.

The principal subjects studied were Greek, Latin, French, mathematics, and foreign languages. Apart from the pale, enticing nudes on the back of the little mirrors sold by the barber, the teaching of fine arts was limited to imitative drawing, and for two hours each week the masks of Juno, Caesar, and Hermes set out as models seemed, with their blind eyes, their fixed expressions, and their lifeless flesh, like the dusty, graying materialization of the hundreds of lines of Latin or French verse that the students were expected to learn by heart, as if they saw appearing before them, taken from the glassed cases to which they were returned at the end of each session by the student in charge of materials (the same one who during recess sat behind a grillwork window selling chocolates, and who pumped up the soccer balls on Thursdays), the bloodless phantoms of heroes, goddesses, or Roman emperors, and as if, overseen by the priests in black gowns and the drawing teacher with his faunlike goatee, the entire history of the world, the armed clashes, the rhetoricians' speeches, and the tears of Bérénice had ended up there in a jumble, blending together over time into that single unchanging plastery substance in the form of a crowd of decapitated heads, emptied of their contents, condemned to silence and blindness.

At the school they also taught, albeit in exchange for a fixed supplement, fencing, music, English boxing, and horsemanship. Boastful, speaking too loudly, slapping their leggings with their whips but accompanied by priests in black gowns, a few students went to a riding school near the Bois de Boulogne every Thursday, returning in the evening, still enveloped by or rather haloed with the prestigious odors of horse sweat, litters, manure, and sawdust, peering out the windows, as they passed by in the elevated metro, nudging each other with their elbows, at the closed shutters of a house on the Boulevard de Grenelle all too quickly hidden from view by the metal arches on either side of the tracks.

"It was only 1700 hours, the machine guns in turrets 555–556–557 and 558, the six nearby support posts, i.e., six machine guns in log huts, open fire, equaling two sections. Intense fire coming from the installations at LA PERCHE A L'OISEAU, LA GOBINETTE, TRIEU DU CHENEAU, LA FERME AUX PUCES, LES AUNIAUX, FERME MIQUET, and LES FILS DE FER. Suddenly several tanks that have reached the trench are hit: one of them by the 25 in LA PERCHE A L'OISEAU, two others by the 25 in LES AUNIAUX, two others by the 25 in TRIEU DU

CHENEAU. The tank personnel, trying to flee, are fired on from the turrets, but at 1715 the AUNIAUX installation ceases fire. Two tongues of flame are coming from its openings." (Field log of the 82nd RIF—Régiment d'infanterie de forteresse)

"'And how charming the name is,' said I. 'One would like to know the origin of all those names.'"

Each time it stopped, the special train (a local made up entirely of third-class cars with yellow wooden benches) bringing the young conscripts from Paris to the Eastern garrisons where they had been posted let off one or several groups of soldiers who were immediately met on the platform and surrounded by armed guards, in cities whose names (Château-Thierry, Epernay, Châlons, Bar-le-Duc, Toul), with their armor-clad sonorities, at once medieval and warlike, evoking fortresses, armed camps, and muffled cannon fire, seemed like so many menacing presages. As if, through Champagne, Argonne, Lorraine, the train with its hard wooden benches were little by little entering a region with a particular status which, not only in France but in the most remote villages of the American continent, was synonymous with battles, vast cemeteries, bayonet charges, barracks, trumpet calls, latrine odors, dung, sour wine, and soldiers' brothels.

Here and there above the plain towered high steeples laden with baroque decorations, similar, vertical and knobbed, to some architect's decaying dream, competing in an overcast sky with the smokestacks and blast furnaces, bearing witness, elaborate and nostalgic, to the past greatness of Polish princes and marshals with porcelain names, with lace cuffs, with gleaming black cuirasses ringed with gold, such that in the rooms and hallways of the chateaux that sometimes now served as barracks one might expect to find the traces left behind by the portraits that had hung there, beneath which, under the sanguine or delicate wig-framed faces, one could read some ducal—or even royal—title, evoking (like the name of that city (Baccarat) posted again and again at the crossroads), in a glinting of cut crystal and a virile odor of stables, visions of garlanded cupids, of marquises in low-cut gowns with décolletage edged with swansdown, of the dappled hindquarters of horses, of three-cornered hats and boots with cuisses.

The men of five regiments considered "elite," three of them cavalry regiments, constituted almost a quarter of the population of the small city whose arrogant cathedral erected to the past glory of the Society of Jesus was surrounded by narrow streets and a scattering of bars whose waitresses, wearing too much makeup, with worn faces and crimped hair, appeared on the doorstep when they heard, approaching, echoing off the façades, the hooves of a squadron heading out for some maneuver clopping over the old paving stones. Behind the main building of one of the cavalry quarters lay a riding ground planted with tall trees and enclosed by whitewashed fences. In the winter, dressed in their short ratiné coats, their impassive faces pink with cold, and accompanied by their bluish wading-bird shadows cast on the blinding snow, the young officers, in groups of two or three, speaking together, walked their pureblood horses with their lustrous hindquarters, dappled in the summer with circles of sunlight chopped up by the leafy branches, gleaming in turns over their red-waxed boots, the polished steel, and the elegant spurs. In the yards (or the groves laid out behind the chateau once inhabited by the Polish prince), the recruits, in canvas coveralls, cartridge belts, and helmets, went through their exercises, goaded by noncommissioned officers, manipulating their weapons and doing about-faces in double time. The most dreaded of these exercises was saber training, for which, in spread formation on the maneuver field, the cavalrymen repeated to the point of exhaustion the forward thrust right, forward thrust left, downward thrust for an enemy on the ground. While a large number of the officers belonged to the nobility, the rest were almost exclusively sons of superior officers or generals who themselves belonged to the cavalry corps. The youngest, newly arrived from Saumur and still unsure of themselves, compensated for their blushing timidity and lack of command experience by an icy demeanor and a perverse severity which, together with the prestige of their names (de l'Estoile, Maison-Rouge, de Villiers), aroused a mixed emotion of hatred and respectful admiration among the subordinates. In any case, they were rarely seen: no more than once a week, for weapons or equipment inspection, and, again once a week, for what was called "maneuvers," which consisted of an unvarying and tiresome repetition of the same imaginary battle plans. Furthermore, once spring came, they disappeared from Friday to Monday, taking the train along with their horses and the jockeys they hired as batmen (or aides?) to various tracks in the area, where they tested themselves against the officers of other garrisons in steeplechases from which they sometimes returned limping dramatically, with a dislocated knee or wrist. Except that they were only allowed one horse now (some of them, in peacetime, had up to three) and could no longer engage in steeplechases, the mobilization and the state of war changed none of their habits, and they continued to maintain the same distant, cold demeanor, more and more distant in fact, more and more absent, leaving it up to the noncommissioned officers to deal with questions of materiel as well as those concerning the troops, riding their one horse during the day with their impassive faces, enlivening the long evenings in the winter camp with interminable games of bridge, discussing strategy, commenting on the right-thinking editorial in the newspaper and waiting impatiently, in a vague daydream of trumpets and charges, for the moment when fate would allow them to prove their courage and exalt their names and their family tradition by some glorious exploit and, if necessary, by their death.

"'She has asked you to lunch,' the judge said to me sternly when the carriage had passed out of sight and I came indoors with the girls. 'We're not on the best of terms. She feels that I neglect her. Good heavens, I'm easy to get on with. If anybody needs me, I'm always there to say: Present! But they tried to get their hooks into me. . . . When you reach my age you will see that society is a paltry thing, and you will be sorry you attached so much importance to these trifles. Well, I'm going to take a turn before dinner.'

When I had said good-bye to Rosemonde and Gisèle, they saw with astonishment that Albertine was staying behind instead of accompanying them. 'Why, Albertine, what are you doing, don't you know what time it is?'"

The bronze lace hands of the Roman-numeraled clock were probably pointing to about nine or maybe ten o'clock then. Night had fallen. The doormen had probably stopped dumping their wheelbarrows full of archives onto the fire where a few little red specks continued to glow, a few little dying flames coming to life, leaping up again, flickering, going out, now only with their last glows lighting the parlor with its profusion of acanthus leaves and cherubs invaded by darkness, awakening some last glint of gold, some last dying glimmer among the cornices, the garlands, around the easel, now useless (or which the doormen might have returned to the school from which they had taken it).

Toward eleven o'clock the squadron receives the order to pull back as silently as possible. The corporal has the unlimbered machine gun removed, the gunner folds up the two back legs, unscrews the front support, and hoists it onto his shoulder to stow it in the shed where the horses are kept hidden. They have not been unsaddled and, feeling their way in the dark, some of the cavalrymen are doing their best to wrap their hooves with rags, pieces of blankets, and anything else they've managed to find in the houses and tear up. Holding their mounts by the bridle and struggling to make them walk on the grassy shoulders of the road, they travel the first five hundred meters on foot, after which the order comes, whispered from mouth to mouth (or rather not even that: each horse bumping up against the hindquarters of the one in front but, because the fatigue was so great, without setting off any kind of stampede, the horse and rider simply stopping and waiting, here and there from one end of the column to the other), to stop and climb into the saddle. The movement starting up again in the night, the exhausted horses, the exhausted riders, the missiles that sometimes suddenly shoot up from a field as they approach. No one speaks. Hunched over their saddles, their slumped backs oscillating from front to back with the footsteps of their horses, they watch, a little later, as, with a sleepwalker's indifference, they pass by the column of bombed-out vans slowly burning down, the charred bodies, the intersection that they cross through also bombed out. They don't know that they're about to fall into a trap.

The last gleams of the setting sun, coloring the water-lily gulls in mellow shades, are followed by a sort of parodic descent into the underworld, set in the cramped, dimly lit space of the elevator in which Albertine and Marcel are enclosed along with an eager Charon personified by the liftboy, of whom Proust wonders if, as is usually the case, employees do not possess "organs" with a greater power of divination than those of the bosses. "Hence the liftboy had gathered, and meant to inform his 'colleagues,' that Albertine and I were preoccupied. But he talked to us without ceasing because he had no tact. And yet I discerned on his face, in place of the customary expression of friendliness and joy at taking me up in his lift, an air of extraordinary dejection and anxiety. Since I knew nothing of the cause of this, in an attempt to distract his thoughts—although I was more preoccupied with Albertine—I told him that the lady who had just left was called the Marquise de Cambremer and not de Camembert."

The road that leads from Solre-le-Château to Avesnes runs in a straight line between the fields, curving only slightly over the shallow depressions in the terrain, climbing up again imperceptibly, sometimes bordered with fruit trees. It passes through villages or rather clusters of small houses, made of brick, with two floors at most, often flanked with little gardens. Having bypassed Solre-le-Château on the southern side, the German tank columns turned onto the road: "The moon had come up, so that . . ."

From that moment on there will simultaneously occur several events which, despite or perhaps precisely because of their apparent incoherence, constitute a virtually homogenous and coherent whole.

Having been brought back to the Embassy in the Rolls-Royce or Bentley that was waiting for him when he got off the plane (or maybe, for the sake of secrecy, the car of a simple attaché) and without taking the time to touch the sandwiches and tea that had been prepared for him (maybe nothing but a flask of whiskey?), his jaw clenched, probably sucking at a fresh cigar, he dictates the message to his cabinet which is immediately sent off, translated by the accompanying former Indian army officer into the language of that land of jungles and swamps where, from atop her pedestal, sitting in her bronze armchair, the double-chinned Queen, with her starchy demeanor and hollowed-out bronze pupils, seems to contemplate, beyond the vast esplanade, the Empire on which the sun never sets, not even arrogant, not even pensive, but august, widowed and pudgy, inconsolable.

"On the floor which we were passing at that moment, I caught sight of a hideous chambermaid carrying a bolster, who greeted me with respect, hoping for a tip when I left. I should have liked to know if she was the one whom I had so ardently desired on the evening of my first arrival at Balbec, but I could never arrive at any certainty. The liftboy swore to me with the sincerity of most false witnesses, but without shedding his woebegone expression. . . ."

And no longer blood, fire, fear, hunger, courage, or fatigue, but only words set out on sheets of paper filed in yellow cardboard folders kept shut with thin olive green ribbons and stored on several kilometers of shelves, inventoried, numbered by order, date, regiment, branch (artillery, cavalry, sharpshooters, miners, infantry, engineering, service corps) dating back to the Imperial wars and even, for certain regiments, well before, when they bore the names of sovereigns, of provinces, of cities, or of the princes who kept them at their expense (Toul Artillery, Royal Dragoons, Lorraine, Lambesc, Artois) and, once the ribbons are untied, sheets of grayish paper, typewritten characters, also grayish, and this:

"*Having learned of the death of General B—— and of his replacement in the command of the 4th D.L.C. by Colonel M——, Commander of the 4th Brigade, the Colonel leaves by car for the Division command post, taking Major H. A——-B—— with him. On the way, he meets Captain Ch—— in a sidecar. The latter informs him that since that morning Colonel C——, who had taken over as commander of the Brigade, was missing, and that consequently he was taking command of the Brigade.*"

. . . .

"*The Regiment is scheduled to move at 2200 hours.*

"*Itinerary: NALINNES, HAM, THUILLIES, LEERS, MONTIGNIES, BOUSSIGNIES, COUSSOLRE, AVESNES area.*

"*A few shells in the direction of the Regiment command post at the moment of departure, a few isolated shots, even some machine guns.*

"*The Regiment marches in the following order:*

Colonel and his command group.

Major H. A——-B—— and his command group.

3rd Squadron (M——-R——)

1st G.E.

4th Squadron.

"*Moving by night is difficult; as soon as they have set off the motorized units that were to have led the column disappear from sight.*

"*The colonel puts two officers at the head of the column, alternating, on bicycle: Lieutenant M—— then Lieut. du Ch——.*

"*The column has difficulty keeping up, the horses and the men are very tired, gaps in the column passing through villages and alongside convoys that are still burning. Everyone is hoping to find some rest on the other side of the border, in the shelter of the Maginot Line.*"

". . . swore to me with the sincerity of most false witnesses, but without shedding his woebegone expression, that it was indeed by the name of Camembert that the marquise had told him to announce her. As a matter of fact it was quite natural that he should have heard her say a name which he already knew. Besides, having only those very vague notions of nobility, and of the names with which titles are composed, which are shared by many people who are not liftboys, the name Camembert had seemed to him all the more probable inasmuch as, that cheese being as universally known, it was not in the least surprising that a marquessate should have been extracted from so glorious a renown, unless it were the marquessate that had bestowed its celebrity upon the cheese. Nevertheless, as he saw that I refused to admit that I might be mistaken, and as he knew that masters like to see their most futile whims obeyed and their most obvious lies accepted, he promised me like a good servant that in the future he would say Cambremer."

After a last stop in San Juan where two lackadaisical Black men dressed in green jumpsuits and long-visored caps refuel the airplane with kerosene, the flight linking Santiago de Chile and New York does not reach the coast of the United States until after night has completely fallen. Flying over the ocean, the airplane moves parallel to the coast, and, on the left, starting at Miami, a string of cities, one after another, begins to parade by in the dark. Glowing red in the centers because of the neon lights, and surrounded with glitter, they look like rivers of molten metal cracking through the shadowy surface of the earth, strange, like a bubbling eruption of lava, passions, and violence.

"But the liftboy's anxious gloom continued to grow. For him thus to forget to show his devotion to me by the customary smiles, some misfortune must have befallen him. Perhaps he had been ''missed.' I made up my mind in that case to try to secure his reinstatement, the manager having promised to ratify all my wishes with regard to his staff. 'You can always do just what you like, I rectify everything in advance.' Suddenly, as I stepped out of the lift, I guessed the meaning of the liftboy's air of stricken misery. Because of Albertine's presence I had not given him the five francs which I was in the habit of slipping into his hand when I went up."

The general's suicide, the debris of the brigade still in Belgium, lost in the night, trundling along on their worn-out horses, some of them limping, one of the two colonels on foot, his horse dead, cut off from his regiment (or rather from what remained of it), the brigade now far behind the column of German tanks advancing down the Avesnes road ("There was nothing left but to climb into our command tank and start off. The road west was now clear"), moving slowly at first, with no other obstacles but the refugees' cars, quickly driven into the ditch by the first tanks, until the moment . . .

He doesn't say if he told the ambassador, although he probably had to explain the reason for the thick black smoke which, from the windows of the Embassy (it wasn't that far away) they were surely able to see. Nor does he say whether after having sent the bulletin to his cabinet he finally touched the sandwiches and cakes prepared for him or if he simply stayed there, not walking nervously back and forth (which his awareness of what he was, represented, forbade) but sitting, imperturbable, in a chair, chewing on a fresh cigar (or perhaps it (the cigar) was only an obligatory accessory, the exterior sign, reserved for crowds and photographers, of opulence, placidity, and invincibility, as others brandish a marshal's baton or wear feathers on their heads): he waited.

. . . until the moment when, suddenly, and although no projectile had reached them, two or three flashes appearing in the darkness on their right made them believe that they were under attack, whereupon, immediately, and as if they had been dragged into it ("In these first engagements and especially in the case of tank attacks, it has been demonstrated that the act of firing immediately toward the zone which the enemy is presumed to hold, instead of waiting for several vehicles to be hit, generally decides the outcome of the combat"), the drivers accelerated at the same time as the gunners opened fire, first of all toward the right, where they thought they had seen the light, then both on the right and on the left, at the cannon straight ahead of them and the machine gun to the side, firing at everything and nothing, at shadows, at bushes, at clumps of trees, houses, the moonlight reflecting off the windows, the refugees' cars that hadn't got out of the way quickly enough, the bolting horses dragging overturned carts, the spray of tracer bullets setting fire to the tarpaulins on the trucks whose gas tanks then exploded, the road now like a streak of fire in the night, the clanking of the tractor belts, the roar of the engines, the detonations, the crackling of the machine guns, the shouts, the cries of the women throwing themselves into the ditch with their babies, and the whinnying of the wounded horses dissolving into a deafening uproar above which, as he later told it, sealed away inside his tank whose odometer, from time to time, he watched successively indicate one thousand, then two thousand, then three thousand meters, the German general unable to make himself heard, going hoarse from shouting, trying in vain to call off the shooting, and when he managed to do so it was only to see, all around him, the silhouettes of soldiers throwing down their weapons, raising their hands, surrendering, stupefied, still half asleep, emerging from the houses, the barns, the tents where they'd been sleeping, the courtyards, the sheds, the intersecting roads full of cannons, machine guns, gun carriages, tanks, all sorts of materiel, intact, abandoned (the journalist exclaiming: But that's impossible! You mean that . . . that they . . . that . . . But that's incredible! It's . . . You . . . I mean: they . . .).

Yes, it was May again, and surely, with his elegant wristwatch, his elegant little briefcase from which he had taken his miniature tape recorder, he hadn't yet been born then, and the affable

Queen with her hydrangea hat to whom the former railway employee with the pressing debts raised his glass was then only a young princess posing in a mechanic's jumpsuit for the photographers, her hands stained with grease, leaning over the engine of an ambulance, and no doubt the newly surfaced road was now edged with two white stripes, carefully painted, perfectly aligned, with a dotted line in the middle which, since it is very straight, allows the cars to move along, pass each other, and meet at great speed, and long since nothing remained of the bold-faced German general but a mask of bone pierced with holes where the eyes and nose were, the bony hoops scarcely lifting up the parade uniform (or its rags) in the darkness of the crypt where to the shrill sound of fifes and the hammering of drums they had laid the coffin covered with a red-and-white flag with, at the center, in a circle, something like a black spider, his assassins walking solemnly at the head of the procession, just after the family, as is customary, dressed in their luxurious uniforms with torsaded epaulets, with wide lapels of an immaculate white, their gold-and-ivory-handled daggers swinging at their sides, and diamond crosses in place of neckties, the journalist looking at his host, saying "You mean that at the very moment that the cavalry brigade . . ."

"Its debris."

". . . that the debris of the cavalry brigade, mounted on their half-dead nags, were trying to find their way in the dark, not even knowing that they were thirty kilometers behind him and that he'd already punched a hole in the line of bunkers with funny names that the French . . ."

". . . The general in chief."

". . . the general in chief had manned with only one regiment over a frontier more than twenty-eight kilometers long, which must come to about one man every twenty meters to stop an armored division, and no one between the bunkers to fill in the gaps, until the regiments defending the three or four that were in the way of his tanks were reduced to a pulp, the German general had only to bend down to collect . . ."

"Along a single line. Not surrounded: along a single line, just like that, as he passed by."

". . . along a single line, ten thousand French soldiers who were sleeping peacefully a few kilometers away while their buddies in the bunkers . . ."

"If you count the ones who managed to get away in the dark, there must have been about twelve thousand."

". . . about twelve thousand French soldiers with rifles, machine guns, fixed machine guns, antitank weapons, tanks, cannons . . ."

"The cannons don't count: their shells had been taken out. Just that very morning."

"Taken ou . . ."

"At least that's what's written in the pages they've carefully preserved on those kilometers of shelves. . . ."

"You mean that at the very moment that in the gilt-edged parlor the general was swearing that he had no reserve troops . . ."

"More precisely: no *masse de manoeuvre*."

"What exactly is meant by a *masse de manoeuvre*?"

"I don't know. He didn't say anything more specific. We'll probably never know: he had more divisions at his disposal than his German counterpart. More armored divisions as well. And of better quality. Furthermore there were all those officers parading around in fancy uniforms in the cafés of Montaubon or Toulouse. So . . . In any case he probably didn't consider those ten or twelve thousand soldiers to be worth anything, probably thought them good for nothing more than sleeping in their billets and furnishing free labor to the enemy. Not a *masse de manoeuvre* . . ."

"In other words, at the moment the man with the cigar, as you call him, had finally received . . . In what language did you say?"

"In Hindi."

"I thought the bronze woman perched atop the pedestal was in Calcutta?"

"Hindustan was also a part of her holdings. No less than the

Kohinoor. In any case that was where the military counselor served."

"Right. In whatever language. He had received, then, authorization from his cabinet. No matter what the language. But how is one to imagine all that?"

"The whole thing? You mean to get an idea of everything that was happening at the same moment? Wait, wait . . . Yes: how can one imagine that? For example, that cabinet meeting, and at the same time the cavalry brigade retreating in the dark, still far away in Belgium, and at the same time that stampede of . . . Wait, wait! . . . Like they tried to do in the movies, we'd have to have several screens with different images running simultaneously. It's impossible in speech or writing. But one can try, all the same. So let's say: on one side, five or six (or ten—or twelve: I don't know) of those serious, stuffy gentlemen, among them a few genuine lords, and all of them dressed by Savile Row tailors—except perhaps the Labour Party hostage who was brought in at the last minute—and gathered together in a meeting room—or rather something like a study or rather a smoking room: the sanctum sanctorum of some very exclusive club, its members handpicked . . . Yes: one can try to imagine that: the light oak paneling, the ceiling also covered in light oak, the doors covered in padded leather and hermetically closed, guarded on the outside by a porter—or more likely by one or several agents of the secret services—and on the walls (I mean on the oak paneling) perhaps two or three paintings, a landscape by Constable maybe, or a little genre study or something slightly saucy by Hogarth. . . . No, that's not right. Wait: more probably a battle scene, with a black sky and rows of red uniforms . . . No. That's not right either: a seascape, surely some historic naval combat, of the kind their fleet always won: a dismasted ship listing to one side, being boarded, green waves, gray spume, smoke, the tongues of fire from the rows of cannons lined up in the gun ports and the invincible flag, red quartered with blue, flying high above on a great yardarm, the whole thing (the painting) lit by one of those lamps housed in a copper cylinder of the sort they put over those Empire-style frames 'England expects every man to do his duty' or something like that (they say that those weren't exactly the words used in the message, but that in those days the limited vocabulary of semaphore—with or without flags—did not allow for nuances; so they simplified, and it stayed that way in History)—and maybe, in a corner, a silver tray with glasses and two crystal decanters which none of the five or six figures have touched . . . No, wait, wait: it's worth it to try to imagine, to picture at that same moment the brigade dragging itself through the night, the Huns' tanks moving forward over the road shooting randomly in all directions, ten thousand French soldiers awakened by the commotion and raising their hands, the imperturbable or rather the invincible—like the fleet of which he was once the first lord—man with the protruding lower lip and the cigar sitting and waiting in an armchair in his Embassy in Paris, the five or six serious gentlemen also sitting in the padded leather armchairs—or perhaps wandering to and fro, pensive, tense (but probably too well educated at Eton, Cambridge, Oxford, or by family tradition to allow themselves to express or show any emotion or any sentiment whatever: simply impassive), and each of them, one after the other, setting out his point of view, and at the end the highest-ranking one walking around the table, looking searchingly, by turns, one last time, into the faces with their clenched jaws, and then going to the door, opening it, ordering that the Hindi interpreter be brought in. . . . And, on the other side, still at the same moment, the exhausted cavalrymen half asleep on their exhausted horses, or rather no: not sleeping: this was the fourth night that they've gone virtually without even closing their eyes, but no one can sleep, no matter how worn out they are, no matter that they're being rocked by the movements of the horse, as they ride past a column of vehicles, still aflame, with, at the wheel of the trucks—or rather of the skeletons of the trucks—or astride their motorcycles lying in the ditch, carbonized and shriveled things, which probably, in the coming hours, they themselves . . ."

The journalist saying "Yes of course, naturally . . . Then about midnight, and the cavalrymen not knowing, not being able to imagine, that they are at that moment far behind an entire enemy armored division which is continuing to drive forward thirty kilometers further wes . . ."

"About sixty, even, when day broke."

"But at around midnight only about thirty kilometers, no?"

"About."

"And at that moment the Rolls or the Bentley (or the more discreet car of the third attaché of the Embassy) letting off the man with the Havana cigar at the door of the man with the departmental manager's face, where he was forced to make the chauffeur—or the policeman on watch—knock repeatedly, and then to wait again for quite some time on the landing until the departmental manager appeared in slippers, pajamas, and dressing gown because he had found nothing better to do at that hour than go to bed and sleep like a baby—I know my authors: 'After an interval M. Reynaud emerged from his bedroom in his dressing gown and I told him the favorable news.' That's it, right?"

"Yes. You're well read."

"Which means that in the early morning the cavalrymen still have not found before them anything but the rear rear guard of the column, the medical corps perhaps, or the team of mechanics, or the mess wagon perhaps, with the cooks busy making their breakfast?"

"Perhaps. Unfortunately the cooks apparently knew how to use machine guns. That's what it says, black on white, or rather clumsily typed gray on gray, in the papers stamped REPRODUCTION FORBIDDEN, but which you can have photocopied for just a franc. So in case you might find it amusing, although this is of course purely anecdotal, you might have a look—"

"Toward 0600 hours the Colonel, in order to reunite the Regiment, decides to make a long stop, and all the units are reassembled.

"The troops resume their movement, but before entering

BOUSSIGNIES *an Infantry group by the side of the road warns the Colonel that they have received a communication and that the enemy is in the area of BEAUMONT.*

"*The Colonel, believing that these are only light units or para-chutists, and wanting to carry out his mission in the AVESNES area, gives Major H. A———-B—— the order to flush out . . .*"

The journalist looking up from the pages, saying "To flush out!"

S. saying "Yes, yes. You read right: to flush out."

". . . *to flush out the isolated units with the three platoons making up M———-R——'s squadron.*

"*The squadron sets out on its mission. With the remaining platoon the Colonel and Major H. A———-B—— enter BOUS-SIGNIES, not without having been fired on from afar by auto-matic weapons situated on their left.*

"*The Colonel stops and gives the order to Major H. A———-B—— to go and see if the 1st G.E. is keeping up, to watch the Regiment pass by and to give him a report on it.*"

The journalist interrupting himself, saying: "Here there's a whole line of dots, what does . . . ," S. taking the sheets from his hands, saying "Ah yes. It's difficult to understand why exactly. Even afterward, looking at a map, you can't tell what he did next, what it is that these ellipses are hiding or not hiding, or whether it's simply that one shouldn't ask too much of a cavalry officer, that he write something coherent—or whether that line of dots might not be a sign of the incoherent confusion that had taken over. Maybe, in the end, that's the way it should be taken. . . . In any case it's an official report of the events. After that enigmatic line of dots, here's what comes next: '*I turn around . . .*' (it's still A———-B—— talking—or rather writing) . . . '*I turn around and meet, a little before BOUSSIGNIES, Major de V—— to whom I speak, telling him of my mission, the Colonel's position, the in-cident motivating these steps. I see C——'s platoon from the 4th squadron and I turn around again to make my way back toward the front of the column. Rather than pass alongside the column, I return at a trot to the intersection, where I face fire from dis-*

tant machine guns. I meet Captain P——— and we make our way up the column at a walk, slipping into a gap.

'Leaving BOUSSIGNIES, we pass alongside a column of refugees who have been fired on with machine guns. It is about nine o'clock. Suddenly we see, charging toward us, 50 to 60 of the Regiment's horses, riderless, wounded. We have heard nothing.

'On the ridge the squadron has taken up position among the hedges and is sending its horses toward us. I dismount and recognize the 1st Squadron. 3 German A.M.s are coming and Captain SPRAUEL shows me the A.M.s, turns his squadron toward the horses, there are no officers with him, only the OSTERTAG platoon. He tells me that alongside the Colonel he fell into an ambush, that the Colonel was killed, then gets back on his horse and sets off toward MAUBEUGE at a trot.

'We remain with Captain P———, watch the A.M.s through binoculars in hopes of regrouping the Regiment.

'I cannot see a single unit; the Regiment has vanished before my eyes.'"

The journalist saying "Good lord! So that's how it ended?"

"In cavalry-officer language, reproduction forbidden, yes. That is, more or less . . . Except that in reality the colonel wasn't killed until about two—or three: my watch was broken—hours later. Not very far from Avesnes, where he'd been ordered to take his regiment. Except that at that point he didn't have a regiment anymore, apart from, as I told you, two cavalrymen. But there it all becomes purely anecdotal. . . ."

"Before answering her, I escorted her to the door of my room. Opening it, I scattered the roseate light that was flooding the room and turning the white muslin of the curtains drawn for the night to golden damask. I went across to the window; the gulls had settled again upon the waves; but this time they were pink."

3

No, it is impossible; it is impossible to convey the life-sensation of any given epoch of one's existence—that which makes its truth, its meaning—its subtle and penetrating essence. It is impossible. We live, as we dream—alone. —Joseph Conrad

In the darkness, little by little, you begin to make out, toward the east, the thin pink line that separates the sky from the sea of clouds. It grows wider and longer, changing color at the same time, fiery red for a moment, then salmon, reflecting against the forward edge of the wing and the rounded openings of the engines. Everything is gray. The glow has not yet reached the curdled layer of clouds whose monotonous, parallel rows of bumps extend as far as the eye can see, without a hole, without a crack, slipping by imperceptibly beneath the plane, which seems to be suspended, still, metallic, and weightless, above some gas planet, some dead star, outside of time, uninhabited and frozen.

In the course of his conversation, in the month of May 199–, with a journalist who had come to interview him, the latter asked him insistently if he felt marked (to what extent he felt marked) by the earliest years of his existence. S. asked him, in turn, what he meant by "the earliest years." If he was talking about his earliest childhood (in which case S. couldn't really think of an event from that time—other than the absence of his father—that might have played any decisive role in the rest of his life), the only thing that he remembered clearly was having fallen into a basin in a public park, from which he was pulled by the servant accompanying him, then carried hurriedly back to the house, then quickly undressed and wrapped in something like a blanket or shawl, and that the concrete memory that he retained of that incident was neither of cold nor of water, nor even of fear (the basin was only about twenty centimeters deep), but of the sight of the dead leaves covering the bottom, half rotted away, deep brown in color, some of them already decomposed and blackish, of a sticky consistency under the palms of his hands which he had thrown out before him to break his fall, and which the servant cleaned off as best she could as she carried him away amid the derisive remarks (at least they seemed derisive to him) of the other nannies sitting on the benches and supervising the play of the children in their care. Nevertheless, S. cautioned the journalist that in spite of that mockery he didn't think such an event (although he recalled it in a particular way, with a feeling of humiliation) could have had any serious psychological consequences for him, as one might find, for example, so they say, in a child (years later, E. told him that she had witnessed this sort of spectacle, but with no memory of the trauma that it is supposed to provoke in a young child—she said that she had simply taken it in, no more troubled than if she were watching a game) who sees his mother and father engaging in sexual intercourse when they think he is asleep.

As a matter of fact, said S. to the journalist, in spite of the various shocks or surprises he had encountered with a greater or lesser degree of emotion, such as the death of his mother, his first masturbation by a playmate, or his brief expedition to Barcelona at the beginning of the Spanish Civil War, the only real trauma that he is aware of having undergone and in the wake of which without the slightest doubt his psyche and his general behavior in life proved to be profoundly altered was, as he tried to say, what he experienced in the hour he spent following that colonel, who had most likely lost his mind, on the road from Solre-le-Château to Avesnes, on May 17, 1940, certain that he would be killed in the second to come.

A woman with a monstrously huge form descends the staircase with great difficulty, supported by two crutches. No matter what the season, she is invariably dressed in a sort of gray housecoat, with a black Tyrolean hat, and carries a satchel on one side whose straps cross diagonally over her chest and back. She progresses from one step to the next with the slow, patient determination of certain insects or shelled animals, scarabs or crustaceans, carefully positioning her feet with each step. Her swollen ankles, about as thick as a child's thigh, are enclosed in sagging gray woolen stockings. She emanates a fetid odor of dirty laundry that hangs in the air long after she has passed by. Under the brim of the Tyrolean hat, her eyes disappear behind the lenses of her glasses, between which lies the curve of her short nose, like an owl's beak in the middle of that mass of sagging flesh. When one of the building's other residents is on the stairs she does her best to move out of the way, pressing herself up against the banister, leaving a narrow passage between her body and the wall, saying Go ahead excuse me you're so much quicker than me. Once in the vestibule she moves heavily, leaning forward, the weight of her upper body resting on the two nickel-plated crutches, clutching the handles, dragging her legs behind her like poles, as if they did not support her body but hung from either side of her behind, which wobbles this way and that like a duck's. In contrast with her shapeless form, her voice is almost fluting, clear, simply a little weary, betraying neither irritation nor sadness.

Endlessly, in the stained-glass window of the school chapel, the officer of the pontifical Zouaves sank backward, endlessly the saber slipping from his raised hand fell toward the ground, endlessly the chorus of juvenile voices rose up beneath the vaults whose arches were decorated with lozenges, while amid the crystalline tinkling of the little bells and the heavy odor of incense the students stood, kneeled, bowed their heads, stood up straight, turned another page in the green canvas-covered book of psalms. Sitting here and there on tall thrones, dressed in black cassocks, the priests supervised the boys' behavior and with wooden clappers punctuated the different phases of the service.

From above, the eye perceives the scintillating tangle of lights stretching off to the horizon, amid which the rectangle of Central Park forms a secluded island of darkness, geometrical, strange, unpeopled. A pastel blue fog hovers stagnant, collecting at the bottom of the vertiginous, gaping crevasses between the parallel vertical walls of the tall façades, as if cut with a knife from some single brownish black material. The fog casts a velvety enveloping film over the docile tide of cars, similar to some insect migration. Preceded by the beams of their headlights, also velvety, they gather and accumulate at the intersections, coming to a stop, moving forward again, forming chains, stopping again in a sort of unreal silence, as if that roar rising up from the enormous city, uniform, frozen in place so to speak, covered or rather absorbed, indiscriminately, all the millions of noises, forming one single formidable hum, vaguely disturbing, pierced here and there by the sporadic wailing of sirens (police, ambulance, fire truck?), growing, reaching a peak, strident, fading away, dying. Like the cries of madwomen, of exotic birds, or the horns of ships in distress. As if the city itself were screaming. As if, intermittently, the gleaming, arrogant pile of cubes and towers were agonizing without end in a sort of diamantine apotheosis, now and then shooting long signals of alarm, of panic, into the opaque sky.

His arrival in Paris in the middle of the school year, or rather at the end of the Easter vacation. The school tailor did not have time to deliver his uniform and he is still wearing his short pants when he is sent for in the middle of the afternoon, during Latin class. In the parlor, he finds his uncle, the retired cavalry officer. His thick face, pachydermatous, topped with his inevitable light gray curved-brim fedora, is perhaps a little pinker than usual, the rims of his eyes slightly red. He tells him simply that his mother is not very well and that she would like to see him. He says there's no need to go and pack a suitcase, his raincoat and beret will be enough. They take a taxi directly from the school to the train station. In those days trains still leave from the Gare d'Orsay, silently moving forward beside the underground platforms as they set out. They are alone in the first-class compartment with its seats and armrests of light gray cloth, its walls ornamented with mahogany-framed black-and-white photographs showing the monuments or countryside of the regions the railway company serves: the Rodez Bell Tower, View of the Banks of the Vienne, the Fortified Bridge of Cahors, Old Houses in Poitiers, Bourges Cathedral. His uncle seems to be in a bad mood, grumbling, his face as if swollen. He speaks to him of trivial things, asks about his new life as a boarder, his teachers, if he's made any friends, remarks on the speed of the train, whose line has recently been electrified as far as Vierzon. This is the first time the boy has eaten in a dining car and he admires the virtuosity of the waiters, who, despite the lurching of the train, manage to hold their dish with one hand and with the other manipulate the spoon and fork like tongs. The sun is setting over the Sologne region, its red disk slashed by the leafy branches of the trees, which rush past at a dizzying speed. Back in their compartment, the boy hesitates, then finally asks about his mother. His uncle does not answer right away. His face now almost purple, flushed, remains turned toward the window, beyond which the dismembered silhouettes of the trees continue to flee. At last he abruptly turns to face him and the boy can see the tears glistening on the rims of his eyes when he says, almost barking, Your mother is dead! Between the poles that hold them up, the telephone lines running alongside the tracks slump down under their own weight, quickly climb upward again toward the top of the next pole, and bow downward again. Under the effect of the train's speed they appear as a series of festoons, dancing.

Turning around in their saddles as they retreat the exhausted cavalrymen can see enemy reconnaissance airplanes rising up in the floral-colored dawn sky. They seem to appear one after the other over the horizon like fireflies, like the bubbles of a carbonated drink coming up from the bottom of the glass, like children's balloons released into the air, climbing slowly at first, then more quickly, growing larger as they approach, spreading out to form a fan shape, one or another of them sometimes beginning to turn circles over a given point.

Watching their rose-colored death coming ever nearer.

Picasso resembles a rabbit (that flattened nose, something about his mouth as well and that eye, a coal black diamond, oddly nervous, as if frightened, those sidelong glances, immediately averted, which he casts toward the bewildered visitor, as if, with a sort of inexplicable anxiousness, urgency, he were scrutinizing the effect produced as he exhausts himself in bons mots and buffoonery). Mornings, when on the vast ground floor of the "California" (the overdone exoticism of the name itself, evoking Hollywoodesque mirages, which he did not choose, which he kept out of a sort of sarcastic humor, derision (or simply indifference), like the sunken old leather couch, its horsehair coming out in handfuls, and the stack of cardboard boxes strangled by the string cinching them together, sitting on a café chair in the middle of the clutter like some immigrant's suitcases, and he claims not to know what is in them, that they've been there since he moved in two or three years before, that it might be like the sewing machine and the umbrella and that he doesn't dare touch them for fear that they might explode) . . . mornings, then, when he receives the admirers or favor seekers who bring him more or less distant friends, writers, poets, or art dealers: the sun glistening over the luxuriant vegetation of the yard (park?) through the belle epoque bay window decorated with outlined morning glories, the heat, the light clothes of the women, the atmosphere, slightly corrupt, dubious, sensual, and vaguely roguish, of the Côte d'Azur: something priapic, faunlike, in the manner of those horned heads that he reproduces one after the other, repeating them ad infinitum on the enameled surface of plates, blowing into panpipes beside limp sleeping nymphs. Grapevines, bacchanals, and memories of Poussin, which haunt him. Melancholy. The theme of whores, brothels, and the aged voyeur to which he will return more and more frequently in his drawings. Mocking, masked hetaerae with shadowy bushes until between their proffered thighs the lips of the hidden mouths open, blooming like flowers. With his bald skull colored copper by the sun, his crown of silvery hair, his jowls as if sculpted in bronze, he recalls some Roman senator or rich patrician surrounded by his "clientele": libertines, courtesans, flatterers, parasites, protégés, a court poet like the one who can always be found there carelessly sprawled on the broken-down couch, silent, gazing with the boredom of the insider at the strangers (intruders) who pass through. Pagan festivity. An ambiguous little canvas (a provocation?) propped up, along with a few others, against the foot of a turntable: two men, naked and bearded, plump, one sitting (playing a pipe?), the other lying at his feet in a pose reminiscent of an odalisque (or Narcissus), another iconoclastic evocation of Poussin: head cradled in his folded arm, but obese (drunk?), a fat Endymion. The exuberant vegetation of the garden is echoed by a proliferation of paintings, drawings, sculptures, ceramics piled up on the floor or furniture: two-eyed profiles, monumental bathers, architectural women, still lives, Zurbarán skull. Painting no longer as an asceticism (Cézanne, van Gogh) but as a challenge, as acrobatics, as a tour de force (like those tumblers, those circus balancing acts he painted in his youth). Always landing on his feet. "Astonish me," Cocteau said to him one day, who is in fact here (pointed nose, pointed chin, pointed eye emerging from the ball of wavy hair, cuffs of his shirt folded back over his jacket sleeves, as was then the fashion among homosexuals): a long *abrazo*, pats on the back, spinning around, then leaves. No sooner out the door than Picasso says: "Did you see that old tart?" Embarrassed laughter. Pretends to think for a moment and adds: "Deep down we're all old tarts. That's just what I was saying to Chagall the other day! . . ." He is wearing a black shirt with a gray print (little flowers, polka dots?), unbuttoned far below the neck, canvas pants, and sandals. To the confused astonishment of the visitors, he puts on a false mustache and a bowler hat. It is said that when he met Chaplin they could think of nothing to say to each other and so spent a moment competing to see who could make the most impressive grimace. An old Chinese painter who has come to offer him a series of wash drawings: the eternal stereotypical bamboo plants, birds, a little Mongol horse lashing its India-ink tail. Finally, exasperated, Picasso says: "I do Chinese too!" goes and gets a box from which he pulls an astounding series of wash drawings: long blades of grass made with one supple brushstroke, clambered over (clung to) by imaginary insects bristling with pincers, elytra, stingers, whiskers, proboscises, which the Chinese man (thin face, bony and yellow, white goatee: could just as easily be forty as eighty years old) silently examines, gravely nodding his head. "I'm receiving him because he's been sent from Peking," Picasso grumbles as an aside. "If he came from Limoges I'd send him packing!" (This is the era when for his birthday he affectionately sent the Russian dictator a drawing representing a hand holding a glass of wine with this legend: "To your health, Stalin!") Of a rich young American couple, both of them very tall, he says after they leave: "Apparently they're on their honeymoon . . . ," he raises a hand over his head and adds: "There must be much, much honey, no?" An Italian tailor who during all this runs after him to take his measurements: inseam, waist, shoulders, arms: "I makea you a soot all of leyther. Alla black. A magnifico soot!" Picasso obediently standing still for a moment says: "Yes: a magnifico soot: I canna buy una motocycle!" The entryway is crammed with large flat wooden crates bearing the marks of customs officials or senders. They say: Sydney, Dortmund, Baltimore, Tokyo. Outside, in the shade, on the gravel by the front steps, are parked two large American cars and a Peugeot delivery van, of the kind you see in Gypsy camps. Although they are clean, well polished, the eye instinctively looks for dents or rusting scrapes.

The image of that raised saber will long remain in his mind, brandished at arm's length in the gleaming May sunlight, horse and rider seeming to topple, to collapse to one side as if in slow motion, like those lead figurines, artillerymen, infantrymen, cavalrymen, which as a child he used to melt down by the heat of the flames on the fireplace shovel, beginning to dissolve at the base, the prancing hooves, the thin legs of the horse gradually leaning sideways, sinking into the little pool of liquefied metal, like mercury, atop which a sort of blackish film of fine slag floated, horse and rider forever melded together, the saber melting last of all. The flat surface of the fireplace shovel was flared in a tulip shape, with a rim that became thinner toward the end, so that when it was tilted slightly to one side the molten lead flowed into the basin filled with cold water from which a faint cloud of steam arose with a brief, gentle hiss. The precipitates which he then extracted from the water took the shape of nebulas, more or less clawed, foamy, each of the claws ending in a little silvery ball, like the pearls of a crown.

Once in view of the construction site, and with no other order having been given, the prisoners broke ranks and began to run, in the grotesque way that men can run, at least, when they are hampered by their ragged uniforms, earth colored, dirty, the half-buttoned flaps of their capes or coats whipping at their legs, waddling like ducks in a sort of parody of a footrace, beating the air with their arms, some of them burdened by knapsacks which they had refused to part with, struggling to outrun the others, trying clumsily to get past each other, the line of men, stretched out like a long chain behind the fastest runners, crashing against, clustering around the door of the tool shed, sometimes exchanging blows and insults as they tried to get in.

(The first time, S. does not understand. He watches this inexplicable, savage stampede with astonishment and disdain. When, among the last men, he makes his way into the shed there is nothing left but pickaxes.)

The work consists of digging a deep trench at the bottom of which, as it moves forward, a team lays the conduits for a system of pipes. Here and there, rifles in their slings, the guards stand motionless or pace in a bored way, sometimes letting out a guttural cry and shaking an arm when they see a prisoner not moving. Apart from that, they seem to take no interest in the progress of the work, which is overseen by old foremen with tired, sad faces, wearing leather-visored caps, and their only function is to see to it that no prisoner slacks off. The workday is made up of two four-hour shifts, with a break at noon so that the prisoners can eat a bowl of soup. At five o'clock they are brought back to the camp.

It was a beautiful summer, and many prisoners worked bare chested. The Saxony plain stretched out in the sunlight, undulating lazily, strewn here and there with sparse stands of pine trees. The second day, even though his legs are collapsing beneath him, S. also runs with all his might in order to be among the first to reach the tool shed, where, throwing punches on all sides, he succeeds in getting his hands on a shovel.

A *chapelle ardente* set up in a little room decorated in blue which usually served as a passageway, where, in a recess, she had had shelves installed for books. They had already closed the coffin and the room was filled with the suffocating, peppery smell of the flowers mingled with the burning candles. Only then did he begin to cry. At the foot of the coffin sits a prie-dieu where they tell him to kneel. Someone leans over him, putting an arm around his shoulders, and tells him that his mother is happy now, that she isn't suffering any longer. Maybe he is crying only because all these people around him have sad faces and red eyes. They've forgotten to take down from the wall an engraving depicting the torture of a vestal virgin, who is about to be buried alive. A hole has been dug, and the virgin has already set her foot on the second rung of the ladder extending down into it, not far from the gravediggers, who can be seen leaning on their shovels, ready to cover her with dirt when she has lain down at the bottom. She has draped the veil in which she is cloaked over her head, in a gesture of affliction (or maybe, he often thought while looking at that engraving, to keep the dirt thrown over her out of her mouth or eyes). In addition to the two gravediggers, the severe-faced High Priest standing at the edge of the tomb, and his lictors in their metal cuirasses, there are numerous figures wearing togas, among them no doubt the virgin's mother, shown half fainting, supported by two women, probably relatives. This engraving has always inspired a sort of fascinated horror in him. The shelves hold only books with old bindings, their leather spines ornamented with little flowers, incised and then gilded. Among them are the complete works of Jean-Jacques Rousseau and *History of the Girondins* in several volumes, with illustrations. He remembers that one of them shows a young man in a riding coat, with short turned-down boots, standing on a chair in the gardens of the Palais Royal, haranguing the crowd. During the dinner, at which the entire family is present, no one speaks except to ask him how he finds his new life at school and if he likes Paris. After dinner, as coffee is being served in the drawing room, he wonders if he should go upstairs again and kneel once more at the prie-dieu. He doesn't want to, but he thinks that might be what is expected of him. Fortunately, he is told to go into the garden with his young cousin. At the center stands a palm tree with fan-shaped leaves, pointed like swords, with a dark brown trunk of a rough material, like horsehair. Above that, a tall acacia growing at the corner of one of the buildings spreads its branches and its leaves, like feathers, which the breezes lift, then let fall again limply.

In his *Notebooks,* Erwin Rommel records for the date of September 4, 1943: "Dined with the Führer. He recommends great circumspection as I deal with the king of Italy."

On October 26, he writes his wife: "Even the Italian police are totally impotent today. We must help him."

Arrested by the Italian police and savagely beaten, Gastone Novelli was then sent to the concentration camp at Dachau, in Bavaria. Of the 250,000 detainees held in that camp, only 33,000 survived, and it was probably thanks only to his robust constitution that Novelli managed to be counted among the latter. Apart from that one allusion to the torture (the punishment, being suspended by his bound hands until he lost consciousness) that he underwent and on which he did not elaborate (or maybe he would have if the two women hadn't come out of the water just then) and which S. was able to picture only later, after seeing a photograph published in an illustrated magazine, he never again spoke of what he had endured there, except to say that once he was free he could no longer bear contact with nor the sight of not only a German but any being, woman or man, considered civilized, so that when he was physically healed he boarded the first boat that could get him to South America where he undertook to devote himself to diamond prospecting (or was it gold?). His one other reference to Dachau was to say that it was only because of the experience he had acquired there that he was able to survive an expedition into the virgin forest, where his Indian guide had abandoned him after having robbed him. "Because," he said, "I had learned or rather come to understand two things: the first is that if you seem too strong, they kill you because they're afraid of you; the second is that if you seem too weak, they also kill you, this time just for the sake of amusement." And he told the story: he and his companion (he had, in spite of it all, accepted—or met—a companion: some adventurer no doubt, or some misanthrope like him, whom he met there and with whom, by choice or by the force of circumstances, he had banded together to form a team: because perhaps even a man who can no longer bear the sight of his fellows needs to exchange a modicum of words in the course of a day) . . . he and his companion, then, in the middle of the virgin forest, the companion having fallen ill (or wounded?), unable to walk, the clearing where they had set up camp, the river in which, as the sick man shivered with fever in his tent, he built a sort of dam out of branches (he said there were no stones), which allowed him to catch, by hand, the fish swimming against (or with?) the current. Life—or rather survival—this way: the other one perpetually shivering in the stifling heat, himself busy catching (the Indian guide had naturally taken their weapons with him when he fled) and cooking over the fire whatever fish he could get hold of (the difficulty of lighting a fire in this waterlogged environment, the search for dry leaves, the dead wood rotting and swollen from the dampness, the alcohol stove whose fuel level he sees falling, the phosphorus matches also damp, the flints).

And one fine day, this: emerging from the tent in the morning light (the nights as hot as the days, sticky, finally managing to sleep in spite not only of the sweat but also of the noises (monkeys, birds?) that rose up in the forest of darkness—he said that he never knew what animal it was that every now and then let out a sort of imbecilic laughter that rose progressively higher, ever more drawn out, discordant, mocking, sinister, then falling again in a cascade) . . . emerging one morning, then, from his tent and suddenly freezing, motionless, looking at what he first took to be sticks thrust vertically into the ground at regular intervals, about every three meters, all around their camp, slowly turning his head, his eyes moving from one to the other, as if (he thought at first) someone had begun to build a fence around them, until he realized that they were arrows.

And nothing else. The burning sun, the silence of the thick wall (or rather tangle) of vegetation broken only by the sound coming from the little dam (he said that it wasn't even a cool, fresh sound like a little waterfall or stream would make in Europe, that this one (this noise) was itself warm, as if viscous), and no other sign of human presence than those long arrows planted during the night by invisible figures. It was then, he said, that he was able to put into practice what he had learned at Dachau. He reasoned that if the strangers (the number of arrows clearly showed that there were several of them) had wanted to kill him, they could easily have done so during the night, even though he always slept with one eye open. He concluded that whoever had sown the arrows this way had no overtly aggressive intentions against him and his companion, but that there was nevertheless a message to be decoded in this act, a warning, a threat, or simply a sign. For fear that the invisible men might see his rifle (the thief had left them one after all, not out of a sudden honorable impulse but probably because of the excess weight—and in any case it was the worst one, and at least, he went on to think, he hadn't killed them before running off, which, on the whole, was better than at Dachau) or hear a shot, he refrained from hunting that day (from time to time he shot a monkey or a bird, but he said that, for one thing, and contrarily to what one might expect, game, monkeys or birds, was quite scarce, and furthermore the meat wasn't very good), and that in the same way, once he had emerged from his tent (or climbed down from his hammock) and realized what sort of pickets or sticks were now surrounding the camp, he was careful not to show, either by his posture or by his gestures or in his eyes, the slightest trace of surprise or fear. He went about his usual morning occupations as if the arrows weren't there (cleaning up a little around the tent, checking on the sick man, burying their refuse) and without paying any further attention (or at least without seeming to pay any further attention) to the arrows, went and took up his position in the low spot of the dam, looking for fish to catch. That day he caught more than he and his companion needed, cooked them, and, in the evening, went slowly, carefully avoiding sudden movements, to place a piece of fish on the feathering of each of the arrows. He couldn't sleep that night, with all his senses on alert, but perhaps toward the end sleep overpowered him, because in the morning, and without his having heard a sound, the arrows were all there, but the pieces of fish had disappeared. And nothing else. Still nothing but that thick, exuberant wall of vegetation beyond which nothing seemed to be stirring, nothing could be seen to move.

He said that he was then more frightened than the day before when he had discovered the arrows. If this was a message, it was clear that it had now begun to take the form of a dunning notice: "What you call in French a *sommation sans frais*," he said laughing, the way people laugh about these things afterward: "Or rather *avec frais*," he corrected himself, "because they'd taken the pieces of fish . . ." (He told this story in one of those little taverns in the Trastevere where in the cool darkness they were all four eating that green-colored pasta with the funny name, drinking one of those thick Italian wines, and surrounded by ordinary people: seated at the next table were three workmen dressed in their beige canvas coveralls, spattered with stains, their faces as if from a Renaissance fresco, rarely speaking, and, at the end of the room, two young couples of the kind one can see on the terraces of cafés in the Piazza del Popolo, the women laughing, and as he went on with his story S. watched the animation of his handsome face, slightly square, solid, the face of a Lombardy condottiere, as if he too had come straight from a fresco or had been sculpted in wood, listening to his calm voice, merry at times but as if weighed down by a sort of permanent sadness): nevertheless, he interpreted the disappearance of the pieces of fish as a sign of peaceful intentions, but coupled with a threat (the arrows were still there), that is, an invitation to make himself scarce, which he would have done immediately, he said, if his companion had been able to walk. He would simply have packed up and gone. With his compass, and guiding himself by sketchy maps, or more exactly by sketchy diagrams which, on the basis of equally sketchy information, he had made of the region before penetrating inside it. But to embark on an adventure of that sort with a sick man on his hands was out of the question. So he stayed. He decided not to change his habits or his everyday occupations in any way, continued cleaning up the area around the campground every morning, burying the refuse (not, he said, that he was a model camper, as conscientious as a Boy Scout, but because whatever they didn't eat immediately began to rot with a terrifying speed and to stink in a way which was not only abominable but also attracted flies—even more flies, that is, he corrected himself: tiny flies that sometimes went after his eyes and which, along with the mosquitoes, were one of the plagues of that country, or at least of that spot). So he cleaned up the campground, looked after his companion (he didn't say whether he'd told him about the arrows—nevertheless, for fear that he might make the mistake of showing himself and frightening the strangers, he probably had no choice but to let him know what had happened, if, that is, he could understand anything at all through his fever), went fishing (he now avoided taking his rifle and wandering into the forest, avoided even casting a glance in the direction of the wall of greenery that surrounded them, tried to look as though he had nothing on his mind but the task of keeping up the camp or finding food) and, every evening, nerves on edge, sensing that he was risking his life but outwardly impassive, as if this extra work had now become a part of his daily occupations, set out the pieces of fish on the arrows planted in the ground where they had been from the beginning.

The tenth day (he later tried to determine whether the natives might have had a decimal system, but he found no other sign of it), on awakening (now he slept at night: badly, but he slept—in any case he wouldn't have been able to stay awake for ten days: sleep fell over him like an anvil, knocked him out; also, in any case, he thought that since they hadn't killed him the first night, nor, although they easily could have, in broad daylight when they could see him, alone, unarmed, coming and going in the clearing or watching for fish, there was no reason why they should do so at night) . . . on the tenth day, then, in the morning, the arrows had disappeared. He thought for a moment, then decided not to change his behavior in any way (he explained that every day he had to maintain the drainage system protecting the inside of their tent from flooding: it rained every day, he said, always at the same time, as if the onset of the rain were governed by some astronomical clock: cloudbursts, he said, gray, the color of metal, so dense that at times the other side of the clearing disappeared (he said that then he truly understood why the French use the expression "raining halberds" to describe a heavy downpour), then as suddenly as it had begun it stopped and the sun began to shine again (to shine, not to give heat: the heat never stopped, sunny or not) and everything (the ground, the grass, the forest) immediately began to steam). In any case, again, his companion couldn't walk and he had no choice. Having finished his domestic chores, still avoiding looking toward the wall of vegetation, he headed toward his dam as usual, and as he watched for fish he suddenly sensed a presence near him. He said that he'd heard nothing: neither a rustling of the undergrowth nor some rotten branch cracking under a foot. He said it was as if the little naked man aiming an arrow at him from a few yards away had sud-

184

denly materialized out of thin air, or rather as if the fear that had gripped his entrails over the past ten days had all at once materialized in the form of an almost-dwarf (who, he later said, scarcely came up to his shoulder) pointing a sharpened arrow in his direction. He said that the hardest thing he then had to do (he had already been forcing himself to do so for ten days, but the moment had become even more dangerous) was to control his gestures and move very slowly. He knew a few words of Indian (of a few Indian dialects), but the little copper-colored man clearly understood none of them, seeming only to understand the gesture that he made (still very slowly) to offer him one of the fish he had just caught.

There were about thirty of them, maybe forty or so, women and children included, all of them completely naked (as was he, furthermore—apart from a bathing suit that he wore to protect his genitals from insect bites) except, among the men, for a little rectangle of cloth that protected nothing and, for the women and the little girls, a belt (of pearls, he thought at first—then he saw that they were shells and dried berries) that girded their hips. In the evening they all ate the fish together, along with other things (quite repulsive, he said) which he forced himself to swallow. His companion was slow to recover but now they were on good terms with the tribe, which in the end replaced the guide who had abandoned them. In the time they spent this way, then later (because he came back to see them again, lived with them for a few months: he said he liked them and they interested him: he didn't say why he found them likable, if it was because they incarnated the opposite of a civilization capable of breeding philosophers as well as torturers like the ones who had tormented him in Dachau, or if it was their elementary way of life, blended into nature and in direct contact with it, without philosophers, that pleased him: maybe (he never spoke of it, but how to believe that his powerful sensuality would remain untouched by it?) he had become attached to one of the girls with breasts like little cones with nipples also like little cones of shiny leather and whose belts of shells hung from their slender hips above the bulge of their smooth, hairless vulvas, split like apricots), . . . over this time, then, that he spent with them (he had become used to eating the repulsive things), he learned to understand and then speak their dialect, which, he said, was unknown to the members of the Society of Linguists in São Paulo to whom he later showed the dictionary he had managed to put together, insofar as it was possible to do so with a language practically without consonants and composed almost uniquely of vowels, among them the sound *A* which, modulated and accentuated in an infinite variety of ways, undulating, now deep, now in a more high-pitched tone, now drawn out, now staccato, clipped, signified an incalculable quantity of things, both conceptual and concrete (tree, plant, danger, bird, hatred, relationships, flowers, friendship, snake, etc.) of completely different sorts. He said that even using all the signs that could be borrowed from the most diverse languages, as for instance Greek aspirates, the umlauts or little circles used in the Nordic languages, circumflexes, grave or acute accent marks, it was virtually impossible to convey the variety of nuances (and consequently of meanings) that those sounds, rendered in the Roman alphabet by one single letter, could signify.

Later he would create paintings in which there recurred a checkerboard construction with uneven lines, the horizontals sometimes leading toward a vanishing point situated outside the canvas, disappearing, with, inside the squares, an alternation, along with purely geometrical motifs (triangles, rhombuses, disks, lacework—or else little checkerboards within the checkerboard) of letters, numbers, more-or-less-erased fragments of sentences, vague scrawls in which one can sometimes make out what might be bodies, interlaced limbs, awkward ithyphallic silhouettes, breasts. Once, even, he would fill the entire surface of the canvas with rows of irregularly written *A*s, each of the letters slightly different from the one preceding or following it not only by its shape (spidery, heavy, suddenly thicker or taller, then thin again, lopsided) but also by its color, which he would obtain by first covering the bare canvas with a green that varied as much by its hue as by its variations (that is, tinted sometimes with blue, sometimes with yellow) then, having done that, after it had dried, smearing the canvas with that thick, white, creamy paste whose composition he kept secret, into which, sometimes using the handle of his brush, or a pencil, or a wider scraper, he would inscribe those superimposed lines of uneven letters, wavering like a scream, repeating themselves, never the same:

AAAAAAAAAAAAAAAAAAAAAAAAAAAAAA
AAAAAAAAAAAAAAAAAAAAAAAAAAAAAA
AAAAAAAAAAAAAAAAAAAAAAAAAAAAAA

At other times . . .

The primary concern, taking precedence over all others, will be keeping out the water. The cavalrymen will halt in a stand of tall trees at the end of the day. After a moment (a slight mist will be falling, or rather it will be drizzling) the order is given to dismount, raise the tents, and set up camp. Until that day they had always been housed in billets in villages whose population had fled, squatting in the villagers' houses, sleeping in their empty rooms or in the haylofts of their barns, sometimes breaking up the furniture for firewood. They do not have tents in the proper sense of the word, but only squares of waterproof canvas inside which they have wrapped their standard-issue blankets, rolled up into sausages and tied to the cantles of their saddles. The squares can be buttoned together and, when they are all joined up, form a roof large enough to cover the six men of a squad. Using the campaign equipment they are carrying with them (hatchets and axes) they cut poles from the brushwood and erect a primitive shelter under which they will sleep, having laid their thick saddle blankets, folded in four, on the ground. The horses, wearing their feedbags, will be tied to the tree trunks by their leads, widely separated so that they will not kick each other during the night. More or less sheltered against the rain, which has now begun to fall in earnest, they will eat their cold rations in the dark, and, taking off only their spurs, they fall asleep.

In the morning the thick saddle blankets they slept on are

soaked from the wet ground. Thus, to begin with, they will use their shovel picks to dig a small ditch to drain off the rainwater. But the following night will make it clear to them that this was not enough. So from the brushwood they cut branches which they will lay out crisscross to form a thick mattress under the saddle blankets, which will in this way be insulated from direct contact with the ground. But this will still not be enough. After some discussion, they will surround the tent with a low wall made of dirt piled up between two screens of interlaced twigs supported by poles, hoisting up the tent so that its sides overlay the wall. With this, water and damp will no longer be a problem, provided, that is, that they take care not to touch the canvas roof in a careless gesture or with any sort of object, for if they did the water would immediately begin to flow from that spot.

In the end, the tent will become very livable and S. will be happy there, the low dirt wall serving as a shelf, the saddles as pillows. Aluminum basins will be distributed to serve as troughs for the horses, the rain will fall less often, the sun will shine sometimes, discipline will become more relaxed, and their only duties will be to walk the horses every day, the cavalrymen entertaining themselves by riding them bareback in the evening, galloping to the nearby pond to drink. Gradually the rain will in fact stop completely, the sun, timid at first, will show itself, and from one day to the next the forest will begin to grow greener, buds appearing amid the undergrowth, multiplying, forming a sort of light mist at first, of a pale green color, veiling the thickets, then opening up, becoming denser, soon blocking any glimpse, except through the gaps between the branches, of the pale tents terraced along the hillside overlooking the valley and the mahogany-colored spots of the horses, the blaring sounds of the bugles now as if velvety, filtered through the thick fronds.

Of his last leave he has kept the memory of crowded, noisy cafés: back-line officers in elaborate uniforms, civilians, women with exaggeratedly piercing laughs. Senegalese soldiers, bayonets affixed to their rifles, along the tracks around the train stations. Barbed wire around the marshaling yards. A feeling of exclusion, of banishment. Rejected by the community as if he were already dead, crossed off the list, unwelcome, indecent. Is relieved to return to his life in the camp: tents, bugle calls, horses. Little by little, over the course of the winter, the workers who had been mobilized at the start of the war were sent back to their factories, and now the squadron is made up mostly of young peasants, and he likes to listen to them tell of sowing, harvesting, haymaking, cartages, animals, boasting to each other, like children, of Herculean feats (cartages, sacks, bundles of straw, plowing), quarreling over a curb chain or a lost oat bucket. The enchantment of the forest in springtime. On Sundays, he goes to sit beneath a tall oak tree with a book which he soon stops reading, sitting there, head thrown back, watching the slow clouds drift by, beyond the talons of the branches. This period will remain in his memory as one of the happiest of his existence.

The bathroom floor is covered with vermilion red linoleum. The walls are painted in white enamel. The plumbing, the door, and the toilet tank are painted the same vermilion red. On the bathtub's enameled sidewalls, glints of light reflected off the water, which ripples at the slightest movement of her body, create a pale web that endlessly disintegrates and comes together again. The woman bends one leg, and the knee, smooth and glistening, rises up like a pink mountain over the pale jade surface. Still immersed, the rest of the leg, calf and thigh, colored a greenish white, as if elongated, gelatinous. As on the feathers of a duck, drops of water cling to the taut skin over the knee. They tremble slightly, sometimes join together, and, grown heavy, come unstuck, slide downward, forming little streams that snake jerkily in broken lines, leaving silvery traces on the skin.

The pond where they take the horses to drink is called the Étang de la Folie. The camp is less than three kilometers from the Belgian border. Although neither they nor their superiors ever speak of it, they have no difficulty guessing why they are there, forward of the fortifications on which, across the pond, they can see the soldiers from a native regiment working ceaselessly. On the tenth of May, at five o'clock in the morning, the Germans will attack. The cavalrymen will break camp and cross immediately into Belgium through a hamlet with the flowery name of Eppe-Sauvage, which, less than two weeks later, the survivors will pass through again, moving in the same direction, their clothes in rags, dirty, hungry, and dazed, dragging their feet, thrown together with the remains of other regiments in a long dirt-colored column, surrounded by guards, snaking its way between the emerald fields.

Other titles of paintings by Novelli:

> Nascita et cattura di un millepiedi
> Giornale intimo
> Senza sonno
> Il sole nudo
> Chiuso per restauro
> Cada vez mas

Takes communion. The Lord clasped between thumb and index finger, which the priest sets on his tongue, a damp little circle, flat, whose substance softens little by little as it absorbs his saliva, and which he keeps in his mouth as long as he can before swallowing it, hoping to prolong His presence, so that while he keeps Him prisoner in this way He will be able to hear his pleas (the shooting pains, the sort of surge bursting forth with a quiet growl, then crashing against the back of his ear with each beat of his pulse, awoke him in the dormitory well before the bell rang).

The doctor they had called did not arrive until about nine o'clock, long after he had come to the infirmary, and for more than an hour he waited for him, one hand clasping his beret to the side of his face where the pain continued to throb in a mute and furious ebb and flow (as if inside his head a sort of blunt wedge were digging in, letting up the pressure only to dig in once again, cruelly, ripping through the tissue, the cartilage). Most of the time, the two or three boys who had come from different classes for minor treatment having already left, he was alone in the vast room, pacing to and fro (he was suffering too much to stay sitting down) over the bare floor, as brightly polished as a mirror, waxed with the maniacal thoroughness of concierges or recluses, and whose smell, mingling with the odors of ether or fumigations hanging in the hallways, seemed, severe and monastic, to be the very emanation of some irresistibly cruel force, vindictive and incomprehensible (his terror of the doctor, the adjustable stool on which the doctor made him sit, the rough contact of the fabric of his pant legs clasping his legs between them (he still wears short pants): the doctor pulled on his earlobe and inserted a little metal cone, hard and cold, then cleaned out the pus using a long needle with cotton wrapped around one end, the clicking of the needles as they are tossed away into the enameled metal bean, the blinding lamp on the doctor's forehead, his long yellow mustachios like a seal's, the nun holding his head as if in a vice, the pain, the tears running down his cheeks).

A large bare-topped table, apparently not reserved for any specific purpose but also waxed with the same maniacal care, occupied the center of the waiting room, and wooden chairs of no particular style, their seats covered with olive green moleskin, were aligned, almost touching each other, all along the four walls, which were painted a greenish gray. Sometimes he stopped pacing, stood near one of the windows and, as the pain continued to bellow in his ear, he looked, without seeing it, at the intersection formed by the street where the school was situated and the boulevard that it crossed obliquely. There were few cars passing by at that hour, and also only a few pedestrians, emerging at regular intervals from the metro exit and dispersing. Across the boulevard he could see the gray stone façade, always closed up, like a blind face, upon which the conjunction of three words (*couvent, dames,* and *Sion*) conferred something severe, stiff, and inexorable.

The room's only decoration consisted of a large oil painting, about two meters high, representing the Crucifixion. The sky was almost black. At the foot of the cross stood three figures (two women and a man) in attitudes of affliction. The veil enveloping the Virgin was of a hard, harsh blue, like metal. Wedges had been driven into the ground to stabilize the foot of the cross, probably with blows of a mallet because their heads were crushed and formed a sort of little folded-down collar (the smell of wood polish, the intersection with its few passersby, the *Dames de Sion,* the painting, the chairs, the bare tabletop without the illustrated magazines that one finds elsewhere in doctors' waiting rooms, or perhaps a few issues of a religious magazine (*Le Pèlerin?*), the floor like a mirror reflecting, slightly bluish, the gray daylight coming from the windows).

In the washed-out beam of the headlights, they saw her from afar, standing, draped in white, motionless in the center of the roundabout that the car was approaching, like a sort of apparition, as if in the tropical warmth (the car had all its windows open and they could smell it: the limp air, thick, as if the car and its occupants were enclosed (it was not yet dawn, it had only just begun to seem that dawn was not far off) in the visceral darkness of some stomach, some originary uterus full of the heavy scents of unfamiliar flowers, with unfamiliar names, which, as they rotted, exhaled a subtle, heady perfume of decomposition and death) there had arisen, as a welcome for them, the very materialization, strange, vaguely menacing, of this equally supernatural continent, in the form of that phantom wrapped in the folds of a shroud (awaiting what? the opening of a market? a servant? standing for what reason?): at her feet, wrapped in the folds of other pale shrouds, were three or four others, sitting on the dried grass, who did not even turn their heads as the car circled the roundabout, turned once again beneath the arch of dusty boughs, motionless in the motionless air (boughs whose leaves, one could see, never fell, knew no autumn, no spring, and which formed a long line, identical and monotonous in the beam of the headlights, revealed one after the other, as if flattened, like a series of theater backdrops cut out of cardboard), and through the rear window (turning around, unbelieving, his eyes burning, still sleepy after the many hours on the airplane) he watched her shrink little by little, fade into the distance, still standing, wrapped in her dead woman's shroud. This was India.

"The author unloads his postcards on us": Breton, exasperated by Dostoevsky's description of the money lender's lodgings: "The little room into which the young man was shown was hung with yellow wallpaper; its windows had muslin curtains; pots of geraniums decorated the windowsills; the setting sun illuminated it at that moment. The ancient furniture, made of light-colored wood, included a divan with an immense curved back, an oval table placed before the divan, a vanity with a mirror, chairs with their backs against the wall, and two or three engravings of no real value depicting German maidens each holding a bird in their hands, that was all." For his part, Montherlant declares that when he comes to a description in a novel he "turns the page."

Both eager to learn "whether the baroness will marry the count," Breton the poet, like Montherlant, clearly cares little for the color of the wallpaper, muslin curtains, geraniums, and young German girls, wondering, moreover (so much time wasted!), why the author informs us that they are each holding a bird in their hands.

> La luce nelle mani (Light in the hands)
> Visibilità 2 (Visibility 2)
> Vuole dire caos (Means chaos)
> Ora zero (Zero hour)
> La peur dans le fond (in French)

The Germans had imprisoned the madman in the pigsty adjoining the farm that sat beside the road at the higher end of the large meadow. It was like no animal's cry; it was something else: little by little the voice grew rasping, hoarser and hoarser, sometimes stopping for a few minutes, as if exhausted, then beginning again more violently than before.

(The guards methodically filled up the field stretching gently downhill from the farm, lining up the prisoners in successive terraced rows three meters apart, so that when they lay down it looked like rows of cut wheat stalks, lying parallel. Having been among the first to arrive, S. is lying in a spot where the grass has not been trampled. Stretched out on his stomach, he presses his face into the cool, vegetal smell. He opens his mouth and fills it with the smell. He closes his jaw and begins to chew it between his teeth. He thinks: I am a horse, a cow, a goat. He tries to chew and swallow something rough, with no taste except perhaps a slight bitterness. The Germans have unlimbered two machine guns to guard the field. They let it be known that after nightfall it is forbidden to stand up, and that the machine guns will fire.)

The madman only screamed the first night. Some claimed that the Germans had killed him. They even explained that it was done with a bayonet, since no gunshots had been heard. Others, on the contrary, said that they had sent him away in an ambulance. One of the prisoners (probably one of the NCOs from the supply corps or from some staff headquarters, captured while sitting at his desk or maybe lying in bed: his beard was only three days old, and he was wearing an elegant and immaculate uniform) had brought his dog with him, an enormous beast, about the size of a small calf. The dog disappeared on the second day. It's not clear how (where had they found the wood, since it was forbidden to approach the forest? how had they been able to keep that vessel with them after their capture and all during the march?), a group of North African infantrymen had managed to light a fire under a kettle. The NCO who owned the dog claimed that they had stolen him, but no one dared go to see what was boiling in the pot, carefully guarded by the North Africans, who said that they had picked some rhubarb and were cooking it. The dog owner began screaming insults at them, trying to rally some of the other soldiers, who joined in. Naturally, the real reason for these insults was not that they thought the North Africans were guilty of having stolen and killed the dog, but because they were desperately jealous of them for having been clever enough to do so and for having something to eat. With vulgar epithets (wogs, darkies, niggers) they accused them of having fled the fighting and caused the defeat. The infantrymen answered with more insults, giving them the finger, and a scuffle began to break out but one of the sentinels came running and shouting and when the NCO came forward to talk to him he shouted even louder and made him understand, shaking the butt of his rifle, that he must keep quiet and return to his place. As he passed by, some of the men who had been standing at some distance from the dispute laughed derisively and commented on the elegance and cleanliness of his uniform. Everyone hated each other.

Le cose nell'uovo
Un goccio di vita
Piuttosto Terra che Cielo
L'ultimo suggerimento
Al di là della terra
La grande bestemmia
Cubo oggetto
Gli Dei et gli Eroi
Di che occuparsi se non dell'uomo?

The emperor of Japan is a man of about fifty, with a fine, bony face and an aquiline nose. The empress's face is of the same sort, her nose also slightly aquiline, so that one might take them to be brother and sister. Both of them are dressed in Western style, the emperor, very thin, in a navy blue suit, completely buttoned up. The empress wears a brown dress, very simple, the bodice curiously adorned with a white yoke vaguely reminiscent of the bib of a waitress's uniform. The vast room into which the guests have been shown resembles a sort of hangar with a sloping ceiling, one wall of which, made entirely of glass, looks onto a lawn which stretches off to the first curtain of trees of a densely wooded park, or rather of a forest. The floor is covered with a thick rug, the walls decorated with lacquerware against a yellow background.

There is no furniture other than two low tables on which two cigarette boxes of engraved silver lie open, inviting the guests to serve themselves. The American physicist is the first to dare, then the others follow his lead. The cigarettes bear the emperor's emblem, the four-petaled cherry flower, which appears in gray on the slender cylinders. Naturally, no one goes so far as to light one, and they simply slip them into the little pockets of their vests. In the photograph commemorating this audience, S. is standing near the famous Russian dissident nuclear scientist. He is tall, almost a giant, his shaved skull is shaped like the nose cone of a missile, strangely pointed. The nape of his neck forms a thick roll of flesh, like on one of those marshals with their thick faces, their chests covered with rows of decorations, and their artificial jaws of chrome-plated steel, who can be seen on the tribunals presiding over military parades beside men with scowling faces wearing astrakhan hats. Here too a photographer is at work. He takes a picture as the colossus with the missile head bows obsequiously to offer the emperor a Japanese translation of one of his works. It is clear from the expression on the emperor's face that he is speaking cordial words to him in return. Before his entrance (through a little door at one end of the wall facing the park) the six guests and their companions were lined up in a row. The day before, they had been requested to wear dark ties, since the period of mourning for the preceding emperor, who had already been dead for a year now, had not yet come to an end. At the far end of the row, the American physicist leans forward a little in order to watch this scene, toward which all the other heads are turned as well. S. also leans forward slightly, with curiosity. He is wearing glasses. A slight down remains on his skull, made silver by the light coming from the window behind him.

"Kyoto": a pond in delicate pastel almond-green shades, rushes, pink and blond reeds, as if drawn with a plume. "Japanese women," but black and white this time, seven of them dressed in kimonos posing for the photographer a bevy standing with hands around each others' waists leaning forward slightly heads turned to one side with the same vapid smile. Orient, Malaysia, Singapore "Saint John's Church," "Colombo: lake by moonlight," mangroves, pirogues, Cairo Street, postcards which throughout her engagement she had received from all over the world ("Langson: Great Wall of China," "Aden: The Reservoirs," "Somali Coast: Typical Natives," etc.). Three bundles found years later, each of them held together by a ribbon in the form of a cross, faded blue with yellowish streaks. The two photographic enlargements life-size sepia with gradated background hung on the wall to the left of her bed a sort of two-headed divinity wearing on one head a kepi decorated with a marine anchor, the other in civilian clothes vest buttoned up to the top, narrow lapels, center part, bangs, same square beard, identical wide frames, concave, made of brown wood. Letters that she wrote there dying too weak probably for inkwell and plume, so pencil each letter, each curlicue, each stroke laboriously inscribed "My dear child . . . ," the address in ink on the envelope but in another hand: name of the school, street, class, *division Cinquième verte:* "I am writing your uncle Paul and asking him to buy you those roller skates . . . ," him clumsy at first staggering, ataxic, from one tree or one pole in the playground to another, struggling, then growing bolder, joining the others, cracking the whip the last one in the line tossed sideways in the curves, then, as he passed from one grade to the next, ball games, *balle au chasseur, balle au mur,* scuffles sometimes, blow of the whistle a warning from the supervisor, then no more rubber balls, no more noisy games, no more scuffles, only little groups in discussion, three or four with superior airs, studying philosophy, math, dirty stories, boasting, pretty cousins, one claiming his young aunt or a friend of his mother's, some of them beginning to shave. He no longer rides horses, plays on the rugby team. In the spring he wears the school colors in track meets. Sprint. Minor stardom. Humiliation of the 4 × 100 through his fault. Lackluster efforts in middle-distance running.

The journalist and S. are sitting on either side of a low table with a tape recorder placed on one corner. They have been speaking for some time. The journalist asked S. how they managed to live with the fear. S. tried to explain that from the moment when, without preamble, a bomb dropped from an airplane suddenly lands just next to you, the fear inhabits you for good but is shoved into the background by the fatigue, a fatigue which no circumstance (no exploit, sporting or otherwise . . .) of normal life can allow you to imagine, so that the fear becomes something almost forgotten so to speak, like the shirt you're wearing on your back, but whose stench you don't even notice anymore, and certainly not at all when your body and your mind are taken over by the urgency of combat (jumping off your horse, throwing yourself to the ground, crawling, running, mounting the horse again, galloping, etc.), but the journalist asked the question again, asked him if in fact nevertheless when S. was following that colonel . . . Those two colonels, said S. Those two colonels, the journalist continued, at least one of them, according to what S. had said, half insane, pushing forward along a road where they now found themselves no longer facing the enemy but overtaken by the enemy, as if they were speeding in their pursuit in hopes of catching up with them and . . . What do they say in the cavalry? Hacking at their rumps, right? Only the rumps in question were if I've understood rightly made of armored steel and . . . No forgive me I'm joking, not very tasteful, but if I am remembering the field log you showed me correctly, on that very morning, before the ambush, when he was warned that there were a few ("a few!") enemy troops up ahead, did the colonel not order an officer to take a cavalry platoon with him and go "flush them out"? Excuse me again if I . . . And S. said No That the journalist is right, that the most tragic events often have a laughable side and that the laughable itself heightens the tragic see Cervantes, Shakespeare "my kingdom for a horse," not to mention the Bovary woman . . . Because, he said, yes, it was perfectly laughable: the splendid spring morning, the sky a transparent blue, the fields in flower, the green countryside where the only trace of the war was that road which looked like a public dump or rather one of those junkyards you sometimes see on the outskirts of large cities, the only difference being that instead of being piled up one atop the other the wrecked vehicles and all the different sorts of debris were lined up as if with a ruler along the road except sometimes for a few . . . how to say it: fumbles that had rolled into the fields but as for the houses (the farm buildings with their slate roofs and brick walls, sometimes set close together to form a sort of street) there was just a broken window here and there, with one of those net curtains hanging through it (you know, the ones with a design of a peacock, or a mythological character, or a basket of flowers?) fluttering in the breeze, or blown back against the façade, clinging, undulating, twisting, then falling straight again, and S. said No he isn't losing sight of the question he was asked, no he couldn't even say that he was afraid when the regiment fell into that . . .

Before you said: was thrown . . .

Thrown. Yes. Or more precisely led. Headed up by its colonel, proudly, as if for the Bastille Day parade, but no time then either to be afraid perhaps just something that clenches up suddenly somewhere in your stomach something flashing through your brain which might be translated as This time this is it we're all going to ge . . . , and not even time to finish the word, already down on the ground, already groping with one hand behind your back between the gunshots, explosions, shouts, and whinnies to try to unhook the rifle, the journalist saying Right. Combat. I understand. But when a little later you found yourself for the second time in five days riding a dead man's horse, as you told me, and all alone with another cavalryman on that public-dump road following the colonel considered already dead in the regiment's field log and with nothing else to do but sit there straddling the horse simply at a walk not even a trot like a living target I don't doubt what you're saying but all the same then you must surely have felt something like fear it's impossible for a man . . . and S. said that No it was much worse than that and the journalist Worse! and S. said that once again if one hasn't lived through such a thing oneself one can't have any idea of it Because, he said, everything seemed to be happening in a sort of fog of unreality No it's not, as the journalist might think, the effect of time more than fifty years now the clouding of the memory, that on the contrary he (S.) has kept a very precise recollection of the whole affair and that what is precise is exactly that feeling of unreality that seemed to hang over everything that was happening and over the people making their way through the wrecks alongside the road, refugees or more probably looters (because, said S., he can still picture a woman trying to decide if a dress she had pulled from a gaping suitcase was her size, holding it up to her shoulders with her two hands her chin touching her chest as she stretched a leg out in front of her to see if she would have to hem it up or not), both of them (except that woman who clearly didn't give a damn about anything but the question of whether she would be able to alter this dress to her size) standing upright abandoning their search to watch in stupefaction as the four riders passed by, shouting out to them that they were on their way to getting shot up that a column of enemy tanks had gone by the night before dropping off some marksmen who were lying in wait and doing a hell of a job on anything in a uniform that they were all four quite a sight on their knock-kneed horses, the two colonels still calmly advancing paying no more attention to their shouts than if they were dogs barking as they passed by or than if a group of street thugs had dared address them, and S. said that in fact he also remembered a man trying to pull something out from under an overturned cart his face red and contorted with rage who called them worthless fucking officers where were they yesterday isn't it a lovely morning to go for a stroll with their two flunkies and . . . The journalist saying But there must have been dead bodies did . . . and S. said that Yes of course but a few not many just here and there but not very spectacular in a way no good as material for an enticing book jacket that is not dismembered an arm or a leg blown off or maybe disemboweled but visibly killed by a single bullet pushed onto their sides by the looters and demurely rolled back onto their stomachs so that with those khaki uniforms they looked like nothing more than bags of sawdust although even more motionless than a bag of sawdust if the journalist sees what he (S.) means but that he didn't look at them too closely perhaps the journalist can understand why and that the journalist might not believe it but in the seven days since all this had begun and since the regiment had melted like if one can say this snow in the sun and apart from the North Africans fried in their vans (but then it was dark and you couldn't see very clearly) this was the first time that he (S.) had had the leisure to look at dead bodies—Because, he said, virtually all they had ever done was retreat (what in military terms they demurely call "pulling back") and most often at a scramble as when they had to cross the Meuse and that day the regiment lost about a quarter of its men so you understand that those who fell wounded or dead or simply unhorsed . . . I found that out for myself when I was left alone half knocked out running (running if you can call it that) along that railway trench watching the last members of the squadron disappearing at a gallop far off in the distance, it's like those trees . . .

The journalist saying What trees?

The ones that the designers of eye-catching book jackets always show as black, charred, decapitated, pathetically brandishing their broken limbs: in seven days I only saw one like that, no more no less. The day before. And not black or burned: hit by a shell, broken in two, the yellow wood of its trunk bristling with splinters, the fallen part still connected by the bark, the mass of its foliage, still green, half crushed against the ground. So no trees with broken limbs, no dramatic red and black sky, no piles of dead bodies, no rutted road full of puddles: beautiful sunshine, the green countryside, only that string of wrecks, and as for deafening warlike tumult nothing but the quiet clopping of the hooves of the five horses accompanied by the echo, weaker and weaker, of a cannon which you might have thought had been put there purely to provide some atmosphere and which was shooting at who knows what at regular intervals, every two or three minutes, metronomic so to speak, and maybe, in the hedges, the birds chirping faintly, silence, the dazzling springtime morning, until there not explodes but so to speak crackles, laughable, like a child's toy, the insignificant coughing or rather spitting of that machine gun which . . .

At regular intervals, about every four or five minutes, an airplane (probably taking off from La Guardia) slowly crosses the square of the windowpane, moving from right to left and climbing little by little. The surface of the small sinuously shaped lake on the south side of Central Park is frozen, black, covered with a thin layer of gray dust. It is streaked by a few straight lines, also gray, coming from the banks and converging more or less toward the center, where a sculpture sits, but never reaching it, sometimes crossing over each other and ending in little blocks, like stones. Looking at them closely, they appear to be pieces of ice thrown horizontally (by children?) from the banks, which left a sort of wake behind them before coming to a stop. A row of calèches (or landaus?) is parked along the sidewalk. The horses are protected from the cold by blankets, some of them brightly colored (striped for example with yellow, red, or green, sometimes solid, putty colored, edged with a brown band). The horses' heads are also protected by a hood that encloses each ear in a sort of cone. Some of the coachmen are sitting, bundled up, on their benches. Three of them stand talking in a little group on the sidewalk. In the street, automobiles with gleaming bodies move in both directions, among them a few taxis. Also at regular intervals they all slow down and stop at the light on Sixth Avenue to let the pedestrians cross. From the eighteenth floor you can't hear the noise they make when they start up again and everything seems to be happening in an unreal silence, or rather to be melding into a uniform roar, muted, unchanging.

From the bed where he is lying next to the woman, only by raising oneself up can one see the tops of the park's trees, stripped bare by winter and forming a violet brown mass. They're still breathless. The woman has long thighs. The setting sun is reflected in the windows at the corners of the tall buildings bordering the park on the west and seems to be boiling like molten gold. After a moment the woman says: But I'm only your mistress. He says: You have the best part. She says: But I'm only your mistress. He says: You have the best part. She says: But I'll never be anything but your mistress. He says: But you have the best part. She doesn't answer. Another airplane crosses the windowpane from right to left, climbing slowly. In the gathering dusk its running lights can be seen blinking on and off. After a moment she says: It's already midnight in Europe. I'm sleepy. He says: Me too but we have an invitation from that Swede. I've never understood why people here have this need to invite you to dinner the evening of your arrival. Maybe it's a local custom. Maybe it's a sort of welcome. That's why I wanted us to lie down and rest when we got here. She says: You call that resting? She gets up and begins to take the dresses out of her suitcase. Her smooth, bare back, her buttocks, her long muscular thighs. The short hairs or rather the down beneath her belly when she stands in profile, swatting at a dress with little blows to get rid of the wrinkles, holding it at arm's length before her. She goes to the closet and hangs it up, comes back to the suitcase and takes out some other things, among them a dress which she inspects. She says: I believe I'll wear this one what do you think? She looks at herself in the mirror, her hands at her shoulders, the dress hanging before her, the way women do in department stores. She says again What do you think? He says: It looks beautiful on you. Particularly if you wear it the way you're doing now. You'll be a great success. At least one of the four elevators is invariably out of order and sometimes you have to wait almost ten minutes to go up or down, so that, despite its vast size, the elevator cabin, paneled in mahogany and decorated with mirrors, is always packed and the people squeezed up against each other. S. finds himself pressed breast to breast against a little Chinese man, shorter than he is, with a face more brown than yellow, whose precise age, somewhere between thirty and sixty, would be impossible to guess, impassive amid all these people (perfumed women wrapped in furs, men dressed for dinner) joking in nasal English or other languages about the discomfort of the situation. When they finally emerge from the elevator someone says that the Chinese man had been imprisoned for twenty years during the Cultural Revolution but someone else says that the Cultural Revolution only began eighteen years earlier, so the first one said that he must have had a head start. Wasn't there something called the Hundred Flowers or some other of those elegant names that the Chinese come up with to send each other to prison or up before the firing squad?: he was walking away, back turned, led or rather escorted by one of the organizers of the colloquium, a very tall man next to whom in his ill-cut blue serge suit he had the look of a quiet, docile little child, and someone said that in the end you see these kinds of colloquia are not entirely pointless because with a little luck you might manage to put to death by asphyxiation in an elevator a Chinese man whom twenty years in prison in his own country hadn't managed to kill, and S. went to the front desk and asked them to call a taxi but they pointed outside to a giant dressed in a pearl gray cape and torsaded epaulets, with a red cap on his head, who with a blow of his whistle made them stop and opened the door, S. wondering if a dollar was enough to slip into his other hand but it was probably good enough because the giant with the torsaded epaulets said Thank you sir and raised his cap as he closed the door of the taxi and as they began to drive away they could once again hear the strident, imperious whistle calls resounding ever more distant in the frozen darkness, lacquered and black, as the lights streamed by, and immediately like every taxi driver in that city and all the while driving expertly he asked them very naturally in English as if it went without saying that every foreigner who came to this city must understand English what country they were from very interested told them talkative implacable that he himself was Turkish and that he had only been here for two years but that it was a terrific city where everyone was free and could freely and comfortably earn a living and that he was going to send for his wife whom he hadn't seen for two years and his children one of whom wanted to be an engineer and his daughter a nurse who wanted to be a doctor which in his country was impossible and which, and she said that yes it really did seem to be a terrific city because just now they'd almost managed to put to death by asphyxiation in a mahogany-paneled elevator a Chinese man who had survived twenty-four years of imprisonment in his own country where after all they're experts in torture and the driver said Did they know Chinatown in lower Manhattan where everything is written in Chinese something to see but he didn't like those people and she asked why and he said that they're not people like us you see what I mean and . . .

Maybe the journalist is tired of hearing S.'s monologue or maybe he is worried about how much time is left on the tape in his machine. He glances at his watch with its various dials where the seconds, minutes, and hours succeed each other (as if time, turning on itself, always passing back over the same places, did not run at the same speed, at the same intervals, different every time) and he said: Right: the road, the wrecks, just a few dead bodies, the looters, you on a horse again and expecting to be killed from one moment to the next, forgive me for belaboring this point but really in your head something must have been happening You said it was worse than fear so what was it? Because fatigue, hunger, lack of sleep, right, I get it, but that . . . And S. said that it must be that there's a limit to fatigue, to lack of sleep, and to hunger, that when you haven't eaten anything for three days . . . The journalist saying Three days? and S. said And even longer because for a week, since it had all begun, they'd only just twice seen the guys from the field kitchen and that for three days apart from the jars of fruit in syrup they'd found in the houses that had already been looted they hadn't eaten anything which the journalist could easily verify by consulting the archives so carefully set out along kilometers of shelves in the Château de Vincennes where in the folder containing his regiment's field log he will find one of those little rectangles of paper torn from a notebook on which the commanding officers write things like "I request artillery support" or "Dangerous enemy infiltration on my right" or that sort of thing and on that little paper rectangle, addressed to the general (the one who at that moment might already have blown his brains out), the journalist will be able to read the words, simply scrawled with a pencil, "My men have not eaten or slept in three days," and since that note was written the day before (the day before the morning in question), it had been not three days but four since . . . The journalist saying Four days! and S. said that according to what he had since learned the functioning of the human body including the brain depended on a set of physiochemical reactions, the faculties of perception of the outside world as well as of the inside are no doubt seriously affected when that set is itself . . . The journalist saying Of course of course But that's precisely what interests me: yes: those physiochemical reactions, since that's what you call them, even if they were of course seriously disturbed with respect to their normal functioning, all the same, they were still going on, weren't they? S. saying nothing, looking out the window for a moment at the trees, the sky, finally shrugging, saying It's hard to explain. Even today to myself. All the more to someone else . . .

From outside, although both windows are closed now, comes, muffled but always present, continuous, the dull hum of the city, that quiet roar, unvarying, at once reassuring and threatening, while S. tries to tell of something which, even to him, now seems unreal, saying that, for example, to give an idea of that semicomatose or semisomnambulistic state in which he found himself at the time, it hadn't even occurred to him to ask not the colonel (who would certainly not have answered) but the other cavalryman, the one who was leading the spare horse, how they had managed to survive the ambush into which the colonel had thrown the squadron. He (S.) said that, believe me, in a state like that you've probably reached a point where, without surprise or indignation (as when for the first time a bomb had exploded next to him without warning—but that was already long past! . . .), you simply register things passively. And then, reciprocally, adds S., and this showed clearly that he (S.) was not an unusual case in that respect, neither of the two colonels, nor the man leading the spare horse, had asked him how he himself had come out of it alive and how they had found him sitting by the side of a road about forty kilometers from where the ambush had taken place: none of them seemed to feel any surprise at this, and even less any interest in it, the colonel, when S. stood up and introduced himself (rank, name, squadron, platoon), clicking his heels in accordance with regulations, doing nothing more than bringing his horse almost to a stop and, as if it were the most natural thing in the world, looking at him for a moment with a perfectly inexpressive air, saying simply "Very well. Mount one of the spare horses that the cavalryman back there is leading and follow me," giving the flanks of his horse a slight squeeze and setting off again, and nothing more. As for mental or nervous reactions, since that was what most interested the journalist, S. said that, for example, the leader of the spare horse (who obviously had been and continued to be very afraid) betrayed his by tormenting that poor animal (the riderless horse) whose mouth he needlessly tore with violent tugs at the reins, to the point where it (the riderless horse) sometimes began to trot desperately in place, moving sideways like a crab, its body perpendicular to the direction of movement, long strings of drool and blood hanging from the corners of its mouth, the rider swearing incessantly and cursing it through his clenched teeth, so much so that at one point, said S., the colonel had half turned around on his saddle, saying All right, that's enough! All right, all right! . . . after which the man leading the horse had stopped swearing, his face now sullen, contenting himself with only an occasional underhanded sharp tug at the reins, probably as a way of showing the poor animal that even if he, his leader, was in a position of perfect powerlessness, he still had the ability to make the animal suffer—But I've already told about all that, S. interrupts himself, I . . . But the journalist says that No or rather that Yes but not like that, that S. had covered that whole story with could it be called a novelistic sauce if the journalist might be allowed to say so, that for example S. made of the leader of the spare horse a jockey and that a jockey would never brutalize a horse in that way, no matter how distraught, and that the colonel became a simple captain, S. inventing a whole combination of psychological factors and antecedents such as suggesting that there was some question of jealousy That no, S. shouldn't take that as a criticism, the journalist would never be so bold and that besides it was a very successful text but that it was even more interesting to hear it told without these embellishments (S. shouldn't take that word the wrong way) simply the brute facts in their materiality because But S. said that Nothing is simple, the journalist saying Of course but all the same . . . I mean that between a fiction and the story, the objective, neutral account of an event . . . But S. interrupts him again and says that it is impossible for anyone to recount or describe anything at all in an objective way, that, except in scientific texts concerning for example anatomy or mechanics or botany (and even then there's room for argument), there is no such thing as a neutral style or as some people have also claimed a "blank" writing which amounts rather naively to maintaining the myth of a godlike novelist presented as an impassive observer with a detached gaze, "the world as if I weren't there to speak of it," as Baudelaire already ironically put it, the journalist saying that he wasn't talking about a novel but about a firsthand account, and S. says that six witnesses of an event will in all good faith give six different versions of it, the journalist saying It's a huge question but let's not get off track, that the only thing he wanted to know in a very precise way insofar as possible was how someone can manage to live with fear and S. said that But precisely that was exactly what he was talking about, that if for example the leader of that poor spare horse dealt with his fear by tormenting the animal everyone lived with his fear in his own way or rather lived with different fears because what had struck him (but not right away, he said: he probably needed some time to get used to his new situation—that is, after having crawled and walked alone through the woods, finding himself on a horse again) was that the colonel was riding, strangely, a plow horse, one of the horses that they'd requisitioned, put to work as the off-horse of a machine-gun caisson and whose hames, having been cut (or detached?) dragged through the dirt on either side of a powerful rump, graceless and heavy, the color of cheap wine (or rather pink, because spotted with white) and which, said S. (Another drop of whiskey? he asks: But your ice cubes have melted, I'll . . . the journalist saying No that's fine go on: you were saying: a plow horse with a pink rump?) . . . and with an ugly yellowish tail, dull blond, something like those corn tassels, vaguely wavy, like badly colored hair, if the journalist saw what he meant? Because, said S., while once again because of that semicomatose or semisomnambulistic state in which, as he had explained, he then found himself and which allowed him to register only a small part of what was in his field of vision like for example that pink rump and that dull blond tail, or else those wads or rather flecks of drool, glistening in the sunlight, that the tormented horse sent flying through the air when it shook its head, at the same time, although he was able to see it clearly when they dismounted to drink those bottles of beer, it would be absolutely impossible for him to describe the face of the colonel which, furthermore, previously, since the beginning of the war, he had only had the occasion to glimpse twice but, he said, that the journalist could imagine it: one of those ascetic faces, a mask of wood with flat cheeks and skin tanned by the open air, about fifty years old or maybe a little more, in other words one of those faces you never look at, or forget as soon as you've seen them, interchangeable so to speak, set (hardened?) by the habit of giving orders and being obeyed, not to mention the pride, the intimate conviction of belonging to a superior caste, not so much from the fact of some noble title (he was a baron), nor from his rank, but simply as a cavalry officer, that is once again not so much superior to the men he commanded (since even those of the humblest origins—farm boys or beet farmers—had themselves been ennobled in some sense by the simple fact of serving in this corps) as to any other man, even a general, in any other branch of the armed forces (infantry, artillery—those Polytechnic students who thought they knew how to ride a horse!—engineering, aviation, supply corps), who never learned to sit properly in a saddle or simply to spread their thighs in accordance with the rules, since at that moment and in a manner, said S., that one could call rather ostentatious, he (the colonel) was riding that big Percheron bareback even though he had a saddle horse available (the one that the brute was leading) and even (before finding S. on the road) two: two half-breed Tarbais—which, said S., (that wretched wine-dregs-colored nag) had put a flea in his ear and (if he could be forgiven the bad pun) had made him think that he (the colonel) had doubly *perdu les pédales,* lost his mind, since an off-horse has neither saddle nor stirrups (called *pédales* in cavalry slang). In other words, said S., it was then that he began to realize that what the colonel probably feared above all else and far more than a sniper's bullet was to have to explain to the general replacing the one who had committed suicide how, in full mobile warfare (but maybe he had not yet understood that this was mobile warfare?) and without even taking the elementary precaution, as the most obtuse NCO—or even corporal—would have done, of sending a reconnaissance squad ahead, he had positioned himself at the head of the regiment. Unless . . . Unless what? said the journalist Unless he thought that as a way of saving his self-respect and giving the most flattering possible picture of himself he'd had the idea of presenting himself like that, dramatically mounted bareback on that off-horse, the first mount he was able to catch under enemy fire after his horse had been killed beneath him (always a glorious deed in the cavalry), straddling it on the run . . . Because, said S. . . . Because the worst thing that a man can be asked to bear is ridicule: Raskolnikov turns himself in not because Sonia persuades him to expiate his sins but because he finally realizes that in Porfiry's eyes he is utterly ridiculous. After having patiently read his entire self-serving confession telling the story of the little girl who'd been raped and compelled to commit suicide, Tikhon gently asks Stavrogin if he does not fear ridicule and one might think that this question plays no small role in Stavrogin's decision to hang himself. No, said S., I'm not psychoanalyzing, I try to steer clear of that, I don't know the first thing about it, I'm not Flaubert brandishing Emma's dissected, bleeding heart on the point of a scalpel, I . . .

At that moment, a click comes from the tape recorder and the journalist raises a hand saying Stop, stop, the tape . . . The gusty winds that followed the cloudburst have diminished and the luxuriant greenery of the trees in the square is still now, with the exception of one—one single—leaf that S., in amazement, watches spinning around, rising up, showing its pale green underside, flipping down, beginning to spin again in the opposite direction as if under the effect of a tiny cyclone centered on it alone, S. wondering if they've finished their prayers in the mosque by now and if, in their long kingly robes, they're back in the metro on the way home to their suburbs or to the rooms where they live in groups of five or six in neighborhoods or suburbs where no one ever goes. Many of them are employed by the city sanitation department. They dress for work in bright green jumpsuits, no doubt supplied by the sanitation department, and wear long-visored caps with cylindrical crowns. After the market which is held three times a week they clean the square using long brooms with bristles apparently made of plastic, the same green as their jumpsuits. S. remembers having seen a mountain of garbage in Calcutta, about as high as the third floor of a building, where half-naked children were busy gathering things, trying to fend off the crows and the vultures. They call those birds "the garbagemen" there, and they count on them to keep the cities clean. The tower in Bombay atop which they set out dead bodies for their food. But on that road there were no vultures. Only the looters and, in one place, a swarm of large flies buzzing around the nostrils of a dead horse. S. said aloud: Sorry, I was thinking of something else, you . . . The journalist, who has started up the tape recorder again, sits upright, leans back against the cushions and says But the other colonel? S. says The other colonel? The journalist says According to what you told me, he'd also had his regiment massacred, but he was only obeying his orders, he himself hadn't made any mis . . . S. shakes his head and says No. Not as far as

I know at least. Naturally one could indulge in all sorts of inter-
pretations and expound endlessly on the psychological com-
plexities of a colonel in the cavalry, construct all sorts of hy-
potheses, as for example that even though he hadn't made any
mistakes he might well find himself, after the loss of his regiment
and that long walk through the night, in a somewhat depressed
state similar to the one that the general in command (or who was
supposed to be in command) of the brigade had fallen into the
day before but that he (still the second colonel) was looking for
a solution that would let him out of having to make use (as the
general had done) of his own revolver; another explanation (forgive me if I seem cynical but, once again, as we've already remarked, there is often an element of comedy in every tragedy)
would be: "calm, forward, straight," a principle or rule of the
equestrian art, which might lead us to suppose that in this
morally desperate, unbearable situation the two officers might
have set each other (tacitly, that goes without saying, since this
sort of thing is never spoken of aloud among well-bred men) . . .
might have tacitly set each other something like a sort of challenge a stupid bet as in the story (which the journalist must
surely know) of the two miserly swimmers who bet ten francs
on who could stay underwater the longest without coming to
the surface for air and whose two drowned bodies were found
the following day, so, continues S., the unspoken bet (or challenge) might have consisted in seeing which of them would be
courageous (or obstinate) enough to continue moving forward
calmly at the horse's natural walking speed along that road until the other one is shot—or both of them. . . . You know there
must be a code of conduct among that sort of people that forbids them from openly expressing any emotion at all. Outwardly, then, they were behaving as if they were simply taking
their horses for a stroll. . . .

Except that one of the two was a plow horse, said the journalist.

The off-horse, said S. Yes. But neither one of them seemed to
notice it: still too well bred no doubt: the one riding it content-

ing himself with that sort of exhibitionism, of furious, passive protest. . . .

Protest? said the journalist. But against whom? Who the hell could he find guilty of . . .

No one, of course. I mean no one in particular. Fate maybe, bad luck, the injustice destiny had dealt him of having led his regiment to its downfall . . .

And the other one?

The other one? Well perhaps as I've just told you too polite to allow his companion to see that he considered him if not mad then at least slightly deranged . . . So anyway: half-breed or huge Percheron, it was as if they were out for a stroll in the riding ground of a cavalry quarter or a pathway in the Bois de Boulogne, chatting calmly between themselves. But I don't think there was anything affected about it. Certainly what they were speaking of between themselves was the situation (not speaking about it would have been an affectation), but in a measured tone, detached, as if they found themselves not on a road where they might be killed at any moment, but on maneuvers, or in the officers' mess, or at a lecture in the École de Guerre discussing such and such tactic, and S. says that he remembers perfectly that at one point, as one of them was turning his head toward the other (but S. says that he couldn't specify which of the two it was, that he remembered only the sound or rather the timbre of his voice: one of those high-pitched nasal voices, suffused at the same time with smugness, detachment, as well as interest, a vague, so to speak, professional admiration), he heard him say "Apparently they use their tanks as . . . ," the end of the sentence eluding S. but, he says, spoken like a simple statement, nothing more, of . . .

The journalist erupting, saying But what else could they have done, what could you expect . . . Since they'd received orders to fall back to Avesnes, what . . . And S. says To fall back along with their regiments: not just followed by two cavalrymen and a riderless horse, pretty paltry, don't you think? the journalist saying But really . . . , and S. says that Listen once again he doesn't have a degree from the École de Guerre but that all the same the regiment had not completely "vanished" to use the term of the major who was looking for them with his binoculars and that even though from that moment on there was no longer a regiment as an organized unit nevertheless there remained a few shreds of it mingled here and there with those or rather with the scraps of other regiments sharpshooters infantry artillery without cannons miners etc. scattered throughout the countryside so that while naturally after that point there is no longer one single regimental field log one can nevertheless have a look at the logbooks of the shreds or of the scraps and that apart from a particularly stupid lieutenant who could think of nothing better to do than once again throw his platoon straight into the jaws of the wolf and get half his men killed, other officers, even though they had no liaisons and no orders, had when it was possible sent out reconnaissance teams questioned lost soldiers civilian refugees or looters and learned from them that Avesnes was to be avoided some of them trying to go around the city on the north the others trying to take cover behind the Sambre and that while in the end none of that had had much effect on the final outcome of this mess it was on the whole still better than insisting on walking "calm, forward, straight" not to mention that instead of "forward" it was more "backward" since the two colonels were traveling west on that pigeon shoot of a road where assuming that one of the snipers missed them it was obvious that they wouldn't have long to wait before the supply corps of the tank column (and in fact the column was an entire division) that had passed by there twelve hours earlier happened along in turn and that they would politely ask them to let them through For Christ's sake yes anything rather than going on parading around on that damn pink horse as if . . . The journalist coughing, timidly clearing his throat and saying You don't think much of him! and S., startled, not speaking for a moment, reflecting, finally saying that But no! No the journalist was wrong! First, once again, how to judge? From a purely military perspective it was obviously idiotic. But, in human terms, once again, how to judge? No, he (S.) had nothing against him. Poor man! And even . . . Falling silent

again, leaning forward, picking up the box lying on the table between the glasses in which the ice cubes have completely melted,
saying You don't want one of these little cigars? No? You don't
smoke? saying Ha ha you don't smoke you don't drink: no vices
good for you Personally I . . . Do you mind? pulling the lighter
to him, puffing on the cigar, sitting there pensively looking at the
incandescent end where a shred of tobacco is twisting in a curl,
saying I beg your pardon What? And the journalist You said And
even . . . And S. shakes his head, shrugging his shoulders, finally
saying I can still picture those legs. That woman's. Along with
that horse's strings of drool glistening in the sun and the big pink
rump and piss-colored tail of the other horse in front of me, it's
one of the images from that sort of fog or daze that I've kept with
me. . . . It happened when we stopped in the courtyard of a bar
and he bought us a beer—although in reality I think it was more
to let the horses drink. Because it was closer to something like a
barnyard, with a drinking trough: you know, those northern bars
that are half tobacconists, selling stamps and rotgut, and it may
have been that when we came in the woman was feeding her
chickens (yes: in the middle of all that, life—a certain sort of life,
at least—went on): that yard, then, with a henhouse, rabbit
cages, and piles of crates, and that woman, halfway out of her
mind with terror, who brought us four bottles of beer in . . . The
journalist saying You're not going to try to make me believe that
in the state you were in you were interested in a woman's legs!
and S. again lets out that laugh which is not a laugh and says No
of course not! It was a middle-aged woman, I would be completely unable to describe her for you except that she had on a
sort of grayish smock with little flowers maybe of the kind
women like that wear but she hadn't put on any stockings, only
thick checked slippers: thick legs, and what struck me were the
varicose veins that you could see snaking green and blue beneath
the unusually white skin of her calves and . . . But the journalist
interrupts him again, he repeats You said And even: even what?
And S. says Yes. Because when he was finished paying (and S.
says that he remembers that as well: that he (the colonel) had in-

sisted that the change be counted out sou by sou, could the journalist imagine such a thing?: sou by sou in the middle of a catastrophe for four bottles of beer? the journalist saying that that
showed the colonel clearly had not lost his reason, S. saying that
on the contrary, no matter how cheap a person might be he
would never think of having the change counted out sou by sou
for four bottles of beer in such circumstances, that that showed
quite to the contrary that the colonel had gone completely off his
head, that he had become a sort of robot, just as he rode robotically down that goddamn road), but, S. says again, it's not that,
it's not the change, it's that when he had finished putting it in his
pocket and was preparing to climb back onto that ridiculous
horse, taking up the reins (or what served as reins for that off-
horse), then he probably realized that we were the only ones (I
mean the soldier leading the spare horse and me) to have continued following along behind him and that the two cyclists (but
I might have forgotten to tell you that the remains of that regiment or rather of that brigade also included, when I stumbled
across them, two cyclists who were slowly pedaling along behind) . . . that the two cyclists had disappeared into the countryside. . . . You'll never guess what he did! the journalist saying
What? and S.: Well today I wonder if at that moment he didn't
suddenly feel something like pity for us, some remorse, some regret at taking us with him where he had decided to go Because
he turned to us and said: What about you, young men, are you
going on? . . . The journalist saying And? and S. saying And do
you know what I said to him? No, believe me, it had nothing to
do with bravery, or courage, or heroism, or duty: those words
had long since ceased to have the slightest meaning for me: I suppose that it was simply an abdication, an abandonment, or else
the ingrained reflex to obey, although now I wonder if there
weren't some other reactions involved as well: pride, an idiotic
vanity, if I didn't feel stupidly stung to the quick by (but maybe
I only imagined it?) a certain inflection of his voice, maybe I
thought I sensed a sort of challenge in it, a vaguely condescend-
ing tone—or maybe no such thing: simply because I too had

reached the point of behaving like a robot, I don't know, I don't know anything, don't ask me why, but suddenly I heard myself answering: Yes, colonel!

No city is more accurately described by the words "arising from the earth" than New York (or perhaps it would be more fitting to say "spurting"): and not exactly upright, static, but exploding, always expanding not in its surface but in its height, as can be seen from certain photographs taken from an airplane (or a helicopter) with a wide-angle lens (fish-eye), where, for a fraction of a second of course, it seems to have stayed still when in fact it has not stopped growing, rising upward, the sort of lens that exaggerates the perspective, so that its multiple skyscrapers seem to be not vertical, parallel, but obeying a divergent force, like those bouquets of crystals that spread further apart as they grow, shoving against each other, pushing the towers of all different heights toward the sky, the least lofty ones not resigned to their fate but having simply gathered their momentum a little later than the others and hurrying to catch up, the whole thing as if thrust into the bulging rotundity of the earth, starting from a narrow base, something like a sort of solidified explosion, a sort of natural phenomenon, anarchic, tumultuous, and geometric.

The opposite of Saint Petersburg, laid down horizontally all at once, entirely designed in advance, on the flat, by the same architect, down to the smallest of its rococo ornamentations, its entablatures, its Atlases with their bulging abdominal muscles, their brawny pectorals, hunched beneath the cornices for the rest of time. Built on a flat swamp by the strength (and death) of men. The Hermitage Museum has a life-size wax mannequin representing Peter the Great. He is sitting in an armchair, one of his legs half folded beneath the chair, slightly forward of the other one, wearing buckled shoes, his calves covered by sheer pink stockings, wearing a pearl gray frock coat and breeches. Although there is nothing particularly disagreeable about his face (but is it the contrast between the bright pink of the stockings and the austerity of the gray, the life-size scale of the mannequin, as if this were the man himself, embalmed?) there emerges from the whole thing something terrifying.

On one of the walls of S.'s room (Hotel Astoria, rm. 4) hangs a medium-size oil painting of an izba in a snow-covered birch forest. The execution is heavy handed and vulgar: the shadows of the birches, extending over lemon white snow, are of an acidic blue color, the izba is yellow and brown, the sky also a garish blue. To prevent the guests from walking off with them, the keys to the rooms, already heavy, are weighted with a massive pendant. This precaution does not originate with the Communist regime then still in force there, because the pendants, molded in bronze, bear the very visible high-relief inscription "Hotel Astoria—Saint Petersburg." The room's window directly faces the Cathedral of Saint Isaac, built by the Frenchman Auguste Montferrand in the style of the eighteenth century. It contains 114 granite columns, each weighing several tons. The interior, where services are no longer held, is cold, too vast, empty. From the top of the highest cupola hangs a Foucault's pendulum, with a weight at the end that describes a broad circle, about eight meters in diameter, along the surface of the tile floor. Around the perimeter of the circle wooden markers (cubes) have been set up, which the end of the pendulum nears, first brushing against them, then knocking them over, and so demonstrating the phenomenon of the rotation of the earth, as a teacherly woman explains in a piercing voice to a group of visitors. Her voice resounds through the large hollow space. At the Hermitage Museum, groups of visitors with high cheekbones and slightly slanted eyes pass noisily through the rooms, following a female guide who makes brief stops before the most significant paintings. The interpreter accompanying S. proudly points out that together the rooms, stairways, and corridors add up to a length of four kilometers. The stairways are made of white marble, decorated on the landings with basins made of onyx, porphyry, or other rare minerals, red or green, weighing several tons. One can also see in one of the rooms a monumental clock with a complicated set of decorations, in the English style. On the mantelpiece of one room of the

Winter Palace sits a clock whose hands have been stopped at the precise moment the October Red Guards entered and informed the gathered ministers that it was all over for them. The interpreter-guide has S. stop before a large painting, the work of a minor Flemish master, showing a vast spread of fish (rays, lampreys, turbots, eels, etc.). She remarks on the abundance amid which the rich lived, alongside people who were dying of hunger. The museum also owns one of the most beautiful works of Veronese, which is *The Conversion of Saint Paul* or *The Road to Damascus*, unfortunately impossible to see in its entirety because of a bad lighting arrangement, and the *Tancredi and Hermione* by Poussin before which the interpreter becomes irritated at the time S. is taking. At one point, between the city and the airport, the car drives for a few hundred meters past a succession of glass-walled greenhouses, on the left. The interpreter-guide explains that thanks to these greenhouses the people of Leningrad will never lack for fresh vegetables, even in winter (and even, she goes on to say, tomatoes). She speaks in a voice that is at once peremptory and groaning. Although from what she says it appears that she has recently finished her studies and is probably not yet thirty years old, she looks forty. Her thin, grayish face has the crumpled look of someone badly nourished since childhood. She is wearing a plaid suit in ocher tones and a black turtleneck, all rather worn. Halfway to the airport, the driver points to a line of low hills in the distance which, she translates, marks the furthest point of the German advance. He says he was a captain in the artillery. He is wearing a blue suit, baggy, to whose lapel are pinned a number of military decoration ribbons, in a fan shape, their colors bright but faded. S. asks if he can smoke and offers him a cigarette which he declines. When they arrive at the airport, the interpreter-guide asks him to wait for her while she goes to take care of the tickets. When he is sure she's out of sight, the driver turns to S., lifts two fingers to his lips and moves them away in an expressive gesture but S. has to insist to get him to accept the pack which despite his protests he slips into the pocket of his vest under the little multicolored fan of faded ribbons. He has an intelligent face, but also worn, wide, with sagging skin. The airport buildings now hide the grayish line of hills which the Germans never managed to cross.

What the hell! said the journalist. He was giving you a chance to save your life, and out of vanity, out of pride, you . . . The two men, one thinking, trying to remember precisely something that happened (that he experienced) more than forty years before, which in his memory is now only a magma of images and sensations, almost as incredible for him as for his interlocutor, the two men, then, sitting in the room which the echoes of the multiplicitous world penetrate only in the form of that tenuous and tenacious hum (or rather whisper) of an engine in neutral, idling but obstinate, and S. repeating I tell you I don't know anything about it: vanity, pride . . . Or simply gregariousness, stupefaction . . . Or maybe by that time I'd come to hate him too much to accept anything he offered me. Or maybe I was irritated at having been caught up in this idiotic game myself, I wanted to play the role of the third swimmer, to show that I too, no less than two colonels, was capable of staying underwater until they fish out my drowned corpse. Who knows what one might be thinking or not thinking at a time like that? Assuming that one is even capable of thinking . . . Of course, said the journalist, of course (he is speaking in a conciliatory tone, as people speak to a sick person or to someone who has lost control of his mind): I understand, you've told me: fatigue, lack of sleep, hunger. . . . But S. says No. Not hunger. Believe it or not. It's strange, in fact, when I think back on it. Listen: hunger, believe me, I know what that is. As a prisoner, God or rather the devil knows I suffered from it: a rat devouring your stomach. But at that moment I don't have even the slightest memory of it. . . . In fact, believe it or not, when that animal of a colonel finally managed to get himself shot and we (all of us, that is the other cavalryman—the brute—and me) did an about-face, galloped until we reached a secluded farm, put our horses in the barn, broke a window, found civilian clothes, after we were screamed at by the owner who caught us and then led us across the fields to a café (yes: a café, another café open in the middle of this pandemonium—not on the road, of course, but not very far off—with three or four regulars calmly discussing what was going on and the barmaid who also chimed in with her opinion even as she served the customers, like the one with the varicose veins selling beers! . . .), well believe it or not it never occurred to me to ask for something to eat, an omelet, or bread and sausage. Even though I had money on me. So I sat there on the bench, completely numb, obediently throwing back one after another of those little conical glasses filled to the rim with genever, which the peasant and then the barmaid kept setting down in front of us. I think the tension had become too great and that at that moment . . . So yes, precisely, what about that tension? . . . said the journalist, how . . .

The Japan Air Lines flight that takes off from Tokyo on April 9 at 5:25 P.M. arrives in San Francisco the same day, April 9, at ten o'clock in the morning.—At New Orleans the Mississippi, the color of milky coffee, flows between tall dikes. It is about 500 meters wide and there are ocean-going ships (freighters) anchored or moored on it. You can buy a ticket for a pleasure boat which passes through a lock and into the bayous for a tour. From the branches of the trees hang long green mosses, like beards. The most interesting thing is, on the way back, an enormous mountain of empty metal barrels (gasoline, diesel oil?) piled up on a dumping ground, in all colors: brown, blue, rust, yellow, green, white.—The Queen invites S. to admire the silverware on the table. Between her and the King, who is facing her across the table (they have to lean to one side if they want to see each other or talk) sits a tall silver urn with three veiled nymphs standing with their backs to it. The whole thing is vaguely reminiscent of those *fontaines Wallace* you used to see in Paris squares. The long dining room's vaulted ceiling is decorated with brownish paintings which make the gilded arches stand out. The valets serving at table are wearing white stockings, short breeches, and black frock coats embroidered with a silver ribbon.—S. is invited to dinner in a restaurant beside the Thames, upstream from London: his host tells him that in the past the judges from the court used to come to dinner here and watch as condemned men were hanged on the other side of the river.—On the way back from Athens, the car breaks down between Tito-Veles and Nis. It is night. S. repairs the carburetor using a pair of tweezers borrowed from R., who provides illumination with a flashlight. A peasant cart passing very close by on the dirt path that runs alongside the road, invisible in the dark: only the squeaking of the wheels and the crackling of the gravel. Rows of men crowded together on the sidewalk, in Nis, silent, before the hotel, looking in through the windows into the lobby where three prostitutes with plaster white faces, made up like geishas, indifferent, are sitting in armchairs smoking cigarettes. At dinner, a German traveling salesman in the large dining room, empty and freezing, decorated in worn Socialist luxury. Asks permission to come and sit at S. and R.'s table. Immediately shows pictures of his family which he pulls from a fat wallet. Says business is good here. Says it's a country with a future.

The afternoon is moving on. Through the gap between the two buildings adjoining the west side of the square the setting sun now thrusts a bronze wedge into the pale green of the motionless boughs and S. is trying to explain once again to the journalist who always comes back to the same question that in the end fear destroys itself or at least neutralizes itself precisely because of its magnitude: Because, he says, as far as he can remember what was going through his mind during the whole time he spent following that colonel along the road expecting at any moment (at any second) to be killed . . .

"But you volunteered," says the journalist, "when he asked you paternally . . ."

"With disdain," says S.

"In a voice that you found disdainful . . . Disdainful or not, he asked if you were going to continue following him and you said yes!"

"Fine," said S. "OK. Mechanically or out of vanity, or stupidity, or simple exhaustion . . . Don't condemn me. In any case, it didn't last long. About five minutes. Or less. Because he was killed just after we left the village, not even five minutes after he'd had the change for his four bottles of beer counted out sou by sou and put it in his pocket. Meaning that for the thieves who must have come along and gone through his pockets that was something, anyway, and . . ."

"But," the journalist interrupts him, "supposing that he hadn't been killed within five minutes, you would have gone on anyway?"

"Gone on?" says S. "You mean would I have gone on following him? Well of course! I'd said yes. What would I have looked like? . . . But before that I was obeying: it was on his orders that I'd followed him, that . . ."

That road in India: camels, elephants walking along under enormous loads, chained bears letting out roars of pain when in hopes of getting a few rupees their masters pulled brutally on the ring through their snouts so they would stand up as we passed by. A palace entirely sculpted (acanthus, interlaced leaves) in ocher stone, down to the merest square centimeter, the king's or maharajah's bedroom built in the center of a basin for fear of assassins, the maharajah assassinated anyway (by his servants?), deserted courtyards, silence, a tiny man, entirely naked, atop the ramparts shouting to attract the attention of the tourists before diving into the moat full of dirty green water.

. . . that I'd had to confront that thing, that, what to call it, trial by ordeal? that situation in which there's nothing left to do but, as the expression goes, "commend your soul to God." The problem, S. goes on to say, is that he doesn't believe in God—which must be very helpful in this sort of situation. I wonder if the colonel believed in Him? Very probably: in a cavalry garrison, on Sunday, at Mass, you can traditionally see the colonel and all his officers in the front row—at least, those who aren't busy that day breaking their necks on some nearby racetrack. Nevertheless, God forbids suicide. That's probably why, unlike the general, he (the colonel) had found in that place a means of making peace with his conscience. With his conscience as a Christian, at least. Because, militarily speaking, does a general or a colonel have the right to commit suicide? Or to get himself killed deliberately? But . . .

Roger C——, standing in the Valparaiso market, armed with a little spoon, eagerly sampling the orange and violet flesh of those urchins as large as small melons that can be found there. His face always slightly flushed, his black forelock hanging to one side, his bulging eyes underlined with bags, his mouth open like a fish out of water, half asphyxiated. In the evening, some Chilean friends take him and S. to a dive in the seedy neighborhood near the port. A room of about seven meters by seven, at street level, covered in yellow paint. A bar on the right as you go in. A minimal dance floor surrounded by four or five tables. On the left as you go in are three little "private rooms" separated by walls made of wooden boards and closed off by orange curtains hanging from a rod, only partially hiding the interior, which is furnished with a little table and two chairs. In the corner opposite the bar, a tiny quarter-circle stage holds the orchestra, made up of a pianist, two violinists, and a bandoneon player. Pushed up against the wall, the piano just barely fits, taking up the entire length of one side of the quarter-circle. The musicians' faces are devoid of expression. The bandoneon player is blind, and a thin white veil can be seen beneath his lowered eyelids. All four of them are wearing grayish, threadbare suits, their shirts also grayish and kept shut at the neck by a stud. The Chilean friends claim that one of the two violinists is a well-known assassin, released for lack of evidence (?). The blind man coaxes shrill sounds from his instrument. At one point, from one of the private rooms emerge, pushing back the curtain, a little man with a beaky profile, in his forties, and a woman of about the same age dressed in a black skirt and a white silk blouse. After talking with the musicians, the couple begins, alone in the middle of the little deserted dance floor, a dance in which they stand face-to-face, arms in a circle above their heads like flamenco dancers, but without castanets or stamping of the heels. They move in a circle this way, at a slow pace, and, now and then, exchange a white handkerchief laid over their left shoulder. The Chilean friends can't explain this strange ritual, no doubt symbolic. Valparaiso (Valley of Paradise), once the first stop for ships that had rounded Cape Horn, was ruined by the construction of the Panama Canal. A squeaking funicular railway hoists itself up to a belvedere from which one can see the entire city, the suburbs whose little houses are terraced along the hillsides, and the port, three-quarters empty, where a few freighters sit, rusting, beside the deserted docks.

But S. says that No he is not making a value judgment, that he is simply asking questions, such as whether the lives of the commanding officers belong to them and are they not accountable for them (as they are for the lives of the soldiers below them) to those who bestowed their command on them and, beyond that, to their homeland? Not to mention that making war is supposed to be their trade (for which they are paid, furthermore), and does the "art of war," as they say, not presuppose an ability to evaluate in battle the unexpected elements of a situation and modify the initial plans or orders accordingly? Is it not the duty of a commanding officer, if he judges an order to be foolhardy, to refuse to follow it, even if it means asking to be sent back to the most dangerous battleground as a simple soldier? For example, was the colonel obligated to "blindly" obey the general (the general who'd committed suicide the day before) who had ordered him to pull his regiment back toward Avesnes, when a little earlier he had thrown that regiment into an ambush so that all that remained of it were two wretched cavalrymen and all those people by the side of the road were shouting out to him that the Germans had already been there for twelve hours (and even, in fact, far beyond)? And if he had left those two cavalrymen absolutely free to continue to follow him or not, did that not show that he implicitly recognized that his actions no longer had anything to do with military operations and were now purely a matter of his own personal conduct? Excuse me, says S., I'm thinking out loud. Not at all, not at all, says the journalist: it's very interesting: I've never heard anyone talk about the defeat that way, but, and I'm sorry to come back to this: you yourself, at that moment . . .

S. and his little cousin (she is about seven years old, as is he) entice the daughter of the tenant farmer into the "little house" to play and forcibly raise her skirt to confirm that she does not wear panties: a soft, hairless little vulva which he touches with surprise, thighs, legs stamping, bursting free: flees in tears, humiliated. A month later, S., on vacation with his family, receives a postcard on which his cousin has written: "M——tte is wearing panties." Years later, S. asks what became of her. "Same as her sister! . . ." they answer with a shrug (the sister, living in the city and kept by some rich landowner, sometimes came on Sunday to visit her parents: getting off the tramway alone, twisting her high heels in the alleyway that ran alongside the garden where the family was having tea, scarcely responding with a nod of the head to her timid greetings. Very beautiful, always dressed in dark colors: a black diamond. Dora M—— also a black diamond).

In the Serbian villages of the Sava plain, garlands of red peppers are hung every fall over the walls of the whitewashed houses. When S., standing on the embankment by the road, tries to take a photograph, a woman whose head is covered with a scarf hurries to hide behind the corner of a house. The hamlets are surrounded by a palisade made of pointed stakes thrust into the ground. Apart from the woman who hid, there is no one to be seen other than a few children, barefooted despite the rainy weather and the cold, and who come and hold out their hands.

The magnolia in the corner of the garden is having difficulty recovering after being transplanted. Despite continual watering its lower branches have lost several leaves. They turn yellow and fall to the ground at its base, stiff as cardboard and soon brown.

A damp warmth hangs in the bathing cabin which is set up every summer on the beach, where he is undressing. The under things (panties, slips, bras) of the girls who have changed before him hang from coat hooks. They shout at him from outside, asking isn't he ready yet, does he still need a nanny at fourteen years old?

S. tells the journalist that as Julien Sorel is led to the guillotine Stendhal writes that he finds himself "in fine courageous form" and that "walking in the fresh air is a delicious sensation for him" (Jesus how can anyone write—and what's more read—such inanities!), whereas the "fresh air" in which the four riders advanced (the bright sunshine, the peaceful countryside, the chirping birds) on the contrary made the thing shall we say . . . infinitely more shall we say . . . unbearable than it would have been if it had all happened at night, or in the rain, or in that mud so dear to the hearts of illustrators, or even in the middle of a bombardment, or in the frenzy of a charge, an assault, circumstances in which the mind might find (S. says "might" because he has never had the opportunity to take part in such things) some support in a certain giddiness, a certain exaltation inspired by action. But good God . . .

In Dallas, the professor at the university where he is invited to speak is more than anything else eager to show him "the biggest department store in the world" (bigger than Macy's in New York, he says) of which S. retains the memory of kilometers of false Louis XV or Chippendale living rooms, of cretonnes, of interminable ranks of vests, shirts, motorcycles, and farming machines, and only after that does he take him to the place (a sort of square) and show him the window from which the President's assassin fired, and S. says he must have been a hell of a shot, because at that distance, even with a telescopic sight, imagine trying to put a bullet into the head of a pin, a ping-pong ball at best, and in a moving car, not very very fast of course, but all the same faster than a walking horse. . . .

. . . Good God! To say that walking in the fresh air is a "delicious sensation" for someone who is about to die, good God! The sun, the birds, the green fields, the blue sky, the sweet air! When from one minute to the next he'll become nothing more than one of those horribly motionless things like bags of sawdust! . . . The journalist saying But in the end if it wasn't despair, or abandonment, or abdication, or . . . , and S. saying that No it was nothing like that, that there might be a word for it, but that it's usually given a meaning which . . . Hesitating again (and for a moment he can once again make out that same indifferent and threatening hum, that sort of ambient noise, that unwavering rumble, with no more substance than a weak, single vibration in which all the agitation of the world outside melds together, in which all the violence, the passions, the desires, the griefs, the terrors are neutralized), and finally he says Melancholy, the journalist exclaiming Melancholy! . . . looking at him from behind the rimless lenses of his doctorlike glasses, eyebrows raised, with a look grown skeptical again, disapproving, almost irritated . . .

Narrow mouth hidden beneath the bush of hairs, which the finger penetrates. Like a little animal endowed with its own life lurking there as if awaiting prey, a trap growing moist, sometimes already open, lips, folds, little tongue. In French slang compared to a cat or a mussel "'Oh how I'd love to eat mussels!' says Albertine. 'But my dear,' says Marcel, 'mussels were the thing to eat in Balbec!'" (Balbec, where he suspects her of having had an affair with a woman.) "Little slit" for Luther (he is warned that if he goes to Worms there is a good chance he will be burned alive (the scandal of the Indulgences): he goes anyway). Like the other students at summer school in Cambridge, one night S. takes a girl

228

to the river that flows beneath the medieval edifices (a hump-backed bridge where one can see, in a stone ball that ornaments the parapet, the dug-out spot where, it is claimed, a queen used to hide the key to her room for her lover—Elizabethan era: another little slit under the heavy, pearl-embroidered skirts). Upstream, the river snakes lazily through the countryside. Invisible in the darkness, some of them almost touching, the long flat punts moored along the banks under the low branches of the trees. No sound comes from them. Sometimes a muffled murmur, a weak splashing in the dark. After a few caresses the girl lets her panties be removed without too much difficulty, even raises her bottom to let them slip off. The inside of her bare thighs, softness, the bush, the slit, the warm, damp little animal. The first time, he is too overwhelmed to do anything. Mortified. Then a misunderstanding with the girl, to whom he apologizes for his impotence (he tells her he is "ashamed"). She misinterprets his words, believes that he is asking her forgiveness for having tried to force her, consoles him. During the day he skips his courses (Magdalen College), plays tennis on the lawn, spends hours watching the cricket matches on the esplanade in the center of town, surprised at the shouts of the spectators, whose enthusiasm he will never be able to understand, or else respectfully goes punting on the same river (upstream there is an inn where tea is served in a garden) with the rich German, Danish, or Italian girls he has met at the university (Kirlsten, Helga, Gina), who intimidate him. The English girls at the dance hall: salesgirls, secretaries, waitresses (Daisy, Winnie, Maisy). He gets their faces mixed up as well as their names. The next day takes to the river another one (a friend of the first) whom in all good faith he believes to be the same one. At first she seems surprised, slightly astonished, but lets him go on. This time it all goes smoothly.

Dressed in a toga, he delivers a speech on literature and art at the University of Bologna. There are more than thirty kilometers of streets lined with arcades in Bologna.

Punishment at the prison camp: clasping together the four corners of a tarpaulin, carry from one end of the yard to the other (about three hundred meters) a few shovelfuls of dirt, dump them, load them again, then carry them back. Not tiring but thought to be demoralizing.

The journalist repeating: Melancholy! Simply melancholy! You . . . and S. saying Yes. Simply, immediately afterward saying No it's not that simple either, not at all. Because it's an ambiguous word, easily misunderstood, saying that probably for the journalist . . .

In Austin, Texas, in a scrupulously maintained park, the first working oil well, long since out of use, still stands like a monument. In that same city, a few months before S.'s arrival, a madman armed with a rifle, shooting from a window, killed six or seven passersby. Before certain houses in the "Vieux Carré," in New Orleans, where most of the streets have kept their French names, you can still see the iron posts, topped with a little horse head in blackened bronze, to which people used to tie their horses. This neighborhood is now a tourist attraction where nightclubs and bars are lined up one after the other almost without interruption. In some of them, behind the bar, almost within reach of the drinkers resting their elbows on the counter, nude dancers wriggle, their nipples hidden by little cones of silvery cloth with fringed tassels hanging from them. One of them skillfully imparts a rotational movement to her breasts, so that the fringes of the silvery tassels whirl like little comets. Decked out in a cowboy hat, short white leather boots, and gauntlets, she finishes her dance arched backward, her knees half bent and spread wide apart while at the same time, in one quick gesture, she moves one arm behind her body and, from between her thighs, thrusts the barrel of a large nickel-plated revolver which she aims at the customers.

saying that probably for the journalist, as is generally the case, the word melancholy calls up those kind of more or less mawkish images beloved of the English Pre-Raphaelites, the washed-out colors, languid women, dreamy eyed, or else, at best, that angel draped in a long robe, sitting pensively, head resting on one hand, the other hand about to drop a useless compass, surrounded in the engraving by a multitude of allegorical accessories whose accumulation recalls the poet's lamentation, *"La chair est triste, hélas, et j'ai lu tous les livres,"* and S. says that it was in fact exactly the opposite: not those mauves, those pinks, those pale greens, those irises, those chlorotic Ophelias, nor that allegorical jumble of discarded books, useless compass, that bitter reverie, but something violent crying out in protest, furious, gagged but screaming: I'd never wanted so much to live, I'd never looked so hungrily, so marvelingly, at the sky, the clouds, the fields, the hedges. . . .

Everyone has seen photos in illustrated newspapers or magazines showing that main street in Las Vegas which by day stretches out like some temporary and rather unimpressive row of fairground attractions, as you see in the outskirts of some cities, but which at night suddenly streams with lights, diamondlike, dazzling, and artificial. One of the principal establishments is named Caesar's Palace, approached from outside by something that resembles, on a smaller scale, the esplanade that extends out from Saint Peter's in Rome, half embraced by a copy, scaled down but nevertheless imposing, of Bernini's colonnade in which, between the shafts, marble reproductions of ancient statues are set out, discoboli, nymphs, goddesses, or satyrs. Inside, in a vast rotunda, stand rows of tables used for various games: roulette, baccarat, *trente et quarante,* blackjack, among which the waitresses circulate, wearing short Roman-style white silk tunics and gold belts, with one shoulder bared. No less than theirs, the faces, made up and porcelainlike, of the tuxedoed croupiers presiding over the games are impassive, like masks permanently set, young or old, made of the same material, like vulcanized rubber, as insensitive (or alien) to boredom as to murder or pleasure. Along with the other gamblers, S. lays down a random bet on the green surface of one of the tables, and the figure standing at the far end almost immediately makes it disappear, wielding his rake robotically. S. bets again on another number and the same thing happens. Other establishments, more or less luxurious, follow one upon the next along the diamond street. In one of them whose sign reads THE CIRCUS, the betting tables are set out beneath a large net with trapeze artists flying overhead. In another, less opulent and with an old-fashioned decor, aging poker players, with the faces of farmers or traveling salesmen, sometimes in shirtsleeves, silently observe each other, sitting at round tables in a vast room whose walls are covered in red wallpaper and decorated with large paintings in heavy frames, depicting, in an overdone style, naked women lying on couches. Outside, in the night lit up as if it were broad daylight, beneath the intersecting beams of the searchlights, the steeples of little chapels can be seen here and there, symbolically topped with a giant wedding ring, set edge-on, which slowly turns on its axis atop a luminous sign indicating that the ceremony can be held at any hour and listing the prices, with or without the ring.

At the roulette table of the Divonne-les-Bains casino Dostoevsky loses everything, down to his wife's earrings. In *The Gambler,* he draws an amused portrait of the passion that possessed him for many years, to the point of forcing him to borrow a hundred talers from Turgenev, against whom he then turned all his hatred for having consented to the loan. In *The Idiot,* he tells of an execution he witnessed in Paris and describes the condemned man's terrible walk to the scaffold. He himself had felt the sensations experienced by a man facing an imminent violent death when he was the victim of that simulated execution toward which a group of supposed conspirators, him among them, was led. He describes that devastating, melancholy hunger with which the condemned man looks at the world around him (the glint of the sun on the gilded onion dome of a church, the houses, the people) which will continue to exist whereas in a few moments he himself will be nothing.

To the eyes of the traveler whose airplane approaches Japan from Anchorage, the first islands appear like oyster shells, brown, laid out atop the glimmering ocean. Unlike the oysters eaten in Europe, with their soft shapes formed by an accretion of calcium carbonate, the ones they serve you in Japan, like its islands, are in the form of broad cones, folded into a fan, with pointed spines fitting neatly into each other. Once open, the sharp edges of the shells form a sort of lacework of points linked together by nacreous membranes. On the other side of the Pacific, between Bogotá and Lima, the airplane flies over a stretch of the Andes cordillera which has that same look of folded, arid cones linked together to form a chain of pink pyramids, adjoined at their base by the thick carpet of the virgin forest, which then fades away.

The journalist is gone now, him, his tape recorder, his Swiss watch with time spinning in circles at different speeds, his face at once curious, interested, and puzzled. Closing the door behind him, S. goes to the window and opens it in order to air out the room, where a bluish layer of smoke is hanging. It is about six o'clock and the roar of the traffic now slaps him full in the face along with the fresh air from outside. He tells himself that he smokes too much and one of these days something is going to happen to him. The star-shaped leaf that was twirling around is still now and the shadow of the buildings to the west has covered the entire square. Resting his elbows on the window ledge he watches the cars streaming past below him, as they stop at the red light to let the pedestrians cross and then start off again, their engines roaring louder than before. Through the leaves, he can see the city workers taking down the poles of the tents that shelter the display cases for the market, carrying them to the trailer behind the truck and loading them inside. The uprights are steel tubes, about four centimeters in diameter, set vertically at regular intervals into sockets installed for that purpose in the concrete of the esplanade. They support horizontal crosspieces, not as heavy, to which are attached the waxed canvas tents, which they roll up and also carry to the trailer. Tomorrow afternoon they will perform this task in reverse. The market is held three times a week: Sunday, Wednesday, and Friday. The workers put up the poles and tents on Saturday afternoon, they take them down on Monday, they put them back up on Tuesday, they take them down once again on Wednesday, and put them up once again on Thursday, taking them down on Friday afternoon, and so on. The support rods used to be made of wood. Now they are naturally much heavier. Walking with long strides, like mountain men or peasants, the workers, with agile, mechanical movements, never pausing, use their right hands to position (or remove) the poles and tents which they carry in bundles on their left shoulder. They do not speak, do not address each other except to shout to the truck driver to move forward as their work progresses. From nearby, one can see their expressionless faces, absent, their gaze as if absent as well, fixed a few meters in front of them on the sockets into which they will insert the uprights or on the trailer as they walk toward it. In the past, also, these workers wore something like wooden buskins on their feet, about ten centimeters high, so that they could easily reach the crosspieces and tents when they raised their arms. Nowadays they are probably hired on the basis of their height and seem to have no difficulties with their task. Above the sound of the traffic, S. can hear the metallic clatter of a carelessly dropped upright (or crosspiece) rebounding over the concrete. At first the workers, trying to save their strength, proceeded by noisily dragging the uprights and crosspieces behind them over the concrete, holding one end of the bundle under their arm. But there must have been complaints about the noise from the neighbors, because now they always carry them over their shoulder. The esplanade forms a square of about fifty meters on a side. There are twenty parallel rows of uprights. Each row holds twelve of them, except for eight rows cut off by the subway entrance, which reduces their number by four. The total number of uprights is thus $12 \times 12 + 8 \times 8$, thus $144 + 64$, thus 208. One of the magpies comes swooping down into the thick foliage concealing the nest and disappears. She must be bringing food to the young born in the last season. The shadow of the buildings bordering the square on the west now cuts across the mass of leaves at its peak, almost horizontally. After a moment, the roar of the traffic becomes too much. S. closes the window and suddenly there is silence. On the way to the bathroom, he notices that the journalist has forgotten his umbrella.

After a stop in Athens, where it is raining, the airplane flies (above Cyprus?) over a sea of iron gray clouds as night falls. About an hour later, you can see the fires of torches twisting here and there in the darkness (the desert?). A little later the airplane flies over Abu Dhabi. With its squares and its arcade-lined streets, its English lawns, its palm trees, the city, lit up as if in broad daylight, deserted, looks like one of those scale models cut out of cardboard, like the pavilions in the colonial expositions. At the airport, the passengers continuing on to New Delhi are not allowed off the plane and, with Roger C——, S. goes out for a moment onto the platform of the gangway. The air is warm, damp. A new crew is coming on board. Pilots, stewards, and stewardesses carrying little bags meet each other. One of the stewardesses coming on board says she's spent a wonderful day at the beach where the water was wonderful. One of the young stewardesses from the departing team asks if there are sharks. The airplane is being refilled with kerosene. Roger C—— loudly sniffs the air and says: Ahhh . . . You can smell the oil here! . . . Everyone laughs.

A brick smokestack stands on the other side of the bay. "Pituitary sea." Between the Tower of Daedalus and the little rocky peninsula across from it, the sloping ground is now covered with cement. Something like a seal was swimming in the gray-green water, sending out a spray of gray foam, then emerged, completely naked (it is November and S. does not feel overdressed in his raincoat), balding, his hair and his gray beard dripping with water, his pubic hair also clinging to his body because of the water, his member pink and retracted ("the sea was coming out his ears"). In town: a punk with three safety pins through one cheek.

The first time, he is in the middle of waxing his leggings, one foot on the rustic bench of untreated wood that the cavalrymen built in the clearing along with a table. The sergeant and two men from the squad are discussing harvests and hay baling. At the same time as he hears the sound of the trumpet, he sees the corporal on duty running toward them, twisting his ankles in the deep mud of the path leading to the pond, rutted by the horses' hooves. As soon as he is within shouting range, he cries out: Alert! S. freezes, his can of wax in his hand. He looks, inside the little crater dug by the repeated passage of the brush through the red wax, at the metal of the can, which shines like a silvery moon.

The second time, eleven years later, he freezes again, leaning over the bathroom sink, his toothbrush in one hand, the glass in the other. He watches a deep red blood clot slide slowly down the enameled, concave surface, like a little piece of veal liver, leaving a pink trail behind it. Outside, the weather is fine and he can hear the voices of the children playing in the park.

The third time, forty years later, he only just has time to run from the elevator to the door of his room, struggle to fit the key into the lock, kick open the door, quickly undo his fly, and, before he even has time to pull down his underwear, already red, to feel the warm spray of red urine which he watches spattering over the toilet bowl, his ears thrumming, buttoning his trousers again and going to sit down in one of the armchairs in the room. After a moment, he pulls his chair near the table and calls the Embassy to say he won't be able to come to dinner. He puts the telephone back into its cradle and stays sitting in the wing chair. He has lit only one lamp and the huge room is bathed in a grayish half light. Two years before the same thing happened to one of his friends, who died shortly after. He knows the name: hematuria. He waits for someone from the Embassy who will take him to the hospital. He sits in the same armchair, motionless, for some

236

time. Finally he looks through his pockets, pulls out a cigar, and lights it.

Each of the three times he thinks: Now. Now. Now. . . .

At nightfall of the first day, the cavalrymen, who have been riding since morning, arrive in a little village where there are not enough barns, stables, and cowsheds to house the entire squadron and S.'s squad is forced to sleep on the tile floor of a kitchen. At dawn, the woman brings them steaming coffee. She is accompanied by a little boy, about three years old, with curly blond hair. He is not fully awake and he looks curiously at the cavalrymen. He says What are you doing here soldier? S. gaily rubs his head and says: As you see, we're out for a stroll. The squadron has gone about three kilometers when, behind him, he hears the echoes of muted explosions, sending shockwaves through the air. The sky is overcast, the ceiling of clouds quite low, and no one has seen the airplanes. As they turn around in their saddles the riders cannot see the village they have just left, situated in a slight dip in the terrain. A thick column of gray smoke rises from the spot.

The fine pearl gray serge of those riding breeches under which you could see the moving lump of his hand as he pocketed his change purse after having paid the terrified woman for the beers (or maybe it was only the handkerchief he'd used to wipe the foam from his lips). Blood soaked just five minutes later? Or maybe not, since he fell to one side. The bricks of the walls: not smooth like the mechanical bricks they make today but pockmarked, rough: red-brown, violet brown, some of them almost blue, a gray blue, ferrous. Pulled from the depths of the earth. Mining region not far away.

As they advance the regular echo of the cannon becomes more muted. One of the five horses (fatigue, wound?) shoes, which means that the shoe on the hoof of one of his back legs strikes that of a front leg, producing a bright, metallic sound. This ringing is not regular, with every footstep, but only occasional.

Melancholy. S. thinks that he ought to have told the journalist it was like when the surgeon stops making just the one ritual morning visit in the company of his staff of interns, and, at seven or eight o'clock in the evening, on the pretext of having forgotten his hat, or his gloves, or of going to dinner at the home of some friends who just happen to live near the clinic, comes into your room accompanied only by the rustling of the nun's starched skirts, "just on a whim," "for a quick good evening to our patient, since I was in the neighborhood," and, from the way he looks at you, his face split by a broad smile, you understand that the dear patient is not well at all and a little later the nun comes back with the same papery rustling of her starched skirts, now holding a syringe in the air, its needle pointed upward, her thumb on the piston, and you say But you've already given me my shot this evening and she answers This one is to help you sleep better, and as she goes out she leaves the door of the room half open and you stay there alone looking at the distorted rhombus of light projected onto the ceiling by the nearest street lamp and the shadow play of the tree leaves which now and then appear, trembling, at the lower, narrower end, with the one difference that on your horse you did not have a raging fever, the air entered and exited your lungs without your even knowing it, and your body was full of life.

Lying on his bed, eyes open, thinking of that thing inside him, red (or what did it look like? cavern, darkness). Watching the sky slowly grow light in the frame of the window, listening to the first noises of the day inside the clinic, the nuns' quiet footfalls on the linoleum, the rustlings of their heavy skirts, the door of the *tisannerie* creaking. Little by little also the first cars outside on the quay. Then full daylight, the thin ray of sunlight on the wall facing the bed, first orange, then yellow, then lemon colored, growing thinner, then only a thread which seems to sparkle for a moment, then going out. A little later the cool, husky voices of the fishwives, singing . . .

For four months he will remain in this bed, forbidden to get up. It is summer. He's been brought home from the clinic. In the frame of the window, he can see the top of the house next door, its tile roof and one of its windows. Dawns, sunny or rainy days, sometimes thunderstorms, in a slow progression. Above the roof he watches the clouds rise up and gather together, the sky growing black, the light changing. The rain spattered over the tiles in a profusion of plumes, the roofs changed color, became shiny, as if varnished, reflecting the newly returned blue of the sky, dried, pink ocher, then spotted yellow in places by the lichens. Certain evenings, once a week, he could see the neighbor girls preparing to go out. During the day, they set their shoes on the window ledge to let them dry, covered with whiting which they had applied with a toothbrush. Then they turned out the lights, left, and everything was black, window and façade. Late at night the rectangle of the window lit up again, yellow, as if hanging in the dark, and he could follow their comings and goings as they got ready for bed, or rather (the window was set higher than his) the brief passages of their upper bodies separated by more or less long moments during which he could see only the dihedral formed by the ceiling and the back wall, against which the moving shadows of their invisible bodies could be seen in profile, sometimes climbing up to the ceiling, overflowing onto it, stretching out, broken in two. Finally they turned out the light, everything was black again, and he began to think once more of the thing, that blood red hole inside his chest where tiny animals gnawed, gnawed, gnawed. He was not suffering. He waited. Every day he saw the sky grow pale, first imperceptibly, then the black profile of the roofs and chimneys, then their colors returning little by little.

Later they moved him to the country. It snowed. He could see the mountains with their sparkling snowcaps in the distance. Toward the end of the winter it rained a great deal. He listened to the sound of the rain in the orchard. Now he could get up, go and sit in an armchair near the window, first for one hour, then two. On the bare branches, black and glistening, the diamond-like strings of water drops slowly slipped along. They chased each other, gathered together, came unstuck, dug little craters in the ground as they fell, uncovering gravel more brightly colored than before. There was a large apple tree in the garden and, in the spring, he watched it slowly cover with flowers. At night, at the end of the valley, he could hear the trains coming nearer, slowing down, stopping with a long shriek of their brakes. In the silence, as the locomotive regularly let out jets of steam, he could hear the voice of the railway employee announcing the name of the station, walking alongside the wagons, sometimes slamming a door. The train whistled, started off again. A little afterward the iron bridge could be heard groaning under its weight. Then the noise shrank away, grew more distant, stopped. Well before dawn, on market days, he could hear, like a hum, the engines of the trucks bringing the calves and cows to the marketplace, the little noises of the vendors setting up their displays. The peasants sold poultry, eggs, and goose livers which the black-dressed women presented on immaculate cloths with long hollows in the creases left by the iron, like those anatomical models made of colored wax (red, blue, green, yellow), spleen, pancreas, lungs, that you see in the windows of the specialized shops around medical schools. Toward the end of April, at night, the nightingales began to sing. They called to each other here and there, echoing through the silence of the valley. The nights were full of fresh odors. In the darkness the flowering apple tree seemed to glow faintly, as if phosphorescent.

4

With the stride of time,
vast as the stride of some infernal giant.—Flaubert

After the Secretary General had taken his leave of them, and although there was only a small distance left to travel, the same bus that had brought them here, running red lights at the intersections, left the fifteen guests before an edifice in the form of a Greek temple, and as they got off the bus one after the other, the one who had played Nero in the movies said that speaking as a Roman emperor and as the literary great-grandson of Tolstoy he could recognize in this massive edifice what was called here (by the one or several satraps who had had it built more than a century before, in imitation, with its pediment and its columns, of an ancient sanctuary—except that it was four times as large) a simple horse ring, and let's hope, he said, that no one (none of the one or more satraps of today) will ask them to gallop snorting through the sawdust. But that wasn't it, although (with the one difference that there was no sawdust and that they were not asked to run) what was planned was indeed a spectacle—or an exhibition—for which, lacking thoroughbreds from Kyrgyzstan or imported at great expense from England (but they themselves (the fifteen guests) were also imported products in a way—although temporarily so), they were here as something like the exotic animals (the two Blacks from Harlem, the Ethiopian painter in tribal costume, the one-time husband of the most beautiful woman in the world, the elegant Hispanic diplomat no doubt expected to play the role of ringmaster) that traveling circuses exhibit for the delectation of the people of the countryside, who come running to watch passing by, among others, the giraffe, the zebra, the dromedary, and the couple of mischievous chimpanzees, parading in single file between the twin rows of an indistinct crowd pressed together in the dark, hundreds of pale spots which, blinded by the beams of the floodlights aimed at them, the fifteen guests could distinguish or rather vaguely make out amid what looked like propaganda posters, doubled by the inevitable haunting bands of red calico with their incomprehensible Cyrillic characters, the same ones that could be seen, tenacious, educational, and imperious, spread out on the lawns of the parks or the façades of the colossal edifices raised to the glory of the workers, of the giant rockets, of the police corps, or of the public transport system: the subway (also monumental, made of precious marble), its entryways through which flow those same workers with their inevitable carryalls, plastic bags, or (for the more well-to-do) briefcases, in which, says the merry Nero of local origin, if one were to open them, one would find, just as in the carryalls or plastic bags, the pickled herring, the four potatoes, or the pair of shoes (even two times too large or two times smaller) bought like the herring or the potatoes completely at random as currency for later exchanges, according to the whim of chance, depending on the goods for sale at market that day, sometimes not even in a store but directly on the sidewalk where a truck was being unloaded.

Then, still blinded by the spotlights, squinting, sitting in a row on a dais, the circus parade, all together, above the turbulent tide of faces scrutinizing them as they would the woman shot from a cannon, the belly dancer, the savage crowned with feathers, and the wrestler with tattooed arms, while they crossed and recrossed their legs, listening uncomprehendingly to the last of the interminable speeches that had punctuated their encounter, from time to time discreetly pulling up the ends of their sleeves, casting a quick glance at their watches, trying to gauge how much time they would need to reach the airport.

Then at the hotel, now no longer with the fourteen others but alone, suitcase fastened (and to tell the truth no more alone—or rather less alone—than he had been among them over the past two days, ever since he had protested against that (but that what? declaration, appeal, motion?) which was supposed to cap off the verbose exchanges of accumulated speeches: a black sheep, the object of a silent but insinuating ostracism (or suspicion, reproof, repulsion), alone, then (because as it happened his airplane was the last to leave) in his room (he told the story a few hours later in the bathroom with the vermilion pipes, as he was brushing his teeth, laughing, the foam of the toothpaste overflowing his lips as he looked in the mirror, over his shoulder, at the naked body sitting on the edge of the bathtub), alone again in the car parked before the hotel, beginning to lose his patience, trying to speak to the driver who understood neither French nor English, thrusting his wristwatch forward before his eyes and tapping it with a furious finger, then saying Ah finally! the female interpreter with the gray, tired, ageless face appearing in the doorway, walking down the front steps, saying I've been looking for you everywhere what a shame you could have watched it on television with us We saw you when HE shook your hand it was, and S. saying Yes it was very nice very nice HE is very likable very great honor Head of State very amiable very Shall we go What are we waiting for? the interpreter woman saying Right away right away don't be anxious we have all the time in the world, saying the name (the one he'd never been able to pronounce himself but which he had finally, by ear, come to recognize as that of the head interpreter), saying that he was eager to accompany him to the airport himself, saying Oh there he is! the fat jovial man coming down the front steps in turn, also saying Don't worry we have all the time in the world, settling in, closing the door behind him, the car finally driving through the city then along the road leading to the airport, the city, the new Jerusalem, the Mecca of future ages above which (above the marble catafalque where, guarded by armed sentries, had been sleeping for the past sixty years (awaiting what resurrection, what Melusina with her magic wand?) not a mummy but that embalmed body, dressed in a three-piece suit, his goateed face dusted off, made up—or freshly repainted—the first of every month), the indifferent red silk flag still fluttering in the snowy beam of the spotlights, fading into the distance behind them as he (S.) responded, without listening, to the head interpreter's words, the car bouncing over the potholed surface of the road, and only the inky darkness now, the head interpreter repeating Don't worry we have all the time in the world, and you . . . , the headlights of the occasional oncoming vehicle illuminating the inside of the car from time to time, the fat man's jovial face and the woman's faded face emerging from the darkness for a moment, sculpted, then submerged again, then the lights of the airport, then the interior, too vast, with only a handful of travelers, as if empty, silent, uninhabited, then, still accompanied by the head interpreter and the woman with the tired face, sitting in one of the plush armchairs of the VIP lounge, the woman with the tired face saying No don't trouble yourself: how many rubles, dollars? Caviar? Fine . . . , disappearing, coming back soon after, saying No caviar but this is very good a salmon you'll see, setting on the table something flat wrapped in newspaper and tied with a string, then the waiting room for the flight, like all the waiting rooms in all the airports in the world, with the one difference that in order to get in you had to show your passport to an armed guard who would unlock the door and lock it again immediately afterward, made entirely (chairs, floor, walls, ceiling) of one single material, artificial, synthetic, which was so to speak something like the opposite of material, that is, not leather, iron, wood, stone, or brick, but something uniformly brown, uniformly smooth, uniformly shiny, and still that sort of emptiness, of silence, the passengers (almost all of them men in severe suits) alone or in little groups, arriving one after another, equally silent, with closed faces that also seemed like the very materialization of silence, sitting down, sometimes taking a document from a briefcase and examining it, sometimes exchanging a few words in low voices, their gaze mechanically following the worker, his face equally inexpressive, sitting on the motorized sweeper, who, seeming to take no notice of them, endlessly ran his machine over the already gleaming floor, its quiet purr melding with the occasional whispers of the passengers and the words, also whispered now, of the head interpreter (as if in this place—or rather in this sort of box—the wait was like the prelude to some secret ceremony, semiclandestine, reserved for a small number of initiates), then, the silence still unbroken by any call or signal—none perceptible at least—the passengers putting away their papers, standing up, heading toward the glass door unlocked by another policeman with a revolver on his hip, the passports checked a second time (and while, deaf to any protest from the head interpreter, a second policeman examined, with a sleepwalker's slowness, page after page—including those without a single stamp on them—the passport that he had held out to him, he (S.) turned around, once again watched the worker, his face more expressionless than ever, he too as if sleepwalking, as he continued to turn in circles, sitting on his little machine, in the now empty waiting room), then, delivered at least of the woman with the tired face but still accompanied by the fat interpreter, making his way down the ramp, then finally in the cabin of the airplane (belonging to a foreign airline), the fat interpreter getting him settled into his seat (as if, he later said, he wanted to make sure that he (S.) was well and truly on board and to be certain that he was finally rid of him but, he said, I'm joking Surely it was nothing more than courtesy—although he (the head interpreter) insisted on securely buckling the seatbelt himself), handing the newspaper-wrapped package to one of the stewardesses, then warmly saying his good-byes, and S. finally alone, looking at the cabin around him, three-fourths empty, distractedly paging through a brochure, the other passengers also settled in, still silent, their faces still as inexpressive, then the door of the cabin sealed shut, the access ramp moving away from the side of the airplane, the airplane beginning to back up slowly, then turning (and still silence inside the cabin, the passengers absorbed in reading foreign newspapers distributed by the stewardesses), slowly moving toward the runway, lurching, turning, finally standing still, then a pause, then the roar of the engines, the airplane trembling in place, shaken, then liberated, rushing forward, gathering speed, the lights of the airport streaming by horizontally, faster and faster, outside the windows, the airplane no longer vibrating, the lights now streaming by diagonally, sinking away, disappearing, and suddenly voices, laughter, the passengers addressing each other, some of them already in shirtsleeves, already on their feet, calling out, the busy stewardesses coming and going along the central aisle, still steeply inclined, and soon the clinking of glasses tapped together, exclamations, bursts of laughter—and him now trying to tell everything pell-mell as he brushes his teeth and as if he himself were finding it difficult to believe all these things which (although they had only ended for him a little less than two hours earlier, strapped solicitously into an airplane seat) already seemed unreal, if not slightly fantastic: the fifteen guests—or rather the fifteen sideshow phenomena—brought together (chosen, selected —according to what criteria, what references?) by, it seemed, some functionary thumbing through some mysterious Social Register or simply letting his hand wander idly over a map (New Delhi, Hollywood, Addis Ababa, Detroit, Madrid, Harlem, Istanbul, Havana . . .) and pointing at random with a mischievous index finger: but why me? . . .), and as for the question of why it was necessary to send these fifteen samples or specimens by a chartered jet to the very heart of Asia, to that place where the steppe, as flat as a croquet field, abuts the fantastic mountain (or rather heap, pile, chaos of rock, snow, and ice) whose base was once a meeting place for caravans loaded with silks, jewels, or damascened weapons and was now the site of the city whose central square was ornamented with the statue of the proconsul wrapped tightly in his leather jacket, with a leather hat, brandishing his philosophical Bible in one hand, the other resting on the butt of a cylinder machine gun to which he had given his name: and now no more camels, no more caravansary, no more tents, bundles of silk, no more merchants in turbans or not, Turkomans, Mongols, Chinese, Persians, Chechens, or Greeks, no more markets, no more trails: broad shady avenues (at least

248

in the part of the city that foreigners were allowed to see) above which (there were also some on the lawns) limply undulated the inevitable haunting red banners on which nevertheless the Cyrillic characters set out their proclamations (or injunctions) in two languages (although, it was said, the million inhabitants who now peopled the city included more than forty communities, including Jewish and German), the militia dressed in the same brown uniforms as the men who pored over passports at the airport, in boots, with revolvers at their hips, controlling with their expansive gestures, in the oversized intersections, nothing more than the circulation of buses with peeling paint, with dented bodies, weighed down by their overflowing cargo of travelers and scraping the roadway with their undersides as they left a stinking wake of black smoke behind them, and, finally, after the exchange of speeches, after having each planted a tree before the municipal library, were taken for a ride in an airplane furnished like a salon over the fantastic mountains, that banquet hall, those cups of caviar, those sturgeons, those smoked tongues, those bottles of vodka, that top table presided over by the current proconsul, also from the West (but no more jacket or leather hat, and the machine guns now invisible—at least in the banquet hall), dressed in an elegant suit and surrounded by the members of the government—or who were at least supposed to be the local government: twelve men also dressed in three-piece suits topped with the same round face, flat and yellow, with the same slanted eyes, the same outraged (or maybe simply patient) dignity, the same mute, permanent smile, and then, at dessert, that declaration (or motion, or proclamation, or what . . .), that grandiloquent, ridiculous capstone to five days of boredom in which one verbose, hollow address followed another, and how he (S.) had stood up, had left the room, and the hero of labor drowsing on his sofa, and the furious interpreter, the Hispanic diplomat, the other interpreter, the classic good cop bad cop routine . . .

And maybe, trying to tell of all that, he'd been speaking for a longer time—maybe he'd begun well before brushing his teeth:

in the car, perhaps, as she drove (interrupting himself, saying You're right it stinks, turning around in his seat, reaching into the back for the flat package wrapped in newspaper and tied with string, with Cyrillic letters printed on it: he rolled down his window, threw it out, saying Sorry She said there was no more caviar, There was no perfume shop either and in any case I don't know if they even make any there or else it stinks too I should have given it to the guy on his electric sweeper At some point he must stop turning circles and go home Still the good old fat interpreter did suggest to the stewardess that she put it in the refrigerator but maybe sixty dollars worth of salmon (no she said they didn't want rubles they only sold in exchange for dollars) . . . sixty dollars worth of rotting salmon might make some dog here very happy?—now the car had left the airport parking lot: he could see, appearing and disappearing in the white glow of the headlights, the birch trees with their black-spotted, silvery trunks, the pines, the pink granite walls of the trenches that the ice had not yet veiled with gray, then the lights of the city glinting like diamonds in the dark)—or maybe he had begun even earlier, as soon as he had sat down in the car, as soon as she had started off, saying What a day! About twelve hours now, eleven counting the time change but twelve counting the fact that, as in the army when the colonel came for inspection, we had to be ready an hour in advance and wait all that time for the bus that took us to the Holy of Holies, and then that guy with his port-wine birthmark sitting at the end of the table as if he were presiding over a Cabinet meeting and the rest of us—I mean the fifteen sideshow freaks bearded lady hermaphrodite Negroes five-footed calf dromedary trained crocodile etc.—all around him listening to the simultaneous translation delivering his speech we the representatives of the global intelligentsia No more vodka now only little bottles of mineral water and plates of tea biscuits Apart from that for one of the two most powerful men in the world he's very likable very well bred Educated in Switzerland maybe while the others let themselves get caught done in with bullets to the back of the neck but anyway even if he himself never used a pis-

tol to do in one of his former associates he nevertheless must have
sent some of them to be frozen alive somewhere near the Arctic
Circle or in central Asia because in their country you can't reach
the position he holds without in one way or another stepping
over a few corpses Having said that, very nice really very proper
very elegant apparently he has his clothes made in Italy No more
field marshal's tunic or zinc-colored gabardine overcoat look of
a sullen Pekinese on the contrary a blue suit well cut tie in the
Italian style Italian collar and all the rest underwear as well no
doubt Apart from that maybe a few gaps in his vocabulary for
example dixit values of humanism must now come before values
of the proletariat his country now wide open to everything:
American books American records American music American
films in a word all Culture with a capital C except he said Except . . .

The deafening 105s continued firing almost until nightfall. For
about an hour, the sound of hoarse voices came occasionally
from the radio car, speaking indistinct, brusque words and alternating with dance music or sopranos singing. Then, an order
having been given, the artillerymen busied themselves around
their weapons which were hooked up to the trailers and when
everything was ready the column lurched forward in the dark.
The moon had come up, bringing out a bluish gleam on the polished leather of the saddles of the horses gathered in the clearing.
A rumor had spread that the enemy paratroopers signaled to
each other and regrouped by imitating the hooting of an owl. The
cavalrymen stood around the horses, their carbines on their hips,
fingers on the triggers, starting at every tiny nocturnal noise coming from the forest. Earlier in the evening, they saw the camou-
flaged, trembling lights of a convoy slowly approaching, but
someone called out not to shoot.

To the right of the mirror above the sink hangs, behind glass, the
chubby-cheeked face of a cherub, with wings on either side, cut
from one of those chromographs popular at the end of the last

century and glued to a background of the same red that covers the heating pipes and the plumbing. The feathers of the wings have glints of gray green, pink, and lilac. The left side of the rectangle of the mirror is taken up by S.'s face. A sinuous line forms the boundary of the right side of his head, his neck, the connection to the shoulder, and the contour of the latter, which stands out, violently lit by the frosted ceiling lamp above the mirror, against the red panel of the half-closed door. The lower edge of the mirror cuts across his chest a little above the nipples. Beyond the little vials, the jars of cream, and various toiletries lined up on the ledge, he can see, behind him, the body of the woman sitting on the edge of the bathtub, her legs stretched out, her ankles crossed, her two hands lying flat on her long thighs. Still golden from the summer sun, her skin is colored a pale ocher, slightly pinkened, her breasts, protected from the sun, a pearly white. When she laughs the triangular shadows they cast play over her upper body, encroaching a little onto one of her arms. The water glass sitting on the ledge immediately below the mirror is of an emerald green, decorated with spiral fluting. Next to it sits a smaller vial, shiny black, with a gold label and topped with a cylindrical cap, also gold. When he brings the glass to his lips to rinse his mouth, his bent forearm hides the body of the woman from him and for a moment a ray of light glints off the rim. The toothpaste has left a white aureole around his lips. A second time he brings the glass to his mouth, sets it down, and a second time the reflection of his arm hides the woman sitting there, then reveals her.

"This, then, is the sad portrait of a man who, visibly, does not confine himself to writing poems in which gibberish, pessimism, and pornography follow one upon the other, but who at the same time turns his mind to thoughts of treason.

"Nevertheless, by reason of Brodsky's youth, he was forgiven many things. A great course of education was undertaken for him, and he was reminded more than once of the responsibilities he had assumed by giving himself over to antisocial activities.

"Brodsky did not draw the conclusions that were plain to see. He continues to live as a parasite."

(Leningrad Evening News)

Danger of arrest. His flight to Paris. In the southern city where he had taken up residence after the escape his past in Spain came to be known and caused him to be considered an extremist and denounced to the police. At the end of the nightmare he had lived through (that caricature of a war: the massacre of the squadron, exhaustion, hunger, captivity in the prison camp, his hunted flight through the woods, but especially that walk following behind the mad colonel), he feels nothing now but a sort of quiet indignation, indifference, and is content to follow the battle taking place to the east only as a spectator, hoping for a mutual exhaustion of the two sides, both of which he hates. He reads a great deal (all of Proust, the complete works of Balzac which he'd found in a leather-bound edition in a second-hand bookshop), does some painting, and in summer goes swimming at the beach where armed sentinels pace. (The heavy black boots making a hissing noise in the sand, the machine guns on their straps, the sweating faces under the round helmets; some days the ones not on duty mingle with the swimmers; scars, sometimes, on their boyish bodies, white, fragile.) At the request of friends, he sometimes houses an underground agent passing through town, or stores a more or less heavy suitcase (tracts, arms?) in his lodgings for a few days, neither asking nor seeking to discover what it contains.

To his amazement, the German police never made enquiries at his home in Paris after his escape. The best hiding place, he thinks. Paris in February, dark, cold, lugubrious. The elevated metro car dimly lit, the Montmartre tough in his unbuttoned SS uniform, his cap at a rakish angle, a girl on his knees. He conspicuously runs his hands over her breasts, slips a hand under her skirt, staring brazenly, his mouth twisted into an imbecilic fixed smile, at the handful of passengers, who pretend to look outside where everything is dark, except the yellowish reflections of their faces in the windowpanes (Glacière station).

During the day, the sky iron gray, an iron cold, the deserted streets now traveled only by the trucks or cars of the occupying forces, also iron gray. In one corner of his cellar he finds a little pile of coal left over from before the war and he parsimoniously burns it to heat one room of the apartment. When after a very short time the pile dwindles, he scrapes his hand along the floor of the cellar to collect the coal dust, which he forms into something like little lumps and wraps like big bonbons in packets of newspaper. Later, some friends will sell him a suitcase full of coal which he will carry or rather drag home in the metro.

He goes to an art school to draw, and when he can get hold of some coal he pays a few models to come and pose at his apartment. The little redhead funnily tries to interest him in coffee éclairs, which she sells. Another whose skin is of such a quality that when she undresses the light seems to flow from her pearly body, with transparent jade-green shadows. Another one, from Brittany, who posed for an old painter and who, naive, at his request (he ingeniously showed her reproductions of nudes by Ingres), shaved her pubic area. At the home of a painter friend, he meets a very young one with whom he falls in love (more precisely she is the one who entices him to her home while her lover, a riding master (or groom?) in a riding school, is away). Only just grown up: little round breasts, smooth hips, scarcely flared. Makes love like a greedy child. Naked in the blink of an eye. Doesn't even leave him time to caress her, starts to come right away as soon as she has put him inside her, one leg folded back, her arm alongside her buttock in order to grasp his member, which she holds in order to guide it precisely, looking him in the eye with a complicitous smile. Funny way of saying "I come too much." Jumps out of bed, graceful and childlike, as soon as he has overflowed inside her, and runs across the room to go and wash. A douche syringe with a long black tube, with a brick red bulb. The wall of the room decorated with a panoply of stirrups and spurs, bits, curb chain, riding crop. Exciting feeling of going to seed in this dubious Paris, vaguely sordid, where apart from the cars of the occupying forces the only things driving through the streets are bicycle-taxis pulled by men with gray, gaunt faces, filthy caps on their heads, transporting characters with faces that seem too prosperous: men in capes and women in turbans.

At the home of the friends who had sold him the coal he makes the acquaintance of D. M. Member of the old Surrealist group, she asks him to let her read the lines in his palm (the supernatural, hidden forces, occultism, etc., so dear to Breton). Gives a sudden start when she examines it but refuses to tell him what she has seen there. The apartment where she lives alone, on the Rue de S——: she also paints: the large room which serves as her studio, bare and empty except for two easels, canvases turned around and leaned against the wall, lying flat on the floor, and, a gift from Picasso, one of those masterpieces that artisans used to have to undertake before they could be admitted into the guild, this one a tour de force of woodworking, consisting of a spiral staircase in mahogany, about a meter high. On Picasso's recommendation (or order?), she endlessly returns to the same still-life subject: a pot full of aspidistras sitting on a table next to an alarm clock. The colors are emerald green for the plant's long leaves, brick red for the pot, white for the face of the alarm clock whose hands are also depicted, brown for the tabletop. The background is gray, modulated by black crosshatching. Depending on the canvas, the edges of the pot and the clock face are round or square. The form of the leaves and the austere colors also display minuscule variations. An austerity that fits with her custom of dressing in clothes made by (or rather her custom of being dressed by) that great couturier with the Mediterranean name (Balenciaga), and with his unfussy, rigorous style (*Espagne noire*).

At about the same time, a chance meeting in the street with one of the members of the underground he'd housed in P—— for a night. The dry face of a career soldier, inexpressive, without warmth, without coldness either, simply inexpressive. Tells him that the information network he directs has been suddenly forced to leave the headquarters where they were based. He asks him if for a few days—not long, he says, they have another possibility in sight—he could let them use his apartment. S. is unable to refuse. Starting the next day, four men also with a military air (bearing) will come and close themselves up every day in the room that he makes available to them. They encode dispatches that a young courier takes away every evening. The "few days" evolve into an occupation that will come to an end only with the departure of the enemy. The perfect location of the apartment, on the seventh floor, reached by a secondary staircase that continued up to the maids' rooms. On the pretext of the frequent power outages, it is agreed that every morning S. will tack a sheet of paper to his door with the words "Please knock loudly" written on it, so that should the Germans come and arrest him in the night and stay there lying in wait, the ones who arrive in the morning and do not see the notice will have only to keep climbing the stairs to the hallway leading to the maids' rooms, follow it, and come down again by the building's main staircase.

Apart from the obligation of getting up early to tack up the warning on the door, S. has no responsibilities, knows only by sight and by code name the four characters who come into his apartment every morning, and does not know how the messages that someone comes and picks up every evening are sent on. It was for no particular reason, only to amuse him, that one of the four strangers one day showed him how, with the help of two coordinates and some simple algebraic formulas defining lines and curves, it is possible to transmit a map (marshaling yard, barracks, junctions, artillery placements, etc.) by radio. Once acquitted of his morning task, he continues to lead the life of an indolent loafer in which his brief experience of combat (the pathetic, deadly role they made him play: an impression that they were ridiculing him, "they" referring not to one or several personages, some human or social category (politicians, generals), but to a sort of vague, facetious entity (History?), impersonal, mindless, and pitiless) remains as a trauma now so to speak encysted inside him like a foreign body, lodged there forever. Acts as he does only through a sort of automatism: neither a sense of duty, of a moral obligation, nor as a game, nor out of defiance (as is the case with the young courier from the "mailbox" who comes every evening to pick up the bulletins), not even out of pride. No more than he would have thought of throwing away his rifle and raising his hands as he ran through that railway trench like a rabbit under fire or of walking away from that lethal road where he followed along behind the colonel. The first time he heard the sirens, he went with everyone else living in the building down to the cellar where in awkward silence they press together, peer at each other, hastily dressed, their faces puffy with sleep, fearful. After that he stays in his room, listening to the sirens warbling and the antiaircraft guns firing, stretched out on his bed on the seventh floor, looking through the frame of his open window at the luminous flat surface that hangs motionless then slowly sinks in the sky through the searchlight beams, hearing a hail of steel shards falling and bouncing over the zinc rooftops here and there. Once, for some time, his gaze follows a dark red spot, like the glowing end of a cigarette, which slowly crosses the frame of the window from right to left along a slightly diagonal line, descending, then all at once plunges downward. The smoke from his cigarette suddenly takes on an acrid taste. He stubs it out and lies motionless in the dark, licking his burned finger.

He continues to paint, sees friends, goes out at night. Curfew, the black density, as if palpable, of the night, when the weather is cloudy: feeling one's way through the streets, bumping into benches or streetlights, counting the intersections to determine one's location. As in any country under some form of oppression, domestic or foreign, the fashion in the theater is for academic works that laboriously dust off the old myths, in which, dressed in chlamyses, peplums, with buskins on their feet, the grease-painted incarnations of Power, Right, and Justice confront each other by way of allusions with double meanings, briefly applauded by a knowing audience (sometimes, sitting in the best seats or strolling in groups of two or three at intermission, and theatrical themselves, a few uniforms with torsaded silver epaulets and red braid, with parade daggers, also proplike, on their hips, corseted, stiff, the collars decorated with oak leaves, a cross worn at the neck, topped by weathered faces with thin smiles, eaglelike eyes, like the delegation of some overly formal barbarous land, at once barbed, impassive, and Goethean).

And against this (against the laborious and erudite plays full of buskins, chlamyses, veiled allusions, and subversive winks), something which was like subversion itself, total, snickering, and worse, derision, execration not only of that glacial, haughty, metallic order, that stiff barbarity in suede gloves (or cloth for the underlings) but also (repudiation, derision, execration) of every sort of order, with or without torsaded silver embellishments, beginning with language itself, with every sort of propriety. And this: not the magical scene of a theater set, the magical costumes in ancient style, but a simple apartment, a drawing room (not a cellar, some secluded clandestine hideout: a drawing room, a cozy place, luxurious even, at the very heart of that city transformed into an armed camp, into a prison), and gathered inside, in a discreet well-bred murmur peppered with tinkling laughter, also well bred, not conspirators with the clothes and faces of reprobates but, amid the vague, subtle effluvia of costly perfumes, men and women in equally costly clothes, prosperous (not prosperous in the manner of the characters who had themselves driven around town, sitting on a bench, pulled by starving bicyclists: simply prosperous, because it was in their nature to be so, as it was in the nature of their companions to be perfumed and wrapped in costly dresses), and him (S.) in his coarse clothes (although he had bought them at black-market prices—but probably not at sufficient expense), unsophisticated, sitting there a little dazed, taking refuge in a corner, after the woman who had brought him there (maybe, he thought, as one exhibits a dog found in the street, a provincial cousin, as an elegant woman might find it piquant to bring with her, rather than the little beribboned Pekingese held under one arm, a grubby spaniel picked up from the sidewalk—or maybe as an act of defiance, as a way of getting back at someone? she who, as the official companion of the one whose long-awaited outpouring of execration and derision we were about to enjoy, was like the mastermind of all this, the queen of the day) had abandoned him: it was already July and things were beginning to come to an end, the tribe (what else could they be called, since that was what they wanted to be, the way they saw themselves: a race, a bloodline, an ethnic group, a primitive clan with its own shamans, customs, tortures, and ritual murders), the tribe of Huns, as they were contemptuously termed by the man with the cigar, with the fat baby face, pink and arrogant, who for almost a year had stood up to them single-handed, armed only with his jowls, his obstinacy, and his protruding lower lip, the army of barbarians in black boots and silver stripes who had advanced straight to the furthest end of the dusty or icy plains at the edges of Europe (if, that is, those snowy or parched expanses, those giant rivers, are still Europe . . .) now retreating, at bay, but still dangerous, like a dog backed into a corner, toe to toe, its chops pulled back over its silver teeth, submerged by the great numbers or rather the tidal wave of the ancient Horde pouring out of inexhaustible Asia while to the west a team of engineers and clergymen in mechanics' uniforms went about methodically or rather technically wearing down its rear guard: and in the middle (that is, between the two, between the bespectacled mechanics and the crashing waves of high-cheek-boned faces), between the two, then, that drawing room, that muted oasis of muted laughter, of costly perfumes, where men and women conversed in muted voices, their opulent clothes owing nothing to that black-market commerce in flour, cheese, or nonferrous metals but to the production and trade (buying, stockpiling, selling) of another sort of goods, such as books, paintings, poems, ideas, talent, success, all more or less full-fledged members, anointed, of a sort of secret society, some coterie or circle of initiates united also, in addition to success, talent, or fortune, by an unconditional and so to speak philosophical (he was moreover—or aspired to be—an expert linguist) veneration for a modern, bloodthirsty potentate incarnated in the appearance of a park watchman, with a jolly mustache and smile, with crew-cut hair topped not with a Caesarian crown of laurels but with a retired man's cap, the cap, the mustache, and the head sculpted in marble or stone, cast in bronze, in lead, or simply in plaster on the scale (the head alone) of a man standing upright, which, later, over the paving stones of the squares in which the pharaonic statue was erected to the applause of the same crowds, would roll, decapitated, lying (the head) on one cheek, or falling facedown, or faceup, carried away in the handcart of some scrap-iron dealer or on the planks of a simple garbage cart, still mustachioed, smiling, jolly, staring into space with his hollowed-out pupils, sly, metallic.

Later he (S.) would remember this: that sort of polite, muted aviary, the polite voices sometimes breaking through, the tinkling laughter, the muted conversations, little by little growing more muffled, little by little more discreet, then fading away entirely, then finally silence, with some sort of breathless excitement hanging in the air, some breathless curiosity (like, he later said, a girl awaiting, in trepidation—or rather, as they say, in anticipation—the man who will come and rape her: not her husband, her lover, or her fiancé: the brute to whom she will succumb in a rapture at once horrified, delicious, and brutal): and no chlamyses, no cardboard cuirasses, swords, no illuminated set, but only four chairs in a row occupied, along with two stooges (or so it seemed to him (S.), just arrived from his distant province: he didn't know them, maybe they were celebrities as well . . .) by the mistress and the master of the house, him with a skull not bald but shaven like a convict's, with the tortured face of a convict, twisted or rather convulsed, above the severe dandyish collar, the dandyish tie, and the dandyish suit, by some bizarre, guilty, and irremediable suffering, the young fashionable writer standing to the left and a little to one side, also elegant, as if pomaded, whose heavy chin vaguely recalled that of a movie comedian then in fashion, with a horselike jaw, but not as bony, encased in or rather softened by a slight pudginess and who, when he began to speak, to read, impassively, the scabrous stage directions, seemed to be savoring, rolling it around in his mouth, one of those soft Eastern sweets dusted with powdered sugar, in dull pastel colors—stage directions, onomatopoeia, insults, maledictions, or shouts which, like

260

the names of the characters (Big Foot, The Onion, The Pie, Silence, Thin Anguish), were to the subtle and erudite allusions of the ancient-style dramas what pebbles or rather paving stones might be to those melting, slightly acidic bonbons wrapped in waxed paper, pink, lemon, or gold, that they sell at intermission in movie theaters.

Then, the last tirade, the last enumeration, the last hail of stones ("sow tits"—"*gras double*"—"sausage"—"tripe"—"blood pudding"—"chancre"—"*fille de joie* and rhumba") thrown out or rather articulated by the readers, applause, enthusiasm, pearled shouts, embraces, the aviary now jabbering, deafening, swept or rather stirred by eddies above which, towering over them by a head (not that he was taller than most of the other people randomly squeezed together there, laughing, calling out to each other, congratulating each other: he might have been shorter in fact, maybe he counterbalanced or compensated for his inferior height by his assurance, his diction like that of an actor accustomed to projecting his words at full volume all the way to the back wall of vast theaters, his self-confidence), seemed to sail, disappearing and surfacing again as if carried along by the eddies, one of those marionette masks vaguely recalling (hooked nose, angular face, ringlets) that of a Polichinelli (and maybe he had had that job in one of those Italian-style parades atop a stage mounted on trestles), but also that of a Brutus or of some Sforza (roles, characters, heroes that he could incarnate at will), tossed, then, resonant, inviting in that falsetto voice Big Foot, The Onion, The Pie, and their partners to appear soon on the stage of his theater with its satin-shod characters; and someone who was next to S. said that now we'd seen everything, that it was really very odd to go just like that hey presto from an old poet-ambassador to howling anarchy, and someone answered not at all that every true poet (and forgive me but church hen or not that old ambassador was one) is an anarchist and that every anarchist is a poet, and the first one who spoke said that nevertheless it wasn't long ago that at least half of the people in that room were calling the old poet a bastard, a dog, a purveyor of weevily beans, and the one who answered him said that nevertheless a lot of water had gone under the bridge since then and that the other was twenty years behind the times, that that was all ancient history, and the first one said that nevertheless . . . But he (S.) is no longer listening, is no longer there: beyond the row of chairs, empty now, turning their backs to the windows, he looks at the sunlit trees, the yellow, sunlit river, and, on the other side, the long, decorative alignment of false columns, entablatures, pediments, pilasters, cornices: the old palace the color of the ages, like some cenotaph, the haughty façade behind which he thinks he sees, wandering, the melancholy ghosts of kings and queens with necks encased in pearls or ruffs, surrounded by jesters, cardinals, favorites, discalced monks, minions, poisoners, spies, bankers: the assembly, the long opulent cortege, stiff, and bringing up the rear, like the clown who capers at the tail of a circus parade (but sad, without capers, wearing a carnivalesque gendarme's hat and more melancholy still), the operetta emperor with his cheeks powdered pink, with a painted mustache, pensive, fortuneless, and dysenteric: a mausoleum, a sepulchre, an architectural riot at the foot of which he (S.) can see, heading toward the west, an endless line of covered trucks, iron gray, regularly spaced, and decorated, as if for some funereal festival, with tree limbs whose branches undulate behind them like long peacock tails. They are too far away for their drivers to be made out, and their tied-down covers also conceal, sitting face-to-face inside, shaken by the jolts, their cargo of young flesh, of young bodies in black boots, in black harnesses, with the juvenile, fresh faces of children in steel helmets. He (S.) is no longer there. It is night. In the darkness one can vaguely make out the group of horses gathered in the clearing. The only noises are now and then those of a horse sneezing, making his bit and his curb chain rattle, or of a hoof hitting the sheath of a saber (and from time to time, here and there, the gentle modulated hooting of an owl). He approaches one of the vans of the column which has just stopped on the forest road and whose officers, at the head of the column, are consulting an ordnance survey map in the glow of a flashlight. Two rows of soldiers can be made out inside the van, sitting face-to-face on the benches, with helmets on their heads, their rifles vertical between their knees, silent. They do not answer the cavalrymen's questions. In the silence you can almost hear them breathing, see their dark African faces deep in the shadows, their white eyes shining in the dark. They sit there, panting soundlessly, with, between them, on the floor of the van, between the two rows of feet framing the rifle stocks, something coiled, dangerous, deadly, and stinking, recalling that nauseating and insipid odor that hangs over the reptile pavilions in zoos. He sees them again, from atop his horse, the next night—or rather by the light of the canvas covers, slowly burning out—in the form of shriveled, carbonized little monkeys, still obediently sitting on the benches from which the airplanes did not even give them time to rise, still holding between their knees what remains of their rifles, which they did not even have time to use. He no longer hears the laughter, the exclamations, the polite animation of the salon behind him. He thinks about the four characters whose names he doesn't even know who slink into his apartment every morning, about the dispatches that the young courier comes to pick up every day, with his happy child face, as if he were playing cops and robbers. He thinks about the system that allows them to transmit maps and the locations of barracks, marshaling yards, intersections, troop movements, by radio. He still vaguely perceives the aviary sounds behind his back, noisy, ecstatic. He thinks: poor bastards, poor bastards, poor bastards, poor bastards. . . .

The man who was waiting for him in the early morning when his train from Paris arrived at the Narbonne station was about fifty years old. Dressed in a well-cut overcoat, his genial face only slightly plump, his hand adorned with a wedding ring, he reminded you of one of those provincial notables, president of a sports club, a former player himself, surrounded on all sides by esteem and respect. Nevertheless, when in the course of the conversation he happens to refer to his wife, he will be careful to call her his companion. Later, S. would learn that he owned one of the largest pharmacies in the city. The sunny early-December morning, cool, the transparent air, the bare gray hills, soon the sea: calm, flat, glimmering. The man drives quickly but calmly in his big car, never taking a risk. Keeping his eyes on the road, he listens as S. explains the situation: the freighter loaded in Marseilles, the Norwegian government's decision, the captain finding himself forbidden by his company to put in at a Spanish port. He asks what's on board. S. tells him machine guns and field mortars made by Brandt.

As they approach the border the road becomes more and more deserted. Finally, the car is all alone as it climbs up to the pass. Two flags, one with three stripes, violet, yellow, red, the other half red, half black, divided along a diagonal line, flutter in the sea wind above the little house of the Spanish customs agents where, their rifles leaning against a wall, three men warm themselves in the sun, wearing threadbare uniforms with cartridge belts slung over them. The view extends far over the bright blue sea where like a toy the steamship coming from Oran slowly drags its wake behind it as it nears the coastline.

One single flag, the red-and-black flag of the Anarchist Federation, was hanging in Port Bou over the door of the building (town hall, *ayuntamiento,* requisitioned hotel?) before which the car came to a stop. Later, S. would remember a room just off the entryway, two propaganda posters tacked up on the wall and a long central table with a thick wooden top in that sort of medieval style, as were, among the unmatched chairs surrounding it, two armchairs with high backrests covered in embossed leather, like the ones bishops occupy in old paintings. The pharmacist introduces him to two young men, thin, also dressed in threadbare suits, one of them wearing a pistol on his belt in a tawny holster. In the late afternoon, after driving once again, in the opposite direction, along the corniche's unending sequence of hairpin turns (in the meantime night has fallen, and when they enter the city the lights are lit), the pharmacist and S. find themselves sitting in a café in P—— speaking this time to a fat man, about sixty, alone, slumped on a bench before a glass filled with an opaque yellow liquid. Located at the border of the city center and the outskirts, it's one of those brightly lit cafés (fluorescent lights?), three-quarters empty, with marble tables and brown moleskin benches running along the bare walls, painted pale green, ornamented only by advertisements for various brands of aperitifs. With his hat pushed back, his unbuttoned overcoat, the folds of his badly shaved double chin overflowing onto a formless necktie, the fat man looks like some office worker or wine merchant, tired and nearing retirement. Afterward, S. will learn that he is one of the teachers in the school. As he listens to them, his eyelids drooping, the ashes of the cigarettes he lights one after the other with slow movements fall onto the accordionlike folds of his vest, which he sometimes brushes off with a mechanical gesture, leaving a light gray streak behind. He exudes a feeling of sadness, at once good-natured and weary, his gaze nevertheless sharp under his half-closed lids. Outside, on the other side of the glass, in that reddish, melancholy light that street lamps cast in late dusk at the end of fall, schoolchildren pass by loaded down with their satchels, along with a few cars, black silhouettes. When the door opens to let customers in or out, the draft sometimes brings in a few dead plane-tree leaves, curled, dry as cardboard, reddish, brown. The taciturn fat man sometimes agrees with a nod to what the pharmacist says to him. Finally, he will point them to the hotel on the Avenue de la Gare, where they can find the man who calls himself Comandante.

With the sound of many wings beating a cloud of pigeons comes to earth at the feet of a man sitting on a bench, who throws them crumbs from his sandwich. Alone or in couples, middle-aged men and women, most of them well dressed, sitting here and there on the benches, are also eating sandwiches or sometimes things in cardboard baskets into which they dip their little plastic forks. They move furtively, seeming slightly ashamed, avoiding eye contact with the strollers. When they are done, they stand up, roll the greasy wrapper into a ball, and throw it in the steel trash cans set out for that purpose. Even in winter, in harsh cold or light rain, they are always there, every day, except Saturday and Sunday. Sometimes, on certain benches, homeless people stretch out to sleep, motionless, indifferent to the sun burning their faces. Elsewhere, in various positions, young people kiss and caress each other. They pay no notice to the people strolling by, nor to the joggers who, alone or in groups, run along the paths at regular intervals, dressed in skintight multicolored suits: cherry red, black, azure, or decorated with yellow-and-red geometrical motifs. The girls generally run alone, moving their hips in awkward rotations, their breasts bouncing beneath their light shirts. A few Blacks or people of mixed race quickly pass by, also alone, scarcely skimming the ground, slender and silent. They meet or pass couples with tired faces, clothes, and bodies, pushing babies in carriages or with older children riding tricycles or running after the pigeons. Clinging to the fences surrounding the bear pit, the strollers, lovers, or children watch as the enormous animals move about inside their concrete prison where a barkless tree trunk stands next to a basin of dirty yellow water. Either standing upright, muzzle raised, awaiting some morsel of food, or sometimes playing among themselves, their supple movements contrast with their great mass, as if the formidably muscular bodies moved independently of the thick fur that seems to float on top of them like an overly large garment. From some cage inside the Zoo, an invisible exotic bird lets out a long discordant cry at regular intervals, which climbs upward in steps, ever more drawn out, then falls again, like malicious laughter, at once frightening and sarcastic. The pigeons bumbling around in search of the crumbs that people throw them thrust their heads forward with every step, like pendulums. Their annulated feet are coral pink, made gray by the dust. Copper and lilac glints play over their breasts. In the buildings of the Museum the skeletons of giant animals are displayed, such as whales or prehistoric monsters, crystals, also giant, and collections of minerals: porphyry, basalt, carnelian, obsidian, onyx. The Zoo houses wolves, hinds, bison, gazelles, eagle owls, monkeys, rare birds, and in a pavilion where a fetid warmth hangs in the air, caimans, sea tortoises, boas, and pythons, whose brown-and-sand-colored scales form geometric motifs. Taking refuge in the opposite corner of the glass cage where a horned viper is coiled in stony immobility, a little rabbit is shaken by a continuous tremor. Two life-size statues, of Buffon and Lamarck, stand at either end of the French-style garden with its rectangular lawns and flower beds framed by long straight walls of plane trees pruned in perfectly square forms every year, and the adjacent streets bear the names of famous naturalists: Linnaeus, Cuvier, Geoffroy-Saint-Hilaire, Jussieu, Lacépède. The Allée Cuvier, about four hundred meters long, is lined with chestnut trees whose leaves begin to turn orange very early in the fall. Far in the distance the groups of joggers first appear as light, jumping spots. As they approach one can make out the colors of the suits that sheathe their bodies. The circles of sunlight filtered by the boughs slip over them. One can hardly hear their breathing when they pass by with long strides, making the pigeons fly away then immediately afterward return to land. Again, shooting out from among the thick green fronds of the acacias, the poplars, the ash trees, the plane trees, and the beech trees, the bird throws out its laugh, strident, mocking, and catastrophic, rising up in steps, unfurling, and falling again in a cascade.

Rommel (final installment): Faithful to his ethos of force, he prepares, once defeat proves inevitable, to betray the dictator to whom he has pledged an oath and whose will he has served with such enthusiasm. A plot with Stülpnagel and Von Kluge. Three days before the event, his injury on the Normandy front and his evacuation interfere with the realization of the coup d'état planned in the west, for the purposes of which the three generals have already had a number of Gestapo members arrested in Paris. Failed suicide attempt by Stülpnagel, who succeeds only in blinding himself. Hospitalized in Germany, then confined to his home by a long convalescence, Rommel will have to wait until mid-October before Hitler decides his fate. He senses that he is doomed. Nevertheless, his vanity is such that he still believes he might be offered a command position on the Russian front. So strong is this belief that his first thought, on seeing the two generals sent from Berlin appear one morning at the entrance of the estate where he is slowly recovering, is that they have come to give him the good news. In fact, it was only because of his rank of field marshal and his renown, both in Germany and abroad, that Hitler hesitated over the proper way to kill him. Finally, as is customary with rats, they decided to use poison. Specifically, the news consists of a cyanide capsule. Threats against his family or appeal to what people of that kind call honor or duty? They warn him that the house is surrounded. Goes up to tell his wife that within a quarter of an hour he will be dead ("It's a matter of three seconds"—account later given by his son). The car in which he takes a seat with the two general officers stops not far from the house, at the edge of a forest. Then the driver and one of the two officers get out and stroll along the road (or through the forest?) for a moment. When they come back and open the door Rommel is slumped forward, doubled over in his seat, his hair tousled, his cap and his marshal's baton fallen at his feet.

The water in the bathtub is pale green. The body appears as if through a fogged-up window. Stretched out, it seems to float like a pinkish kind of seaweed, invertebrate, spotted in the middle by a brown tuft. From a bar of soap fallen to the bottom of the bathtub slowly rises a sort of milky smoke that moves lazily, dissolves little by little in the water, making it paler still. Its coils, its suspended serpentine undulations drift slightly from side to side without disintegrating, at the whim of the imperceptible currents brought about by the tiniest movements of the limbs, propagating from one end of the bathtub to the other, setting off again in the opposite direction, crashing together with a quiet lapping sound. Sometimes the breasts emerge like two islands, with their lilac peaks, their pink skin made brighter by the heat of the bathwater. On the pale surface of the almond-colored water the thin layer of soap cracks up, remains accumulated in deposits over the cliffs of the bathtub sidewalls before the next little wave comes along and washes them away. When the bather stands up the water seems to be torn, luminous, beneath her thighs, trickles noisily in a thousand cascades as she rises, unfurls herself. From the arm stretched out toward the towel falls a chain of drops that give rise, over the surface of the water, now churned up by waves, to a series of little circles, lined up in a row, which immediately vanish. The wet skin is crisscrossed by a network of sinuous fringes that slide quickly toward the ground, leaving silvery streaks behind them. The water mats down the brown patch, where it remains hanging in scintillating pearls. As the bather raises her hands to tie up her hair, the fine down under her arms seems to be sprinkled with little diamonds. He touches her. She totters and grabs hold of the bathtub faucets. She lets go of the pink towel from which she had made a turban and which she was adjusting.

It happened after the last houses of the village, a little after they had passed by a dead horse half covered with an ocher liquid mud (but how the hell since it hadn't rained for several days?) lying on its flank crosswise in the ditch its front legs folded back as if it were jumping an obstacle or saying its prayers a sort of praying mantis the neck and head with its long yellow teeth across the edge of the road. It seemed to S. that the burst of gunfire was coming from a hedge to the left of the road the colonel being ahead of him to the right. S. still not understanding today why it was not the other one who was on his left in any case he was the one who caught it all Years later he thinks he can still see him tragically (or laughably?) raising his saber at arm's length as he and the horse collapsed in slow motion and S. wonders also how the one leading the spare horse managed to turn tail without letting go of it since he was leading it on its left so that he must have gone all the way around it all that under fire from an automatic weapon or maybe while the sniper was putting in a new clip because he (the one leading the spare horse) did after all have one thigh grazed by a bullet nevertheless in less time than it takes to say it S., the one leading the spare horse, and the latter, now between the two of them, found themselves galloping side by side, as for the other colonel he later wrote in his field log that he took his revolver from its holster killed a German then jumped over a hedge and took off across country Quite a feat under automatic weapons fire, but still . . .

"Monsieur,

"I have just read The Flanders Road *with a rigor full of pleasure. But what strikes me more personally are the scenes that so closely recall what I saw in 1940, and as I read them I remain stupefied (as Racine says). This is what I mean: I traveled back over the 15 kilometers beyond the Meuse at great speed. My general (B——) committed suicide and I fell into an ambush in which my comrade (Colonel R——) was killed or rather, as you say, assassinated. This episode faithfully recounts the facts, down to the smallest detail: the beer we drank in the courtyard of an inn, the terrified infantryman that I forced to dismount from a spare horse, and finally even the horse with its trace cut, which R—— was riding.*

"Perhaps you smile as you read these reminiscences of an old cavalryman. If this is the case, I do not regret writing this letter. It offers me the opportunity to pay you my respects and to observe that a horse's legs are not referred to as pattes, *as those of ordinary animals are, but as* jambes.*"*

Signed: Colonel C——, ex-colonel of the 8th Dragoons

This letter, to which S. will sometimes refer on various later occasions, will provoke a variety of readings and reactions. Thus, to the editor of an important daily newspaper which will publish it in the course of an interview, some readers, among others, will write:

"It is with indignation that I read C. S.'s remarks on the rout in Flanders in May 1940, calling into question the valor of the military and the honor of my father Colonel R——, even going so far, shamelessly, as to make of him an object of ridicule, etc."

Or:

"I have read with great attention and also with indignation the pages you devote to the battle waged on horseback by the 4th DLC, and in particular by the 31st Dragoons, commanded by Colonel R——, etc."

And a few years earlier, in the course of a colloquium on the novel, S.'s disclosure of this letter had aroused another sort of emotion (of alarm?): had S. not violated the basic rules of a certain literary movement? By making such a document public, was S. not contravening the theories ascribed to by the adepts of that movement? Was he not thereby excluding himself from the community of thought that presided over the group's research? By showing how a text must be constructed purely on the basis of the combinations offered by language referring only to itself, did Raymond Roussel not open (prescribe) for the novel a path from which one could not diverge without falling into the errors (the pitfall) of a vulgar naturalism? Was this truly the place for S., who was expected the next day, and was the invitation that had been extended to him not sent off a little too lightly? Was it proper to welcome him as a member of the community or rather to consider him as an occasional and uncertain "traveling companion"? Was it not time to put an end to this ambiguity?

As is shown by the tape recorded during the debates, of which a transcription was later published, these questions gave rise to an interesting discussion:

A participant: . . . if one reads *The Battle of Pharsala* or *The Flanders Road*, there are certain sequences that suggest something real, even if, obviously, they acquire their full meaning and function only in relation to other passages within the confines of the book. But C. S. himself, who will soon be among us, one day showed me a letter he had received from an old cavalry officer who had lived through the 1940 defeat, saying of *The Flanders Road*: "How can this be? How were you able to see that? That's exactly what I went through!" Thus, not only is there a mimetic illusion but even, in certain cases, it can be confirmed outright by a reference.

J. R.: I would have expected the devil, of whom you have made yourself the advocate, to prove a little more cunning than that. . . . (Laughter). Given that this is a question of theory, I must admit that letters from a cavalry officer mean little to me. . . .

A. R.-G.: But R., what about the banknotes, of which C. S. himself has provided the photographs here? . . .

J. R.: We all know that one of the primary illusions of which reading must free itself is the illusion of projection. . . . Thus it is in no way curious that a former cavalry officer projects himself into *The Flanders Road*. . . . There are two ways in which people do this: by eliminating the literal dimension (in this case through a projection that replaces the text with fantasized memories) and allowing oneself to become fascinated by a supposed "life itself"; by eliminating the referential dimension (an illusion more rare in practice since it runs counter to the dominant ideology) and allowing oneself to become fascinated by the pure materiality of an ordered set of letters. The first would be the referential illusion, the second the literal illusion.

The participant: Well, I'm in complete agreement with you. . . .

J. R.: Allow me not to be so, not completely, on the other hand: there stands between us, unless you are making a very abrupt about-face, a certain cavalry officer to whose testimony we do not attach the same degree of importance. I am not unaware that this is a delicate problem, and R.-G. was right to bring it back to the fore by mentioning the photographs. What S. has provided are the referents of the fiction: in no way does this mean that fiction obtained by the text is the equivalent of the referent provided for the purposes of documentation.

A. R.-G.: We agree with you, in reality, R. When someone sets a "trap" of that kind for you, it is in order to make you state the problem more clearly: personally, I do indeed find that, as you remarked a little earlier, each of us is subject to the temptation of a certain referentialist past, and C. S., among us, is the only one who felt the need to allow the banknote referent to be hung on the wall. . . .

A speaker: I would like to make it clear that the referent of

C. S.'s text is in part the banknote, but only in part. It is in part, also, the referent of the sign which is the banknote. The text creates a sort of confusion between the referent of the banknote and the banknote as a referent. The result, I think, is not to valorize the referent but on the contrary to devalorize it.

A. R.-G.: It is nonetheless the case that C. S. constantly gives us his referents. . . . Thus, we really must believe that S. attributes to referents a greater importance than do the other novelists at this meeting.

Originally built of wood like most Scandinavian cities, Göteborg has burned to the ground several times, and today, with its broad central avenue lined with bland modern buildings, it offers nothing of any great interest except for a major ship works, its workers continually in motion, illuminated by powerful spotlights beneath the towering cranes. The ships under construction are lined up in parallel rows, surrounded by a forest of scaffolds from which sprays and cascades of sparks shoot here and there. The windows of one of the city's best restaurants overlook this fascinating spectacle. On Saturday nights, cars full of young people race along the streets, their tires screeching, the passengers letting out wild shrieks. They seem more or less drunk, and fights must sometimes break out, because in the morning the gutters are strewn with beer cans, broken bottles, and one sometimes sees a large pool of blood in the middle of the sidewalk.

Continuous rainfall confines S. to his hotel room for an entire Sunday afternoon. Bored, he turns on the television set and randomly runs through the channels. On the black-and-white (or rather grayish) screen there appear, depending on the channel:

A tennis court surrounded by stands. The court is covered with a tarpaulin and the camera zooms in on a puddle that has formed between two creases, in which the unending rain makes little circles. In the stands sit a few groups of spectators, wearing raincoats and sheltering under umbrellas.

A blues pianist who accompanies his playing with various gesticulations and poses, sometimes hunched over the keyboard, his back arched, his nose grazing the keys, sometimes throwing himself backward, his grimacing mulattolike face raised toward the heavens as if in the throes of some great torment. The concert, which has been taped earlier, is given outdoors, at night. In the background one can make out a crowd of young men and women sitting on the grass and listening reverently.

A man dressed in a dark, shining wetsuit, apparently made of rubber, clutching the support bar of a sailboard, rising and falling over gray waves covered with a gray foam.

A voice-over provides a running commentary on these various events in Swedish.

A promenade lined with palm trees (coconut trees?) running horizontally along the bottom of the screen. Beyond the trunks, one can see a silvery expanse of water (sea, ocean?) glistening. A light wind makes the branches of the palm trees shake limply. There is no one in sight. A bass voice says in French: Theh': you all stand oveh theh', laïk thaht. The President weel come ahlong from oveh theh'. He'll walk ahlong the ocean and you cahn feelm heem. No: he won't stop, but you'll have plennty of taïme: he'll be walkeeng slowly. Yes, that's raït: stand heeh': he'll come ahlong from the left and he'll walk ahlong theh' by the ocean, and then you'll feelm heem. OK?

S. tries several times to find a new channel but each time falls back on the same scenes: the bather on his sailboard tossed by the gray, choppy sea, the grimacing pianist, the group of spectators under their umbrellas, and the promenade lined with palm trees, still deserted, with the offscreen voice of the organizer of the ceremonies.

In the vestibule, around noon, S. met the old elephant woman who lives on the second floor as he was going out. She was coming home after buying her groceries. Her dark, backlit silhouette almost completely obstructed the opening of the left-hand swinging door in the front entrance, which is fitted with a spring mechanism to bring it back to its closed position and which she awkwardly pushed aside with one elbow, her motions hampered by

274

her nickel-plated steel crutch. He quickly walked across the vestibule to hold it open for her, so that she could catch hold of the black-rubber handle of her crutch again. She said Oh thank you you're very kind and headed toward the mailboxes, dragging her legs, thick as posts, leaning forward, supporting herself on her two crutches. She was wearing her usual Tyrolean hat, dark gray, decorated with a black ribbon, and her gabardine coat, also dark gray, with, strapped across her upper body like a bandolier, the enormous brown canvas bag, the edges bound with a strip of reddish false leather. She leaned her right crutch against the wall, looked through her pockets, took a key ring from one of them and opened the little lock on the box. The box was empty. She said I'm checking just in case the mailman might have come by with today's second delivery while I was at the market. Her coat was shorter than her black skirt which in this position (leaning toward the mailboxes) pulled up in back, revealing her calf, about as thick as a thigh and sheathed in a bandage (varicose veins, fitting for an artificial limb?) that showed through the weave of her black stockings. She locked the mailbox door with a turn of the key and said in her lisping Auvergne accent I was at the hospital yesterday. The Specialist showed me to his pupils. He said I was doing very well. If it hadn't been for that accident! . . . She picked up her crutch with her right hand and headed toward the glass door between the vestibule and the foot of the staircase. This door was also controlled by a spring mechanism, and S. went ahead of her to hold it open. First she moved forward a crutch, then a foot, then the opposite crutch, like a sort of four-legged animal, being very careful to keep three points on the ground at all times. With her thick, ravaged face, her round steel-framed glasses, and her short, slightly hooked nose, she looked a little like an owl, her mouth squeezed between two drooping jowls. As she slipped slowly into the narrow opening she said again You're very kind thank you The Specialist told his students I was an interesting case. If it hadn't been for that car accident! Don't trouble yourself Thank you thank you again thank you very much. Having reached the foot of the staircase, she took her two crutches under her left arm, grasped the banister with her right hand, and began to slowly climb the steps. Her upper body was bent forward again and at the level of her enormous rump a sort of armature, like the inside of a lampshade, no doubt the lower edge of a corset, formed a half circle from which hung the folds of her coat and skirt, swinging from side to side each time she pulled herself up to a new step.

31st Regiment of Dragoons
    Sprauel Squadron   *Suggestions for citations*

· ·

    Sergeant-Major   *Ostertag Auguste Mle 1918.*

                                    Holding a position at the Les Fontaines halt near Assesse on the 12th of May and surrounded by the enemy, did not hesitate to jump a deep railway embankment, thereby protecting his platoon from certain capture. A noncommissioned officer of calm courage and great initiative.

· ·

The ruins of the Médinet-Abou Temple stand on the left bank of the Nile, not far from the foot of the cliff overlooking the narrow band of irrigable, fertile fields that extends between the river and the desert. A little before the ruins one passes by the two colossi of Memnon that once guarded the entrance to a sanctuary, since disappeared. They are seated, parallel, as tall as a six-story building, their knees together, their hands lying flat on their stone thighs, their faces flat, noses broken off, eyes staring into emptiness. Time, the wind, sand, the centuries, the alternating brutal heat and brutal cold of the night have amputated an arm, a foot, sometimes an entire limb, have cracked the blocks they are sitting on, through which, it is said, the desert wind once made, at certain times, a sound like that of a harp. Monumental, strange, and solitary, they tower over the fields of tobacco and beans like the guardians of some nonexistent enigma. In their shadow sometimes rest the women armed with scythes and the little donkeys whose loads come down to their toes. A few kilometers away, the temple covers a square of about four hundred meters on a side, and its enclosure has long served as a protective wall for an Arab village. On the high walls framing its entrance, the wind and sand have also eaten away at the light bas-reliefs, half erased, where one can just make out the forms of horses, chariots, crushed bodies, warriors with lances, bows, and arrows. On the inside there alternate monumental columns, round or square, against which the light splashes or softens, clinging to the profusion of deeply engraved hieroglyphs which seem to populate these piles of stone with myriads of birds, with a silent and deafening chirping resounding off the Cyclopean stones under the stifling, gray sky of the desert.

bottom of the basin lined with a layer of dead leaves red-brown rust prune rotting sticky under his hands he doesn't remember feeling the cold of the water only the amused laughter and taunts of the other nannies sitting on the benches while his own carried him away undressed naked wrapped in a blanket or maybe her shawl the basin not very deep at the foot of a little mound decorated with ornamental boulders between which yuccas or dwarf bushes (boxwood? go and see but almost eighty years later! so??? ...) public park lawns palm trees medlars lindens laurels a culvert whose concrete balustrades imitated interlaced branches (bark depicted by means of short gouges) crossed the little canal connecting two other larger basins flat-beaked swans gliding over the water pushing fine little silver waves before their breasts, the waves extending outward making a triangle in their wake little island with a house up to which they sometimes climbed waddling their webbed feet orange then swimming again suddenly capsizing forward decapitated their short tails in the air their necks thrust into the water the beaks searching through the black-green mud (dead leaves also at the bottom) against which stand out motionless the tapered forms of the goldfish scattered here and there like jackstraws ducks also Chinese pathway cathedral of tall hundred-year-old plane trees their trunks smooth as columns white spotted standing out brilliant against the blue of the winter sky swept by the wind slowly swaying their disheveled summits convulsive floating like seaweed in a current above the lawns where the peacocks promenaded their long horizontal gray tails a male sometimes unfurling in a fan shape its plumes the color of emeralds sprinkled with sapphire eyes stamping in place turning alternately one way then the other fatuous throwing out at intervals the two notes of a long white and yellow cry Léon . . . on . . . on . . . drawn out there were also two eagles in a large cage back wall of piled rocks again their talons curled over the barkless branches of an old tree trunk crusted with droppings motionless again their wings folded or sometimes on the cement floor busy tearing apart some carcass of rotting meat red and yellow more droppings in the form of a skullcap fringed and dripping on the head of the dark bronze blacksmith naked muscular bent over hammering into the form of a plow a bundle of weapons swords broken sabers the statue's title *The Age to Come* engraved on the pedestal surrounded by a flower bank covered depending on the season with blooming pansies tulips cinerarias hyacinths another sculpture not far from the eagle cage white marble bas-relief three meters by two more or less onto which the leaves from the medlar tree fell *The Dream* man and woman nude soapy half lying side by side the body of the man in the foreground partly covering that of his companion brother and sister one would think rather than lovers chaste their profiles parallel turned toward the right in the direction of vague shapes (clouds?) also soapy the sculptor's signature chiseled in elegant script in the lower left corner recalling that other one among the multicolored signs on the movie-house curtain which covered the screen before the show began singing the praises of the stores in town hardware jewelry clocks fashion "Sam—*Au gaspillage* Ladies' clothing" alarm clock SUZE Gentian Aperitif gray-green capital letters with black shadows standing out as if in relief against a yellow background but the sculptor was SUDRE Funerary Monuments the *S* like a standing snake with a forked tail the whole thing underlined starting from the final *e* by an artistic flourish also with a forked tail

S. is in discussion with a director who is planning to bring one of his novels to the screen. Together they consider (review) the various possibilities and the various difficulties that might come up (characters, sets, exterior locations, the style of the acting, etc.). Concerning the episode of the four cavalrymen traveling along the road where one of the two officers will be killed, S. describes their exact positions and especially the movements of the one leading the spare horse which, despite the interdiction of one of the two officers, a lost infantryman obstinately tries to mount.

Plan, as precisely as possible, the framing, the various camera movements, and the shooting angles for this entire episode.

S. suggests, in this order:

1. Motionless close-up of a flower in the fields (umbel?).

2. Backward zoom revealing a flowery meadow in the light of a beautiful sunny May morning at the same time as the camera (mounted on a car) begins to move: tracking shot over the meadow, the hedge, a grassy ditch in which successively appear a bashed-in suitcase, the carcass of a burned-out truck, a sewing machine lying in the grass, the body of a dead horse whose head, lying on its side, rests against the edge of the road.

3. Slow tracking shot over the body of the dead horse half covered by an ocher liquid mud. The back legs are extended, the two forward legs folded back, as if for a jump. The head. The open mouth reveals the long yellow teeth.

4. Shadows of riders pass over this head (we can hear the sound of the hooves striking the pavement—until then, only a few chirping birds and, at regular intervals, fairly widely separated, the sound of a single distant cannon, muted).

5. The angle of the camera rises upward and reveals the four riders and the spare horse moving down the road.

6. The camera follows them, a little behind and to their right.

7. The woman in the bathtub bends one leg, raising one knee, which rises above the water like a mountain. Pinkened skin, the smooth knee a slick shining rock what Chinese stone onyx or what of a delicate, transparent pink the rest of the leg undulating invertebrate under the jade-colored water the brown spot of the pubis moving side to side with the lazy eddies of the soapy water.

8. An infantryman (leggings, one of which, half undone, trails behind him, no weapon, no helmet, bareheaded) appears, emerging from a ditch (or from behind a hedge) on the left. He crosses the road, limping, running clumsily, and heads toward the two officers shouting Captain, captain! Take me with you! I've lost my regiment! Take me, take me. . . .

9. In the foreground, filling the right side of the screen, the pink rump of the officer's horse and the upper body of the officer, still riding forward, giving no reply to the infantryman running along below him and to his left (in the background), his head raised toward the officer. We can see his mouth opening and closing but we do not hear his pleas: only the sound of the hooves.

10. A man in a black wetsuit hunched over the frame of a sailboard, rising and falling over the gray waves flecked gray, spitty foam. He is filmed not from the shore but, it seems, from a helicopter apparently hovering at low altitude over the sea (or a telephoto lens?).

11. The camera still to the right of the group, following along with them but moving more slowly, so that, in profile, the upper bodies of the two officers and the rumps of their horses pass out of our field of vision to the right, allowing us to see the infantryman from the waist up, no longer running alongside the officer's boot, now watching as the three horses (the corporal's horse, the horse of the man leading the spare horse, and the latter) continue moving forward and soon block our view of him.

12. The backlit silhouette, in the frame of the open door, of the huge woman leaning on her crutches. In the background the illuminated display cases of a market.

13. The four men on horseback now seen from the front (the camera mounted on a car ahead of them, moving at the same speed as them): the infantryman, hopping clumsily, is trying to put his foot into the stirrup of the spare horse. He has grasped the pommel of the saddle with his left hand and is trying to fit the stirrup over his foot with his right hand.

14. The upper body of the officer, seen from behind again (between the heads of the spare horse and of the man leading it): he turns around in his saddle; we see in profile his hard, impassive face under his helmet. He says, raising his voice a little: Leave that horse alone: I forbid you to follow me! then resumes his previous position.

15. The upper body of the infantryman suddenly appearing over the saddle of the spare horse, lurching forward, his stomach on the saddle, his hands on the pommel and the cantle.

16. He thrusts his arm into the water. She stops soaping herself. She looks at him silently with a questioning gaze, amused and avid, with her mouth slightly open she breathes a little faster and her eyes dim as if from a sudden film over the enamel blue of her irises. She closes her eyelids and throws her head back. She is still holding the bar of soap in her raised hand, her arm bent, her hand level with her shoulder. The pink towel knotted like a turban around her head comes undone and slips into the water. Soaked, it takes on a dark pomegranate color. Close-up of the towel gradually unfurling like a sort of bird, undulating slowly, beating its wings, its color a red that is nearly black.

17. Close-up of the upper body of the officer, now turned fully around in his saddle, saying in a loud voice: Get off that horse at once! I have forbidden you to follow me! Get off at once! Then he resumes his normal position. (At regular intervals, and still

rather widely spaced, the distant cannon continues to resound. Still the small sound of the hooves, birdsongs.)

18. The mulatto pianist: he is dressed in a white tuxedo, now he is playing with his shoulders thrown back, his face thrown back as well, raised toward the heavens, almost horizontal, grimacing as if in the throes of a violent anguish, of profound concentration, his eyelids closed. The glow from the spotlights extends to the first few rows of the audience, made up of young men and women of Nordic type sitting on a lawn. The men are wearing ties, the women are in summer dresses, light and cool.

19. Close-up of the man leading the spare horse (seen from the front, in three-quarters profile), who is shouting at the infantryman: Dyou hear what he said to you, dyou hear? Get away from here! Clear off! (in the background the upper body of the infantryman leaning forward, his stomach against the saddle of the spare horse).

20. A group of spectators wearing raincoats and sheltering under umbrellas, motionless in the stands of the tennis court.

21. Close-up of the upper body of the infantryman, still in the same position. Shooting up from the lower right corner of the screen, the boot-sheathed foot of the man leading the spare horse (legging, large hobnail sole, spur) strikes the infantryman's face several times. At the same time the man leading the spare horse shouts: Jesus Christ you deaf or what? Didn't you understand what he said? Will you get off? Get the fuck out of here! Groan of pain from the infantryman whose torso slides toward the ground.

22. Fixed shot: the camera frames the wall of a small white-painted room with a window on the right side. To the left of the window hangs a glass case, inside of which are pinned several rows of butterflies. The casements of the window are closed. The window is of an old-fashioned type, with a catch whose oval handle is decorated around the edges with grooves whose raised

parts, having taken on a patina with use, appear black against the original white paint (close-up of the handle of the catch). Backlit, the uprights and crossbars of the window stand out in dark gray against the bright exterior, before which the ironwork of the balcony, painted black, unfurls its ornamental volutes. Behind their decorative forms (spirals, stylized vegetation) appear the thick, soft green boughs of the plane trees shading the square. A light wind tosses them in contrary movements which can be described in this way: (1) the incessant slight palpitation, individual so to speak, of every leaf, (2) the slow swaying of the thick branches and of their masses of leaves, which bend downward, then come up again, even as their extremities, more flexible, continue to follow their earlier path, curving in the opposite direction, (3) the swirling winds strike the various trees and the various branches at different moments, the entire group moving under the influence of opposing currents.

23. Only the head and hands of the infantryman, the latter still clutching at the pommel and the cantle of the saddle, can be seen. The man leading the spare horse returns to his normal position, leans to the left and hammers at them with his fists. Hands and head disappear. The man leading the spare horse turns toward the corporal (the upper body of the latter in the foreground, to the left of the screen) and says Jesus how do you like that! Dyou see that asshole! Those footslogger assholes! . . .

24. The promenade lined with palm trees running along the sea. The same offscreen voice says: All raït now Theh's the President. Go on and feelm heem! A tall Black man appears to the left of the screen. He walks slowly and deliberately. He is thin, dressed in a long coat (or robe?) buttoned up to the neck, of the kind Hindus wear. His head is topped with a sort of leopard-skin forage cap and in one hand he is holding a heavy sculpted cane which he handles gracefully. He walks straight ahead, never looking toward the cameras that are filming him as he crosses the screen from left to right and disappears.

25. The camera now stopped (fixed shot) behind the group of cavalrymen, who slowly ride away, still at a walk. The infantryman in the foreground to the left, standing beside the road, sniffling, sobbing, and awkwardly wiping away with his sleeve the blood flowing from his face.

26. The mulatto pianist, his back now arched, his nose against the keyboard.

27. Close-up of one of the half-moons that ornament the plumes of the peacock: its center, apple-shaped, is black. It is surrounded by an irregular sapphire blue ring, itself bordered on the lower side by an auburn oval, it too surrounded by a ring of light green (English green). On either side of the shaft extend, in a fan shape, the long barbs of the plume (of the same green, but darker), fluttering in a soft breeze.

28. Same shot as number 22 (the walls of the room, the case with the butterflies, the window). On the left side of the screen appears the backlit silhouette of a man. It moves past the butterfly case, heading toward the window, turning the catch, and opening the casements. A deafening roar of traffic invades the room, which has been silent until then. The figure (seen from behind) stands for a moment with his elbows on the railing of the balcony, bending forward slightly, looking below him at the movement of the pedestrians and cars in the square. Beyond his dark silhouette we can see the boughs slowly waving (this shot will have to be a rather long one, even at the risk of boring the viewer, the roar of the cars is very violent). Finally the man stands upright and closes the casements. In the sudden silence, he crosses the screen from right to left and sits down at a table placed before a second window, this one fitted with a sheer curtain. He leans to his left over a manuscript page, sits upright and begins to hit the keys of a typewriter. In the silence we hear the clattering of the machine which little by little becomes a clattering of hooves.

29. The camera far ahead of the cavalrymen, who move toward it along the road, gradually growing larger.

284

30. Two players walk onto the tennis court from which the tarpaulin has been removed, each of them carrying several rackets under his arm. They are dressed in long white pants, whose cuffs seem to be clasped by the ankles of high-top shoes. They prod the ground with their feet and seem to be engaged in some sort of discussion.

31. The camera behind a soldier lying full-length on his stomach in the grass, his head near a hedge. Zoom in on the round helmet painted gray-green. Zoom in on the weapon he is holding ready to fire in the direction of the road through a hole in the hedge. Zoom in on the weapon's telescopic sight.

32. Seen head-on against the light the old elephant woman leaning on her crutches slowly crosses the vestibule, coming forward to meet the camera.

33. The man dressed in his black wetsuit still hunched over his sailboard rising and falling over the gray waves.

34. Seen through the telescopic lens of the rifle (machine gun?), the four cavalrymen approaching along the road, at a walk. Two thin black lines meet perpendicularly at the center, their intersection moving slowly from left to right and right to left over the group of cavalrymen. A sudden glint of sunlight on the stripes of one of the riders' sleeves.

35. One of the tennis players stands ready to serve and bounces the ball three times at his feet.

36. The group of cavalrymen is now very near. The intersection of the horizontal and vertical lines in the gun sight comes to rest on the chest of the leftmost officer. (Sound: the clattering of the hooves coming nearer, slight chirping of birds.)

37. The body of the tennis player stretches out as he lifts the racket, which is about to hit the ball.

38. The figure seen from behind striking the keys of his typewriter.

39. The elephant woman in the vestibule, limping, leaning on her crutches, comes nearer and nearer the camera.

40. The bead of the weapon aimed directly at the officer's torso.

41. The raised racket strikes the ball. Dry clack of the ball against the strings.

42. At the same moment the black mass of the elephant woman finally obstructs the entire screen, on which appear, in white capital letters, the words:

THE END

Additional instructions:

Since the cavalrymen are moving from east to west with the camera following them situated on their right, the greater part of the episode will be filmed against the light. The escutcheons adorning the collar of the infantryman's tunic bear a yellow number 84 against a green background and are bordered with a yellow stripe (check this: the colors of the regiments of the *infanterie de forteresse*). The escutcheons on the cavalrymen's collars bear a sky blue number against a navy blue background. The infantryman is very young. His hair is blond and curly, his face almost childlike. The cannon shots that resound at regular intervals, fairly widely spaced, become more and more muffled, more and more distant. The chirping of the birds is discreet and sporadic. It might be a good idea to have a butterfly (brown spotted with yellow) perching on the flower seen in close-up in shot 1 and it would be by following its flight that the camera would progressively reveal the flowering pasture, the scattered wrecks, the dead horse, and finally the cavalrymen accompanied by the spare horse on the road. In that case, insert into shot no. 22 a close-up of the butterfly case. Slow tracking shot over the rows of butterflies ending on one of them (white wings with black stripes, in a fan shape) which will fill up the entire screen. Also, it would not be bad if as the camera follows the four cavalrymen with a tracking shot, the carcasses of trucks or burned-out vehicles occasionally pass by in the foreground.

Shot no. 7 (woman in the bathtub): it would be preferable to have the film shot in panoramic format, in which case the submerged body, gigantic, would fill up the entire frame of the screen, that is to say several meters in length. The screen would then be divided into three horizontal and parallel strips, thus, from bottom to top: the bright white of the bathtub rim, the almond green of the water enclosing the body whose flesh color will appear translucently as if through a tinted window, then, again, the white of the inner bathtub wall over which the network of reflections from the water will play. The two copper faucets with their heads in the form of crowns (that is, with four spokes each ending in a little ball) will stand out against that background, the camera filming this from above. Note that since the head of the bather is not submerged her face (also seen from above and foreshortened) and hair (or the turban) will be rather brightly colored. Similarly, when, for instance, in order to take hold of the soap, she raises one arm out of the water, it will be violently sculpted by the light and no longer softened with pastel colors by the transparent thickness of the water. Every motion sets off slight undulations which propagate over the liquid surface, beneath which the body itself seems to undulate, without consistency and without weight. If, for financial reasons, the film can only be shot in normal format, that is to say in 24 × 36, a stripe of vermilion red linoleum would be added to the lower part and we could thus see the claw feet of the bathtub, white against red.

Shot no. 28: As has already been said, this shot must be very long (two or three minutes at least), the roar of the traffic growing weaker or stronger (deafening in the latter case) by turns, the smoke from the cigar of the man seen from behind and leaning over the balcony billowing above his head against the limply swaying background of the boughs over the top floors of the mansarded apartment buildings and their bluish zinc roofs.

Shot no. 16: Try to synchronize the appearance of the upper

body of the infantryman above the saddle of the spare horse and the sudden rise of the naked body of the woman standing up in the bathtub amid a sonorous splashing of water (zoom in over the drops of water gliding over her breast and her armpit revealed by the raised arm).

Shot no. 22: One might, by a strong light projected onto the wall and the window, be able to cancel out the backlit effect so that the window frame and crossbars do not appear in dark tones against the background of trees, but in light tones: the colors would then be reduced to three: white and window, green (the leaves on the trees), and black (the ornamental cast-iron motifs of the balcony).

Except for the pink off-horse, all the horses are bays: mahogany coat, black mane and tail. The manes are clipped, including that of the second officer's mount, from which we can understand that he has also lost his own and is now riding the mount of a dead cavalryman. After having forbidden the infantryman to mount the spare horse and during the entire incident that follows (the blows dealt by the man leading the spare horse to the infantryman) neither of the two officers will turn around. Their two upper bodies, very stiff in their saddles, hardly move. They both have a day's growth of beard, their uniforms and boots are relatively clean. The clothes of the two cavalrymen following them are spotted with dust and mud, the corporal's coat is torn. Both of them have an eight-day growth of beard. At times the sunlight will sparkle over the metallic parts of the harnesses (buckles, bits, stirrups) as well as over the spurs, the coquilles of the sabers, and the two officers' helmets, covered with an extremely glossy paint. In order to lessen their sheen, which could cause them to be spotted by the enemy, the two cavalrymen have smeared their helmets with mud, but this crude camouflage might, on film, seem to be the clumsy work of some prop master trying to make it look more "true to life." It would be better, then, to avoid it.

Claude Simon was awarded the Nobel Prize for literature in 1985. Born in Madagascar in 1913, he grew up in Perpignan, France, and after leaving school traveled extensively throughout Europe. At the beginning of World War II he was captured by the Germans at the Battle of the Meuse but escaped and joined the resistance movement. He published his first novel, *The Cheat,* in 1946. His many works include *The Wind, The Georgics,* and *The Invitation.*